THE ORI
MISS LUCY JONES

Liz Shakespeare

LETTERBOX BOOKS

First published 2024
by
Letterbox Books
Littleham
Bideford
Devon
EX39 5HW

www.lizshakespeare.co.uk

ISBN 978-0-9516879-7-0

Printed and bound by SRP Ltd, Exeter

Acknowledgements

As ever, I am grateful to many people for their help with this book, but particularly to Peter Christie who sadly passed away before it went to print. He was always generous in sharing his knowledge of North Devon history and will be greatly missed.

Volunteers at the Bideford and District Community Archive carried out research for me during the coronavirus lockdown; staff at the North Devon Record Office helped with images from The North Devon Journal; volunteers at Torrington Museum gave me their support; Sarah Coull showed me around Castle House Care Home to help me picture the house as it would have been in the nineteenth century, and Torrington Common Conservators sourced a map for me. Moira Brewer's book *Torrington Uncovered* has been a very useful resource.

I am indebted to Alison Harding for her insight, encouragement and advice; to Kate Cryan for her proofreading and, of course, my son Ben who makes self-publishing possible through his skill with images.

I am thankful for Torrington Common; it has been an inspiration.

I am also grateful for my many loyal readers who make it all worthwhile.

Torrington Common

Torrington Common today comprises 365 acres of land and 20 miles of public footpaths.

The Commons are administered by up to fifteen Trustees known as Conservators who are elected every three years. Only residents of Great Torrington are eligible to apply to be Conservators.

Map of Torrington in 1879, drawn by Ben Shakespeare. Based on a map kindly loaned by the Great Torrington Commons Conservators and reproduced with permission.

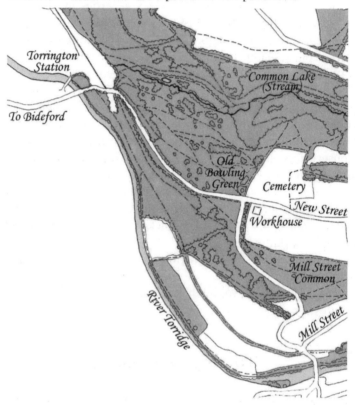

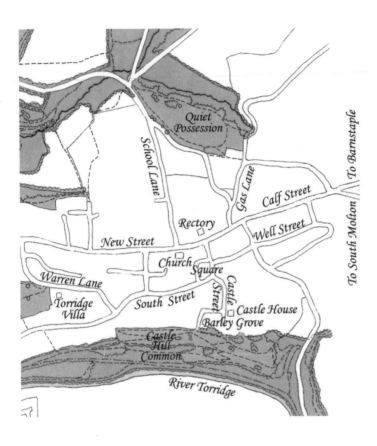

TORRINGTON.

BOROUGH MAGISTRATES' PETTY SESSION.

GUILDHALL, WEDNESDAY (Yesterday).

Before the Mayor (H. L. Mallet, Esq.), and J. Balsdon, Esq.

SERIOUS ACCUSATIONS AGAINST THE CURATE.

The hall was crowded to-day to its utmost capacity in consequence of its having become known that the curate, the Rev. H. O. Frances, would meet in open Court the rumours which have been in circulation for a month past respecting his relations with a lady of this town. Many of the leading inhabitants of the town were present, among them the vicar, the Rev. S. Buckland, and Mrs. Frances, wife of the curate. Mr. Frances was the complainant, and a young man of the labouring class, named *Wm. Balkwell*, the defendant, and the charge against him was that on the 18th August he "indirectly threatened to publish certain false libel, matter, or thing, of, concerning, and touching one Herbert Oldfield Frances, of Great Torrington, Clerk in Holy Orders, with intent then and there to extort money from him."

Mr. J. A. Thorne, of Barnstaple, prosecuted, and Mr. R. I. Bencraft, of the same place, defended.

The witnesses having, at Mr. Bencraft's request, been ordered out of Court, Mr. Thorne made a long opening speech, in the course of which he said that the case was one of a somewhat unusual character; at the same time, it was by no means of the sensational description many persons believed it to be. The matters which were the subject of the summons took place on the 18th August, and since then they had no doubt been much canvassed both in Torrington and the neighbourhood. Rumours had been circulated very freely, some of which were gross exaggerations. The charge against Balkwell was that he represented to Mr. Frances that he had seen him acting improperly towards a young lady, Miss Lucy Jones (daughter of Dr. Jones), who was one of the district visitors of the church, and that he said in effect, "If you don't give me 10s. to hold my tongue, I'll go into the town and publish all that has taken place."

North Devon Journal, 1879

18ᵗʰ August 1879

Lucy Jones walked slowly alongside the wall that separated the town from the Common. She was usually a brisk walker but it was, in truth, far too hot for taking the air and, although it had been her intention to descend the hill and follow the stream through the valley, the thought of the steep climb back up to the town was not inviting. She paused, resting her hand on the wall.

She never tired of the view from here or, indeed, from anywhere on Torrington Common; the green folds of the hills all around, the glint of running water in the deep wooded valleys of the River Torridge and its tributaries below. A blackbird was singing languorously, pausing after each phrase as if the effort required for song in this hot sun was almost too much for him. She knew a tap-tapping coming from the undergrowth to be a thrush striking a snail shell against a rock; she had spent much time studying such matters, and could picture the raising of the narrow head, the glint of the eye, the sudden oblique strike.

There was a movement from the allotments on the hill opposite, and she watched idly as the distant figure bent, straightened, and bent again as he tended his crops. Then the man remained still, seeming to stare across the valley to where she stood on the hill. She did not like to be observed, but he was far off, and it did not seem significant. Hearing the *thunk* of a bat from the boys playing cricket on the Common behind her, she turned instead to watch their studied concentration as they tracked the ball's trajectory, their tense limbs ready to run and catch.

The heat of the sun was relentless. There was perspiration running down the back of her neck, and her legs above her stockings felt damp. It was just too hot to take a walk. She undid the top button of her dress where it constricted her throat and, putting up her parasol to shade herself, she lifted her skirt above the dusty surface of the path and turned back towards the road that led to the town.

But after walking a short distance she paused, reluctant to return home so soon. At breakfast her father had been silent, the tension palpable. Her eldest brother, who was staying at the house for a night or two, had come to the table late, then poured coffee and taken a small piece of dry toast. She guessed that he had again been drinking late into the night. Her father lifted his newspaper and did not emerge from behind it until John had left the table. If she returned home now, it would be too early for her father to be attending his first patients and she would again have to play the part of peacemaker, a role of which she had long grown weary.

She walked on again, slowly, undecided as to which course she should take. Her excuse for leaving the house before listening to her parents' complaints had been the necessity of calling on the curate, Reverend Francis. It was true that she needed to talk to him about the troubled family who had moved into Well Street – the husband had sustained a nasty injury at work, they had neither coal nor sufficient food – and it really could not wait until their fortnightly meeting. In the event, when she reached his house on Warren Lane, she found that he was not at home.

Lucy stopped when she reached the road that climbed from the railway station to the town. She would *not* return home just yet. If she were to continue the walk she had planned, the air would surely be a little cooler in the valley by the stream. She turned again and retraced her steps.

It was then that she noticed the curate in his long black coat hurrying across the Common from the direction of the station. Recognising her, he increased his pace and waved enthusiastically, one of those extravagant gestures that had earned him such ridicule in the town.

And, without a thought, she turned off the path to meet him.

Part One

Chapter One

It was three years since Reverend Francis came to Torrington. When she first saw him, Lucy was sitting in St Michael and All Angels with her parents, her sister and one of her brothers. The family pew was behind those belonging to Colonel Palmer and Mr and Mrs Johnson of Cross House, but in front of the shopkeepers and small tradesmen, whose pews were in turn suitably distanced from the labourers at the back of the church. Everyone was aware of their position in Torrington society. The muted hum of anticipation as the congregation waited for their first glimpse of the new curate died down when they heard the vicar, Reverend Buckland, clearing his throat, indicating that he was about to commence his slow, measured walk up the aisle.

Not wanting to appear to stare, Lucy carefully inclined her head to watch the two men pass by. The new curate was tall, with an eager, mobile face and a long nose which he thrust forward as he walked, as if in a hurry to reach the altar. He was clean-shaven with straight, dark hair cut in a pudding basin style. He seemed a very different character from the diffident Reverend Thompson whom he replaced. Lucy had grown accustomed to the fortnightly meetings with the curate necessitated by her role as a district visitor, and felt a pang of anxiety at the thought of getting to know this new man.

It was not until he turned to face the congregation that she noticed the long stole that he wore over his white surplice, its jewel-like colours as bright as the stained-glass windows amidst the cold, grey stone of the church, and understood the gasps and whispered remarks.

The people of Torrington did not approve of high church practices. Bright colours, candles and crucifixes, bowing and chanting - they had made their feelings on such matters clear. The previous curate had disliked Romish practices, so Reverend Buckland had reluctantly given in to him, but was known to slip into a chant or to carry a candle when he thought he could get away with it.

Lucy's mother raised her eyebrows to communicate her disapproval. As the congregation settled into the familiar pattern of standing, kneeling and learned responses, moving as one in response to Reverend Buckland's deep, calming voice, the sense of disquiet was palpable.

Lucy knelt, her forehead resting on her gloved hands. It was cold in the church, the rays of summer sunlight finding their way through the stained glass bringing no warmth with them. She could, by moving her head just an inch or two, observe the members of her family in church that day. Twenty-five-year-old Polly, just a year older than Lucy, was carefully smoothing the lace trim on her white gloves. She had, as usual, taken all of two hours to dress for church. Her hat, perched above her forehead on an abundance of carefully arranged knots and braids, was new, and Polly patted it gently when she thought she was not being observed. She would not, Lucy knew, be at all interested in the liturgical beliefs of the new curate.

Their mother, resting her head on her arms, had her eyes closed, but was giving the vicar's words her full attention and would be the first to lead the responses, whereas their father's faraway expression indicated that he was probably thinking of one of his problem patients rather than the words of the service. At the end of the pew the second youngest of Lucy's four brothers, Charles, his bearded chin resting on his folded hands, had his eyes tightly closed, but there was no knowing where his thoughts lay. He was a serious-minded young man but had a way of focussing on any matter except the one in hand, much to his father's irritation when trying to explain to him a medical dilemma. Charles had been studying under his father for several years, but was not yet considered ready to qualify as a doctor in his own right. Of Lucy's brothers, he was the one to whom she was closest.

Her reverie was disturbed by Reverend Francis ascending the steps to the pulpit. He lifted the long silk bookmark from the open Bible that lay on the lectern, looked out at the congregation, and gave them a wide and unexpected smile.

'It is a *privilege* to be here at St Michael's and I *thank* you for the welcome I *have* been given.'

His intonation was quite unlike Reverend Buckland's authoritative tone, and caused a ripple of unease amongst the congregation. His voice rose and fell in a sing-song fashion, some words being over-emphasised while others were almost incomprehensible.

'*Sure*ly,' he chanted, 'there can be no doubt that *most* of us regard instruction as the *chief* work of the Christian ministry?'

When Lucy met her sister Polly's glance, they both looked hastily down at their prayer books lest their smiles should turn to giggles. But what was he saying now?

'It is my *intention* to guide my parishioners on *the* true path, and also *those* Dissenters who might repent and *return* from the wilderness. *Be in no doubt,*' his voice was loud now and had lost its affected intonation, '*that any who do not follow the true Church are on their way to eternal punishment*!'

There was a stunned silence. Lucy felt her eyes grow wide. He could not say that! Many in the congregation had cousins, brothers, nephews and nieces who were Nonconformists; a few supported both Chapel and Church, turn and turn about. A murmur of disquiet passed around the church; even Polly looked shocked. Then there was a sudden rustle of clothing, the sound of leather soles echoing on stone and the loud click of the oak door's latch. Had two people walked out, or had there been more? Lucy dared not turn around to look.

Eventually, when Reverend Francis descended from the pulpit, the service concluded with the more familiar tones of the vicar. A low hum of conversation commenced as the congregation picked up their prayer books and retrieved lost gloves and umbrellas from under the pews.

Lucy's mother leaned towards her and Polly.

'Did you ever hear such a thing!'

Lucy knew it would be a long time before they heard the last of this. She was not greatly interested in the rights and wrongs of high church practices, but it could not be right to condemn the many Nonconformists in the town as heretics. As she edged sideways out of the pew after her family, she arrived in the aisle at the same time as her friend Edith, Reverend Buckland's daughter. Lucy gave her a meaningful look, but Edith responded only with her characteristically sweet smile.

'Call in for tea tomorrow, would you? I have a book I think you would like to read.'

Edith would not say anything against the new curate. She taught at Sunday School, was quiet and good, and sympathetic to every living being, or so it seemed to Lucy. She sometimes wished she could be more like Edith.

As she joined the crowd moving slowly down the aisle, she smiled at Mrs Balsdon and Mr Pidgeon, both of whom shook their heads expressively to communicate their disapproval of the new curate. Reverend Francis was waiting in the porch with Reverend Buckland.

'Now, Reverend Francis, this is Dr Jones and his family.'

Some people were pushing past without speaking. Lucy's father shook the curate's hand, but Lucy could tell from the straightness of her father's back and the paucity of his words that he was not pleased.

The extent of his displeasure became clear over lunch. Sitting at the head of the table, he waved his fork irritably in the air.

'Such extreme Romish practices might suit some towns, but they won't be accepted in Torrington! The townspeople won't stand for it. Church and Chapel rub along together well enough, there's no need for him to be creating divisions where there are none. Reverend Buckland should put a stop to it at once, but we all know he's been leaning in that direction for many years, and only wanted an accomplice to help him on his way.'

Lucy saw that a vegetable dish had been forgotten and rose from the table to fetch it. She was glad of an excuse to leave the dining room. For herself, she rather admired the bright colours of the new curate's stole and was not greatly interested in what they represented; she only hoped that he would be a sympathetic presence at her fortnightly meeting.

The long, tiled passageway was cool and quiet, but when she pushed open the kitchen door she was met by a rush of heat, the clatter of dishes and the smell of newly roasted meat and hot oil. Sarah, the cook, flustered and red in the face as she furiously stirred the custard that would accompany their dessert, looked up in alarm when Lucy came in.

'What's up now? 'Tisn't overdone, be it?'

'No, Sarah, it's very good. But there should be another dish of vegetables, carrots, I think.'

'Well, what's her done with them?'

The housemaid, Ann, appeared from the scullery. She and Sarah were cousins, and both were barely twenty years of age. Usually, they were kept in order by Mary Wilcox who had been with the family for more than thirty years, moving from being a nursemaid to Lucy and her siblings when they were small, to becoming the housekeeper, although no one could remember her ever being given the role. Today, she was away visiting relatives. Lucy had taken it upon herself to run the household each Sunday so that Mary could have a day off. It was not a role that Lucy relished but, as her mother was not as strong as she had been, she felt compelled to play a more active part. She feared that it was a duty that would grow and grow unless she could, one day, escape by marrying. Recently, she had felt less hopeful of this ever coming to pass.

'Yer 'tis!' Ann retrieved the dish of carrots from the dresser. 'Must have put it down while I was opening the door. Do 'ee want me to take it in?'

'No, don't fret,' said Lucy, 'I'll take it.'

When she returned to the dining room, the subject of the conversation had not changed.

'I was just saying, Lucy,' said her mother, 'whatever impressions we have formed of Reverend Francis, you, Polly and I must call one day soon to welcome the family to Torrington. We must not shirk our duty even if he has spoken out of turn. Besides, it will be interesting to meet his wife and to see how they are settling in at Torridge Villa. It is a large house for a young family to afford – there are three small children, I believe.'

Lucy opened the window on to the garden to let in some air before sitting down.

'Then let us go soon. I would rather have spoken to him in a social way before I have the first of my meetings with him.'

OUR NEW CURATE.—On Monday last the chief topic conversed about and discussed amongst some of our leading church people was the substance of a sermon preached at our church on Sunday evening last by the Rev. H. O. Francis, M.A., the newly-appointed Curate. From what we are told the reverend gentleman's sermon was intended as a defence, or support, of the establishment of the Truro Bishopric; but in the course of it, it is stated that he characterised all classes of Dissenters, preachers and people, as being on their way to eternal punishment. The doctrines advanced during the discourse have given very great offence to several of the more respectable church people (some of whom have members of their families who are Dissenters), who have gone so far as to declare that they will not sit under such preaching. Dissenters themselves will take no heed to such bigotry and folly, being too well acquainted with the plan of salvation by faith in Christ Jesus, to be moved from the hope of the Gospel; and the matter would not have been referred to, if it were not for the effects produced by the sermon amongst the members of the established church.

North Devon Journal, 1876

Chapter Two

As it happened, she met the new curate the very next day. Her father asked her and Polly to represent him at a garden party at Stevenstone because he was too busy to attend. They would have gone in any case but, as their mother did not feel well enough, it was arranged that Lucy and Polly would go in the carriage with Reverend and Mrs Buckland and Edith.

Waiting in the spacious hallway of Castle House, Lucy called up the stairs to her sister.

'Polly! It's three forty-five! They will be here at any moment.'

A door closed loudly, and Polly ran along the landing and down the wide staircase. She was wearing her new dress with fine navy and white stripes, the overskirt looped and gathered into a particularly pronounced bustle, and a matching navy hat which emphasised her deep blue eyes.

'See? I've turned the waistband over just an inch, so I don't trip on the hem when I run. Does it look presentable?'

She twirled around while Lucy perused her. 'Yes, but I'm sure your racquet will catch on the flounces. You might have done better to wear your pale blue, but it's too late now.'

'I wore that last time! I'll take care to keep my distance from the ball. If I have to stretch to reach it I won't get in a tangle.'

Polly was determined to play tennis. It was not that she had a great deal of interest in the game, but knew that the exercise would give her complexion a healthy glow, and lifting her arms to serve would show her figure to advantage.

'Here's the carriage! Don't forget your parasol.'

Mrs Buckland and Edith greeted them kindly as they climbed into the landau for the short journey. Reverend Buckland sat directly opposite Lucy, his face bearing its usual benign but remote expression. She would like to have asked him his opinion of the new curate; he surely could not be pleased that people had walked out of the service.

'You're looking quite charming, both of you!' The purple flowers decorating Mrs Buckland's hat quivered as she leaned forward to pat Polly's and Lucy's knees. She was Edith's stepmother, and had been like a second mother to Lucy, for the children of both families had spent much time playing together. Mrs Buckland had been a welcome source of wisdom, sympathy and cake when they returned to the drawing room with stories of their adventures and mishaps. Edith had five brothers. Rawlin was the same age as Lucy, and had always been her favourite, both as a child and as they grew up. But he had gone to Australia now. She would like to have known whether there had been any letters from him since the telegram that told of his arrival in Melbourne, but did not want even Edith to know how she longed for news of him.

She was not particularly looking forward to the garden party, but most people considered it a privilege to go to Stevenstone. Although the main residence of the Honourable Mark Rolle was only a mile and a half outside Torrington, many of the townsfolk had only glimpsed the turrets of the house, standing as it did at the end of a lengthy drive. As the horse trotted up the long approach, Lucy leaned out of the landau for the first sight of the house. Someone had once told her that it resembled a French chateau; she was not one of those who had toured Europe so did not know whether this was true, but the sheer size of the house and the turreted towers that stood at each corner was even more impressive than she remembered.

'One cannot help wondering why he needed to build such an enormous house when he has only two small daughters. They must frequently lose their way along all the corridors.'

She spoke without thinking but, as usual, Mrs Buckland smiled at her indulgently.

At least it provided employment for an army of servants, she thought. She tried to count the windows, all of which would need regular cleaning.

When the landau drew up on the gravelled driveway, small groups of people were already wandering along the terrace, or leaning on the balustrade to look out across the grounds to the herd of grazing red deer in the distance. She recognised Mr and Mrs Saltren-Willett from Monkleigh with their two daughters, also Mr, Mrs and Miss Vidal from Abbotsham. The garden party always attracted well-to-do people from throughout the area.

She leaned over to whisper to Edith. 'If anyone should be in need of a magistrate, a solicitor or a clergyman in Devon today, there will scarcely be one to be found, for they have all been invited to Stevenstone.'

Edith suppressed a laugh as they alighted. 'Then let us hope no one here requires a doctor, for they are all too busy to attend.'

It was true; Lucy's father and brothers rarely had time for entertainment.

As each carriage drew up, its occupants were perused by those on the terrace. Lucy began to wish that she had worn her new dress. Which group should she and Edith join? Polly had already hurried over to some young people who were loudly proposing a game of tennis, and Reverend and Mrs Buckland were conversing with Reverend Kempe and his family from Merton. Lucy turned away to take Edith's arm.

'Shall we walk together to the flower garden?'

They passed the garden house where tables covered with pristine white cloths were laden with decorative displays of food, each table attended by a uniformed footman waiting to serve the guests strolling in that direction, but she did not yet feel ready to eat.

The weather was perfect, the sun warm but not uncomfortably hot, the sky blue enough to form a suitable backdrop to the immaculate lawns and stone walls of Stevenstone. The scent of newly mown grass drifted on the breeze, and from somewhere beyond the estate came the distant shouts and laughter of men harvesting in the fields. Now that she was out of the public eye, she could begin to enjoy herself.

She turned to her friend. As usual, Edith's expression was one of benign contentment. Her style of dress reflected her character; sensible, sufficiently attractive, but never flamboyant.

'Now, tell me,' she squeezed Edith's arm, 'what is your opinion of the new curate? He caused quite a stir on Sunday.'

Edith reflected before she replied. 'It was unfortunate that some people took offence, but it is not an unusual reaction to strongly-held beliefs. My father says Reverend Francis will bring energy and enthusiasm to the town; he has many ideas as to how we might increase the congregation.'

'He has had the opposite effect so far! Will he frighten away members of the congregation every Sunday? St Michael and All Angels will be empty before long!'

Edith smiled. 'There are always a few who will try joining the Nonconformists, but they very often return when they tire of the dreariness of the chapel. Reverend Francis believes he can attract those who rarely attend church; we know from our work, Lucy, that there are many of those.'

In the walled garden, closely-mown grass pathways led between beds containing bright orange and pale apricot lilies, multi-coloured dahlias alive with the buzzing of bees, and vivid yellow sunflowers growing taller than a man against the old stone walls.

Ahead there was a familiar figure. Reverend Francis and his wife were walking through the flower garden, the curate carrying a stick which he flourished as he walked, and looking about eagerly while his wife, who barely reached her husband's shoulder, clutched his arm tightly as if afraid that she might lose him.

Edith leaned in to whisper to Lucy. 'There! Now you can form your own opinion.'

Reverend Francis hurried towards them and took Edith's hand.

'Dear Miss Buckland! How pleasing to see you again so soon! Is this not the most delightful garden? And I am so glad to be meeting the right sort of people. Will you introduce me to your friend?'

Lucy had hung back, but the curate reached for her hand and pulled her towards him.

'I remember! We met in church, did we not? I believe it is Miss Jones, and your father is the doctor. You see, I have a good memory!' His laugh was high and unexpected, and quite out of proportion to the occasion. She took advantage of the moment to withdraw her hand, noticing as she did so that Reverend Francis smelled of cologne. Never before had she known a man who used cologne!

'Miss Jones is, like me, a district visitor, so will be present at our meeting next week,' said Edith.

Feeling uncomfortable in the curate's intent gaze, Lucy turned her attention to Mrs Francis. In contrast to her husband's overbearing confidence, she seemed very timid. She was small of stature, with a round, pale face and startled blue eyes. Her childlike appearance made it hard to believe that she was in fact mother to three children.

'How are you settling in, Mrs Francis? I hope you will enjoy living in Torrington.'

Before Mrs Francis could reply, her husband began to extoll the advantages of the town, and to enumerate his plans for improving it, while his wife watched him with admiration. Lucy hardly heard what he was saying, being transfixed by his hands which he moved expressively as he spoke. There was, she thought, something reptilian about the narrow white fingers and long nails.

'And I hope, Miss Jones and Miss Buckland, that you will be able to help me achieve that aim!'

'I'm sorry, Reverend Francis, what aim was that?' She had not been paying attention.

'To encourage more of the working classes to attend church, Lucy,' said Edith. 'We both know that is not an easy task, do we not?'

Lucy had become a district visitor to give aid to those who were sick or malnourished, advise those who had family problems, and use her knowledge of the town for those who were seeking work. She had reminded one or two men who seemed determined to follow a criminal path that they might be heading for eternal punishment, but on the whole she did not dwell on religion in her conversations with the poor. It was wrong of her, no doubt; it was, after all, the vicar who had asked her to carry out the work. Edith was far more diligent. Would she really have to move the conversation from coals and clothing to church attendance?

'Not easy, but necessary!' Reverend Francis was saying. 'I have promised the bishop, with whom I am *very* well acquainted, that I shall continue the fight against Nonconformity and enlarge the congregation, so I shall be most grateful for your assistance! You can do the groundwork, so to speak!'

As they walked through the garden together, Reverend Francis continued to talk loudly and wave his hands around. When the garden path narrowed, Lucy fell back to walk beside his wife.

'Where were you living before you came to Torrington, Mrs Francis?'

'Chatham in Kent. Herbert was curate at St Mary's. It is a very busy town; there are the docks and the army barracks, you know, and Herbert thinks a country town will be better for me and the children. I was brought up in Bridport, Dorset, where my father is a doctor, like yours!' She looked up at Lucy, delighted by the coincidence. 'Herbert is determined to make a success of his time here in Torrington; you see he hopes eventually to find a patron who will get him a living of his own – it is very important to him to have his own parish. And to me too, of course.' She leaned confidingly towards Lucy. 'It would please me, one day, to tell my father that Herbert was to become a vicar. My father does not have a great deal of faith in Herbert, you see. He seems blind to his strengths.'

It was disconcerting to hear such confidences so soon after meeting. Lucy tried to smile sympathetically before quickly changing the subject.

'Look, we are coming to the garden house where food is being served! Shall we eat?'

But Reverend Francis had a fancy for a game of tennis, so they continued on.

Lucy could hear cheering as they approached the tennis court. Polly was holding up her racquet in a pose of mock triumph and managing to look remarkably elegant despite the heat and her recent exertion; her hat was only a little askew and she was certainly attracting many attentive glances from the groups of people on the terrace.

Lucy, Edith and Mrs Francis found a spot in the shade from which they could watch the next game. Reverend Francis' opponent was suitably dressed in comfortable, light-coloured clothing, but it was not long before the curate's narrow black

14

trousers and high-collared jacket were making him look very hot indeed.

'Herbert does enjoy tennis!' said Mrs Francis. 'A friend of my father's has installed a court and he often takes the opportunity for a game when we are visiting.'

It seemed he had more enthusiasm than skill. His loud laughs and uncoordinated leaps, accompanied by peculiar exclamations when he tried to reach the ball, were providing the onlookers with much amusement, but Mrs Francis was too engrossed in admiring her husband to notice.

Eventually Lucy grew tired of the spectacle and, making her excuses, went to join Polly who was talking with a group of friends further along the terrace.

'Lucy! We are planning an outing to Instow next week, you will join us, won't you? If the fine weather continues, we can take a picnic.'

Ever since the railway line was extended from Bideford to Torrington four years previously, it had become the custom to take an excursion every few weeks.

'Which day will you go?' Lucy asked. 'I have my district visits on Tuesday and Thursday.'

'Ah, your district visits! Worthy Miss Jones! If we were all as dutiful as you, the town would be a better place, would it not!' Richard Tapley's genuine smile took the sting out of the comment, but Lucy knew that most were in accord with him. She was perceived as being worthy, but dull.

She did not mind too much. She was used to being the sensible one in her family. Polly was the one who attracted attention.

In any case her friends did not shun her, deciding on the following Wednesday to accommodate her. They went on to plan the details of the excursion - which train they would catch, and whose turn it was to have the picnic basket prepared.

Polly's gaze, she noticed, was on Richard Tapley. Lucy and Polly had known him all their lives. Being several years older than they, he had been a rather remote but greatly admired figure at the children's parties and concerts at which they met, then had been glimpsed only occasionally when home from holidays from school and then university. He had followed in his father's footsteps and was now established as a solicitor at Church Stile House, playing an active part in the life of the town, and accompanying Lucy and their friends on excursions when he could spare a few hours away from his work.

She had been aware that Polly always managed to sit near him on the train and to walk with him whenever she had the opportunity, but when Lucy questioned her gently about her feelings for him, she turned away and changed the subject.

'Richard is a friend, no more than that! Why should you think otherwise?'

She and Polly had never been inclined to confide in each other.

As a rule, Richard Tapley was equally charming to everyone present, but today his gaze returned most frequently to a new member of the group. Marianne Anderson, a fair-haired, fine-featured girl, was the middle daughter of the vicar of Milton Damerel. Marianne seemed quiet and unassuming, but Lucy saw that she often allowed her eyes to meet Richard's with a confidence that suggested she knew her interest was reciprocated. There was surely an understanding between them, of which Polly, laughing prettily at his witticisms, seemed unaware.

A polite round of applause from the far end of the terrace indicated that the game of tennis had finished, and Reverend Francis ran laughing up the steps to join his wife. Edith took the opportunity to take her leave and came over to join the group, then Richard suggested that they all make their way through the garden for refreshments.

'Now that you are better acquainted with Reverend Francis, have you revised your opinion of him?' Strolling towards the garden house, Lucy had deliberately fallen behind the rest of the group so that she might talk to Edith.

Her friend hesitated for a moment.

'He shared many of his ideas with me while you were walking with his wife. There is much that is praiseworthy.'

Lucy could tell that she was searching for the right words.

'But I can't help wishing, Lucy, that he was a different sort of man. I'm afraid that the people of Torrington will not take him seriously.'

'I think you are right. But I am also afraid that if he persists with his high church ideas, they will turn against him. And we know how forcefully they can make their feelings known.'

But that did not cause her any great concern. It was the thought of having to hold frequent meetings with him that was giving her a strange sense of foreboding.

Chapter Three

Lucy bent to lace her walking shoes, lifted Alpheus's lead from the hook in the boot room, and tiptoed across the hall so as not to dirty the tiled floor that was still damp after Ann's work with the scrubbing brush.

'Lucy?' Mary Wilcox appeared from the kitchen passage, the heavy apron she wore in the mornings wrapped around her ample figure. 'Be 'ee going into the town? Mr Short's new boy has only brought one loaf, don't know if he's coming or going, that boy don't.' She paused on the threshold, frowning down at the floor. 'Her uses too much water, 'tisn't necessary and folks'll take a tumble one of these days. I've lost count of the times I've told her!'

'I wasn't intending to go to town, just to go with Alpheus to the Common, and take my sketchbook. But I'll go to the baker first if you wish.'

'No, you have your walk, chiel,' Mary regarded Lucy fondly. 'Ann can go for the bread, and p'raps you'll help me with the week's menus when you'm back.' As she proceeded to bellow up the stairs for the housemaid, there was a clattering of pans from the kitchen and a shriek from Sarah. Lucy knew that her mother, working on the household accounts in the morning room, would be wincing at the unwarranted racket.

She closed the door on the noises of the house. The garden lay still and expectant in the early warmth of the August sun, the peacefulness of the scene intensified by the melodic notes of a blackbird's song and the distant chanting of children from the school opposite Castle House. The lawn, large enough for a sizeable tea party and a croquet lawn, but not for the tennis court that Polly craved, was bordered by her mother's carefully tended beds of dahlias, and at the far end by a shrubbery from which the retriever, Alpheus, now emerged, bounding over to Lucy with wagging tail and giving little, excited barks at the sight of his lead.

She clipped on the lead; he was generally well-behaved but the sight of the geese and hens that roamed the Common sometimes proved too much of a temptation in the first exuberance of a walk.

Castle House, although only two minutes' walk from the shops on the Square, stood at the edge of the town next to the precipitous site of the old Norman castle whose stones had been used in the building of many Torrington walls so, when Lucy turned from the entrance gate, she immediately left the houses of the town behind. She passed the bowling green where the first players were taking their positions on the smooth green sward, and came to the spot that always caused her to stop and stare.

Torrington was set on the summit of a hill which fell away steeply to north, south, east and west, giving panoramic views over the surrounding countryside. Here, on the southerly side, the bracken and gorse-strewn slopes of the Common fell almost sheer to the River Torridge three hundred feet below, giving Lucy a giddy view down to the glistening water snaking through the valley, and beyond to the gentler slopes stretching up for a mile or more to the distant horizon, a vista of ancient pastures and woodlands untouched by turnpike roads or railway tracks, but enhanced here and there by the soft outline of a thatched cottage roof, the whitewashed walls of a farmhouse, or a gently winding lane.

Lucy sat on the bench alongside the path and, having checked for wandering hens, unclipped Alpheus's lead, whereupon he bounded down the steep slope in search of rabbits.

Her eyes travelled over the landscape on the far side of the steep valley. Half a dozen figures moving methodically over a golden field were, she guessed, women gleaners gathering grain left after the harvest of the previous day. From her vantage point, her gaze sought out the source of a repetitive dull *thud*, and identified a tiny figure high on the hill, his arms lifting and falling as he let the weight of a mallet drive a fence post into the ground. The sound reached her a second after she saw his arm fall.

There was no one here to look disapprovingly at her for walking alone on the Common. When a thrush started to sing from a nearby tree, she felt the tensions of the morning begin to melt away.

Last night, as she and Polly prepared for bed, Polly had talked incessantly about Richard Tapley; how he had attained the highest marks of any in his year when he took his final examinations, how he had been so very keen to arrange the outing to Instow – 'He asked particularly whether I should be able to go!' she said, smiling over her shoulder at Lucy as she brushed out her hair in front of the mirror.

Lucy had climbed carefully into bed. 'Polly, has he given you any reason to believe he has a special regard for you? I know you say he favours you, but he hasn't put such feelings into words, has he?'

She spoke as gently as she could but, as she feared, Polly's response was to slam her hairbrush down on the dressing table and turn angrily to her.

'What do you know of such things? You wouldn't even notice if a man looked favourably on you! You are far too serious, Lucy, you don't understand all the little tricks by which one can make one's feelings known! Richard will speak to me before long, that's quite clear!'

Polly had climbed into her side of the bed and turned her back on Lucy. They did not speak again before they slept.

But, at breakfast time, their mother bustled in from the kitchen with some news.

'Do you know what Mary has told me? She met Mrs Yeo who has worked all these years for the Tapley family, and Richard Tapley is to marry! He's engaged to one of Reverend Anderson's daughters from Milton Damerel, isn't that lovely news?'

Their mother left the room again with a vase of flowers in her arms. Lucy looked carefully at Polly who was staring down at the tablecloth, then reached out for her hand.

'I'm sorry, Polly, it's dreadful to be told like that. I'm sure Mother had no idea…'

Polly turned on her with tears in her eyes. 'You knew! You must have known! Why else did you say those things last night! Why didn't you warn me?'

And despite Lucy's protestations, she had run from the room and rejected any attempt to talk to her when she went upstairs after breakfast.

Lucy leaned back on the bench and drew up her knees. It was not the first time her sister had been disappointed. Because Polly was determined that she should marry soon, she looked for signs of interest where there were none, and Lucy feared that, being so eager, she might meet with disappointment again. But it was impossible to reason with her; as the elder sister, Polly always considered herself to be in possession of greater wisdom.

And besides, Lucy thought, as she wrapped her arms around her knees, what *did* she know of such matters? Who was she to advise?

Alpheus appeared on the slope below the path, his nose to the ground amongst the bracken and his tail wagging, but, seeing Lucy, he left the trail he was following and bounded up to her, pushing his nose against her face before leaping away again. It was a clear invitation to join him.

'All right, Alph, I'm coming.' She would walk, her sketching could wait for another day.

The path followed the contour of the hill, dropping gently until it made a sharp turn to zigzag down into the valley. A gentle breeze was drifting up from the River Torridge, carrying with it the scent of the meadowsweet that grew on its banks. Lucy walked as quickly as her long skirts would allow, with a long, confident stride despite the roughness of the path, until an old holly bush caught her eye, and she stopped suddenly. A large flat stone lay at its base.

It was Rawlin who had shown her this place, years ago now, when they were thirteen or fourteen years old. They had been racing down the path to join the other children by the river when he had stopped suddenly, grabbing her hand when she careered into him.

'Wait, Lucy! I want to show you something!'

They had knelt together on the short, cropped grass by the side of the path, and she felt the warmth of his arm next to hers.

'I found this place yesterday. I don't know whether it'll still be here...' And reaching under the holly bush, he carefully lifted one end of the stone.

'There! Look!' His voice was a whisper.

She had known at once what it was. Not a snake; it was a slow worm, the length of its sinuous golden-grey form pressed into the earth so that it lay in a mould of its own making. They had found one near the old castle walls the previous year. This one blinked at them, then slid slowly and gracefully away from its hiding place. She reached out and touched it with the tip of her finger. It was surprisingly warm.

'I daren't replace the stone until it's gone for fear of hurting it,' said Rawlin. 'It'll come back when we've left.' He was so close to her, she could see the flecks of orange in his brown eyes. 'Don't tell the others, it'll be our secret. Edward would only torment it, and Charles'd want to carry out experiments on it, throw it in the river to see if it can swim, or feed it to the geese.'

'They can live up to twenty years,' she told him. 'I read that in Father's book.'

He jumped up and gave her one of those smiles that transformed his normally serious expression.

'You can watch it for me while I'm away at school! See if it nests!'

And as they continued their headlong rush down the steep winding path to the river, she had shouted after him, 'I'll write and tell you!'

But she was alone now. She lifted one end of the stone and peered underneath. Nothing. The long, curving indentation was still there in the earth, so a slow worm still spent some time there, even now, years later; but now, whenever she looked, it had gone.

Continuing down the path to the bottom of the hill, she crossed the road that the Honourable Mark Rolle had built over the old canal bed, and walked over the buttercup-rich meadow to reach the river, feeling moisture from the early morning dew seeping into her shoes. Although the day was not far advanced there was already warmth in the sun; her shoes and the hem of her dress would soon dry. Alpheus ran to the very edge of the riverbank and gave several short, excited barks at the sight of the water, while dashing to and fro until he found a spot from which he could scramble down into the river. Standing chest-deep with his long coat streaming out behind him, he gulped happily at the water while looking up at Lucy as if inviting her to join him.

'This way, Alpheus!' She walked along the riverbank until she found a tussock on which she could sit with her feet above the water. There had been heavy rain just a few days previously, so the river was high for the time of the year, and the sparkling water rushing over the stony bed was inviting. The trees on the opposite bank ensured that she could not be seen from that direction, and there were no fishermen. She twisted around to look back up the hill. It was deserted but for a boy leading a goat along the upper slopes; there was no one who would notice her, no one to carry stories back to the town. Daringly, she reached up under her skirt and eased her stockings down her left thigh, then down her right, rolling them carefully over her calves until her feet and legs were bare. Then she pulled her skirt and petticoats up to her thighs and tucked them under her. Her pale legs glowed in the greenish light that filtered through the leaves.

The water was cold at first and made her gasp. She curled her toes in uneasy ecstasy, but as she got used to the temperature, the caress of the running water on her dangling feet soothed her, and she let her thoughts drift back to the past.

Many of her childhood memories involved the Common. It was on Castle Hill that she, with her brothers and sister and the children from the Vicarage, were most at ease. They considered it to be their own; it was where they built tree houses, and camps amongst the ferns. Mill Street Common by contrast was foreign territory, home to boys who were inclined to pick a fight, and numerous aggressive geese whose droppings were carried home on shoes, to the disgust of the servants. The Old Bowling Green was the playground for children from New Street, the part of the Common known as Quiet Possession home to Calf Street children. Lucy and her playmates explored all these places, but were on their guard everywhere except Castle Hill.

It was not with her brothers but with Edith and Rawlin that Lucy spent most time; together they picked wildflowers to press carefully between the pages of a book, they memorised the names of butterflies, watched a family of young stoats chasing each other on a grassy bank, and found the prints of an otter in the mud of the riverbank. Lucy climbed trees and waded through streams with Rawlin in search of birds' eggs while Edith waited anxiously at a safe distance. On wet days they wrote illustrated accounts of their adventures in notebooks with alternate pages of lined and plain paper.

But then, things changed. Edith often chose to stay at home to help her stepmother with the younger children. Polly, who had never been as adventurous as Lucy, decided she preferred sewing or writing letters to playing on the Common. Sometimes Lucy was joined by another girl from Castle Street, but often it was just her and the boys. She thought nothing of it until her mother started to make discouraging remarks.

'Lucy, you're not going out rampaging with your brothers again, are you? Will other boys be there too?'

'Lucy, I hardly think that is ladylike behaviour. You're not a child now, you know.'

While the boys were away at school, her mother had new, longer dresses made for her. The early pride she took in her new clothes passed when she saw in the mirror that they did not flatter her figure the way that Polly's did; her broad shoulders and undefined waist made her look clumsy rather than elegant. She did not want to disappoint her mother, so she pretended to be pleased, knowing that the clothes had been expensive.

Her mother told her that she must walk sedately, and she found that she had to; the skirts reached almost to her ankles, so she could not run without them tangling around her legs. She practised walking around the garden, and then around the town square, trying to keep her back straight and her chin lifted in the way her mother had taught her, but she longed to be a child again and run on the Common. When the boys returned for the holidays she trailed after them on the paths down to the river, often arriving at the destination just as they were ready to leave. Sometimes she decided not to go, and hid instead in her father's library where she could escape the demands of the household and lose herself in a book.

It was not long before the boys started to change too. Rawlin and his older brothers rarely came out, and it was only Lucy's brother Charles who explored the Common with the younger Buckland boys. Sometimes Rawlin came to Castle House with Edith, or she would see him engrossed in his studies at the Vicarage and would pluck up courage to interrupt him. He always seemed pleased to see her but there was awkwardness between them, especially when they were in company. The spontaneity of their childhood days had gone.

But sometimes they met by chance in the town, and on several occasions Rawlin suggested a walk on the Common, to visit their old haunts, he said. When they were out on the familiar paths together, the discomfort fell away; they laughed and talked together as naturally as they had done as children, and when they sat on a seat together they could be silent if they wished, because the expansive view out across the Torridge valley drew them out of themselves.

She remembered one particular day when they were sitting together at the top of Castle Hill. It was early spring, a couple of years ago. They talked of the goings-on in the town, laughed at the plotting and posturing of people they knew, then Rawlin told her about his work in the Rifle Volunteer Corps; as a lieutenant he had to lead the men, motivate them to do their best but at the same time to adhere to a strict routine. He turned to her, his face alight with enthusiasm.

'I feel I'm doing a good job, Lucy. I try to treat them fairly but firmly; they're ordinary working men, you know, a rough, untutored lot on the whole, but they like me, I think, and respect me. I find more satisfaction in my evenings with the Volunteer Corps than I do in my working day. Sometimes I think I would like to be a leader of men in my work, but what work that might be, I do not know.'

She watched him as he spoke. His face had broadened, and his beard suited him well; there was confidence in his expression, a certainty that he would make his way in the world, but his boyish enthusiasm had not been lost. He was still her friend.

'I envy you,' she said, 'being able to do something worthwhile, I wish I could put my time to better use. Household tasks are so dull, and as for embroidery and mending, can there be anything as dismal as sitting all day with a needle in your hand? But there, someone has to do them.'

He laughed sympathetically and, reaching out, laid his hand on hers. 'Lucy, you never did wish to do as everyone else does, your thoughts and tastes run upon different lines from those of the majority.'

She knew it to be true; she usually kept her thoughts to herself for fear of appearing odd. Even with Rawlin she did not like to express the extent of her difference. If she told him how much she disliked the never-ending task of making life comfortable for her father and brothers, she was afraid he would think her selfish. But it surely must be more rewarding to go out each day and help those who were in need and make one's mark upon the world, as her father did.

She sat very still, intensely aware of the warmth and weight of Rawlin's hand resting on hers.

He was staring out over the valley, and spoke quietly. 'It is your difference that makes you special, Lucy. Don't try to change.'

She could not find the words for a reply.

A mewing cry broke the silence, and they looked up to see two buzzards soaring high over the river. The broad-winged birds spiralled up and up, wing tips touching as they passed each other, then one stooped suddenly at breath-taking speed before spreading its wings and soaring upwards again. It was beautiful to watch, and they sat for several minutes, the stillness broken only by the high-pitched calls of the buzzards. She was acutely aware of Rawlin's presence, and his slow, steady breathing.

'They mate for life, you know,' he said quietly.

It was not long after that day that he moved away for his work. She saw him occasionally when he was home for a visit, but he often seemed distracted. Although she always made a point of calling at the Vicarage when he was visiting, they did not have the opportunity to spend time alone together.

And then she heard that he was to move to Australia. He had obtained a post with the Eastern Extension Telegraph Company, Edith told her; he wished to make a new start in life, she said.

There was a party at the Vicarage before his departure. She spent longer than usual getting dressed, but then berated herself for thinking it important. What did it matter how she looked? Who would notice? And if someone did notice, they would see that her clothes did not hide the clumsiness of her figure, nor her attempts at hairdressing succeed in smoothing her hair.

Rawlin was, of course, the centre of attention. She watched him from her chair near the fire; he moved from group to group and seemed jovial but, at the same time, distracted. Probably she imagined that he glanced several times in her direction. Eventually he came to speak to her; he was ensuring that he spoke to everyone in the room, he had always been well-mannered.

'Well, Lucy.' He sat on the footstool next to her. 'I shall be away next week.'

She nodded. She could not speak.

'It has come around so quickly. There has been so much to do, and I have had so little time to prepare. It is a big adventure, but…'

Was there an honesty in his face which she had not seen when he was speaking to others?

'I don't know what sort of life I will have out there,' he said hesitantly, 'what the living conditions will be like. It may well be that they will be more spartan than that to which we are accustomed.'

'Edith told me that the houses are quite basic,' she ventured.

He stared at the floor, and neither of them spoke for a minute or more.

'I hope I'm doing the right thing,' he said, 'by travelling to the far side of the world. On my own. It seems a daunting prospect, now that I am to go.'

'I'm sure you will be very happy.' It was all she could trust herself to say.

He looked at her, and his eyes were troubled. 'We have been good friends, haven't we, Lucy?' he said. 'Growing up together, exploring the Common, it was always you and me, wasn't it? And I thought it always would be. Did you feel that too, Lucy?'

She tried to keep her voice level. 'I hoped that it might be so. But we can never know what the future holds.'

'No. We cannot. And now, now that I feel compelled to travel, to work at something that will challenge me, to have adventures, it seems more uncertain than ever before.'

He stared at the floor.

'Perhaps, Lucy, one day there will be the opportunity for us to be together.'

Their eyes met, and she knew that her gaze was as anguished as was his.

He stood up suddenly. 'I'll write to you, Lucy.' And he had walked quickly away.

She looked out across the river, now. She could again hear the buzzards calling, as they had when she and Rawlin were here together. This time they were not in the sky above her, but in the woodland upstream; they were the cries of young birds calling for sustenance.

He had been gone for five months now, and still she had not received a letter. She did not suppose now that she would.

Chapter Four

Lucy paused in her reading and looked up. She guessed it must be getting close to three o'clock, the hour at which she was to meet the new curate. She was not much looking forward to making acquaintance with Reverend Francis again.

Sitting opposite her, old Mrs Sandford's eyes were closed, her chin resting on the high collar of her black serge dress, and her open mouth revealing the scarcity of her teeth. Wisps of white hair had escaped from the confines of her black lace cap. It was little wonder that she had dozed off; the small back room in Calf Street where she spent her days was dim, and the atmosphere close on a day such as this. Lucy had tried to open the window when she arrived but found that it was jammed.

'Don't 'ee worry, Miss, 'twill only let the flies in if 'tis open.'

Lucy kept her finger on the paragraph she had reached in the Bible and sat back in the chair. The only sounds came from the ticking of the clock, and the distant voices of men somewhere beyond the back yard. It was a relief, now, to sit quietly. The visit she had made to a family that morning had been difficult, and the shock of it remained with her still.

Mrs Sandford's room might be warm now, but there were signs of damp where the whitewash was flaking from the walls, and there was no fireplace. How ever did she keep warm in winter? Lucy hoped that the woman with whom the old lady lodged allowed her to share her room when the weather was cold. She shifted her weight on the hard chair.

She had decided to start district visiting after Rawlin left for Australia. Edith, of course, had been visiting alongside her stepmother since she was a child, and on her own account for several years, but Lucy had not previously felt drawn to the role despite Edith's encouragement. It was only when the future that she had imagined for herself was snatched away that she thought she might as well try district visiting. Perhaps keeping busy would keep the feelings of hopelessness at bay. It would be something she could do away from the house, where she was growing so weary of the mundane demands on her time. And besides, why should she not perform useful work as her father and brothers did? She could not be a doctor, but being a district visitor was similar, or so she imagined.

Her mother had not approved.

'Lucy, really, must you?' she said. 'It is one thing for Edith, as the vicar's daughter, to go out visiting but I really do not think that you, as a young lady with prospects, should be wandering about in the poorer parts of town by yourself, exposed to the attentions of anyone who presumes to address you.'

The family had been sitting at the dinner table when she broached the subject. Lucy's father was not expecting to rush off to see a patient before he had even finished his dessert as was so often the case, so she had decided to take advantage of the relaxed pace of the meal, guessing that he might support her.

'Your grandmother, of course,' her mother went on, her eyes wide with indignation, 'visited the poorer people in High Bickington, but it was entirely different; it was expected that the upper classes should take alms to the poor and they were honoured for it. People in the town don't feel the same sense of deference towards their betters. You would be subjecting yourself to all sorts of uncouth behaviours. And the work that Edith does, as I understand it, is just that – work! She has a schedule and is expected to bring about change!'

'I should like to bring about change too, Mother,' said Lucy quietly. 'I should like to do something useful. I could tell Father when children have not been vaccinated, and who needs medical care.'

Her mother sighed impatiently. 'Is not helping to run the house useful? I'm sure I think it is. Your first duty is to your own family.'

Charles winked sympathetically at Lucy, and Polly said she hoped that Lucy would still plan the week's menus with Mary Wilcox because *she* had more than enough to do already. Their father seemed intent on his dinner, but Lucy could see that he was considering the matter.

Finally, he reached across the table and patted her hand. 'You're quick enough to help run the house and carry out a few visits too. You can try it, my dear, but you may tire of the work in time, it's not what you are accustomed to, you know.'

Her mother was unlikely to forbid the work once her father had given his blessing, but she had the last word nevertheless.

'No one in *my* family has ever done such a thing. I cannot imagine what your great aunts will say when they hear, Lucy.'

Lucy knew that her mother would soon be distracted by other concerns, and quietly made arrangements to start work as soon as possible. When she had accompanied Edith on several visits, and Reverend Thompson, the elderly curate, had met with her twice to give advice, she was allocated Calf Street and part of Well Street and left to her own devices apart from the fortnightly meeting with Reverend Thompson and her fellow district visitors.

She did not talk much of her experiences. When asked by friends when out walking, or by Charles while she sat sewing flannel petticoats for the elderly, she told them of the satisfaction in bringing comfort to lonely old people such as Mrs Sandford, and the usefulness of her role in ensuring young children were brought forward for vaccination. She did not tell them of how appalled she was by the exhaustion of a mother unable to care properly for her family, or by the dirt and discomfort she encountered. She did not tell them of the distress she experienced from the bold looks from men on the street, the muttered, half-heard remarks, and the laughter when she had passed by. She would have struggled to find words that would describe how she felt.

Her mother had been right, of course, but Lucy would admit it to no one. She was determined to overcome her fears and learn to be of use to the community. Not far from her own home, people of the same flesh and blood as herself were compelled to live in physical discomfort, to undertake hard toil; young girls were exposed to coarse behaviour and talk. How could they not be affected by it? What had started as a distraction from her disappointment became a calling.

She closed the Bible and cleared her throat. Mrs Sandford gave a sudden snort, and opened her eyes in confusion.

'That is a very comforting passage, is it not?' Lucy pretended not to have noticed that the old lady had been sleeping. 'Now, the time is getting on, and I must be on my way.'

Mrs Sandford pressed Lucy's hand, her fingers twisted by rheumatism.

''Tis so good of you to come, Miss, it means the world to me, it does, having you sit with me like this.'

Lucy wrote the date and time of the visit in her notebook, then said a few words to Mrs Blake who was in the kitchen sewing gloves for Mr Vaughan's factory.

When she stepped out on to the street again, the sky had clouded over, and the drizzle-laden breeze had strengthened enough to blow torn newspaper and other rubbish along the street, but it was not strong enough to dissipate the stench from a blocked drain; she must report that to her father who, as medical officer for health, battled against insanitary conditions in the town.

She walked quickly alongside the long rows of terraced houses that faced in on each other, blocking the view of the steep-sided valleys that surrounded the town. The pavement was narrow; she would have walked in the road if it were not so dirty, because she had discovered that men lounging in doorways found it amusing to lean out suddenly as she passed. But she had only to reach the Vicarage, and would then have Edith's company for the remainder of the walk to Reverend Francis' house.

They arrived at Reverend Francis' front door at the same time as Miss Macartney. The third member of their team, wearing a long black cloak despite the closeness of the day, greeted Lucy and Edith with a curt nod. She was more than ten years older than they, and at previous meetings Lucy had found her rather humourless. Edith, who was distantly related to her, said that Rhoda Macartney had not had a happy life, but would not tell Lucy any more than that.

'Come in! Come in and we will show you our new house!' Reverend Francis had pushed past the housemaid who answered the door and ushered them in without giving Lucy or Edith time to introduce Miss Macartney. 'Come through to the drawing room and see the wonderful view that we have – we cannot believe our good fortune in finding such a house!'

The room was of elegant proportions but devoid of furniture, with the exception of a small rug and two armchairs.

'There now!' Reverend Francis had flung open the French windows that opened on to a terrace – and the view across the garden to the Common, and the village of Taddiport far below in the valley, was indeed magnificent. Lucy had not previously had occasion to visit the house, and it was interesting to see such a familiar view from another aspect.

'Such a large garden we have!' he said. 'And, do you see, we can walk directly from the garden out on to the Common! This house is much better suited to a growing family than our previous home in Chatham. Now let me show you the other rooms.'

Miss Macartney had not joined in with Lucy's and Edith's comments on the view, but stood with her hands clasped in front of her and her lips pursed.

'Reverend Francis,' she said eventually, 'there is much business to discuss. Do you not think that we should make a start?'

'Plenty of time for that, dear lady! Let me show you the extent of the kitchens, and the wonderful system there is for the pumping of water!'

Lucy gave Miss Macartney a sympathetic look as they trailed after their host, but it was met only with a frown.

Absurd as the curate was, it was interesting to see the house, but what impressed itself most strongly on Lucy was the absence of furniture. A small parlour was relatively comfortable, but most of the rooms had very little in them, a small table here, a chest of drawers there. Some were altogether empty, and their footsteps echoed on bare floors. She asked Mrs Francis, who had now joined them, whether their furniture had still to arrive from Chatham.

'Oh, it is already here!' Mrs Francis had two small boys clinging to her skirt, and a girl, the oldest, watched shyly from the door.

'Our house in Chatham was much smaller, you see, so there is much that we need.'

Lucy smiled at the two little boys, who had a look of their father about them. There would surely be a great deal of expense in furnishing the whole house, and that would be especially difficult on a curate's salary.

'Perhaps some rooms could be left empty for the time being.'

'Oh, but plans have already been made! Herbert is full of ideas, you see! He knows exactly the sort of cupboards we should have, the measurements of the bookcases and the style of the chairs! The only puzzle will be to find just what he wants!'

When the tour was complete they returned to the parlour where Mrs Francis, having promised to order some tea, left them to their meeting. Reverend Francis leaned forward in his chair and smiled widely at each of them in turn.

'What a pleasure it is to have the company of three fine ladies!'

Lucy shifted uncomfortably. She had hoped his manner would become more serious once their meeting began.

Edith spoke, sounding unusually hesitant, 'Reverend Francis, at our meetings with Reverend Thompson we usually took turns to talk about our visits, sharing our thoughts on what people needed in the way of clothing, food, coal and so on.'

He raised his eyebrows questioningly.

'We would say who we felt would benefit from a personal visit from the clergy, then, when all the cases had been discussed, the priorities were decided upon with Reverend Thompson's help. And we would plan for any shortfall in the Sick and Needy Fund, perhaps by asking for new donors of leftover food or recruiting new members to the sewing circle. Would you be happy to approach things in the same way?'

Reverend Francis looked a little startled. 'Well, yes, if you feel I need to be so involved, then I will be happy to listen. But I hope there will also be time for *me* to tell *you* of my plans!' His laugh was disconcerting, and he leaned so far forward that all three of them instinctively drew back a little. 'So many of the lower classes find church services dull, and I believe that if we are to bring them into the Church, we must reach out to them in different ways! And at the same time, we must conquer the threat that is posed by Nonconformists – just imagine if all those who have strayed could be enticed back to the true Church!'

'Well said, Reverend Francis! I agree that it is the Nonconformists who present the biggest threat. I will be most interested to hear your ideas.'

It was startling to hear Miss Macartney speak with such vehemence; Edith, too, was nodding, and saying that her father would be very pleased if the congregation could be increased. But for Lucy the most important issue was the family she had visited that morning; she could not allow them to be forgotten. Once Reverend Francis started talking of his plans there would be no stopping him. She took a deep breath.

'May I speak first of a family I visited this morning in Calf Street? I feel their need is urgent.'

Reverend Thompson had always invited her to speak and she was not accustomed to pushing herself forward. However, Reverend Francis nodded enthusiastically so she quickly consulted her notebook, then proceeded to describe the visit that had so disturbed her.

She had to choose her words carefully. The plight of the mother who had recently given birth had shocked her. Until she started district visiting she had little idea of the birth process, but the women she visited spared her no details, demonstrating what had happened to them with gestures that left nothing to the imagination and words that she had never heard before, but soon came to understand. This mother was in so much discomfort she could barely stand, but Lucy only said now that the birth had been 'difficult', the word coming out as a whisper, and she felt her face flush as she stumbled over the syllables. She had already, that morning, hurried home to ask her father to visit the new mother and give her something to ease the pain, but there was much else that was needed. She explained that the mother had insufficient blankets and no clothing suitable for a newborn baby; she needed bread and tea, brandy to regain her strength and coal for heating water. The father was out of work; Lucy had sent him to fetch his mother-in-law who lived in a village some miles away, hoping that she would be prepared to give practical aid.

Edith, who listened intently to all that Lucy said, immediately offered help. 'I will ask our cook to make some beef soup, and I am sure there is still some brandy my father bought for the emergency supplies.'

Reverend Francis shifted uncomfortably in his seat. 'The curate, I assume, is not expected to give aid? Because, as I am sure you can understand, with a growing family and all the expenses of moving house...'

There was an awkward silence.

'There are many well-to-do families in the town, Reverend Francis, whose families have grown up, and who contribute regularly to the Sick and Needy Fund,' Edith said at last. 'I'm sure it will not be a problem.'

Miss Macartney was inclined to be critical of the family, asking why they had not been better prepared, but Edith quickly changed the course of the conversation. She would retrieve the box of napkins, tiny shirts and nightdresses that was loaned to new mothers in need, she said, and suggested that more boxes should be available for times when several new babies came at once in the town. Lucy felt a tremendous sense of relief that she would soon be able to deliver aid to the family; she would hardly have slept if it had not been so.

Other cases were then discussed. Reverend Francis lent little to the conversation except to ask if the people concerned were regular churchgoers. Without exception, they were not.

He then held forth on his plans for the parish. There was evidence, he said, that town labourers were attracted to churches where the ritual was elaborate, where the service could be followed with the eyes as well as the ears. It seemed to Lucy that changes in the decoration of the church would do little to bring people in, and would no doubt offend others, and she wondered how anyone would find the time to stage the extravagant entertainments he planned. She kept her thoughts to herself, but Miss Macartney was very enthusiastic.

When it was time to go, Lucy made sure that she said goodbye to Mrs Francis. She found her sitting listlessly in the almost empty drawing room while the three children played around her feet, but she jumped up to speak to Lucy, and said she hoped they would be friends. 'I know no one in the town, you see, and Herbert is too busy to keep me company,' she said.

Walking home on her own, Lucy still felt shaken by having to talk about delicate matters in front of Reverend Francis; there was something in his manner that made her feel particularly uncomfortable. But while she had been indoors the day had brightened and a rainbow arced over the distant hills; the fresh breeze on her face and the hedgerow hawthorn berries shining like jewels in the sunshine soon lightened her mood. Tomorrow was not her day for visiting but she would nonetheless take some clothing and food to the family whose plight had so haunted her. She reached into the hedge to pick a dog rose and, tucking it into her buttonhole, she strode happily along the path.

But when the path emerged on to the street, she slowed to a more sedate pace. There were greetings of *Good afternoon, Miss Jones* and *How are you, Miss Lucy,* and there were raised caps. She stopped to talk to Katherine Colling who was coming out of Mrs Bartlett's sweet shop, promised Mrs Haverfield to take a message to her mother, then turned into the more peaceful Castle Street.

The house was quiet when she entered. She intended to escape to the library to sketch for a while, but had barely crossed the hall when her mother, having heard the front door close, called out from the morning room.

'Is that you, Lucy?'

She was sitting at her writing desk with the accounts spread out before her, and another pile of papers spilling over on the floor at her side. Her hair was coming unpinned and there was a smudge of ink on her nose.

'Lucy, look at these figures for me, would you? I just cannot make them add up today, however hard I try. And your father has lost another patient to Dr Norman and I'm sure I don't know what we'll do if any more go. Lord knows, now that John and Charles are practising, we need more patients, not less.'

Her mother always worried excessively when a patient left. There had been some sort of crisis involving money ten or twelve years previously; Lucy had been too young to be told what was happening and it was never spoken of now, but she thought that her mother had taken over the accounts at that time. She was certain she could remember her father adding up columns of figures when she was a child – had she not sometimes been allowed to sit on his lap while he did so? But he was never consulted about the finances now.

She leaned over her mother's shoulder and, running her finger down the column of figures, added the numbers quickly in her head.

'Here you are, look, you've read this number five as a two, that's where the problem lies. The numbers tally now.' She glanced over the rest of the figures. 'There's a lot owing again, is there not?'

'When is there not a lot owing, Lucy? I've just sent out numerous bills and I'm sure I don't know what else is to be done. If only people would pay promptly it would make my life so much easier, and of course your father will insist on attending to people whether their bills are paid or not.'

'I'm sure the money will come in soon, Mother. Would you like me to call for some tea?'

Her mother dropped into the armchair with a sigh. 'I have such a headache. I'm not sure that tea is going to help.'

She did look very tired. 'Tea always helps, that is what you often tell me! There, let me make you comfortable.' Lucy passed her mother an extra cushion, then tidied the papers on the desk. 'I'll leave you in peace, I'm sure the headache will pass.'

She was determined to have a quiet time alone in the library before dinner.

Chapter Five

Ann jumped away from the door of the morning room and pretended to tidy the hallstand. Miss Lucy did not seem to realise that she had been listening.

'Could we have some tea, Ann, and some shortbread. But I'll have mine in the library please.'

As she marched across the floor towards the library door, she left dusty footprints behind. More work with the dustpan, more bending, and Ann had been up since five o'clock, nearly twelve hours now. Why could people not wipe their feet properly? Miss Lucy was considerate about most things, but not about wiping her feet. As soon as you finished one job another appeared, you could never say the day's work was done.

In the kitchen, the fire in the stove had already been built up ready for cooking dinner, and Sarah was chopping onions, screwing up her eyes to stop them watering. Ann pushed the kettle on to the hotplate.

'They'm not short of a penny or two, this family, be 'em?'

She spoke hesitantly. You had to be careful with Sarah. She might be a cousin, but she didn't always make life easy for Ann; she liked to think she knew the answer to everything. 'That's for me to know and you to find out,' was often her response to questions.

Sarah straightened up from her chopping and pushed a strand of hair away with her forearm. 'Course they'm not.'

'Just that her's worrying about money, the Missus. Has her cause for it, do 'ee suppose?'

'What did her say then?' She had caught Sarah's interest now.

'Oh, just about money that's owed and suchlike. Miss Lucy came in and helped with it.'

'Hmm, makes a change from Miss Nosy Wilcox then.' Sarah swept the chopped onions into a pan and turned away to put them on the stove. She stirred them thoughtfully.

'If I tell 'ee something, you'm not to breathe a word of it, do 'ee hear?' She glared at Ann. 'Clara that works for Colonel

Palmer over Mill Street, her told me that Dr Jones was in trouble, years back. He was bankrupted, and that means all his money was gone and the news was in the papers for all to see, and people went to other doctors instead of he. It was brought about by a bank failing, a lot of people lost their money so 'twan't all his fault, though as I understand it, some of it was. He got over it in time, so Clara said, but 'tisn't something that's ever forgotten. *That's* why the Missis is always worrying. She don't want the family to lose their good name another time. Now, don't you dare tell a soul you know about it!'

Ann put two small teapots on the side of the stove to warm, measuring two scoops of tea into each. She would never have guessed such a thing could happen, not in this house where everything seemed so well-ordered, the rooms so luxuriously furnished. But there was much that she did not yet understand. When she started work two months ago – being offered an interview because Sarah, who had been the cook for nearly a year, had recommended her – she found it different from other places she had worked, not that she had much experience. In her previous job at a farmhouse near Shebbear, it was just the Missis who told her what to do. At Castle House, Mrs Jones was the Missis but she didn't say much, except when you did something wrong. Sometimes Miss Polly or Miss Lucy gave her jobs to do, but it was more often Miss Wilcox who gave the orders; she was the housekeeper, but she was very familiar with members of the family, not like a servant at all. She was strict with Ann and Sarah, and even more so with Harry who was the groom and the gardener and cleaned all the boots each night. Miss Wilcox kept a close eye on him when he came into the kitchen for his meals. In fact, neither of them was interested in him; he was just a village boy.

Ann had been a village girl once, but she was a town girl now. She liked living in Torrington.

She made up two trays with a teapot on each. Had she missed anything? Yes, a teaspoon on each saucer. From the biscuit tin she took four pieces of the shortbread that Sarah had baked yesterday and placed two on each plate. Sarah looked at the trays and frowned.

'Who's that for then? Didn't Miss Polly come back yet?'

'Her's still out with her friends.'

'Hmm, what's her up to then?'

When Ann went to post a letter for Miss Wilcox, she had seen Polly talking and laughing with a group of other well-to-do young people outside the post office. When Ann came to the shop door, Polly had turned away so that she could pretend not to have seen her. She would not want to greet a servant while she was talking with her friends.

Polly had some lovely clothes, nicer than Lucy's. Every morning when Ann went to tidy the young ladies' bedroom, she admired the high, soft bed with its pile of pillows, and pressed her hand into the sumptuous coverlet. Polly and Lucy made their own bed before coming down for breakfast, but she usually had to straighten the cover or shake out a pillow. Before she took the chamber pots downstairs, she loved to peep in the wardrobe to see the bright colours and touch the lace collars. Two of the dresses were made of silk. Today, Polly had been wearing the dark blue dress with drapes gathered up behind and fringing around the skirt. Ann longed for a bustle like the sisters wore under their dresses. One day last week she had noticed that Miss Lucy was wearing an old dress without a bustle so, when no one was about, she had crept up to the bedroom and found the bustle pad on the shelf in the wardrobe. It was a cushion made from linen and horsehair with tapes to tie around the waist. Her heart beating against her ribs, she quickly lifted her skirts and gathered them over her arm while she tied the tapes around her waist, then shook her dress down over her new figure. She turned first this way, then that, in front of the long mirror, looking back over her shoulder and wiggling her bottom in admiration of her transformed outline. Of course, her plain day dress was not designed for such a garment, there was not enough material even when she pulled the folds back, but she could imagine how she would look if she had the right dress. If it ever happened that she was the only one in the house, perhaps she would try on one of the young ladies' dresses. It would have to be Miss Lucy's, she would never get into one of Polly's.

'Ann!'

She had nearly jumped out of her skin and narrowly missed
knocking the jug from the washstand.

'Whatever are you doing?'

What a shock it had been! Every time she thought of it
afterwards, she started to quiver with nerves all over again, but
really, after the first reprimand, Miss Lucy had been very kind.
She had even laughed a little, telling her that bustles were a
nuisance to wear and she was better off without one.

If it had been Mrs Jones or Miss Wilcox, she was sure she
would have been dismissed. She would always think kindly of
Miss Lucy for not telling anyone else.

'I will give you one of my old dresses,' she had said, 'one
that you can wear when you have a day off. I won't do it yet
because Mary Wilcox would scold me and tell me that you have
not been here long enough to have gifts, but one day I shall
choose a dress for you.'

When Sarah turned towards the stove to stir the onions, Ann
took a third shortbread from the tin and placed it on Miss Lucy's
plate.

There were seven for dinner that evening because Dr John Jones
and his wife were joining the rest of the family. They lived on
the other side of the town in Mill Street, a steep, narrow street
leading down into the valley where Ann had walked on her
afternoon off. There were three doctors in the family. Mr Charles
was the youngest, he nearly always worked alongside his father
rather than on his own account, but Mr John, the oldest son, was
a doctor in his own right. She knew that there were two more
sons, but they lived a great distance away and, as far as she knew,
they were not doctors. Just as well; surely three doctors were
enough for any family.

Because there were guests, the family had dressed for dinner,
and in addition to the gaslights there were candles on the table,
their flames reflecting in the silver cutlery that Ann had spent
much of the afternoon polishing. She had to wait at table as usual
but Miss Wilcox was helping as well, and she found fault with
Ann's every move.

'You leaned right over Miss Polly with the gravy boat!' she said when they returned to the kitchen, and 'Put the dishes down *quietly*, Ann, folks can hardly hear theirselves think!'

It was interesting to hear the snatches of conversation as she went in and out. Dr John had a loud voice and an even louder laugh, although the story he was telling did not, to Ann's ears, appear very funny.

'Such was the pace at which he was bowling along, when that spirited mare of his shied at a barking dog, he could not correct it, so – voila! - the wheel caught on that of a passing dogcart, tipped right over and threw him out!'

Standing behind Dr John's wife, Ann carefully reached in for her empty plate, embarrassed by the proximity of the woman's bosom. Her dark pink dress had a lower neckline than any of Miss Polly's or Miss Lucy's dresses.

'I've seen him driving furiously down the hill to the station, so he had it coming to him,' said the woman. She had a strange way of talking, nothing like the rest of the family, or the country people Ann grew up with.

'When I got to him,' Mr John went on, 'I saw at once that his arm was broken, the bone was protruding right through the skin.'

'John, please! You know we do not like that talk at the dinner table!'

Ann had just started to reach for Mrs Jones's plate but jumped back when she spoke out. Lucy, who was sitting next to her mother, passed the plate to Ann with an amused glance.

'Mother, what can you expect when you have three doctors around the table! At least I was there to help the poor chap.' Dr John gave one of his loud guffaws. It wasn't the sort of laugh that made you want to join in.

'John, your mother is quite right. You know the rules.'

'I like Dr Jones,' Ann said, as she carried the pile of the plates into the kitchen. 'He's quiet when he speaks, but you know he means it and everyone takes notice.'

But she had spoken out of turn, so Miss Wilcox looked up indignantly from the pan of custard she was stirring.

'You like him, do you!' She looked up scornfully as she poured the custard into a jug. 'You'm not wrong; you'll not meet a better man than Dr Jones, but since when did your opinion count, Ann White?'

Ann hurried back to the dining room before she could be scolded again. It was a blessing that Miss Wilcox had not heard Sarah's earlier comments about money; she would not like to be reminded of a time when Dr Jones's good name was damaged.

While the dessert plates were passed around, Dr Jones sat back and observed his family. It used to be such a pleasure, when all the children were still at home, to sit at the head of the table witnessing with pride the many ways in which they had blossomed. No doubt most fathers thought the same way when the children were young, but he would not be the only one who experienced more complex emotions when observing his adult children. It was easier with girls of course, they were under their parents' influence for longer; look at Polly there, just as pretty and vivacious as her mother had been at that age, and Lucy, his favourite although he should not have favourites; sensible, serious, and following in her father's footsteps now, as far as she was able, with her commitment to helping the poorer people of Torrington.

He felt Ann lean in carefully to his left, the cuff of her dress inadvertently brushing against his hand, then a bowl containing a generous slice of apple pie appeared in front of him. It looked very good, as did the large dish of thick clotted cream that was soon placed alongside.

John had launched into another of his anecdotes. His eldest son had always been the one Dr Jones worried about most. Perhaps fathers always worried about their oldest child but, as John grew up, he gradually realised that he had more cause than most. There was an instability that John kept in check for much of the time, but which would then erupt, resulting in consequences that they all had reason to regret.

Dr Jones's gaze moved to one of the consequences, John's wife, Rose. He tried, but he could not be comfortable when she was present, and he knew the rest of the family felt the same. Listen to her now, demanding of Polly and Lucy whether they had met any interesting beaux in the town recently, throwing up her hands and declaring with a laugh that they *must now be feeling quite desperate, after all, time marches on, don't it?* Polly tried to laugh off her embarrassment, but Lucy looked down at her lap with her cheeks growing pink.

'My daughters are far too sensible to discuss such things at the dinner table, Rose, and in any case they know my views on early marriage.'

He spoke evenly, but he was perhaps being rather unkind – certainly John looked up at him challengingly – but he would not see his daughters humiliated.

'Here you are, my dear, will you have some cream, or do you prefer custard?'

Rose took the dish from him with a smile and the moment passed; she had not the intelligence to recognise his way of controlling the situation.

John could not seem to take things in his stride; he allowed the pressures from work and from disagreements in his marriage to build up until they could not be contained any longer. And then he would drink.

No one in the family had ever had the tendency to partake in bouts of drinking, so why did John? Dr Jones's attempts at intervention seemed to make things worse, so he had learned to step back and wait, but people in the town were beginning to talk, and it was making his wife ill. Perhaps John's proposed move to Sheepwash would make things easier, but there was insufficient work in the village so he would still have to practise in Torrington for two or three days a week.

Dr Jones leaned back in his chair to allow Ann to take his bowl. Soon, when the ladies retired to the drawing room, he, John and Charles would be able to speak openly about the cases they were treating, communication that was a source of pleasure for all three. But he would keep his eye on the decanter of port.

On Sunday, after lunch had been cleared away, Ann and Sarah were free until suppertime.

Ann changed hurriedly into the dark blue dress her mother had altered for her, then checked her hat in the mirror below the sloping ceiling of her little bedroom. Her face looked pale and puffy, as it always did after leaning over a sink of steaming washing-up water for an hour; she pinched her cheeks hard in an attempt to bring some colour into them, and smiled experimentally at her reflection.

'Be 'ee ready? Us'll be late!' Sarah stood in the doorway. 'I reckon us'll go to Howe Chapel as it's closest.'

Neither of them was particularly religious, but there was nothing else to do on a wet Sunday afternoon. Ann was happy to be lulled by the minister's voice for an hour or two, to sing rousing hymns and, most importantly, to have the opportunity to look around at the congregation. There was always a number of young men who were more interested in catching the eyes of girls than they were in listening to the prayers.

Before she started work in Torrington, she went with her mother to long services at the small Bible Christian Chapel in Stibb Cross, but in Torrington there were lots of churches to try out. They could not go to the parish church attended by the Jones family because the services were in the morning when lunch had to be prepared, but she and Sarah had been welcomed at the Bible Christian Chapel in South Street. They found it somewhat dull, and the services at the Baptist Chapel in New Street were rather late in the afternoon, making them anxious about getting back in time to prepare supper, so the best ones were the Methodist Church in Mill Street and the Congregational Howe Chapel. Both churches were large, meaning that there were more likely to be people of interest in the congregation, and both organised regular entertainments and afternoon teas which Mrs Jones did not mind Ann and Sarah attending.

They ran down the stairs together, secure in the knowledge that Miss Wilcox was not around to scold them. They slowed to a sedate walk when they saw Dr Jones coming out of his study, but he just greeted them with a cheery 'Have a good afternoon, girls!'

The rain was falling steadily, gushing down the drains and dripping from the trees as they hesitated in the porch.

'Us could take an umbrella,' said Sarah.

'Won't it be missed?'

'If we take Miss Lucy's old one, her won't mind.'

So, they hurried down the road huddled under the umbrella together, although Sarah, who was holding it, stayed drier than Ann.

The chapel was already three-quarters full when they slipped into a pew near the back. Ann knelt to say a prayer, or at least pretend to do so, before sitting up to wait for the service to begin. She liked to look up at the roof so high above her, the straight lines of the dark beams reaching up to meet each other at the highest point. She had been astounded the first time she came, having never before been in such a large building.

A woman on the other side of the aisle smiled at her. Most of the chapelgoers were friendly. Then, she saw that a young man sitting in the pew behind the woman was watching her. She bowed her head. Should she look at him? Perhaps he was watching Sarah, but she did not think so, and Sarah was gazing straight ahead in an apparent reverie. She glanced quickly in his direction. He smiled! She smiled back, just a little, then looked down again, her heart racing.

When the first hymn was called, he had to face the front, so she was then able to look in his direction. He was not tall but had wide shoulders and light brown curly hair. She had gained the impression of humorous blue eyes in a broad, confident face. Standing next to him was a younger boy who might be his brother.

Throughout the service he kept glancing back at her, she could see him from the corner of her eye even when she did not look that way. But occasionally she returned his glance; it was a game, they both knew it.

Sarah seemed quite unaware of what was happening. Ann knew that she was interested only in Henry Davey back home in Shebbear. He had married Sarah's best friend, but she had died when their baby was young so Sarah's parents now cared for the small boy. Perhaps Sarah would, one day, return to Shebbear to marry Henry.

The boy across the aisle seemed to have a good voice; she could pick it out during the hymns despite the very loud singing of a man behind her. He glanced back at her again, and she quickly looked down at her hymn book, but she could not hide a small smile. He was sure to see it.

As the service drew to a close, her heart started to thump with excitement. It was usual when the congregation spilled out of the chapel for people to gather and talk on the steps or on the pavement outside; she and Sarah often talked with other servants from the big houses of the town and it would sometimes be half an hour before they made their farewells and headed for home. But today it was wet, so surely everyone would hurry away at once.

At last, the chapel doors opened. When the young man started to move from his pew, she stepped out too so that they met in the aisle. They walked along side-by-side; she wouldn't be the first to speak, but suppose he said nothing? Then, when they reached the double doors, he stepped aside and smiled.

'Do 'ee want to go first?'

'Thank you.'

And then he was beside her again.

'I've seen 'ee here before, haven't I?'

'Yes.'

She smiled, but couldn't look at him. It was pouring with rain, everyone was hurrying away, and now Sarah was putting up the umbrella.

'Here,' he said, 'stand under your friend's umbrella, I don't mind getting wet.'

Sarah looked startled.

'You don't mind if I talk to your friend for a minute or two, do 'ee?' he asked, and he smiled at Ann again. 'Sorry, I don't know your name.'

His name, he said, was George Chapple, and his brother was Milton. They both worked at the tannery at the end of New Street.

''Tis my uncle's business, you might know him, he was mayor a few years back, Mr Nathaniel Chapple.'

Ann shook her head. 'I haven't lived in Torrington long. I work for Dr Jones, just over there, us both do.'

'I know!' He grinned. He had a lovely face, open and honest. 'I'm secretary of the Mutual Improvement Society. Us meets in an upstairs room in the Square every week, a group of working men like meself.'

He seemed very proud of this, and it did sound like an important position.

'Have 'ee heard about the entertainment next week,' he asked, 'it's arranged by the Chapel, Thursday evening. There's tea and then singing and suchlike. Will 'ee both be going? I'm going!'

'Oh! I don't know.' It was much harder to meet his eyes when he was standing so close, but she made herself do it. 'Us is supposed to have an evening off each week, so us could ask...'

Milton was looking rather bored, and the rain was running from his hair and from George's too. The situation suddenly struck her as being rather amusing.

'You'd better go, you'm getting so wet! Look at you!'

And they both laughed then, and held each other's gaze.

'Bye then! Hope to see you next week!'

She hurried along beside Sarah, trying to stay under the umbrella. Sarah was grumpy, and wanted to know how she knew George, but Ann didn't care about Sarah's moods now.

Her world had changed.

Chapter Six

Lucy stepped back into the nave to study the display of fruit, flowers and vegetables. She had placed the wicker basket of shiny red apples in the centre but now the large green marrow was obscured, and Mrs Andrew might be offended. But it did all look rather fine. The golden harvest loaf donated by Short's Bakery was the centrepiece; almost two feet high, it looked magnificent propped against the altar steps. She had placed the sheaves of corn on either side, with a collection of carrots and onions and Mr Hearn's two orange pumpkins to balance the colours. Trays of yellow, green and russet apples made up the foreground. Perhaps the marrow could go just behind them, she needed to get it just right, there was sure to be a large congregation for the harvest thanksgiving service.

'That looks wonderful, Lucy!' Edith was standing on a chair to help her stepmother arrange yellow and orange chrysanthemums on the windowsills. Miss Macartney was on her knees with some lilies at the foot of the pulpit, while at the far end of the nave Maria and Catherine Williams arranged garlands of berries around the font, and Mrs Loveband was building a pyramid of apples at the back of the south transept.

Lucy sat down in the front pew. She liked the church best at times such as this, when one did not feel oneself to be under scrutiny from Reverend Buckland's eagle-eyed gaze or the curious looks from members of the congregation. Unobserved, she could stare up at the arched roof trusses that resembled the upside-down keel of a ship, and wonder about the men who had worked there, so high, and so long ago. She loved the carved stone arches that fell as gracefully as cream-coloured silk from the wide openings of the nave, and the faces of gilded cherubs peeping out from the sides of the pulpit. Then there was the stone-slabbed floor; the smooth polished wood of the pews; the rubies, sapphires and emeralds of the stained-glass windows contrasting with the clear light-filled panes and the tracery of black lead, and the evocative smells of wood polish, combined with a hint of mustiness and damp.

It was very peaceful now, but it had not always been so. During the Civil War, the church had been blown up and many people killed. Nor had it been peaceful in more recent times. Reverend Francis, during a sermon on the Good Samaritan, had claimed that the thieves in the story were Nonconformists. People had again walked out of the service, there were highly critical articles in the local newspapers and much anger in the town.

But at least the fabric of the church was undisturbed; she loved the silence, and how it was broken only by the low voices of Edith and Mrs Buckland conversing as they put the finishing touches to the floral arrangements.

As she got up to finish the display, she caught some of their words.

'It sounds as if he is more comfortable, Mother, does it not? We were quite worried for him after his last letter.'

'I'm sure he meant to frighten us,' Mrs Buckland replied, 'with all his talk of snakes and poisonous spiders, and no secure doors to keep them out. I shall sleep more peacefully now.'

When Edith turned around, Lucy walked quickly forward to busy herself with the display.

'Oh, Lucy, I was going to tell you, we have had a letter from Rawlin! Such a long letter, telling us all about the extraordinary place where he lives!'

'I thought that must be what you were talking about. I'm sorry, I didn't mean to eavesdrop.' She bent over the apples she was polishing.

'Don't be silly!' Edith placed her hand on Lucy's shoulder. 'It was not a private conversation, I just hadn't had the opportunity to tell you. Come home with us when we are finished here and I will read it to you, it is a most amusing letter. Oh, and he wished to be remembered to you.'

Edith walked away just then, so perhaps did not notice Lucy's blushes. What exactly had Rawlin written – was it just that, *remember me to Lucy?* Or perhaps he had said *Miss Jones.* But no, surely not. Had he written something more personal, a promise that he would write to her perhaps? She did not think that Edith had any knowledge of her feelings for Rawlin. If she was sure that they were reciprocated, she would have confided in her friend but, as it was, she did not think she could bear the humiliation.

The display was finished. She would help by sweeping up the leaves and bits of straw that had dropped in the aisle during the decorating; keep busy, that was the answer.

As she walked towards the back of the church where Maria and Catherine Williams were putting the final touches to the font, there was the sudden loud click of the latch, and Reverend Francis put his head around the door.

'Good afternoon, ladies!' He slid through the door while it was barely ajar and closed it behind him. 'I have just come from a meeting at the Workhouse but thought I must see how your work is progressing before I go home for my tea!' He laughed loudly.

'Hush! Really!' From the south transept Mrs Loveband tutted disapprovingly.

He looked around at the displays of fruit, vegetables and flowers, his glance passing over Lucy without acknowledgement.

'Very pretty, ladies!' He addressed his remarks to Edith and Mrs Buckland. 'A very attractive show!' He placed his hand on Mrs Buckland's arm. 'Of course, I would like to see the Harvest Thanksgiving replaced with a celebration of the Feast of St Michael, as the church is dedicated to him it would be most appropriate, don't you think? I have suggested the idea to Reverend Buckland, not for this year of course, not now that you have spent so much time decorating!' He laughed wildly.

Mrs Buckland was always diplomatic, but even she looked startled.

'Harvest thanksgiving is always very popular, Reverend Francis, it would cause great upset if it were to be changed.'

'Well, one day, perhaps, one day!' And he strode back down the aisle and out of the door, waving his hand high above his head.

There was silence for a few moments after the latch rattled into place, but then Mrs Loveband hurried over to where Maria and Catherine Williams stood.

'The Feast of St Michael is *Catholic*!' Lucy heard her say.

Miss Macartney joined Edith and Mrs Buckland. One group supported Reverend Francis and, despite some misgivings, sought to justify his actions, the other was appalled by him. Lucy resumed sweeping the floor. She was weary of hearing the diatribes against the curate at home; she did not wish to listen to more. Besides, she had other things on her mind.

Finally, Mrs Buckland, seeking to heal the rift between her helpers, changed the subject of the conversation.

'There, ladies, I think our work is finished now! Would you all like to come over to the Vicarage for some refreshments? I'm sure you must be ready for some.'

HARVEST THANKSGIVING SERVICE.—This annual event, connected with our parish Church, was celebrated on Thursday last. The Church was most tastefully decorated with sheaves of corn, flowers, fruits, &c., by Mrs. and Miss Buckland and other ladies. At 8 a.m. there was a celebration of the Holy Communion. The evening service commenced at 7.30 p.m., for some time previous to which merry peals were rung from the Old Church bells. There was a very large congregation, and the service being choral, it possessed more than usual attractiveness. The prayers were intoned by the Rev. H. O. Francis, the new Curate, whose peculiar style of intonation was prominently noticed, if not admired. The first l───── w── ──ad by the Rev. J. C. Jardine, Curate of

North Devon Journal, 1876

A month later, Lucy ran down the stairs. It was already almost nine o'clock, she would be late. Her basket containing the washed and ironed hand-me-down clothing was waiting by the hall stand; she hurried through to the kitchen where Mary was making pastry and Sarah peeling apples at the table.

'Mary, have you that leftover pie for me? I'm in a rush!'

'Here, I've wrapped it for 'ee, and a half-loaf too. Be it for the Gent family?'

'Yes, I need boots too so the oldest girl can start school, but that will have to wait. Let me know if you hear of any.'

In the hall, Ann was staring at a letter she had just picked up from the mat.

'Look at this postage stamp, Miss, I've never seen one of they before.' She held it up for Lucy to see.

Under the image of the Queen's head was the word *Australia*. For a moment the room seemed to swim. Could it be?

'Let me see.' She snatched the envelope from Ann and read the handwriting on the front. *Miss Lucy Jones*.

'It's for me.' She stared at it. The letter that had existed for so long in her imagination was here, in her hand.

'Any post for me?' Polly was coming from the dining room.

'I don't know. Ann has the letters. I have to go.' And she was out of the door and walking up the drive, the letter in her basket.

At the gate, she hesitated. She *could* not continue without reading the letter. Glancing back at the house, she closed the gate behind her and turned left towards the Common, walking fast.

The seats at the top of Castle Hill were empty. There was a man on a lower path, but no one else in sight, no one to ask questions, no one to look over her shoulder, but she would have to be quick, it was already so late! Sitting down, she took the envelope out of her basket, held it, turned it over. It was not thin, there must be several sheets of paper inside. *Miss Lucy Jones, Castle House, Great Torrington, Devon, England.* She was not very familiar with Rawlin's handwriting, but of course it *was* from him. She would soon come to know how every letter was formed, every stroke and flourish. To think that this flimsy envelope had travelled from the other side of the world!

She had no letter knife, and it was a shame to make tears in the envelope. Should she keep it intact, safe in her basket until she returned home? But if she did, her anticipation would build and build throughout the morning, and might then end in worse disappointment; if he were writing to say that he would not be returning, perhaps that he had met someone he wanted to marry in Australia, then it were better that she knew now. She turned it over again. Would it be long, or would it be short? Would it be cool, or would it be kind? Carefully she made a slit across the top with her fingernail, causing only a little damage, then she slid the folded papers out, and she opened them.

Dear Lucy. Her eyes flew this way and that, the unfamiliar address at the top, the date, nearly three months earlier. Three months! She knew that letters took a long time to arrive from Australia, but it seemed extraordinary that he had sat down three months ago to write this letter to her. Three months ago he was thinking of her, and all this time she had imagined that he was not.

I hope this finds you well. I picture you sitting at the dining room table or perhaps in your father's library to read this letter. She wanted to shout out, to tell him that she was not, that she was on Castle Hill, on the very seat where they had sat together! *I'm sorry that I have not written before but, as you can imagine, I have been very busy. I hope that my letters to my family have been shared with you.*

She read quickly. She need not have worried. It was long. It was kind. She felt her eyes fill with tears. She read the descriptions of his life in Australia very rapidly – she would savour them later, at her leisure – but she read his closing lines more closely, then read them again.

Lucy, know that I think of you often. I left in great haste, and I did not say things that should have been said. Sometimes I imagine that you are here with me, but I do not yet know this place well enough to be sure that you would like it. Perhaps in time I will know. Meanwhile, if you should find the time to write to me, it would give me the greatest pleasure to hear from you.

She walked fast along Castle Street. The breeze blowing in from the south-west was damp, and she had left home in such a hurry she had not even fastened her jacket buttons. She fastened them now as she walked with her basket on her arm, then she cut through Potacre Street, almost running to reach the house she was to visit.

'Hello? Mrs Gent?' She put her head around the low door.

The woman was sitting on a stool stitching a leather glove. A white cloth covering her lap did not hide the fact that she was with child, and her hair was pulled tightly back from her thin face to keep the work clean. It was the way of working for all the glove makers of the town.

Lucy closed the door. Her gaze had already passed quickly around the room. She knew now what to look for, what to comment on and what to ignore in such a room. She understood so much more than she had in the early days when she would be rendered almost speechless by the unfamiliar sights and smells.

She had the reputation of being sympathetic. Miss Macartney, she was told, would scold if she found the fireplace cold, if the pot of simmering vegetables contained no meat bones for sustenance, if the floor was unswept, but Lucy had quickly learnt that criticism produced defensive anger, not change.

She patted the heads of the two small girls sitting on the floor and seated herself at the table.

'Oh, Mrs Gent, it must be difficult, trying to sew with cold fingers. Has the coal run out again?'

The woman glanced up. 'What's left I has to keep for evenings. My husband has to have a bit of a fire.'

The weather was not yet cold enough to warrant supplying coal, so Lucy just nodded kindly. She asked after the family's health, then, while Mrs Gent went on to speak of her husband's demands – he liked a fire, food on his plate, and well-behaved children when he came home from the tannery – her thoughts began to wander.

Know that I think of you often. Had Rawlin really written those words? Had she imagined it? Thinking of it made her tingle all over from the crown of her head to the tips of her toes. *Sometimes I imagine that you are here with me.* He might be thinking of her at this very moment, just as she was thinking of him. If only he were here and their eyes could meet!

'Miss Jones?'

'Sorry, Mrs Gent, what did you say?' She was back in the dreary room.

'I said he won't leave me be, even now that the child is due in a month or two. Every night he's at me, and me so tired 'tis all I can do to raise my legs!'

Lucy shook her head sympathetically. They loved to try to shock her, these women. She knew they met to laugh about it afterwards. And she *had* been shocked at first, and uncomprehending, and had asked foolish questions which must have led to further hilarity. Now she made sure that her face remained bland and her comments neutral. She wanted them to like her.

'Tell him he must consider your feelings as well as his own, Mrs Gent.'

'When Alice goes to school I'll mebbe feel less tired, though she's a help to me too.'

Mrs Gent had dark circles under her eyes, and looked much older than her twenty-six years.

'I hope to find some boots for her soon. I have some clothes for the children, but once the baby has come and things are a bit easier, you will try to put a few pennies aside for the clothing club, won't you? I can collect it each week for you, and the money soon mounts up. Now look, I have also brought some bread and some meat pie.'

The pie would be a treat. The family rarely had meat, except once a year when their pig was brought in from foraging on the Common to be killed, and then some of the meat had to be sold to raise money for another piglet.

'Why don't you and the children have a slice when I've gone, then Mr Gent can have his later.' Otherwise he might eat it all, she thought, but did not say. Lucy had only met Mr Gent once, but had not been very impressed with him. She knew that he had been fined several times for drunkenness, which was a double waste of the family's meagre income.

She unpacked the children's clothes and called the oldest over to try them against her for size. The dress the girl wore had been mended, turned and darned until there was little left of the original material.

'There, Alice, you can wear this new dress to school.'

The girl's face lit up as she stroked the coarse fabric. 'Will 'ee get me some boots?'

'Yes, as soon as I can, I shall get you some boots.'

The younger girl was tethered by a string, one end being tied around her waist and the other attached to the table leg. Lucy had been horrified when she first saw this, but accepted now that it was a common practice of the glove makers to keep sticky fingers away from the fine leather; none of the families could afford for the materials to be spoiled. There were only so many changes that she could make.

'Have both children been vaccinated, Mrs Gent? And you will ensure that the new baby receives its vaccine, won't you?'

At the end of each day, she reported to her father on any cases that needed his attention.

After promising to call the following week, she stepped out on to the pavement again, reaching into her basket to touch her letter. She had not dreamed it. *Dear Lucy.* She would reply soon, this evening. Already the words she might use began to form in her head, but she must not let him know how she had longed to hear from him. He had asked her something, what was it? She had read that part of the letter very fast, but it was a question about a plant found on the Common. Walking slowly along Calf Street, she hesitated for a moment, but she could not take out the letter and read it here on the street; she must wait.

She opened a small blue door, and called out. The reply was barely discernible, but she went in and closed the door behind her. The old man's bed had been brought into the small downstairs room because he was now too weak to climb the stairs, or even to stand.

'Hello, my dear.' His breathing was laboured. The room was sufficiently warm; his daughter would have been in earlier to light the fire that glowed now in the hearth. Lucy drew up a chair and held the hand that rested on the blanket, trying not to recoil when it reminded her of a claw.

'How are you today?'

'Better for seeing you, my dear; I can't complain.'

The old man's daughter looked after him as best she could, but had not the space to take him in.

Lucy showed him the bowl of jelly she had brought for him, and tried to interest him in the goings-on of the town; he made appreciative noises but she was not sure how much he could follow.

But then he said, 'What of that curate that's causing everyone to leave the church?'

Oh dear, Reverend Francis again, it seemed the whole town was talking of him whether they went to church or not.

'Oh, it is only a minority, you know, who have left; there are many who think highly of Reverend Francis. Would you like me to ask him to call on you one day?'

The old man coughed, the paroxysms wracking his thin frame. When he had recovered, he replied, 'I'd rather have the minister see me, us have always been chapelgoers in my family. I don't fancy having that Reverend Francis in my house.'

In an effort to change the subject, she found herself saying, 'I have had some good news today.'

'What's that, my dear?'

She should not have mentioned it but, the truth was, she could think of nothing else. 'Just that I've had a letter from a dear friend I thought I might never hear from again.'

She was preparing to go when he spoke again and she understood from his hesitant words and discomfiture that he needed to relieve himself, and needed help. 'If you could be so good, Miss,' he said, shamefaced.

She could not; she simply could not. She knew that Edith would do such things, but she was not Edith.

'Could I fetch your daughter for you?' That at least she could do, she thought, as she hurried away to find the house.

There were two further calls to make before she was finally able to return to eat. She did not have to go out again until two o'clock, and Ann was only just laying the table.

'Luncheon will be about twenty minutes, Miss. Have 'ee had a good morning, not too many awkward cases?'

Lucy would never tell their names, but Ann loved to hear about the people she visited; the poorer they were, the more interested she was, but Lucy had other things on her mind today. Returning to the hall, she could hear her mother and Polly in the morning room, and her father in conversation beyond the closed door to the surgery. Moving quietly, she went to the library.

Her instinct had been to keep Rawlin's letter a secret, but then Mary Wilcox discovered her. When Mary appeared, Lucy was tracing the route of Rawlin's journey on her father's globe in the library, cupping its smooth round surface in one hand while she ran a finger around its circumference to link up the unfamiliar place names.

'Well now, Lucy, I wondered where 'ee'd got to. What have 'ee got there? Not trying to hide something from your Mary, be 'ee?'

Lucy snatched up the letter and put it on her lap, but was too late to hide it from Mary's sharp eyes, and she found she wanted to share the news. She had kept her sadness at Rawlin's departure a secret for too long, and Mary would understand.

'I have had a letter from Rawlin today,' she said, trying to keep her voice steady. 'I'd hoped that I would.' She hesitated. 'He hinted before he left that he might have feelings for me.'

'Well, of course he has, my lover!' Mary sat next to her and held Lucy's hand between her own work-roughened palms. 'You've been friends since before you could walk. I always was of a mind that 'e'd marry 'ee one day!'

'Mary! There's no talk of that!'

'Not yet there idn't, but you wait and see! Being on the far side of the world won't count for nothing; you'm made for each other, you two!'

Mary's confidence tended to make Lucy more apprehensive; it was a friendly letter, that was all, she must not think it was more than that.

'Mary, please don't say anything to Mother, I don't want her to start imagining things that will probably never happen.' The feelings she and Rawlin had for each other were delicate, they needed nurturing; they were not for public discussion.

'I won't, but 'tis no good trying to keep his letters a secret, chiel, else when her learns of it, her's sure to imagine all manner of things.'

Mary was right; if Lucy's mother or Polly discovered that she had been writing secretly to Rawlin, there would be a lot of unwelcome questions. She could not always be there when the post landed on the mat, so future letters from Australia – if there were any – might well be noticed.

While eating dinner with her family, she was able to mention the letter without attracting too much attention. John had arrived unexpectedly for dinner. He did not give a reason, but Lucy wondered whether he had again had an argument with his wife, and from her parents' guarded manner it seemed that they suspected the same. John was laughing too loudly and had clearly been drinking.

When there was a lull in the conversation, and the room was silent but for the clink of cutlery, she spoke out.

'I had a letter from Rawlin today.'

Both her mother and Polly looked a little startled. Lucy looked down at her plate; unable to meet their eyes, she pretended to be busy with her meal as she spoke.

'He wrote most interestingly about his journey, and the place where he now lives. Do you know, after the three-month sailing to Melbourne, he had to take another ship to reach Palmerston which took many weeks. It was another three thousand miles – can you imagine?'

'He wrote to you?' Her mother's fork was suspended in mid-air.

Lucy nodded, and put a piece of chicken in her mouth.

Unwittingly, her father came to the rescue. 'Of course! He is up on the northern coast, is he not? It's not yet a civilised part of the country, I believe, though now that it's connected to the rest of the world by the telegraph, no doubt business opportunities and development will come along. A most interesting place to work, I imagine.'

She composed her features. 'He says there have been many improvements in the last few years, there are a few shops now and a library in Palmerston. And he says that the scenery is magnificent, there is a huge and beautiful harbour with rich green vegetation right down to the water's edge, and in the jungle there are waterfalls flowing from overhanging cliffs, and flowers, butterflies and insects such as one can hardly imagine.' She took a sip of water, being careful not to look at her mother or Polly.

'Ah, I would like an adventure such as that!' John got up to help himself to more sherry from the sideboard. 'Imagine being able to leave Torrington and start a new life!'

'John, you've had enough to drink.' Her father spoke quietly, then addressed himself to Lucy. 'The telegraph was completed a few years ago I believe, so what does his work entail?'

'The company is duplicating the cable because there had been several breaks under the water. With two cables, one can be used while the other is repaired.'

'Oh Lucy, you are so knowledgeable! How did you learn about such tedious things?' Polly laughed prettily. 'And why does Rawlin not send you a telegram instead of a letter, seeing that he works for the telegraph company?'

Lucy smiled. She knew the answer to that because Edith had spoken of it. 'It is extremely expensive to send a telegram from Australia, but he was allowed to send one to his family when he first arrived.'

'Will you write back to him, Lucy?' her mother asked.

'I may do so, when I have time.'

'You're a dark horse,' Polly said later, as they undressed for bed, 'you didn't tell me you had an understanding with Rawlin.'

'Don't be silly,' Lucy bent to roll down her stockings, avoiding Polly's gaze, 'I don't. We've always been friends, that's all.'

'Hmm. Well, I've been friends with him too but he hasn't written to me.'

Lucy could tell she was already losing interest in the subject. Polly would not care to receive a letter from Rawlin. He was not sufficiently handsome to attract her, being of rather stocky build with strong, dark features, and Lucy knew that she thought him dull. *She does not share his interests the way I do*, she thought, *she does not see the passion that lights up his face when he talks.*

Polly stepped out of her dress. 'Have you heard that Reverend Francis plans to give an entertainment after Christmas? I'm sure to be asked to sing, so would you be my accompanist? There are certain to be many people there, and it should be amusing.'

She continued to chat about the concert and the dress she planned to wear for it as they climbed into bed together, while Lucy gave sufficient answers to keep her happy. But when Polly finally settled for sleep she was able to turn over, pull the quilt up to her ears, and let her mind wander. She thought of Rawlin, of walking together hand-in-hand past the hanging ferns and curious rope-like creepers of the tropical jungle as he showed her exotic flowers and butterflies bigger than any she had ever seen. They walked until they came to a waterfall flowing from a cliff hundreds of feet high, shimmering in the sunlight that found its way through the trees. And it was there that he turned to her, stroked her hair, and took her into his arms.

Chapter Seven

When Dr Jones had finished packing the saddle bag with medicines and dressings, he closed the surgery door and hurried through to the yard, pausing to put his head around the kitchen door.

'I'm off to Roborough, Mary, and Kingscott on the way back. If anyone calls, I can see urgent cases this evening.'

'Oh, Doctor, now, you must have some tea to take with 'ee, 'tis a bit bivverly out there and like enough to rain too.'

Mary Wilcox had already filled a bottle with tea and was cutting a slice of cake. Perhaps it was as well; there would be no tea where he was going.

In the yard, Harry had Diamond ready for him. The horse raised his head when he saw Dr Jones approach, knowing that a carrot would have been supplied from the kitchen.

Harry held the back gate open for him while he rode out on to Castle Street. Although a fine drizzle was falling, a glance at the sky suggested that the rain would not come to much, despite Mary Wilcox's warnings. Sometimes he arrived home wet right through to his skin, but he preferred the freedom of travelling on horseback when he went out into the country, some of the lanes being so thick with mud it was difficult to make progress in a carriage, and so narrow the paintwork was susceptible to scratches.

Torrington Square was congested with carts, carriages and packhorses; by the time he reached the post office he had nodded so many times in reply to greetings, he would surely develop a stiff neck. Although not a native of Torrington, he had grown very fond of the place during the twenty years he had lived there, particularly the centre of town where the jumble of grand eighteenth century houses, Georgian mansions and early cottages blended to form a most pleasing prospect.

'Afternoon, Doctor, I hope you'm well!' This was shouted from across the street, but he did not shout in reply; his patients, knowing that he was a quiet man, were satisfied with a smile and a nod.

When the post office boy had run out to take his letter, he turned his horse's head towards Well Street to ride out of the town. He would like, he mused, to visit more of the grand houses on South Street and Warren Lane. Some wealthier patients would please his wife, for she had not been raised to count the pennies, and it would help to establish the future of his daughters, and to pay Mr Rolle the annual rent of seventy pounds which Castle House commanded. But, unlike Bideford, Torrington had not become a magnet for retiring army officers and fund-holders. Perhaps John would meet with greater success, but only if he could maintain sobriety.

Soon after passing the main entrance to Stevenstone, he took the track that acted as a service road to part of Mark Rolle's estate. He felt the change in temperature immediately; there were no high hedgebanks here to shelter him from the wind that blew unimpeded from the looming bulk of Dartmoor on the southern horizon and on towards Exmoor to the north. No leaves remained on the occasional saplings that had been planted alongside the fence, but further down the hill the rare and beautiful trees in the more sheltered woodlands around Stevenstone House were still displaying a medley of yellow, russet and gold, illuminated suddenly by a shaft of sunlight which managed to penetrate the low cloud. He adjusted his woollen cravat more closely around his neck and pressed his horse into a trot.

Riding through the village of St Giles in the Wood he admired, as usual, the neat rows of stone cottages with attractive gabled windows built by the Rolle Estate for its workers. If only all cottages were as warm and dry, there would be far fewer cases of fever and respiratory problems.

'Good afternoon, Doctor!' A familiar figure strode from the church, and Dr Jones reined Diamond in as Reverend Buxton approached. He was an open-faced young man whom everyone liked; his sense of humour could melt the resolve of the most pompous churchman.

'Dr Jones! I had thought I would see you in St Giles before now!'

It was clear that he spoke in jest. 'And why is that? Have you need of a doctor?'

His eyes twinkled. 'No, but I think you have need of a church! Are not all the parishioners leaving St Michael's? You would be welcome here anytime, you know, and I promise you will hear no stories about Samaritans and Nonconformist thieves!'

Ah, that tale again. Reverend Francis' notoriety was spreading far and wide, for his claims had outraged many people. Perhaps it was as well to laugh about it; one could not be angry all the time.

'If I do ever leave St Michael's, Reverend Buxton, then your church will be my first preference! But I will not let a curate drive me away, I intend to stand firm. I would rather change minds than churches!'

The young man grew more serious. 'It is a sad business, Dr Jones. As I understand it, Church and Chapel in Torrington have overcome many of their differences in recent decades. It is a retrograde step to be introducing division where there was harmony.'

Their eyes met in sympathetic agreement, and Dr Jones rode on, his friend delivering a friendly slap to Diamond's haunches.

It was true, in a town like Torrington many of the old enmities between Church and Chapel had gone, and people worked together harmoniously irrespective of their beliefs. How dare Reverend Francis disturb that tranquillity! And why would Reverend Buckland not stand up to him? The answer was, of course, that the curate had the support of the Bishop of Exeter who had great sympathy with high church practices, and the vicar could not defy the bishop even if he had wanted to.

It was not altogether true to say that Reverend Francis was bringing about division however, he mused; it was more a matter of the people of Torrington uniting against him.

His road took him down into a sheltered valley, past a small farm where a black-and-white collie ran out to bark and wag its tail at him, and then across Dodcott Brook. As the lane started to climb again, he pressed Diamond into a trot, for the sun was already low in the sky. It would not be long before all his return journeys were completed in the dark, but Diamond was sure-footed and knew his way home however steep and stony the lane.

It was four days since he had been to Roborough, and he was hopeful that the scarlet fever epidemic that had raged for three weeks would now be coming to an end. Despite his order to close the school as soon as the severity of the outbreak became clear, eight children had died. Eight young lives lost. There were others who were at risk, but he was optimistic that the essentials he had ordered for them and careful nursing would have enabled them to recover.

His first call was at a large cottage between Ebberley and Roborough known as No Place, a name that always made him smile. It stood end-on to the narrow lane, another cottage standing directly opposite as if the two huddled together for company, the only houses visible for miles around.

John Smale, who lived at No Place with his family, appeared to be in a better position than most paupers the doctor attended, because not only did he rent an acre or two of land, he also owned a cow and a donkey. However, he had seven children to support, his rent was high, and he was not always given a full week's work by his employer. Even the donkey was a necessity for his work and had to be paid for from his wages which, in a good week, he had told Dr Jones, amounted to twelve shillings. It was clear from the interior of the house that there was no money to spare.

The door was opened by an older woman. He did not recognise her as one of the village nurses, and she stared at him blankly.

'Dr Jones,' he informed her, 'to see the children.'

She continued to stare, before replying in a whisper, 'You'm too late.'

He felt a chill run down his spine. 'Too late? Can I come in? I'm sorry, I don't know you, are you the nurse?'

She stood aside to let him in. 'Us haven't had a nurse. I be Honor Tucker, Elizabeth's mother.'

So, the grandmother. 'But I asked for a nurse to be sent!'

She shook her head, 'Us haven't seen no nurse.'

She led him through the living room where the oldest boy sat silently by the fire, and up the narrow staircase to a bedroom where two small corpses lay on the bed. He recognised the oldest girl, and the small boy who had been somewhat frail since birth.

'When…?'

'Samuel in the night, Ann this forenoon.'

Afterwards, she took him into another bedroom. The mother lay on one bed, sleeping fitfully with the baby by her side, while from another bed the three remaining children gazed up at him, their eyes wide and dull. He examined them quickly, talking quietly to soothe them. The fever had abated; if they could get through the next day or so, all would be well. The mother, too, was past the worst.

He turned to the grandmother. 'Are they taking sustenance? Mutton broth would be helpful now, they need strength to aid their recovery.'

She could not meet his eyes. 'I do me best, Doctor, but us have so little. John told me you'd ordered vittles, but us haven't got it, none of it.'

He turned away to the window, and he felt a twitch develop in his cheek. How could the order have been turned down? Who had challenged his authority? He thought he knew the answer, and his blood ran cold.

'I will ride immediately to the schoolmaster's house, I know he keeps a supply of beef tea and port wine which I will ask him to bring to you immediately. He is a good man and will do this for me. And,' he added grimly, 'I will enquire as to why a nurse was not provided.'

'I've done me best,' the woman whispered. 'I've nursed 'em best I can.'

'Of course you have,' he placed his hand on her arm, 'you have done well. I believe the rest of the family will recover with your care, so try not to worry.'

It was in sober mood that he rode away from No Place. If there were district visitors working in rural areas, if Lucy were able to travel this far, the tragedy could have been averted. It was not the first time that his orders had been refused; there had been the recent disagreement over the supply of wine and ale to

Workhouse inmates. He had soon learned who was behind the decision.

The Chairman of the Board, Mr Moore-Stevens, had always been a difficult man. He was notorious in his own parish for demanding complete obedience from his tenants and workers; lapses in morality, sobriety or lawfulness being swiftly dealt with in the courtroom that he had incorporated into his house, he being a magistrate as well as the M.P., and at one time the High Sherriff for Devon.

His home, Winscott House at Peter's Marland, had been built in a grand style. He had inherited much land from his father, but he had also expected that he would be Lord Rolle's beneficiary, rather than the young Mark Trefusis. Perhaps that was what made him so bad-tempered.

So powerful and so determined was he, there were few who would stand up to him, and those that did were soon defeated. Dr Jones had avoided confronting him directly, but desisted in the orders for wine and ale, then gradually reintroduced them with the quiet support of the Workhouse Master. It seemed that Mr Moore-Stevens, having demonstrated his power, had lost interest in the subject.

But this was different. Children had died.

The road led down into a small valley before starting its climb towards Roborough, a few scattered cottages at the top of the hill coming into view. A blackbird used its bill to turn over the leaf litter at the edge of the lane in its search for worms and grubs. It paused to stare with beady yellow eyes at Diamond's approaching hoofs then flew suddenly away over the hedge uttering its loud alarm call.

Dr Jones's day was spoiled. Not only had there been two deaths he believed to be unnecessary, but there was the dread of a confrontation to come. Perhaps he should ride straight to Winscott House to demand an explanation and an apology, but he knew he would not, and the knowledge made him ashamed.

He found the schoolmaster, William Bishop, digging his garden in his shirtsleeves. Here, at least, was someone who would help.

He rode on to Pond Close where two cottages stood a short way from the road. Two small girls ran from the first cottage to meet him, stopping suddenly to stand and stare when their courage failed them.

'Who would like to hold my horse?' he called encouragingly, knowing that Diamond would wait patiently in their company.

Children had died here early in the epidemic, the youngest Madge boy in one cottage, William and little Grace Quick in the other but, as he hoped, the remaining children had made a good recovery. However, the schoolmaster would find his class sadly depleted when the school was able to open again.

His three remaining calls were swiftly dealt with, and there remained a little light in the sky as he rode home. So preoccupied had he been, he had quite forgotten the bottle of tea and slice of cake so, knotting the reins, he let Diamond pick his own way along the muddy, rutted lane while he ate and drank. Mary Wilcox would not be pleased if she found her offerings had been ignored.

How was the situation with Moore-Stevens to be resolved? The thought of confrontation was abhorrent, and certain to fail. A vision came to him of Mr Moore-Stevens' intimidating gaze, the set of his mouth. No, he needed the support of others. He would write to the Local Government Board; the problem was not his alone, it affected the whole district and should be shared.

His road led along an exposed ridge, giving him no shelter from the cold wind which now carried with it a light drizzle that formed droplets on Diamond's mane, but he could see the spire of St Michael and All Angels in the distance. For miles around, it was the marker of the town, and it gave him comfort at the end of a long day. At home, there would be dinner, a discussion with Charles and then, he decided, he would write that letter to the Board. Only when it was done would he be able to relax by the drawing room fire.

Chapter Eight

Mr Copp's omnibus waited in the Square outside the Black Horse, the two horses standing patiently while the driver chatted to passing shoppers on the pavement. A farmer's wagon and a donkey cart manoeuvred around the obstruction, accompanied by a shouted disagreement over the right of way. A little light rain fell slowly as if threatening to turn to sleet, but the sky had lightened since Lucy first looked out of her bedroom window. The rain was sure to pass. It did not matter if the air was a little cold; there should be a nip in the air for Christmas shopping.

''Tis a job to keep up with you two! There's no need to rush, you know he never leaves before ten past ten.' Mary Wilcox was breathing heavily as she hurried along behind, attempting to hold her skirt away from the wet pavement.

'Don't worry, we will save a seat for you.' Mary Wilcox would want to sit inside, whereas Lucy preferred to ride in the open air for the view it gave her.

Emily Rudd and Katherine Colling were already seated on the lower level of the omnibus, and when Lucy mounted the stairs, she saw Edith crossing the road with her brothers, Maurice and William. Were they coming to Bideford also? Their company would be welcome. They vanished from view for a few moments, but then appeared again, climbing the twisting stairs.

'Are we to have the pleasure of your company in Bideford?'

Maurice took her gloved hand, and with a self-consciously affectionate gesture, raised it to his lips.

'We would love to accompany you around the shops, Lucy, but we plan to travel beyond Bideford. I have decided that it is time William learned to play golf, so today is to be his first lesson.'

'Are you sure you would not rather come shopping with Edith and me?' she teased William. She was fond of Edith's second youngest brother but rarely saw him now that he was away at school.

'I'd like to say I would prefer it, but...' He laughed, embarrassed. He had a look of Rawlin about him; it was in the eyes, and the mouth.

When Mr Copp spoke to the horses, the omnibus moved off, creaking and swaying gently with the load.

'Lucy,' Edith said, 'have you heard Maurice's plans – do you know I have to say goodbye to yet another of my brothers?'

Maurice explained that he was going to join his older brother Ernest in the Argentine. It was a beautiful country, he said, with rivers, lakes and mountains, the like of which could not be seen in England, but the farming was hard; there were many challenges for pioneers in ranching, not the least of which was having to fight off the Indians who were persistent in their efforts to return to the land.

'We offer them work but they continue in their belief that independence is preferable. There has been considerable violence which makes our work so much harder.'

She tried to picture such a place. 'Will you not miss Torrington?' she asked.

They had reached the point where the town was behind them, and a steep hill led down across the Common to the railway station; the view of wooded hills and deep valleys was very fine even on a damp December day when the trees were bare and the colours muted. She wondered whether she would ever want to leave it to travel to the far side of the world.

'Why is it, Edith, that all your brothers have the desire to travel?' She turned to William, forcing a little lightness into her voice. 'Will you leave too, and Charles, when you are old enough?'

Why did they all have to go? Why did Rawlin have to go? Her brothers did not leave the country; even those who had left Torrington were not so very far away.

'I don't know yet,' said William shyly. 'I don't think I want to go into farming, but there are many opportunities to be found overseas.'

Mr Copp steadied the horses as they started to descend the hill.

'Who is that?' William laughed.

A tall figure dressed in black was hurrying down the hill with arms swinging as if he would soon take off and fly.

'Why, William,' Edith said, 'even from the back you should recognise Reverend Francis! He is walking so fast I don't think even Mr Copp will catch him up. Do you suppose he is going to board the train?'

Clouds of steam billowed between the distant trees and soon the huffing of the engine could be heard, then a loud whistle as the train rounded a bend and came into sight. By the time their omnibus drew into the station yard, the brakes were hissing and the train creeping to a standstill.

It soon became apparent that Reverend Francis intended to join their party. Mary Wilcox, standing close to Lucy on the station platform, whispered, 'Was 'e *asked* to come?'

'Ssh, Mary, I don't know, but we must not be uncharitable.'

Having heard Lucy's parents complain about Reverend Francis, Mary Wilcox had made up her mind that she would not like him. Despite her admonishment, Lucy did not particularly want his company either, but she soon found herself sitting opposite him in a compartment with Polly, Mary Wilcox and Katherine Colling.

He talked incessantly. He was going to Bideford, he said, to visit Reverend Granville. It was so important to make the acquaintance of men of influence when one was new to the area, he said. Reverend Granville, despite being a young man, was very learned, and was sure to have important connections. He had managed to fix Lucy with his gaze as he talked, and it was very difficult to look away without appearing rude; while she nodded and smiled, she longed to look out of the window. As the train ran close to the River Torridge she could see from the corner of her eye that they were passing over the first of three bridges that crossed the meandering river. She often spotted a grey heron staring intently into the shallows alongside the riverbank.

'Reverend Granville is descended from a most noteworthy and historic family and, as we know, *historia vitae magistra*!' He laughed loudly, and looked around the carriage to share the joke. Lucy quickly turned her head towards the window as if a sudden movement had caught her eye. When she glanced back, she saw that his gaze was now on Polly.

'What of your family, Reverend Francis?' Polly asked, with her sweetest smile. 'Do you too have illustrious forbears?'

'Ah!' For a moment he seemed nonplussed. 'Yes. I do, I do! My father was the head of a very important business; he exhibited at the Great Exhibition and travelled a good deal abroad, his transactions extending to all parts of the world. My brother now follows in his footsteps, although his strides are somewhat foreshortened!'

'What was that business then, Reverend Francis?' asked Polly.

'Cement.' He grinned, but without humour. 'He had great experience and scientific knowledge in the manufacture of cement.'

'A very useful trade,' said Edith kindly. 'Were you not drawn to follow on in the family business?'

'Well, I was the younger son, you see, and in any case it is not always a good thing for two brothers to work together.' His chortling laugh really was quite unsettling. 'And personally, I was drawn to the studious life, *ex scientia vera*!'

Mary Wilcox was frowning at him incredulously.

The train rattled over the long, iron bridge that spanned the Torridge at Landcross where the river broadened as it ran down to the estuary. Lucy looked out to see a little weak sunlight catching the ripples on the surface of the water as it eddied through the arches of the bridge; the weather was improving and it was likely that they would have a dry day for their outing. Black-and-white oystercatchers probed the mud enthusiastically at the river's edge, and slower-moving curlews with long downward-curving bills stalked through deeper water; if it were not for the rattling of the train perhaps she could have heard their bubbling calls. But they were approaching Bideford Station now, the rhythmic chugg-chugg-chugg of the train slowing as it wheezed and swayed to a gradual standstill.

Usually, she and her friends walked over the ancient long bridge to reach the High Street, but Mary Wilcox declared that she would be quite fagged if she had to walk all that way in addition to trailing around the shops, so they took the omnibus which was waiting to take passengers into the town, and which would then continue on to Northam, taking Maurice and William to the golf links. Reverend Francis, rather to their relief, declared that he would walk over the bridge and up the hill to visit Reverend Granville.

They watched him stride away.

'I imagine he needs to save the fare,' Lucy said. 'His house is still largely unfurnished.'

'And there is another child on the way.' Edith leaned in and spoke quietly so that the rest of the party would not hear. 'Father is quite concerned for their wellbeing, but Reverend Francis insisted when he first took the position that he would not consider a smaller house.'

'Is your father pleased with the work he is doing?' She spoke carefully, having already discovered that her friend would not discuss the disquiet that was felt in the town.

'Yes, Father feels that he will do much good among the working people.' Edith's expression was inscrutable. 'Have you heard yet about the entertainment he intends to put on after Christmas? He is asking around the town for performers. He feels it will attract many people.'

Reverend Francis was soon forgotten when they descended from the omnibus and walked as a group into the High Street.

'First of all, I *must* visit Mrs Jones and Miss Sanders in Buttgarden Street to see their new designs,' declared Polly.

'Polly! The purpose of our visit is Christmas shopping, not looking at hats!' Lucy took her sister's arm. 'And besides, there is no sense in climbing the hill yet, we will be going up there later for our dinner.'

'Katherine, Emily, I'm sure you want to look at hats, do you not?' Polly twirled around to talk to them, blocking the pavement.

Emily indulged her. 'I'll come with you providing we can look at other shops on the way, but I do prefer the milliners in Barnstaple.' Katherine smiled but declined to answer; Lucy knew that she would not be able to afford a new hat.

Lucy wanted to go to Mrs Puddicombe's bookshop. It had a bigger stock than Miss Fowler's shop in Torrington, and also sold sheet music. She had several ideas for presents, and thought she might buy a book for herself also. It was such a pleasure to walk into the hushed atmosphere of the shop, to stand and peruse the names on the spines of the books while savouring the smell of paper and leather. She hoped she could go in alone or perhaps with Edith, who also liked to read. One felt that one should whisper while in the shop because there were already so many words held between the pages of the books.

But first they went into Miss Green's china and glass shop. It stood on the corner of Allhalland Street, its grand, dressed stone exterior matched by the impressive displays within.

'Keep your elbows in and your skirts close!' warned Mary Wilcox, 'us don't want breakages.' She often forgot the age of her charges and imagined that she was still their nurse.

Lucy chose a vase for her mother, a pale yellow one with a hand-painted decoration of deeper yellow flowers. She was sure her mother would like it. Mary Wilcox returned several times to look at a china dog which was not unlike Alpheus, so Lucy quietly asked Miss Green to wrap that also when they had left the shop, and said she would pick up the parcels at the end of the day.

After luncheon in the Buttgarden Street refreshment rooms, an inevitable trip to the milliner's where they quite crowded out the shop, and a foray into Mill Street, they collected up their parcels and took the omnibus back to the station. Sitting on the platform awaiting the arrival of the train, Lucy checked the contents of her basket, and fingered the brown paper parcel containing her favourite purchases. She had spent almost an hour in the bookshop with Edith. She had bought *The Heart of Midlothian* in a fine leather binding for her father. Having recently persuaded him to overcome his reluctance to read novels, she was now sharing his enjoyment of works by Sir Walter Scott. She had bought Mr Hardy's *Far from the Madding Crowd* in a cheap cloth binding for herself, an attractive edition of Mr Trollope's new book *The Way We Live Now* for Edith, and books on fossils and history for her brothers. Now, sitting on the platform with her friends, and warmly wrapped against the chill air, she could look forward to an evening at home by the fire with a new book to read.

'Ah! We meet again!' The laugh was unmistakeable. Reverend Francis' hat was askew, and he was looking rather red in the face. 'I almost ran across the bridge thinking I might miss the train – and look! Here it is now!'

Lucy should have acted more quickly as the train thundered into the station. She again found herself in a carriage with the curate, Polly having grabbed Mary Wilcox's hand and ushered her into another compartment. He had spent a most interesting time with Reverend Granville, he said, though rather shorter than he would have liked. He had then explored the town, particularly admiring the houses in Bridgeland Street, and had passed an interesting hour telling the men loading boats on the Quay about the docks at Chatham. Lucy had chosen a seat alongside him this time so that he could not hold her in his gaze, but she saw how Katherine's and Emily's eyes glazed over as he talked.

'But now, dear ladies, I must tell you about the entertainment I plan to hold after Christmas. I need your help!' His aim, he said, was to attract people who did not, perhaps, attend church regularly but, by meeting their curate and other churchgoers in an informal setting might be persuaded to swell the congregation. 'I have discovered that the Nonconformists have an annual entertainment after Christmas in the schoolrooms attached to the Howe Chapel, and I intend my event to be grander and more amusing! Your father thinks it a good plan, Miss Buckland.'

He grinned, looking at each of them in turn for far too long, while the train wheezed and puffed out of the station.

'Now, which of you can sing? All of you, I hope!'

Lucy's heart sank. She was told that she had a good singing voice, and she had sung in public before, but did not enjoy it. To stand exposed in front of a crowd of people all of whom had their eyes fixed on her, and knowing that despite their smiles they were waiting to pass judgment, had made her want to run and hide.

'Both Miss Rudd and Miss Colling have contributed to previous entertainments,' Edith glanced sympathetically at Lucy, 'and might perhaps be persuaded to do so again.' She looked at them enquiringly.

'But what of you, Miss Jones?' She flinched as Reverend Francis put his hand on her arm. 'I'm certain you have a charming voice!'

'You might accompany others on the pianoforte, might you not, Lucy?'

'Well, perhaps…' She would rather be a spectator, but as an accompanist she would at least have her back to the audience.

Reverend Francis still had his hand on her arm. He turned to her. 'You could give a reading! Recite a poem!'

She had had enough. 'No, Reverend Francis. I will accompany Miss Rudd and Miss Colling if they wish me to, but I will not perform.'

He withdrew his hand at last. She knew that she had been rather outspoken, but how else could one discourage him?

'I'm sure my uncle Mr Haverfield, and Major Macartney, would give some readings.' Edith was ever the peacemaker.

'And we would love you to accompany us,' said Emily, 'wouldn't we, Katherine? But what of you, Reverend Francis, what will you do?'

'Ah, I have plans, Miss Rudd! I will be the master of ceremonies and will keep the audience entertained between the performances with my amusing stories!'

When the train drew into the station the sky was beginning to darken, and the air felt chill as Lucy stepped down on to the platform. Mr Copp, waiting in the station yard, had already lit the lamps on the omnibus. She ascended the stairs with Edith, the rest of the group choosing an inside seat, and she sat behind Mr Copp.

'He's a strange one, he is,' observed Mr Copp, watching Reverend Francis stride off up the hill. 'Though not as strange as the goings-on in town while you've been away.'

'Oh? What has occurred?'

He turned in his seat to address them. 'Well, it seems as Mr Fletcher, what's Mr Rolle's steward, put up notice boards on parts of the Common.'

'Oh!' said Lucy. 'My father saw one! He was called out to a sick patient late last night and, hearing the sound of hammering while walking along Rack Park Lane, went to investigate. He guessed the boards would cause trouble.'

'Ah, so they was put up under cover of darkness,' said Mr Copp, 'I guessed as much. And these signs told folks that they weren't to remove turf, soil or stones from the Common, and if they did they'd be prosecuted. So, of course, word soon got around.'

The people of Torrington had always strenuously protected their Commoners' rights. Lucy had heard of the uproar many years ago when the late Lord Rolle cut his canal through part of the Common, and the fierce arguments over compensation that followed.

'So, what has happened today?'

''Tisn't over yet, Miss Jones,' Mr Copp shook his head in wonderment, 'Us'll see more of it when us goes up the hill, I don't doubt. When the men got home from work, they started to gather by the cemetery and they tore up the board that was there, and the ones down School Lane and Rack Park Lane. Then they sent the crier out into the town to ask people to gather on the Common by the Warren. While I was waiting in the Square, a large crowd, rough as you like, came marching past and went right around the town, then I got out just in time 'cos they were headed for Halsdon Terrace. I could hear 'em as I went along New Street, such a yelling and hooting as you've never heard. They was outside Mr Fletcher's house by then, see, and I must say I have some sympathy for 'em, 'Tisn't right to take away what people have had all their lives.'

'Will it be safe to go into the town?' It was hard to imagine the usually peaceful streets so transformed.

'Don't worry, Miss, 'tisn't my bus they have argument with. But if they'm still in Halsdon Terrace I'll go round by Potacre Street 'cos the horses don't much like all that shouting and noise.'

They started up the hill.

'I'm surprised that Mr Rolle allowed this to happen,' Edith said quietly, 'in fact I wonder whether Mr Fletcher acted without advice. It was bound to lead to trouble.'

Lucy guessed, from the exclamations coming from below, that news of the disturbance had spread to the other passengers, but then it fell unusually quiet, the silence broken only by the rhythmic clopping of the horses' hoofs and the rumbling of the wheels on the road that wound up the hill. A tawny owl called breathlessly on the Common down to their right and, when she turned to look, she saw that the sky behind them was suffused with red from the setting sun, and heavy with storm clouds.

They heard the shouting first. It started as a distant rumble, growing louder as the omnibus drew nearer to the town, then as the road made its final turn, they saw the crowd. In the fading light it appeared first as a large billowing mass like a stormy sea, then, as they drew closer, individual men could be discerned; three at the front holding up large placards which were, no doubt, the signs that had caused such offence, other men on the periphery of the crowd running to catch up with the leaders, and some carrying flaming torches that they held high above their heads. There must have been two or three hundred men, and even a few women. A sudden movement catching her eye, Lucy turned to see a figure in black hurrying across the rough grass of the Common to her right; Reverend Francis was seeking a safer way home.

Mr Copp stopped the horses at a safe distance. 'Us'll wait just here,' he muttered, 'I doubt they'll come closer,' and he spoke quietly to the horses when they threw up their heads and snorted at the unfamiliar sight.

Suddenly there was a roar and the crowd lurched to the right. A man on horseback was coming up Limers Hill; seeing the crowd, he halted, but it was too late. The crowd surged around the horse which reared, almost unseating its rider and bringing forth a gasp from the passengers on the omnibus and cheers from the crowd.

'It's Mr Rolle!' She recognised his upright posture and tall hat, and the horse was unmistakeable, a fine chestnut hunter which Lucy had often admired. Mr Rolle struggled to regain control as the horse reared and plunged but, as she watched in horror, and Edith reached out to take her hand, another horse appeared and pushed into the crowd, this one ridden by Mr Rolle's groom with his whip hand raised. Together they turned and at a fast trot the two horses descended the hill again accompanied by jeers and shouts of 'Shame!' from the mob.

'That could have turned nasty,' Mr Copp exclaimed, soothing his horses as they moved restlessly. 'I've an idea what they'll do next, then perhaps us can get through.'

The leaders moved up on to the Common to the left of the road and, as the crowd poured after them, Lucy saw that many of the men were carrying stakes and poles. Two men did not move with the rest but remained close to the cemetery wall, standing very still while they watched the proceedings; she gasped when she saw who they were, and pointed them out to Edith.

'Look, it's the town constables! They're not even trying to put a stop to it!'

Edith shook her head in wonder. ''There is just too many in the crowd, what could they do?'

When the crowd reached the Old Bowling Green, the wood was piled high and the men with torches stepped forward. There was a brief pause before flames started to lick around the base of the bonfire. The three leaders, holding the placards high above their heads, made a proclamation, the words of which were indistinct to the passengers on the omnibus but resulted in a huge cheer, louder than any heard before. Then, the signs were thrown on to the fire.

'Will Mr Rolle or Mr Fletcher dare to erect more signs after this?' Lucy whispered to Edith.

The crowd now safely off the road, Mr Copp clicked his tongue and the horses moved forwards, hesitantly at first, tossing their heads as the smoke from the fire drifted towards them. Lucy took out her handkerchief to hold it over her nose and mouth as they passed within fifty yards of the fire, its crackling and spitting plain to hear. She watched in astonishment as the fire roared around the offending placards until they splintered and disintegrated, sending the flames so high that they lit up the sky.

She would never have thought that the people of Torrington were capable of such lawlessness.

Chapter Nine

While Mr Haverfield's voice droned on during the second half of the Christmas concert, the Town Hall was growing decidedly warm. The many gas jets that lit the room, and the heat given off by the crush of bodies meant that even here, in the front row, there was very little air. Lucy wriggled uncomfortably in her seat. The chairs had been placed very close together to fit in as many people as possible, so with Polly on her right and her mother on her left, she felt she was cocooned in yards of warm fabric. She raised a hand to her mouth to hide her smile. It would surely have been wise to ask the ladies and gentlemen to sit in alternate chairs so that the ladies had more space to accommodate their skirts.

Polly sighed and moved restlessly, no doubt growing nervous now that her turn to perform was approaching. Lucy gave her a nudge and a sympathetic glance, and Polly pulled a face in response. She was clearly finding Mr Haverfield's reading as dull as Lucy did. His dramatic rendering of *A Christmas Carol* had held everyone's attention at first, but his delivery was not sufficiently varied. Why must his voice always fall that way at the end of a sentence? Lucy suppressed a giggle. Surely he could make some effort to vary the voices of the characters – Tiny Tim would not have such a strong, deep tone! The shuffling and fidgeting from the seats behind her told her that she was not the only one to think so.

Most of the concert had gone well. Katherine and Emily had sung beautifully, Major Macartney's dramatic monologues were amusing, and the choir had received a standing ovation. But Reverend Francis' anecdotes in the first half, and his showman-like introductions to each act, were not what Torrington was accustomed to. There had been much delighted laughter from the back of the hall, but Lucy could sense the disapproval around her in the front rows.

As soon as Mr Haverfield finished his reading she would have to rise from her seat, for she was to accompany Polly on the piano. They had practised frequently, but Polly had insisted on choosing a new song, *The Lost Chord*, and it was not an easy piece to play.

Mr Haverfield reached the part of the story that compared the Christmas pudding to 'a speckled cannonball'. It would not be long now.

Ann could only see the man who was reading if she leaned towards George until her head was almost resting against his; she could then see between the couple sitting in front. In truth, she was not much interested in the reading, but the pretence enabled her to move closer to George and, in response, he had put his hand on hers. She was not sure whether to turn her hand over so that he might hold it, but decided against it for the time being. It would not do for him to think her too forward.

He smelled of soap and something deeper and more masculine. She could feel his body move as he breathed, and she matched her breath to his so that they were in harmony. His coat sleeve was rough against her wrist, and his hand pressed firmly on hers.

This was the third time they had met. The first time was when she had gone with Sarah to the entertainment at the Howe Chapel schoolroom and George had been waiting at the door with his brother, just as she hoped he would be. They had sat together for the tea, and they talked a little between the various acts. Then he had invited her to meet him for a Sunday afternoon walk on the Common instead of going to chapel. Miss Wilcox allowed her to go because George's uncle had been the mayor, and was well thought of in the town. Even Sarah seemed quite impressed.

They had walked along Castle Hill and down to Taddiport, then to the stream known as Common Lake, but there was a cold wind with a flurry of rain from time to time.

'Be 'ee warm enough?' he had asked anxiously, 'Us can go back if you want,' and she had assured him she didn't mind a bit of rain.

He had been brought up by his uncle and aunt, he said, his parents having died when he was very young, and he and his brother now had lodgings in Calf Street. Another uncle had given him employment and told him that his prospects at the tannery were good.

When they were walking past the Old Bowling Green, he surprised her by pointing to an area of charred earth.

'That's where us burnt the placards that were put up on the Common.'

She stared at him. 'You was there?'

Miss Lucy had told her about the huge crowd of people and the policemen who just stood and watched while the placards were burnt.

'I carried one of the signs, wouldn't have missed it for anything!' George said, grinning. 'Us showed Mr Rolle a thing or two that night, and his steward, Mr Fletcher. I reckon they won't try nought like that again. 'Tis our Common, no one else's!'

She withdrew from him a little then; Dr Jones had said that the men involved with the burning were 'lawless', and she had thought that meant they must all be very rough types.

She glanced doubtfully at George. 'Suppose some folks had been hurt? Or the police might have arrested you!' He did not look like a rough type, he had a lovely face, and he was well-dressed.

He laughed. 'There was too many of us to arrest! And us made sure no one got hurt, 'tisn't as though there was any fighting, us was all in agreement. I don't need to take turf or soil from the Common meself but there's those that do, and I'll stand up for 'em. Us all sticks together in Torrington, always has done.'

The doctor had also said that the men could not be blamed for protecting their rights, so perhaps George had not done anything too bad. She decided to forgive him, and before long they were again laughing together. He was easy to talk to, and kind; he took her hand to help her up the steepest paths.

'You'll learn Torrington ways in time,' he said sympathetically, ''tis different here. Out in the villages there idn't so many of 'ee so you have to do as the vicar or landowner says.'

Towards the end of the walk, when there was no one around, she had let him kiss her.

The audience was applauding now. George took his hand away from hers so that he could clap.

'Look,' she whispered, ''tis my young ladies' turn now.'

When Miss Lucy sat at the piano with her back to the audience, she disappeared from Ann's view, but Miss Polly stepped on to the platform. She looked so pretty in her blue dress that the audience made a soft 'Ahh', and there was a brief outbreak of applause. Miss Polly stood with her hands clasped in front of her and her gaze fixed above the audience's heads; Ann could tell that she was nervous.

Lucy and Polly had practised the song again and again in the drawing room. Ann thought it rather dull, but Miss Polly did look lovely standing there on the platform, her chest rising and falling as she sang, and her mouth opening very wide as she held the long notes. When she reached the end, the applause was very loud and, one by one, the audience stood up as they clapped until everyone on the hall was on their feet. Miss Polly, looking very pleased, bowed several times whereas Miss Lucy just gave a quick nod and returned to her seat. Ann clapped as loud as she could because she felt so proud of them both.

'Her's got a beautiful voice,' said George.

When the audience settled down, Reverend Francis, the curate, returned to the stage. He had introduced all the acts, and told such a funny story in the first half that everyone sat up to see what would come next, and some of the men at the back cheered. Reverend Francis looked delighted and pulled a funny, laughing face like a clown. It was strange to see a curate act that way, but it made people cheer even louder, until he waved his arms to tell them to quieten down and listen. Ann leaned towards George, and he took her hand again.

'There once was a young gentleman,' Reverend Francis paused, raising his eyebrows in a comical way which made the men cheer again, 'who fancied he would take a swim in the river. He looked this way,' he turned to face the left, 'and he looked that way, and as there was no one to be seen he proceeded to remove his clothes, and he instructed his dog to guard them.

However,' he paused dramatically, 'when he returned from his swim, his dog, being unaccustomed to seeing his master unclothed, did not recognise him and barked most ferociously.'

George was chuckling, but Ann kept quiet. It *was* funny, but thinking about naked men when she was holding hands with George made her feel uncomfortable.

'The poor man had therefore to run about until almost broiled by the sun, and he got the cramp in his legs. At length, however, the dog fell asleep, upon which its owner took it by the tail and flung it across the river and then got on his clothes as quick as he could, by which time the dog returned and recognised him.'

When the crowd roared with laughter Reverend Francis laughed as loudly as any of them, bending forward with his hands on his knees. What a strange way for a gentleman to behave!

Lucy raised her hands to clap, then quickly replaced them in her lap. She felt she should applaud out of politeness but there was silence around her; all the applause and cheering came from the back of the hall. She glanced along the row. Her mother was tight-lipped, her hands clasped firmly in her lap. Not a single person was clapping. On her right, Polly was looking quite upset, and of course it was natural that she should be distressed that her singing – which had gone so well – should be followed by such distasteful nonsense. Reverend Francis, grinning, seemed quite unaware of the effect of his story on the front rows, and was now embarking on another. Surely this one would be more appropriate.

'There once was a boy,' he started, 'who swallowed a musical box.' The men at the back roared with laughter. 'The effect of the comic tunes, when he visited church with his family, was extraordinary.'

As he went on, it became apparent that this story was not as objectionable as the last, but merely foolish. An impatient sigh coming from the row behind would, no doubt, be her great-uncle, Colonel Palmer. He had already made it clear that he objected to Reverend Francis' high church practices and this performance would not help him to regard the curate more favourably.

'There once was a man,' again that pause and rolling of the eyes, 'who came downstairs in his nightgown. While going outside to check on the weather, the front door closed behind him, trapping the hinder part of his nightgown.'

Lucy's fears were realised; the story went on to relate how the man was too tightly caught to turn around, so had to remove his nightgown in order to ring the doorbell. She could sense the tension around her which was surely increased by the rapturous response from the back of the hall; men were now shouting out rude comments which led to further hilarity.

How could Reverend Francis do it? How could he not realise how entirely inappropriate this was? He reminded her of a small boy who, excited by a crowd of admiring relatives, starts boasting and playing to the audience; she wanted to reprimand him as she would have rebuked her youngest brother years ago. *Reverend Francis! That's enough! You are becoming foolish now!*

But she could not do that, and as he continued, getting himself into even more trouble, she began to feel sorry for him, and for his wife who was sitting a few rows behind. This would be the talk of the town for many days to come. He would surely be mortified when he realised what a bad mistake he had made. Where was Reverend Buckland? Would he not strongly disapprove?

She turned her head carefully. Edith, sitting at the end of the row behind, was looking uncomfortable but her father sat very upright, gazing with an inscrutable expression at Reverend Francis on the platform.

At last, the farce came to an end. There was a final bow; Reverend Francis left the platform and eventually the cheering ceased. Those around her stood in silence, gathered their gloves and umbrellas without a word and started to move towards the exit. Only the meaningful looks and raised eyebrows hinted at their displeasure.

THE CURATE'S REMINISCENCES (or, as they have been vulgarly styled, "RUMMY NUISANCES").—On Tuesday evening last, the 9th instant, a Christmas entertainment of readings, music, &c., took place at the Town Hall, on which occasion the Rev. H. O. Francis, M.A., curate of this place, gave some reminiscences, the character of which called forth great surprise and disgust in the minds of many respectable persons, and a very strong feeling prevails that the unseemliness of such a performance on the part of a clergyman ought to be exposed, in the interest of public decency, good taste, propriety, and even morality. It appears that, almost at the close of the entertainment on Tuesday night, the reverend gentleman was called upon (according to the programme) to give more of his personal reminiscences, when, (owing to the fact that he had at a former entertainment on the 18th ult. given the first batch of them,) on rising to his feet at the call, he was greeted with uproarious applause from those occupying the back seats. It is hoped that if on any future occasion the curate should be announced to give more "reminiscences" of a similar character, respectable married ladies will, on the ground of common decency, discountenance the same by refraining from going themselves and prohibiting their sons and daughters from going to listen to such demoralising foolishness.—It has b—— stated to us that ——

North Devon Journal, 1877

Chapter Ten

Lucy sat in the library consulting one of her father's books on botany. From the surgery next door, she could catch the low rumble of his voice, the higher, more plaintive tones of a woman, then the door opening and his commanding 'Next!'

It was always quiet in the library but the books had a presence, like friends waiting in silence until invited to speak. She rose and ran her hand along a row of cloth and leather spines. Many of them were medical textbooks or dull tomes of ancient history, but she liked the Greek myths, and had passed many hours with the works of Shakespeare and the volumes of poetry that her father had favoured when he was younger. Today, however, she had been looking for something special. She scanned the shelves again. It was no good; the information she wanted was not here.

In his second letter, Rawlin had described some of the exotic flowers and trees he saw in Australia. He knew the correct names for one or two, and a few amusing descriptive names told to him by the natives, but there were many he could not name. He had made sketches for Lucy of some of the more extraordinary examples with twisted, creeping stems and leaves as big as umbrellas. She had hoped to find their names in one of her father's books but, after leafing through several and studying the illustrations, she finally thought to consider their titles. *The Flowers of Europe. The Trees of the Northern Hemisphere.* She should have realised that there would be no books about Australia.

She had spent a week composing her first letter to Rawlin, carefully considering each phrase to ensure that it could not be misinterpreted. *I was pleased to receive your letter* she wrote. *My family were amazed to hear of your arduous journey.* No, that would not do; he would not write anything personal if he thought it would be shared with the whole family. *I was surprised* would be better. She puzzled for days over the way she should respond to his declaration that he thought of her often. She could not possibly write that she thought of him day and night, so she substituted a careful *I often think of our times together on the Common*. It was with much trepidation that she finally took the letter to the post office, dreading Mrs Fowler's curious questions when she noticed the name on the envelope.

Rawlin had asked her for stories about the town. She told him how the telegraph wire to the post office had broken in a storm – imagine if a telegram should travel all the way from Australia only to fail when it reached Torrington Square! – and she would like to have written an amusing account of Reverend Francis at the Christmas concert, but making fun of the curate might reflect badly on Rawlin's father for having agreed to the appointment. She wondered what the family told him about the goings-on.

She told Edith that she had received a letter from Rawlin, mentioning it casually when they were shopping together in Barnstaple. Edith stopped abruptly and took her hand.

'I thought that he would write to you. I'm glad, Lucy.'

She was embarrassed. 'Oh, he probably won't write again,' she said.

Then, after only three weeks, a second letter arrived. *I hope to receive a letter from you, Lucy*, Rawlin wrote, *but if I wait for one to arrive before writing again, my letters to you will be six months apart.* After describing the extraordinary plants and trees close to his new home, Rawlin wrote how he would miss seeing the bluebells on the hills of the Common. *Endymion non-scriptus – do you remember any of the Latin names I shared with you when we were children?* he wrote. It would be some weeks before the bluebell leaves would start to push through on the grassy slopes near the Common Lake, but Lucy had a sudden thought; the snowdrops might now be in flower, *Galanthus nivalis* they were called, she could remember the Latin names of the most common flowers. She jumped up from her chair; she would look for them now so that she could tell him whether they were flowering.

Ann was singing quietly as she swept the stairs. Since she had been walking out with young George Chapple she often sang as she worked, and had lost the weary, pinched look she had when she first started work. How wonderful it must be for her to look forward to a weekly meeting with him! Lucy could scarcely imagine how she would feel if Rawlin still lived in the town.

'Where will you go with George this Sunday, Ann?'

Ann looked startled and straightened up, the dustpan in her hand.

'Oh! I don't know, Miss. 'Twill be all right, will it, for me to have the afternoon off?'

'Of course, if Miss Wilcox agrees. I'm taking Alpheus out now, I'll be back for luncheon.'

She paused at the gate. The quickest way to reach the stream was across the town, but then she would have to stop every few yards to pass the time of day with people, and today she wanted to be alone with her thoughts. She turned left towards Castle Hill; she would walk right around the town on the Common.

The wind was cold but the clouds were moving quickly, sending shadows racing across the hillsides, and when the sun appeared there was a semblance of warmth which probably, she thought, existed more in her imagination than in reality, given that it was only January. It was the start of the wet season in Australia, Rawlin had told her, with daily temperatures of ninety degrees, and so humid that everything in the house became damp and mouldy; his books were already beginning to rot. Every day there were thunderstorms, the sky becoming almost black while the thunder rumbled nearer and nearer, and the trees quivering as if in fear. Then the thunder roared and the lightning flashed continuously for perhaps twenty minutes until the rain, heavier than had ever been seen in Devon, arrived without warning. Rawlin wrote of it with wonder; she wished she could be with him to see it.

She walked fast along the path that followed the contour of the hill, calling to Alpheus when he leapt down the slopes after a rabbit, then she took the drangway that passed between the houses on Mill Street to reach the Common on the other side, breathing heavily as she climbed the steep slopes. Alpheus walked obediently at her side; there were too many hens and grazing sheep here to allow him to run freely, quite apart from the lure of the duck pond.

Polly would be shocked if she could see her striding up the hill with her skirt gathered in her hand. *Lucy, the way you carry on is barely respectable, walking alone as you do, and all that district visiting too, going in such dreadful houses!*

But Rawlin would not think less of her for being busy, and in his letters had shown interest in her work. They had always enjoyed talking on serious subjects, and she had tried to keep up with her reading since he left. Naturally her education had not been as thorough as his; history had consisted merely of the learning of dates, geography the names of towns and rivers, and consequently there was so much that she did not understand, but she wanted to learn. Recently, she had read Mr Darwin's *The Origin of the Species*, which had both sharpened her appreciation of the wildlife around her, and diminished her fervour for church doctrine.

Down in the valley, the silence was almost complete; no birds, no breeze to rustle the dead leaves. She stood still and listened. At this time of year, only robins would sing, a quiet, subdued song that some said presaged the death of a child; there was no robin today but she could just make out the faint tinkle of running water at the bottom of the valley, and then from the far slopes the croak of a distant pheasant seeking safety from Mr Rolle's guns.

The path alongside the fast-running stream was muddy. After a few minutes of trying to pick her way around the worst of it, she lifted her skirt above her ankles and ploughed through; the mud would brush off her boots and hem when it dried, but she would have to return by another circuitous route rather than through the town if she were not to become the subject of gossip.

Above the stream the grass was sparse between the bare, scattered trees, and littered with dead leaves and fallen twigs, but ahead she could see fresh green shoots pushing through and – yes! – the bright white flowers of snowdrops. She hurried over and crouched to admire them. The stems stood tall and proud, but the faces of the flowers gazed demurely down, the green-tipped petals glowing in the wintry morning light, a sure sign that spring would come. She wished she had brought her sketchbook; she could have included a drawing with her letter.

She was continuing on her way and planning the words she would write to Rawlin when she saw a figure approaching along the path. If he had been proceeding at his usual hurried pace, she would have recognised Reverend Francis immediately, but he was walking rather slowly with his head downcast and did not notice her until they were only a few yards apart.

'Oh! Miss Jones!' He looked startled. 'I'm sorry, I was deep in thought.'

She could have wished him a good morning and continued on her way, but something made her stop. She had been curious, since his dreadful performance at the Christmas concert, as to whether he had any awareness of the embarrassment it had caused. He had not appeared to notice the reaction of those in the front rows but surely someone would have told him, his wife or Reverend Buckland perhaps, and if he read *The North Devon Journal* he would have seen the damning report of the concert.

'Why, Reverend Francis, I hope there is nothing worrying you?' It was not like her to be so forthright; she felt quite daring.

He gazed past her, his mouth working. 'Miss Jones, you have lived in this town all your life, I believe. Would you consider its people intolerant? Opinionated? Because I have to confess I am finding it difficult to make headway here, at least with a certain sector of the population.'

She was taken aback. She had not expected him to speak in such a way.

'I may be wrong, Reverend Francis, but is it the reaction to the Christmas concert that has caused you to feel this way?'

'It is, Miss Jones, and I feel it is most unfair. There were many in the audience who enjoyed my stories very much, the very people whom we wish to bring into the church. Everyone agrees that the congregation is smaller than we would wish due to the actions of the Methodists, yet when I succeed in influencing the lower classes, people turn against me. It seems the only support I have comes from the bishop, and Reverend Buckland of course.'

'But those who enjoyed your stories, Reverend Francis, have they attended church?' Perhaps she was being too bold, but he looked surprised rather than annoyed.

'Well, no, they haven't, not yet, but these things take time, Miss Jones.'

'But meanwhile,' unable to face him, she gazed away up the hill, 'others are offended, and the congregation is reduced still further.'

'Were you offended, Miss Jones?'

'Yes, I was! I found the stories improper and foolish!' There, it was said. 'I'm sorry, but I have to speak my mind.'

He looked downcast. 'Thank you for your honesty. It would appear, then, that I overstepped the mark. But, Miss Jones, I will never admit such a thing to those who criticise me in public, nor to the Methodists, nor to the editor of the local paper who is himself a Nonconformist and loves to find fault with churchmen.' He smiled at her, although it was more of a grimace. 'That I realise I have made a mistake must be our secret, Miss Jones.'

Emboldened by her success, she plunged on. 'My father is the Workhouse Medical Officer – you know that, of course, being chaplain there. The nurse told him, and others in the town, that you snatched a tract from her hand and threw it on the fire. She was greatly upset. The news has now spread around the town and I'm afraid it has not increased your popularity.'

His brow wrinkled, like a child who has been reprimanded. 'But, Miss Jones, it was a *Methodist* tract! I am determined to root out the atrocious criminality of dissent within the Workhouse, we should work to bring those unfortunate people to the shelter of the true church!'

'All I can say, Reverend Francis, is that people have the right to worship as they choose. Church people and Nonconformists have lived quite happily as neighbours in Torrington!' She was feeling hot and flustered; the conversation had gone on quite long enough.

'Miss Jones, I believe you have much good sense.' He was looking downcast. 'You have helped me, and I shall think carefully about what you have said. I do not wish to create discord, but there will continue to be changes in the church services, Reverend Buckland and I are resolute on that issue despite some opposition. Do you know, Colonel Palmer stopped me on South Street today to complain of what he called Romish practices in the church? "I *will* put a stop to it," he said, though how he imagines he will do that, I do not know.'

What could she say? She could not allow him to continue in that vein.

'Colonel Palmer is my mother's uncle, Reverend Francis. He has a great deal of influence in the town.'

'Oh, then I have made another *faux pas*.' With a dramatic gesture, he struck himself on the forehead. 'It seems that everyone is related to one another in this town. But may I ask a favour of you?' He took her hand and squeezed it as he talked. 'My wife is finding life in the town quite difficult; she cannot go out visiting because of the children, and is lonely at times, I fear. Would you be so kind as to call on her one day? I know she would value your friendship.'

'Of course I will, Reverend Francis.' She withdrew her hand from his grasp. 'Perhaps I will call on her this week.'

She was glad when two labourers passed on the path, staring curiously at her, for they gave her an excuse to hurry away before he had time to say any more.

She was not sure that she wanted more involvement with Reverend Francis or his household, but she felt sympathy for Mrs Francis and did not like to think of her being unhappy. The next day was a long one with eight visits to make in Calf Street, including a long vigil at a death bed, but on Wednesday, after helping her mother check the household accounts and accompanying Mary Wilcox to Pearce and Burnell's in the Square to buy some new bed sheets, she set off for Torridge Villa.

The oldest child, a girl of about six years, opened the door and stared shyly at Lucy.

'Mama's in the kitchen,' she replied, after a long pause.

'Would you tell her that Miss Jones is here to see her?'

The girl nodded and ran off, leaving Lucy on the doorstep. After a few minutes Mrs Francis hurried into the hall, untying a long white apron and trying to straighten her hair.

'Miss Jones, I am so sorry, do come in. I was just making some cakes but Lizzie can put them in the oven. I do what I can, you see, because really, in a house this size and the children as well, two servants simply aren't enough.'

The drawing room was still very sparsely furnished despite the addition of a new rug and a couple of rather faded watercolours on the wall. After calling for some tea, Mrs Francis told her about the jams and pickles she had made in the autumn from the fruit in the garden, and the clothing she had sewn for the children.

'It is all new to me, Miss Jones, I never had to do such things in my parents' house, but you see a curate's pay is not high so I must help to make ends meet!' She laughed, seemingly delighted with her new role. 'Until Herbert is able to get his own parish – and the bishop has promised that he will – we must do what we can.'

She chattered on while the three children looked on seriously. The youngest boy's raised eyebrows gave him a comical expression reminding Lucy rather disconcertingly of his father.

Mrs Francis' pregnancy was now quite advanced, a fact she acknowledged by placing her hand on her abdomen and laughing self-consciously.

'Herbert would like a son again, but I would prefer another girl to keep me company, and you would like a sister, wouldn't you, Jessie?'

'We cannot choose, Mama,' the girl said levelly, 'you know that.'

'Well, of course, you are quite right, Jessie!' Mrs Francis laughed, and turned to Lucy. 'Isn't she adorable?'

Lucy agreed that she was although, in truth, the girl's watchful demeanour was rather unsettling.

As the conversation continued, it became apparent that Mrs Francis had little awareness of her husband's reputation.

'He is so pleased to have found a position where he can make improvements and show how able he is!'

Had the anxieties he had expressed on the Common not been shared with his wife? The thought made her feel rather uncomfortable; perhaps Reverend Francis did not want to add to his wife's worries when a birth was forthcoming, but she felt uneasy about being party to information that had been concealed from his wife.

Despite these misgivings, Lucy promised to call again. Mrs Francis appeared to be much alone with only the two servants and the children for company.

It was not long, however, before there were further difficulties for Reverend Francis' family. At the dinner table a month later, when the meal was finished, her father reached into his inside pocket.

'Colonel Palmer passed this to me today,' he waved a paper. 'He has had enough of Reverend Buckland's refusal to take his complaints seriously, so he has drawn up this petition. Mr and Mrs Loveband have already signed, and I think we should all sign it.'

He read out the declaration which was strongly critical of the superfluous ornaments in the church, the saying of the Litany in a tone not understood by the people, and the Romanising tendency of the preaching.

When he had finished, her mother laughed, and clapped lightly.

'I knew my uncle could be trusted to express our complaints clearly! I will sign it, of course, I am tired of the curate's fiddle-faddery, it is theatrical and distasteful and I much prefer a simpler service.'

'Charles?' Her father raised his eyebrows at her brother.

'Yes, Father, I'll sign. I'll come to your study later, shall I? I have notes to write up now.' He pushed back his chair and left the table.

'Polly? Lucy?'

'Oh, it's no concern of mine, Father,' Polly said, 'but I'll sign it if you wish.'

Lucy looked down at her lap. The petition was addressed to Reverend Buckland. Edith, her best and oldest friend, would be upset by it. Rawlin might hear of it. How could she sign it? And if she did, how could she face Reverend Francis at their fortnightly meeting, and his wife?

'Lucy?'

She twisted her napkin in her lap. She could not meet her father's eyes.

'Father, I cannot. Not when I work with Reverend Francis, and Edith is my friend.'

There was silence as her mother arranged the knife and fork on her plate with great deliberation, and her father drank the last sip of wine before replacing the cut-glass goblet on the table. His reply was slow in coming.

'Do you not think that people will find it strange that you are the only member of the family not to sign?'

She glanced up. He was looking at her kindly but, as she suspected, her mother was less sympathetic.

'Lucy, don't be ridiculous, of course you must sign. What would your great-uncle say if you did not? Edith will soon get over it, and as for Reverend Francis, it would be better if you did not have anything to do with that man. It is time you gave up district visiting; I always said it was quite unsuitable for you.'

Anger rose up inside her. 'Last week, Mother, I sat with Mr Beer for three hours when no one else could.' She gripped her napkin tightly to stop her hands shaking. 'He died the next day. The work I do is valuable. I'll not give it up, not yet.'

She would not cry; she must not.

'How can you be so wilful, Lucy? Charles, will you not support me in this?'

Lucy stared stubbornly at the table, then felt her father's hand on her shoulder as he rose.

'We've always encouraged strongmindedness in our children, Charlotte. I'm glad to see Lucy so determined.'

'Oh, really!' Her mother left the room, knowing that she had lost the argument. Lucy sat at the table reliving the disagreement, until Ann came to clear the table. Had she made the right decision?

> **TORRINGTON.**
> **RITUALISM AT TORRINGTON.**
> Since the present curate (the Rev. H. O. Francis) came among us, various innovations, of Ritualistic character and Romish tendency, have been introduced in the services of the parish church, which have been very offensive to many of the parishioners. A letter of remonstrance was addressed to the vicar (the Rev. S. Buckland) on the subject, under date the 5th March, which was signed by the following 36 parishioners:—John Palmer, Lieut.-Col., M. R. Loveband, Mrs. Loveband, Chas. R. Jones, Mrs. Jones, James Balsdon, Mrs. Balsdon, Edward Wills, Mrs. Wills, Gabriel Fisher, W. E. Price, George Doe, Charles Doe, John Hooper, H. L. Mallet, John Lake (parish churchwarden), Hubert H. Pidgeon, G. Walkey, Frederick Brede, C. Colling, William Toms, John Rude, Thomas Copp, W. P. Ashton, George Stoneman, Maria Williams, Catherine Williams, Mary F. Lake, G. D. Adams, John Tapley, Elizabeth Bartlett, George Baker, John B. Reed, Eliza Williams, Charles Brailey, and J. Petherick.
> The points chiefly dwelt on in their letter were—the "decorations" of various kinds set up in the church; the early celebration of the Lord's Supper; the "saying" of the Litany in a *tone* if not "in a tongue not understood by the people"; and the Romanising tendency of the curate's preaching. To this letter the vicar wrote a reply, which he published in "Holy Week, 1877." The vicar's tone compares unfavourably with that of his correspondents. There is little of the kindness or love of the pastor in it, but much that is sarcastic and acrimonious. On the most important point—that of the Romanising ten-

North Devon Journal, 1877

The next day, as she walked with Edith to Torridge Villa for their fortnightly meeting, she told her friend about the petition.

'Yes, I have heard.' Edith, walking arm-in-arm with Lucy in her neat, deliberate way, sighed and made a rueful face. 'I know that Colonel Palmer is your great-uncle, Lucy, but I do wish people would leave Father alone and allow him to make decisions about the church as he sees fit. After all, he cannot go against the bishop's wishes.'

A steady drizzle was falling. Lucy glanced up to make sure that she was holding the umbrella equally over them both.

'My father says that Torrington people are always determined to have their own way, they will not be told what to do, and he thinks it a good thing. It is the same with their Commoners' rights, they will not give them up, and he believes they will not give up this fight either.'

'Have you signed it, Lucy?' Edith looked troubled, and Lucy squeezed her arm.

'No, I haven't. But I do wonder whether it might be better to keep the services the way they used to be. After all, so many people are leaving, some attending church in Frithelstock or Little Torrington instead of St Michael's!'

'I know, but Father thinks they will return, and he has said that he will not reverse any of the changes. He intends to write a letter to the newspaper about it. He is in a difficult position, you see, because the bishop has wanted him to make alterations to the services for some time, but he was reluctant to do so, knowing that the congregation would not approve. But now he has Reverend Francis' support too. I would not say it to anyone else, Lucy, but Father can be quite stubborn too. I'm afraid he does not listen to the parishioners as well as he might.'

They reached Torridge Villa and rang the bell. Almost immediately, the door was flung open by a dishevelled-looking Reverend Francis.

'Oh!' His hair was wild, and he wore no necktie. 'I'm sorry, you cannot come in! Dr Norman is here; my wife – it seems her time has come, but we were not expecting it to be so soon!' He looked confused and ran his hands through his hair. 'Were you making a social call?'

Lucy saw that his little daughter, Jessie, was standing behind him, her eyes wide and frightened.

Edith quickly took control. 'Reverend Francis, we will go.' She reached out and touched his arm. 'I hope all will be well.'

They turned away and heard the door close behind them.

The next morning when Lucy was walking Alpheus, she found herself at the lower entrance to Torridge Villa where a small gate led into the garden from the Common. She looked up at the house. Above the terraced lawns, the windows gleamed blankly in the weak March sunlight. Why should she not call in and enquire? Yesterday might have been a false alarm, but if the baby had arrived Mrs Francis would be glad to show it off. She decided to walk up through the garden and call at the back door so that she would not disturb the new mother if she was sleeping. Perhaps there would be somewhere to tie Alpheus's lead while she went inside.

The kitchen door was opened by a startled-looking maid.

'I have come up from the Common, hoping for some news of Mrs Francis, and to see her,' said Lucy. 'Is she well? Is there a new arrival?' She felt quite excited; would it be a girl as Mrs Francis hoped?

'Oh! No, Miss, no, I'm sorry but 'tis best you don't come in.' She looked most alarmed. 'The child – it didn't live, Miss, no more than an hour or two, and the Maister's beside himself and the Missis too!' She started to cry. 'It was a boy, you know. Oh, 'tis dreadful, Miss, and those poor children, Jessie especially!'

Lucy felt stunned. 'I'm so sorry. Please tell Reverend and Mrs Francis – well, if it seems right to say something, please give them my condolences.'

The maid, now sobbing openly, nodded and closed the door. Lucy hurried back across the lawns, hoping she would not be seen from the windows. She had intruded, she should not have gone, but how was she to know? Her heart went out to poor Mrs Francis.

At home, she went straight to her father's surgery. The door was open, and he was writing at his desk.

'Father, may I speak with you?'

She had to fight back the tears. 'Mrs Francis has lost her baby, it lived only for an hour. Father, it is dreadful, and that petition *cannot* now be sent, imagine them discovering that so many in the town are against them, now, of all times! It would be too much to bear. Will you tell Uncle that it cannot be sent? Please do, Father!'

He shook his head. 'Lucy, it has already gone, one copy to Reverend Buckland and one copy to the newspaper. I'm very sorry to hear about the child, but the petition is not being sent to Reverend Francis.'

'But it is directed against him! It makes particular mention of his manner of delivery and of the decorations in the church that he has arranged! It is cruel to attack someone at such a time!'

'That is as may be, but there is nothing that can be done about it now. Perhaps Reverend Buckland will delay a day or two before telling him of it. And Lucy, try not to take things so much to heart, life *is* hard, I see it every day in the suffering of my patients, but I have to brush it aside if I am to continue to help them.'

He meant well, she knew that, but she could not stop thinking of Mrs Francis, and of Reverend Francis, too, who had wanted another son. As she mounted the stairs to her room, she determined that she would continue to be a friend to them both, even if the rest of the town turned against them.

BIRTHS, MARRIAGES, AND DEATHS.

BIRTHS.

BLATHWAYT.—April 24, at Chulmleigh, the wife of the Rev. C. R. Blathwayt, of a son.

DAVIES.—April 22, at 19, James's Walk, Clerkenwell Green, London, the wife of Mr. J. M. Davies, watch-maker and silversmith, of twins.

FRANCIS.—March 17, at Torrington, N. Devon, prematurely, the wife of the Rev. Herbert O. Francis, M.A., of a son (Basil), who only survived his birth a few hours.

FULFORD.—April 24, at Woolbury, the wife of the Rev. F. L. Langdon Fulford, of a daughter.

HOWARD.—April 22, at Queen street, Barnstaple, the wife of Mr. C. Howard, tinman and plumber, of a son.

THOMAS.—April 15, at Ivy Cottage, Cooney Bridge, Barnstaple, the wife of Capt. W. Thomas, of a son.

North Devon Journal, 1877

Chapter Eleven

The Castle Street cockerel had been crowing for at least half an hour when Ann finally swung out her legs to sit sleepily on the edge of the bed.

'Bring me a cup of tea when you come up, would 'ee?' murmured Sarah from under the blankets.

Ann pulled on her clothes, then tiptoed past the main bedrooms and down the stairs.

In the kitchen she lit the gas lamp before sitting for a moment at the table, yawning loudly. Perhaps when the mornings were lighter it would be easier.

The back door opened suddenly, and Harry walked in. 'Haven't 'ee lit the stove yet? Do 'ee want me to clear it out? You look done in.'

''Tis all very fine for you, Harry, you can go to bed early. But 'tis good of 'ee, if you light the fire I can tidy myself and sweep the hall before the kettle boils.'

She got up and gave him a quick hug; he would do anything for her if she gave him a hug, but she drew the line at a kiss, despite his occasional shy requests. As long as she was quick, he did not try to kiss her but just stood as if stupefied, his ankles and wrists protruding from his clothes as if he would never stop growing.

She swayed her hips as she walked out of the room, knowing that his eyes were on her.

In the drawing room she cleaned out the grate and relaid the fire, thankful that there was only the one to do now that the weather was warmer. She opened all the curtains in the downstairs rooms and swept the hall quickly, being careful not to bang the broom against the skirting board lest she wake anyone, then, unlocking the front door to sweep the porch, she paused to watch the sun rise, a huge half-globe above the hills to the east. She did not often see it at just the right moment, especially on a cloudless day when it was clearly visible. Under its gentle light the vivid greens of the garden emerged from the gloom and a blackbird started to sing. Perhaps he, also, knew that today was Mayfair.

'And 'twill be dry for it, too,' she murmured, her heart lifting. She had only the morning's work to do, and then she would go to the Fair with George.

The kitchen was empty; Harry must have gone back to clean out the stables and feed the horses, but he'd made a good fire, the stove was already giving out heat and the kettle coming to the boil. She made a pot of tea, filled the kettles for the washing water, and carefully carried two cups of tea up the stairs.

Miss Wilcox was lying on her back, fast asleep and snoring gently with her mouth open, the white cotton cap she wore in bed askew over one eye. Ann suppressed a giggle as she placed the cup and saucer on the bedside table.

'Morning, Miss Wilcox, 'tis a fine day for Mayfair.'

She woke with a snort. 'What's that? Oh! Oh, thank you, Ann.'

She took Sarah her tea, hurried down to drink her own, then started to dust the downstairs rooms, but her mind was elsewhere. She was going to wear her new dark blue dress for Mayfair, the one Miss Lucy had given her. It was not designed for a large bustle of course and was fairly plain because that was Miss Lucy's style, but the lighter blue ribbon Ann had sewn around the lower tiers of the skirt had transformed it. The dress was a little tight over her bust and, along with the bustle, served to emphasise her curves, especially once she had taken it in at the waist. George was sure to make admiring comments, but she would pretend it was nothing, as if she had a new dress every day.

She had been counting the days until Mayfair. The three occasions she had attended in the past were highlights in a childhood almost devoid of treats; she could still remember the mixture of utter exhaustion and delight she felt, aged nine or ten, by the end of the three hour walk back to Shebbear through dark lanes with a toffee apple still in her hand. The family could not, at that time, afford the carrier's cart.

But now, she lived in the town, and the Fair took place just a few paces away. She paused in her dusting of the glass-domed clock on the mantelpiece and smiled to herself as she remembered what had happened the previous day. Hearing shouts and the loud rumble of wheels from the kitchen, she had run out to see three enormous brightly painted wagons coming along Castle Street, each pulled by four heavy horses with huge shaggy feet, while in every doorway people stood to see the cavalcade pass by. As the horses threw their weight into their collars, two men in rough working clothes jumped down from the first wagon to guide them up the narrow lane to Barley Grove where the Fair was to be held. As Ann stood by the gate with a dishcloth in her hand, one of the men had shouted out to her in an unfamiliar accent.

'Come back tomorrow, lass, ride one of them!' He gestured at the red and gold horses painted on the side of the wagons. 'I'll ride with you, eh lass!' He winked and broke into a laugh.

Embarrassed, she had hurried back to the kitchen, but in the evening went to watch from a safe distance as the men, with much shouting and good-natured swearing, assembled a large contraption with brightly painted horses fixed to poles around its circumference, and a roof rising to a peak. A sudden blast of harsh music made her jump back in surprise.

Never before had there been a steam roundabout in Torrington.

By the time the kettles had come to the boil and Ann had dusted all the downstairs rooms, Sarah finally made an appearance to prepare the breakfast.

Ann filled two large jugs with hot water from the kettles. As usual her wrists ached horribly by the time she reached the landing, and it was a relief to put them down on the tiled side table. She took one jug to Miss Wilcox, now sitting on the edge of her bed drinking her tea, then knocked on Dr Jones's bedroom door.

'Come in, Ann.'

He was sitting up in bed reading with his spectacles perched on the end of his nose; it was rare to find him asleep.

''Tis a fine day for Mayfair, Sir.'

She poured the water carefully into the china bowl on the washstand and opened the curtains, frightening off a seagull sitting on the railings of the balcony.

'Mayfair.' Dr Jones said. 'Yes, of course it is; you will go, Ann?'

'Oh yes, Sir, I'm looking forward to it.'

Removing the bed pan and covering it with the cloth she held over her arm, she closed his door and hurried down the stairs to fetch two more jugs.

Miss Lucy was still in bed, gazing thoughtfully at the ceiling with her hands behind her head, but Miss Polly was brushing out her hair at the dressing table. There was a hint of perfume in the room.

'Ann, would you plait my hair at the back like you did before? I want to wear my new hat for Mayfair and the pinned plaits sit nicely below the brim.'

How ever was she to manage that, along with all the other things she had to do?

'I'll try, Miss Polly, perhaps when breakfast is done and cleared away.'

Back in the kitchen, Miss Wilcox appeared from the pantry.

'Now then,' she stood with her hands on her hips, 'you must watch yourselves today, the pair of 'ee, I know what goes on at Mayfair, I've seen it time and again, and there's many a young maid who's found herself in trouble. There's some rough ol' types in Torrington and even the best of the lads get a bit wild-ified after a few drinks. You've heard what happened to that maid last year when her was walking home to Langtree, and her won't be the last, I don't doubt.' She took side plates from the dresser and stacked them on a tray. 'So mind you keep George in his place, Ann, he's a good boy but no different from all the rest when it comes down to it, and all the excitement of Mayfair.'

Ann exchanged an amused look with Sarah before they continued with their work. She would have her day at Mayfair, a whole afternoon *and* evening to enjoy.

'Lucy, let us go out this morning to see the livestock sale! Life has been so dull lately and I want to enjoy every moment of Mayfair!' Polly, her hair around her shoulders until Ann could put it up for her, ate the last mouthful of egg and replaced her teaspoon neatly on the plate. 'It's amusing to see New Street so transformed! You will come with me, won't you?'

Lucy looked dubiously at her sister. 'Surely, cattle and sheep are not very thrilling? And the state of the road may spoil your dress. Would you rather not wait until this afternoon?' She would then have plenty of time to read the letter from Rawlin that lay on her lap under the tablecloth.

'No!' Polly patted her mouth with her napkin. 'I will get dressed now and hope that Ann can do my hair. You will come, won't you? It is sure to be fun and one never knows who might be there.'

It was late in the morning before they set out, Polly having changed her mind about her dress at the last moment. Lucy had dressed quickly before escaping to the library with her letter.

'Let's not stop to look at the stalls now,' Polly declared, taking Lucy's arm, 'we'll save that for this afternoon when more people are here.'

Stalls were already set up along the length of Castle Street to entice people along to the amusement fair at Barley Grove, quite transforming the usually quiet road. From midday a constant stream of countryfolk on foot, on horseback and in carts would converge on the town until all the streets were thronged with people, their voices raised to make themselves heard above the neighing of horses, the shouting of cheapjacks and the blasts of mechanical music.

'Wouldn't it be better to look now while it's quiet?' The thought of the afternoon crowds was not very appealing.

'Let's just glance as we walk past so that we know which stalls have the nicest things, and we can return to them this afternoon.'

There were stalls selling fairings, small buns, lollipops and sweetmeats, and one offering a mound of oranges; there were ribbons and braids, laces and buttons, flutes, penny whistles, posies of flowers, decorative china and pots and pans; all this before they turned into the Square where many of the houses had been whitewashed especially for the occasion, and booths decorated with colourful flags lined the pavements to await the afternoon crowds.

'Come along, we'll go straight to New Street to see the livestock fair.' Polly took Lucy's hand and hurried her past the attractions. She was behaving most strangely.

In New Street the bellowing of cattle, neighing of horses, bleating of sheep and barking of dogs combined to create more noise than would be found in a dozen farmyards, with the insistent voice of the auctioneer, who stood on a chair in the middle of the street, cutting through it all. Pens were erected along the length of the road and strong bars placed in front of the houses to protect the windows, even the church gate had been blocked by cattle pens. There must have been six or seven hundred head of cattle, some of which, when sold, would be driven down Station Hill and taken by rail to grazing lands in Somerset. The sweet, milky scent of cattle was overladen by smells of straw, hide and dung.

Lucy had been to the livestock fair before, but always with her father or one of her brothers.

'Polly, you surely have no interest in this!'

'I do; come on, let us see the horses being auctioned.'

Further along the street, twenty or more horses had been tied to a railing. It was a relief to notice a couple of ladies in the crowd as she and Polly trod carefully to avoid the frequent piles of manure.

Many of the horses were unremarkable and in poor condition, but there was an attractive grey, and a lively-looking chestnut.

'Look at that one; I'm sure he would be a fine ride.'

'But, Polly, you hate riding!'

'Oh, I don't want him for myself, but I do like to admire a good horse.' She was casting her eyes around the crowd. 'Let's go this way to look at the grey.'

A man was running his hand over the haunches of the grey horse, while Polly pulled Lucy through the crowd. As they approached, he turned.

'Miss Jones! How good to see you!'

'Good morning, Mr Boxer.' Polly was putting on her most expressive voice. 'My sister and I thought we would take a look at the horses because our brother has expressed interest in buying a new hunter.'

The man bowed politely to Lucy. She nodded to him, trying not to show her confusion. Whatever was Polly talking about? As far as she knew, none of her brothers intended to buy a new horse.

Mr Boxer was a smartly dressed man of rather slight build.

'Your brother might like the chestnut over there, but I've decided that there isn't one here to suit me. Shall we look at the chestnut?'

'Oh, I'll tell my brother that there is not a great deal of choice today, I don't think he is in a particular hurry.' She smiled sweetly at Mr Boxer.

'Then shall we walk away from this throng? I would not want you ladies to spoil your dresses, and the road here is quite filthy.'

They returned to the Square, Polly talking with Mr Boxer while she walked arm-in-arm with Lucy. She must have known he would be at the livestock fair! When they passed a stall selling buttons and ribbons, Lucy let go of her sister's arm.

'I am going to stop here to have a look.'

Polly waved casually at her and strolled on with Mr Boxer.

Absent-mindedly, she picked up some buttons, too cross to concentrate on what she was doing. Polly had not told her the truth; she had no interest in the livestock fair. And who was Mr Boxer? Lucy had never seen him in the town before. She glanced up. They were standing on the other side of the Square, Polly leaning back to look up into his face. They were both laughing. For a moment, she imagined how things might be if Rawlin were to come home for Mayfair; an absurd thought, he was on the other side of the world. But it was hard not to think of him. In his letter he had written of the previous year when they had met at Mayfair and walked around the stalls together; he had said he wished he could be there with her. It was extraordinary that he had written those words three months previously, hoping that they would reach her in time for Mayfair.

She did not, she reflected, draw as many gazes as did Polly in her pink and cream dress smiling up at Mr Boxer, but she was used to that; she was Dr Jones's younger daughter, the less pretty one but pleasant enough and entirely respectable. Was that the way Rawlin thought of her, his very ordinary childhood friend? Did he write to her merely because he was homesick for Torrington?

'Would you like the blue ones or the white ones, Miss?' The woman behind the stall was smiling determinedly at her.

'Thank you, I might come back later.' She hurried away. Polly and Mr Boxer were no longer on the street corner and she felt a moment of panic – but then someone grabbed her hand, and there was Polly, laughing.

'Thank you, Lucy, it was thoughtful of you to stop at the stall so that we could have a few minutes alone! Don't you think he is handsome? And we are going to meet again this afternoon, by the drinking fountain at three o'clock! He might have been too shy to ask if you had been there also.'

'Who is he, Polly? And why did you not tell me that you planned to meet him?'

'Oh, I knew that then you would not come! You would find some reason to disapprove!' She laughed carelessly. 'But there is no need for it, he is perfectly respectable. He is the new accountant at the National Provincial Bank and his father is a Commander in the Royal Navy, he just told me so. I met him on Tuesday when I went to the bank for Father. I knew he intended to look at the horses.'

'You must tell Mother that you mean to meet him this afternoon. I suppose I shall have to come with you, but Edith will be with me also.'

'Mother is in bed with a headache! I'll not worry her with it now. Do you think I should change my dress for this afternoon? Oh, look how prettily those cakes are decorated! Should we take some home?'

'If you wear a different dress he will think you have expensive tastes, beyond those that an accountant can afford, perhaps. You can brush the horse dung off the hem when it is dry.' She spoke tersely, but her annoyance was beginning to pass. How should she describe the morning's events to Rawlin? He would like to hear about Mayfair, and she could surely make it an amusing story.

When Edith arrived at Castle House, they set off together for the Square, arriving at the drinking fountain just as the hands of the clock on its southern side reached three o'clock. Mr Boxer spoke nicely to Edith, who had heard of his appointment at the National Provincial Bank, and they wandered along South Street together until Lucy and Edith stopped to look at a book stall. Although the books were second-hand, most were in good condition. Scanning the upended spines, Lucy found a copy of *Agnes Grey* by Anne Brontë.

'Have you read this one? I have only read the novels by her sisters, Charlotte and Emily. I will buy it, I think.'

Edith leaned over her shoulder. 'May I borrow it when you have finished?'

Lucy counted out the pennies for the book. 'I think we could let them go on alone, don't you?' she asked, nodding in the direction of Polly and Mr Boxer.

'Yes, we can stay nearby for form's sake.'

Earlier, Lucy had gone upstairs to her mother, who was lying on her bed with the curtains closed, to tell her of Polly's meeting with Mr Boxer. She had been greatly interested in the news and, when assured that he was respectable, sat up and seemed rather better.

Mr Boxer had now offered Polly his arm, and they were laughing and talking together.

'I didn't tell you earlier, but I have had another letter from Rawlin today.' She was now more open with Edith about his letters; it did not seem right to hide her feelings from her friend, especially as she was his sister. Sometimes she even dared to think of Edith as her future sister-in-law, but would then reprimand herself for thinking such a foolish thing.

Edith turned to her with pleasure. 'Lucy, the letters are becoming even more frequent! I'm so glad.'

'Oh, there is no significance to it, I'm sure. He wanted to fill some time, I expect.'

'Now, that is not true, Rawlin has always been very fond of you. I know he left in a hurry, but I believe he will come back one day. And perhaps then you will return to Australia with him.' A shadow passed across her face. 'If you do, I will miss you very much.'

They had not spoken so honestly before. Lucy tried to cover her confusion with a light-hearted reply. 'That is all nonsense, Edith! Besides, by then you will no doubt be married, and far too busy with your husband and children to worry about me!'

'No, I will not, I shall not marry, Lucy,' Edith replied soberly. 'I have enough to do here in Torrington with my district visiting and helping Father, and now that my stepmother is losing her sight she will need me by her side. That is *my* future, and I am quite reconciled to it. But for *you*,' she took Lucy's hand and smiled warmly, 'I believe life will be very different!'

'And you know,' Edith went on, 'you should not be concerned that the years are passing. What would it matter if you were thirty before you marry? You and I, in our work as district visitors, see the results of early marriage, women whose health has been destroyed by having eight or ten children. Better to marry late and only have three or four.'

She was right, of course, but Lucy wished she knew what the future would bring. They linked arms and walked on, following Polly and Mr Boxer at a discreet distance, and stopping to look at stalls when something caught their interest.

'Look, there is Reverend Francis and his family!'

The curate was guiding his wife and children through the crowd, his head held high as if he considered the heathen goings-on in the street to be unworthy of his notice.

'Come along now,' his voice cut through the hubbub, 'follow me!' He had made no concessions to the warmth or the celebratory nature of the day, but wore his usual long black coat and shallow-crowned black hat. Mrs Francis held her two young sons tightly by the hands, and little Jessie was clutching her mother's sleeve.

Lucy had called in to see Mrs Francis about a month after the baby died. She had begun to regain her strength but was subdued, and wept when Lucy tried to comfort her. Since then, Lucy had made a point of spending some time with her following the fortnightly meetings. Mrs Francis sometimes spoke of her husband's future in the Church, but her previous childlike optimism was beginning to be replaced by anxiety. It was difficult to know how to reassure her.

'Shall we walk with them to the amusement fair?' suggested Edith. 'There will be more space there for the children and perhaps we can help to keep them entertained.'

When Mr Boxer and Polly agreed that they too would make their way to Barley Grove, Lucy took Jessie's hand and the party set off, pushing their way through a group of countrywomen in their best dresses and hats who were laughing loudly at the jokes of a cheapjack. They turned when they saw Reverend Francis, and nudged each other.

'See 'oo that be?' said one.

'Oh, 'tis Mr High and Mighty!' shrieked another, 'Thinks as he can tell us common folk what's what! Treats us like muck, 'e does!'

'Well, he bain't telling me! I'd knock his 'at off sooner than have any of that trickery of a Sunday!'

They shrieked with laughter before turning back to the cheapjack.

Lucy moved quickly away. 'Are you enjoying your first Mayfair, Jessie?' The little girl, her long hair tied neatly back from her face with a large brown ribbon, looked up at Lucy seriously. She did not seem to realise that the women had been talking about her father, and Lucy was hopeful that Mrs Francis had been too far ahead to hear the exchange.

'I don't like it. It's too noisy.'

It was indeed noisy. 'Do you have some pennies to spend?' As a child, that had always been one of the aspects of Mayfair she had most enjoyed.

'No. Father does not earn enough money to give any to us children.'

'Ah, I see. Never mind, there is plenty to look at. Let's hurry, Jessie, and catch up with your mother, there is even a steam roundabout, or so I hear!'

Reverend Francis strode ahead of them all, looking up at the sky as if to avoid the attention of the people around him, a strategy that was not proving effective because it was clear that many people *were* noticing him and whispering to each other.

He had been in trouble again just the previous week. Whilst preparing a group of boys for confirmation, he had taught them about Purgatory which, as everyone knew, only existed in the imagination of Catholics. Then, discovering that two brothers in the group had attended chapel, he made them sit apart from the others and lectured them on the evils of schism. Their father, a respectable churchman, was called to the Vicarage and, following an altercation with the vicar who, as usual, supported his curate, resolved that his sons would never be confirmed within that parish. As was to be expected, the story reached the newspapers and became the talk of the town.

Lucy had not seen him since then. He had taken to sharing his troubles with her when he accompanied her and her friends on a rail excursion or when they happened to meet in the town, so she expected he would want to talk to her today. She grew rather weary of his complaints and self-justifications but, as she seemed to be able to help him understand why his actions upset his parishioners, she hoped that he would eventually become less impulsive. It was a strange role that she had taken on, but perhaps by helping him she would also help Mrs Francis.

She also needed to talk to him about an elderly woman in Well Street who had become too unsteady on her feet to walk to church, and wanted 'a man of God' to visit her. Unusually, she seemed to have no objection to Reverend Francis.

'Look, Jessie, the steam roundabout! Have you ever seen such a thing?'

Jessie let go of Lucy's hand and ran to where the other children stood spellbound.

Left alone at the edge of the crowd, Lucy turned away from the crush of people to walk a few steps to the edge of the steep hill overlooking the valley. The growth of fresh, new grass on this May afternoon was brightened still further by bluebells flowering amongst the stands of gorse, oxeye daisies alongside the path and red campion that had been missed by grazing sheep. A path led along the contour of the hill to the seat that gave a giddy vista of the river below; no one sat there today. She ran her thumb along the embossed title of the book in her hand; it would be very pleasant to sit on the seat and read, even if it was Mayfair, and she took a step forward, but her musings were interrupted by a hand on her arm; it was Reverend Francis, of course, and he wished to talk.

Chapter Twelve

Ann clung tightly to the gold-painted pole that rose from her horse's neck, the deafening music and the sensation of moving up, down and around being thrillingly unfamiliar. It was easier for George sitting astride on the horse in front, but being side-saddle on the slippery horse was terrifying as well as exciting. She didn't dare to turn around even when a woman on the horse behind her gave a shriek that turned to laughter.

The faces of the crowd flashed past again and again, everyone smiling. If it had been allowed, she would like to have ridden with George sitting behind her, close enough for her to feel his thighs against her and his arms keeping her safe. But when the music ceased at last and the ride came to a gradual standstill, her horse was out of view of the crowd, so no one saw when George lifted her from the saddle and kissed her.

She clung to his arm as they made their way across the green, her head still spinning from the movement. They stared at the painting of the Fat Lady but agreed they did not want to pay to see her, then both took a turn at the Aunt Sally before wandering on.

'There's your young lady,' George said, indicating where the green fell away to Castle Hill, 'with Reverend Francis, the silly bugger.'

'George! You mustn't talk like that!' She punched him playfully on the arm.

'Well he be, bain't he, you've heard the talk, there's not a soul can say aught good about him. And your young lady too they speak of in the same breath.'

She stopped dead. 'What! Miss Lucy? What can they say about Miss Lucy?'

'Well, look at them now! Standing so close, you'd never think as the world was watching.'

'But he's married!'

George winked at her and laughed. 'He wouldn't be the first, nor the last neither! That's what folks say of 'em!'

'It's not true!' She saw that some women standing nearby were listening and she dropped her voice. 'Her'd never do aught wrong, my young lady! Her works alongside of him with her district visiting, that's all!'

'Well, I dunno. But if it were out in the villages I know what'd happen, there'd be rough music to shame 'em, it don't take much for folks to get started when they'm crying out for a bit of excitement.'

She knew what he meant, for there had been an incident of rough music when she was living with her family near Shebbear. The fields around their cottage were usually silent but for birdsong and the bleating of sheep, so when the family heard a great commotion, they had all run out to see what was happening. There, coming up the lane, was a crowd of twenty or more men, some with faces blackened with soot, some wearing masks, women's clothing or coats worn back-to-front, and all making a tremendous din produced by cows' horns, whistles, the banging of saucepans and kettles and, in addition, chanting and jeering by all those present. Ann had stood in shocked silence as the gang strode past and around the corner to reach the lane that led to the village. When they had gone and the noise began to fade, her mother, with a deep, sighing breath, murmured the names of a man and a woman in the village, two people who were believed to be having an illicit affair. The group would march to the house of each person in turn to shame them into mending their ways.

Probably *they* had been guilty, but it was preposterous to think such a thing of Miss Lucy! She would never behave in such a way, and a display of that sort could surely never happen in a street such as Castle Street – it was unthinkable!

George took her arm. 'Come on, don't glare at me like that, I didn't mean no harm by it. It's just what folks are saying, that's all.'

'What folks? If I ever catch anyone saying such things they'll wish they'd never opened their mouths! And you must do likewise!' She pulled George around to face her. 'Tell 'em it idn't true!'

He promised that he would, and they walked on. George stroked her hand and, in time, her anger subsided. Probably he had misunderstood; people would never say those things about Miss Lucy. But after they had walked around the green, stopping to look at the weight-lifter and the wheel of fortune, and after George had taken a turn at skittles and bought some gingerbread, she saw that Reverend Francis and Miss Lucy were still standing on the edge of the precipice, and were still deep in conversation.

During the remainder of the afternoon they browsed the stalls in the Square, talking with George's friends and people Ann knew from Shebbear, until they met Ann's family and went to sit on the grass beyond the bowling green together, George putting down his coat so that her new dress would not be spoiled. She felt some trepidation when she saw how her mother was quietly scrutinising George, but he must have met with her approval because soon she was laughing as she joined in with the stories of Mayfair in years past. He told them about the Mutual Improvement Society of which he was the secretary, how the men in the group helped each other with reading and writing, and shared any knowledge they had. He had given a talk recently, he said, all about the Battle of Torrington during the English Civil War, when the church had been blown up by gunpowder; it was a story his uncle had told him. Ann's stepfather looked at George admiringly, saying he wished there had been such a society when he was growing up in Milton Damerel.

George looked relaxed and handsome as he leaned back on his elbows, chuckling along with the family. It was the best day ever.

When the evening cooled, and mist began to gather over the river in the valley below, Ann's parents decided to go in search of a hot drink before their journey home, so she and George walked with them to the Square before making their farewells.

When they had gone, he pulled her close, his body warm and familiar. 'What shall us do now? Shall us go in for a drink?'

They were standing on the pavement outside the Black Horse, warm air infused with the buzz of voices and laughter spilling through the open door on to the street.

She hung back. 'I've never been in a public house before.' She knew that some women did go into inns in Torrington, but it was hardly respectable to do so and certainly Miss Wilcox would not approve. 'And what do 'ee want to go in there for anyway, you told me as you don't take strong drink, you've signed the pledge, you said.'

'Well, yes,' he looked rather shamefaced, 'but 'tis Mayfair, everyone has a drink at Mayfair.'

'Well, I don't know that I want to.' She leaned against him and looked up into his face. 'Shall us go for a walk instead?'

When he looked at her searchingly, she had to turn away. She knew what he was thinking. Last time they had gone for a walk he had taken her to a secluded part of the Common, a little dell in Furzebeam Wood. They had sat and kissed but he had been more persistent than usual, running his hand up her leg and reaching inside her blouse. She removed his hand laughingly at first, teasing him, but he had become quietly determined until finally she jumped up, a little frightened, and shouted at him to stop. They had walked home in silence until, at the gate of Castle House, she asked him to forgive her, even though she had not done anything wrong. She had no choice – she did not want a child out of wedlock and George did not yet earn enough to support them. Besides, he had not asked her to marry him.

Of course, he understood why she could not meet his gaze now.

'What's the point in going for a walk?' He spoke challengingly, then turned towards the inn door. 'It's Mayfair, look, Milton's in there, and Will too. And Will's got his girl with 'im so you won't be the only one.'

When he took her hand, she followed him reluctantly.

There was a crowd of men at the bar who laughed loudly as she and George walked in, causing her to hesitate but, as their backs were turned, they were surely not laughing at her. The long, low room smelled of ale, pipe smoke and the stale smell of male bodies; she was relieved when they went to a table near the window where a young man and woman sat.

'Will.' George nodded at the man. 'And Lizzie too. This is Ann, my girl.'

He had owned her, she thought with some irritation, so had perhaps got over the earlier awkwardness. He went to buy them some drinks, leaving Ann next to Lizzie, a neat-looking girl who seemed familiar.

'I've seen 'ee about town, I reckon,' Ann ventured.

Lizzie said that she often shopped in the Square for her mistress, and they agreed that they must have seen each other several times.

'I've never been in this inn before,' said Lizzie, ''tis only this once, 'cos it's Mayfair.'

'Me too.' Warming to each other, they pulled rueful faces in acknowledgement of their discomfort.

Lizzie had heard of Dr Jones of Castle House, which was no surprise because everyone knew the doctor. 'Where do you work?' Ann asked.

'Torridge Villa, down Warren Lane. For Reverend Francis.'

'Oh!' She didn't know what to say.

Lizzie laughed. 'The whole town's talking about him, I know. But he's not a bad man to work for, and you can't help liking the Missis. She lost a little child, you know, 'twas so sad, just a few hours old it was.'

'I know, I heard.'

Lizzie did not say anything about Miss Lucy, so surely George had been wrong to say everyone was talking about her and Reverend Francis.

George came back with his brother, Milton, and it was not long before the three men were laughing loudly enough to rival the hubbub from the bar but, while she was talking with Lizzie, Ann became aware of a familiar voice cutting through the noise.

'There he was driving the cart towards Peter's Marland at a gallop, when what should he meet but Mr Moore-Stevens' carriage, near as dammit crashed into him!' A roar of laughter went up from the men around the bar. 'Well, he was summonsed on the spot and goes to court next week, you don't argue with Mr Moore-Stevens!'

When the man launched into a song, his voice was quickly joined by others.

Ann leaned past George so that she could see the man; she was right, it was Mr John! He was standing at the end of the bar, his eyes bloodshot and his cravat askew. She could see that as the only gentleman, he was the focus of attention, as if the working men around him felt both honoured and amused by his presence. When the song came to an end, they shouted for another.

'Come on, Dr Jones, us want more!' One man slapped him on the back.

George turned around to see what had caught her attention. He laughed. 'There, see, 'tidn't such a great family you'm working for. He's been seen in yer before, so I'm told.'

She did not reply, and sipped her ale slowly, unsure whether she liked the bitter taste. Suppose Mr John should see her and come to the table? She turned towards Lizzie so that he should not see her face, hoping that she would soon be able to leave with George.

But George rose to his feet. 'Who wants another drink, then?' he demanded loudly. He looked exhilarated and his face was slightly flushed. She was not sure she liked him quite so much when he was in male company. While he bought another drink for himself and his friends, more men came into the inn, including some she guessed to be traders and fair-workers, one of them bumping into her chair and almost falling in her lap.

'I think I'm ready to go,' Lizzie whispered.

'Me too, but us'll have to wait until our men have finished their drinks. I don't want to walk home alone.'

'Me neither.'

'George,' she put her hand on his arm, 'Me and Lizzie'd like to go home when you'm all done.'

'Done! 'Tis Mayfair, us won't be done for a good many hours yet!' His laugh was rougher than she was used to hearing from him. 'But us can take 'ee home and come back.'

She and Lizzie exchanged rueful looks, then sat in companionable silence while Ann listened to the boasting, the loud laughter and the arguments that were developing around the bar. When George, still talking to his friends, reached out his hand, she took it gratefully.

Lucy could not sleep. When Polly's breathing had slowed and deepened, she carefully pushed back the bedding, slid down on to the soft rug and moved silently to the French window.

The stone floor of the balcony was cold beneath her feet but she could feel through the sleeves of her nightgown that the wooden rail still retained some warmth. There was no moon, but the dark shape of the beech tree at the end of the garden was just visible, and beyond the tree and the old stone wall that marked the boundary of the garden the darkness was less intense; the smooth turf of the bowling green lay there and beyond, the Common, falling away into the valley.

The scent of lilac drifted up from the garden, a scent associated since childhood with the excitement of spring and the warming of the season. She inhaled deeply. There was a faint rustling and snuffling, a hedgehog perhaps in the shrubbery, a squeak from some other small creature.

She tiptoed back into the bedroom, pausing to listen for Polly's still-sleeping breath, and pulled a shawl around her shoulders. She was not ready for sleep yet, and the night air soothed her churning thoughts.

A faint breeze stirred the leaves of the lilac tree. It was a relief to be alone, to be quiet. She had tried to be patient with Polly but had grown rather weary of hearing how interesting Mr Boxer was, how well-attached his family, and that surely a brother who spoke so thoughtfully of his sisters was a true gentleman. It was true that he seemed to suit Polly well. Their mother, having recovered sufficiently from her headache to come down for dinner, warned Polly to be cautious, but Lucy could tell from the light in her mother's eyes that she was no more inclined to caution than was Polly.

She could not help feeling a little jealous; it must be wonderful to feel such excitement. Suppose Rawlin returned to England – would she then feel as Polly did? Despite his increasingly affectionate letters – *my dearest Lucy*, warmth spread through her as she remembered his words – she feared she would find, should he ever return, that she had overestimated his feelings for her.

'Just think, Lucy,' Polly had said as she climbed into bed, 'Mr Boxer is just a few hundred yards away, just over there,' she waved expressively, 'in the Square.'

'Indeed he is,' she had replied kindly, indulging Polly, and longing for Rawlin, too, to be in the Square rather than on the other side of the world.

A tawny owl called from somewhere on the Common, a sharp *keewick!* answered by the soft, wavering call of a second owl. When she had first tried to sleep, the noise of the pleasure fair was still loud in the room, but Mayfair was finished now; there was only distant shouting and laughter from the direction of the Square. Poor Mr Boxer, he would have trouble sleeping. No doubt the public houses throughout the town were full; it was not uncommon for her father to go out late on Fair night to tend to a badly injured head or an arm broken in a fight.

The entrance gate clicked open; from the whispered voices she guessed that it was Ann returning from her day out with George Chapple. The back gate opening from the street into the yard was kept locked on Fair day, so Ann would come to the front door below the balcony. Lucy stepped back a little, but they would not see her up here in the darkness. There were whispers and a low male laugh, then silence, and a soft sigh.

Lucy leaned back against the French window, and closed her eyes. Would Rawlin ever return?

Chapter Thirteen

Another year passed, and Lucy increased her district visiting to three days each week.

'I will call in again on Tuesday.' She crouched down beside the bed, raising her voice so that the old woman would hear her. 'I've left some more broth for your husband to heat later; he'll take good care of you.'

She took the hand that reached towards her, so thin, it was merely skin and dark blue veins stretched over bone, and felt a squeeze of gratitude.

'Thank 'ee, Miss, I don't know what us'd do without 'ee.' The voice was no more than a whisper.

Lucy patted the woman's hand and stood up. Mr Rattenbury was standing by the low front door, tears in his eyes. He did his best to keep the house clean and to cook simple meals, chores that had been foreign to him before his wife fell ill. He had promised that she would never go to the Workhouse Infirmary and Lucy was determined to support him, but it would be hard. She hoped the old woman would not linger, otherwise her husband's health would be at risk also; he was too old and frail to withstand the strain for long.

'Now look, I have left some rice and jelly too, but it is for you as well as for your wife. Will you promise me that you will eat some? You must, so that you have strength to care for her. And do send for me if you need me. Would you like Reverend Francis to come in and say a prayer with you?'

'Oh no, Miss,' the man looked uncomfortable, 'I don't reckon so. He came in the once, but 'e would leave the door open, for health's sake he said, but it let out all the warmth. And he read the Service for the Sick so fast us couldn't follow'n, then 'e was gone, and us didn't feel any the better for it. Not that I'm not grateful. But us'd like to see *you*, Miss, anytime, when you'm passing.'

Once outside, she paused to regain her equilibrium. The atmosphere inside the cottage had been close, the stench of illness almost overpowering. She took a deep breath and looked up at the sky; it was a clear blue, out here was a beautifully warm June day. She had only one more visit to make, her eighth, then she would be free. She would take home her empty basket, call Alpheus, and walk on the Common before dinner. In her next letter, she wanted to be able to tell Rawlin whether the Painted Lady butterflies had arrived.

The next visit was to Mary Gilbert. She was only twenty-one years old, but had given birth to her third child a week previously. She had a two-year-old girl living, and had lost a boy shortly after birth the previous year. The latest child was not feeding well, and was weak and listless. Lucy's father had visited to give the child a tonic, but there was little more he could do.

When Lucy knocked, the door was opened by Emma, Mr Gilbert's seven-year-old sister who lived nearby.

'Come in, Miss. The little chiel's still not viddy, her's had a suck but puked it up again. Ma says her don't hold out much hope. Do 'ee want a cup of tea, Miss?'

Emma was as good as any nurse, Lucy mused, as she climbed the stairs. Despite being so young, she could undertake most of the household tasks and would run to her mother for help if necessary. The neighbours, too, looked in when they could.

The infant was a pitiful little thing. It lay listlessly in Lucy's arms while Mary Gilbert spoke of her efforts to persuade the child to take some milk.

'Perhaps, Mary,' she said gently, 'it might be as well to ask the curate to baptise her, just in case, you know.' She held the young mother's hand. 'Would you like me to arrange that?'

The young woman, still weak from the birth and her eyes dull with grief, lay back on the pillows and nodded her assent.

'You'll come by to see me again, won't 'ee, Miss Jones?' she whispered. 'Whatever happens?'

Lucy left the parcel she had prepared for the family containing a loaf, a meat pie and a jar of jam, then walked out on to Calf Street again, turning to wave to Ellen watching sadly from the doorway.

''Ave 'ee got a parcel for me then, Miss?'

The man had crossed the road to stand in front of her, blocking her path. Instinctively, she held her basket up in front of her.

'Are you expecting one? I don't know you, do I?'

'I knows you, Miss. I've got two little chiels at home and they'm always hungry. Why do folks in Calf Street get parcels? Us is in Well Street and us has never had a parcel.'

He was looking at her directly, almost rudely in fact, as if weighing her up.

'I don't cover all of Well Street. Miss Macartney is responsible for the rest.'

He gave a harsh, humourless laugh. 'Miss Macartney! 'Tis like getting water from a stone, getting a parcel from she! Why don't 'ee come down my end of Well Street, Miss?' He leaned back against a cottage wall. 'My wife 'ud make 'ee welcome. Do some mending for 'ee if you gave us a parcel or two.'

'I've told you, I don't work there, I've enough work already. Now please excuse me, I have to go home.'

When he did not move out of the way she had to step out into the road to pass him, and she sensed that he was watching her as she walked away. Perhaps it was foolish to feel unnerved, but she was not accustomed to such rudeness.

Looking up, she saw Reverend Francis striding towards her, and her heart sank. She had to speak to him about the baptism, but she had grown very weary of Reverend Francis in recent months, and she wanted to go home. During the past year he had continued to ask for her advice. At first, he had seemed to listen, speaking out less against Nonconformists and toning down his high church leanings, but more recently he had reverted to his old ways. He had delivered a scurrilous sermon against dissenters when a tent for Methodist preachers was set up on Barley Grove; then, with the help of Major Macartney and Mr Haverfield, he had organised entertainments to raise money for a highly ornamental reredos for the church in which the majority of his parishioners had no interest. Indeed, many thought the money should be spent on renovating the churchyard, which was in a disgraceful state.

'Why not donate the money to the Indian Famine Appeal!' her father had complained, 'The Baptists have raised a great deal of money for that worthy cause rather than spending it on fripperies!'

Some admired the reredos when it was installed, but when Reverend Francis added a two-foot-high brass cross above it, there was not a single person who would accept such a flagrant symbol of popery. Reverend Buckland was forced to remove it, but both church wardens resigned as a result of the upset. And, of course, every time the curate did something ridiculous, the local newspapers revelled in the details of the story which only served to turn more people against him.

Exasperated at his stupidity, Lucy had tried to distance herself from him, but he was persistent in his efforts to talk to her. Recently, when she had been travelling to Exeter to attend a funeral on her father's behalf, Reverend Francis had entered her carriage when the train was at Barnstaple Station, claiming he had travelled from Torrington on an earlier train.

'The carriages were too crowded,' he declared, 'I believe on account of so many people travelling to the Agricultural Show in Exeter. But what a pleasant surprise to find you here!'

She had known, then, that he was not being truthful, for she had mentioned at a meeting the previous day that she would be travelling to Exeter. He sat with her all the way there and on the way back too, despite not being able to give a plausible reason for his journey. On arrival at Torrington Station, he accompanied her across the Common and back to the town although it was out of his way. She had not confided her suspicions to anyone because she feared it would sound too foolish but, the truth was, she felt that he was pursuing her.

And now here he was again, striding towards her with a foolish grin on his face.

'Miss Jones!' He threw up his hands. 'How good to see you! What was occurring just then? Was that man bothering you?'

She continued walking in the direction of her home. 'Oh, it was nothing. He asked for a parcel, but I know nothing of his circumstances.'

'I will talk to him.' And he marched off, so she felt compelled to wait.

The man, still leaning against the wall and watching them, did not stand up straight even when Reverend Francis addressed him.

'Now then, my man,' he sounded absurd, 'have you been bothering Miss Jones? If you are in need, you must speak to Miss Macartney, and she will consult me or Reverend Buckland. Are you in work?'

'When I can get it.' His manner was quite insolent.

'Then I suggest you go in search of more, rather than lounging about the streets causing a nuisance! Or go and dig the allotment that I know you have been given!'

He strode back to her, looking very pleased with himself.

'I know of that man, Balkwill; nothing but a troublemaker. Come, Miss Jones, I will accompany you home.'

'There's no need, I am perfectly all right.'

'It is no trouble at all, in fact it would be helpful to me, Miss Jones, because there is a little matter I would like to discuss.'

They turned into Potacre Street together, Reverend Francis jumping into the road when the pavement became too narrow for them to walk side-by-side.

'You know, do you not, Miss Jones, that I am planning a concert of church music. It is to raise funds towards my salary, voluntary contributions having fallen off in recent months.'

She looked at him, alarmed, but he was gazing at the sky. Edith had told her something of the situation, but she never imagined that he would speak to her about it.

'I am rather afraid that the concert will not raise a great deal of money so I am wondering whether I will have to let one of my servants go. Do you suppose, Miss Jones, that we would manage with just one servant?'

Lucy was lost for words. He should not consult her about such a personal matter! A house the size of Torridge Villa needed at least three servants to run it, and an additional nursemaid would be preferable with four small children to look after, for Mrs Francis had given birth to a healthy boy a few months previously. She could not imagine how one servant could possibly manage even if Mrs Francis worked the entire day herself, and how could she do that?

'What does your wife think, Reverend Francis?'

'Oh!' He waved his hand as if swatting a fly. 'I haven't told her yet. I fear she may be disappointed, so I thought I would consult you first.' He stopped and took her hand. 'You have an innate intelligence, Miss Jones, and always identify the best course for action. I do not know what I would do without you.'

She replied coldly, withdrawing her hand. 'Then why have you not followed my advice? Through your actions you have driven many people away from the church – Mr Doe, Mr Pidgeon, Mr Mallet for instance, people who gave generously and whose contributions to your salary are now lost!' She walked away along Castle Street, but he scurried after her.

She stopped and turned to him. 'Reverend Francis, you must discuss this matter with your wife. But I cannot see that Torridge Villa can be run with just one servant. If your financial situation is really so difficult – and it isn't right that I should even know about it – then I think you should find a smaller house.'

'Oh, I couldn't possibly do that!' He looked at her sadly, as if disappointed in her. 'My wife has always lived in a large house, and the garden is so ideally suited to the children. I am hopeful that this situation is temporary, and that before long we would be able to again employ a second servant. I have tried offering Latin tuition, thinking it might bring in a little extra *pecunia*, but there appears to be no appetite for self-improvement in Torrington despite such lamentable ignorance in the town. May I talk to you again on the subject of servants, Miss Jones? Perhaps we could meet to discuss things?'

'It is your wife you need to talk to, not me, Reverend Francis. Now please excuse me.'

She hurried down the driveway to Castle House, leaving him standing at the gate, her afternoon spoiled.

Lucy could not stop thinking about Mrs Francis. The poor woman had been as confident of her husband's success as a child is of having a happy Christmas, and Lucy hated to think of her facing such grave disappointment. Lucy could do nothing to alter the dreadful financial situation, but could at least continue to be a friend to Mrs Francis so, having not seen her for several weeks, she decided to call on her.

The opportunity arose the very next day. Reverend Francis was taking a choir practice in the church, so she was able to call at Torridge Villa knowing that she would not have to see him.

The door was opened by Lizzie, the servant she had met on previous visits. She was a sensible girl who was a hard worker and good with the children; perhaps she would be the one to be kept on if one servant was to be dismissed, but of course neither she nor Mrs Francis knew anything of that yet. It was a very awkward situation.

''Scuse me, Miss, coming to the door like this,' Lizzie gestured at the rough apron she was wearing, 'I was out the back doing the washing – there's no end to 'n – and Amy is upstairs doing the rooms. Us is that behind today.'

Mrs Francis was in the drawing room, walking up and down with a crying baby on her shoulder while the other children played with some toy animals on the floor.

Jessie jumped up when Lucy entered. 'I'll hold Bertram, Mother, so's you can talk to Miss Jones.' She took the baby and sat on the floor rocking and talking to him while regarding Lucy warily.

Mrs Francis apologised for the disarray of the room. 'The baby's teething and I just haven't been able to put him down. Shall I call for some tea? – but I believe Lizzie to be too busy with the washing to make it, I'm so sorry.' She seemed close to tears.

'I don't mind about tea, but if you would like a cup why don't we go to the kitchen to make it together? That is what I do at home when the servants are busy.' Jessie seemed quite capable of looking after the younger children, and Mrs Francis would have the opportunity to talk if they were alone.

The kitchen was tolerably tidy, and a kettle was simmering on the stove. They made the tea together and, at Lucy's insistence, sat at the table rather than return to the drawing room.

Mrs Francis stirred her tea slowly. 'It's so good of you to come and see me, Miss Jones. I am rarely in company now and the days are so long.' Her previous enthusiasm seemed to have given way to a profound weariness which was upsetting to see. 'The nights too, I don't sleep as well as I used to.' She looked appealingly at Lucy, as if hoping she might provide an answer to this state of affairs.

Lucy took her hand. 'I'm sorry to hear that. Does the baby keep you awake?' She hesitated, guessing the real reason for the insomnia.

Mrs Francis shook her head slowly. 'He sleeps well generally, it's only the last few days while he's been teething that he's been waking. No, it's… Miss Jones, you know how clever my husband is, what high hopes we had for his future, but it is not going to plan. For a long time he wouldn't tell me why the congregation was so small but I heard things, and I know now that it's true; Torrington people don't like him, they are going to different churches, chapels even, rather than listen to him at St Michael's.' She looked at Lucy imploringly. 'And I don't understand why it has happened or what he can do to change it. He says the bishop supports him and Reverend Buckland, but how can he get a living of his own if people won't come to hear him preach? Does he have to stay a curate forever? Move to another parish perhaps? Miss Jones, please don't tell others what I am telling you – I can't bear to think of people talking about us even more than they are already.'

Lucy tried to comfort her, saying that Torrington people could be very determined, but would perhaps get used to Reverend Francis in time and return to the church. What else could she say?

Later, as she walked home, she decided that even if she could not do anything to change the family's fortunes or avert the coming financial difficulties, she could at least continue to be a friend to Mrs Francis. The unfortunate woman had few others in the town.

Next page: articles from *The North Devon Journal*, 1878

ANOTHER SCENE IN CHURCH.—The erection of the new Reredos in our Parish Church, and its dedication on the 27th ult., have naturally created amongst church people, and especially amongst subscribers, a desire not only to see at a distance the effect produced by its erection, but to more closely inspect the Reredos as a work of art. On Sunday morning last, Mr. John Rude, a well-known and highly respectable Churchman, paid a visit to the Church some little while before the time fixed for commencing the public worship, and ventured to take up his position within the altar rails for the purpose of inspecting the various figures, and also the letters (the Ten Commandments and Belief) inscribed on the Reredos; whilst Mr. H. Hooper, draper, and his daughter were standing near the rails (outside, we believe). The trio had not been there very long before the Rev. S. Buckland, vicar, entered the Church. On his seeing the above parties occupying positions within the rails, and close to the altar, the reverend gentleman became indignant at the audacity of the intruders, and in a most authoritative manner informed them that they had no right there. The style in which the Vicar administered his reproof was too much for the party concerned, especially Mr. Rude, who at once left the Church in disgust, and in a later part of the day was found worshipping at Howe Chapel, Castle-street. The above affair has been the cause of much talk in various circles, and the general opinion prevails that the Vicar, since the arrival here of his present Curate, the Rev. H. O. Francis, has begun to carry things with a high hand, so that his High Church principles are becoming more fully developed, and the result is that many respectable persons have left the Church, some of whom may be seen on Sundays wending their way towards some adjacent village Church, whilst many others attend Nonconformist places of worship here. The new Reredos has been much talked about in the last few ___ and ___

THE CURATE AGAIN.—For some time past the Rev. H. O. Francis has to a considerable extent refrained from making himself so ridiculous as he did in the early part of his curacy in this town, when he seemed to do all he could to prejudice the minds of his audiences against Dissenters and Dissenting places of worship. On Sunday evening last, however, the reverend gentleman preached what several of his respectable hearers call a most extraordinary sermon, on the subject of Christ entering the Temple and driving out the buyers and sellers therefrom. During the discourse (which a gentleman stranger who was present has described as the merest twaddle), the curate argued that the Established Church alone was the real house of God. There were other places where persons pretended to preach the gospel, &c., but these were not really God's houses, for they were not consecrated, and could be bought and sold. He therefore in effect charged his audience against frequenting Dissenting places of worship, where they would be ___ ___ their feelings wrought upon by men ___ to preach. The Curate's foolish ___ect of general talk after the ser___ very much displeased, if not dis___ to listen to such nonsense. Some ___ at the fact of the gospel services ___ n the tent at Barley Grove by ___bot may have induced the Curate ___gainst Dissenters, and that his ___ock from wandering away from ___he prevailing excitement of these ___ he miserably failed to accom___ediately on leaving church the ___bers of respectable church peo___ flocking to the tent, where for ___ listened attentively to an earn___red by Mr. Abbot on the sub___ in the window; " on which ___ed, and scores had to stand ___r.

TORRINGTON.

SACRED CONCERT.—During the past week or more, large handbills have been well posted in the town, announcing that a sacred concert on a grand scale is to be given in the Town Hall on Tuesday evening in next week. The parties concerned in getting up the affair have failed to state for what object the concert is to be given. It is stated in some quarters that the funds for paying the curate's salary have greatly fallen off lately, and the fact of "the Major himself" being announced as treasurer to take charge of the proceeds of the concert has led to the supposition that its object must be to provide funds for covering the deficiency arising from the want of voluntary subscriptions in aid of the curate's fund. If so, or if for any other special object, why not inform the public thereof? It is stated by some good Church people, that the curate has consented to take £25 a year less for salary, rather than give up his curacy here: if so, such self-sacrifice ought to be taken into consideration and rewarded by his few admirers. ___ ___ Sessions Town Hall. Wednes-

Ann strolled through the pannier market with her basket on her arm. It was not often that she had the opportunity to leave Castle House during the day, because either Sarah or Miss Wilcox usually insisted on doing the shopping themselves. The high-roofed market hall was abuzz with shouted greetings and the exchange of pleasantries as people moved between the rows of stalls searching for the freshest vegetables and the brownest eggs, while the farmers' wives stood smiling behind their stalls. Pushing through a group of women who were gossiping in the aisle, she stopped to look at a stall selling strawberries, a carefully written sign declaring that they were from Weare Giffard. The village was said to grow the very best. She had to buy four punnets, and these looked to be good quality, a bright, glossy red, ripe but not soft or bruised. She carefully counted out the right money and placed the punnets in her basket.

She sometimes wondered whether she should learn more about cooking in order to obtain a better position, but then she would remember how anxious Sarah became when she had to cook for visitors. Today, the solicitor Mr Doe and his wife were coming to dinner with Mr and Mrs Loveband – he was the bank manager – and of course Miss Polly's fiancé would be there too. Miss Wilcox looked forward to dinner parties, but kept reminding Sarah how important it was for every detail to be perfect so, in the kitchen, you could cut the air with a knife. Probably Ann was better off as she was; she would not have to be a housemaid forever; one day she would get married.

She stopped to look at some fine speckled hens packed together in a wicker basket on the stone floor. They were clucking loudly as they tried to push their red-combed heads through the gaps in the basket until one of them became flustered and flapped wildly, its squawks reaching a panic-stricken crescendo.

George had not exactly *asked* her to marry him, but when he talked of one day becoming a superintendent in his uncle's business and earning enough to rent a house, he seemed to be including her in his plans. She did not like to question him, and she did not quite know how she would reply if he did ask her to marry him. Probably she would accept. She often daydreamed of having a little house of her own to keep clean and tidy without anyone watching over her, of having time to sit down and read a paper in the afternoon, then cook a meal for her husband, ready to put on the table when he came home from work and kissed her.

She had to marry someone, one day, but she was not always sure that it would be George.

Last month she had been very annoyed with him, and not for the first time. The bowling club was to start playing on the Castle Green for the summer season; she knew all about it because Dr Jones and Dr Charles played bowls and talked about all the work that went in to preparing the ground. But then the town crier was sent around to announce that a game of football would be played on the green to assert rights over that part of the Common. The bowling green was ruined, and Dr Jones had been very angry that the game had been spoiled. And then George told her that *he* had been one of the footballers!

Them bowlers, they think theirselves important enough to walk up and down on the green wearing hats – that bain't sport!

She told him there were plenty of places on the Common that were better for football without spoiling things for the bowlers, and it was as well that Dr Jones hadn't heard he was involved in the rabble. She might even have been stopped from seeing George, and it would have served him right.

Remembering her shopping, she went next to Mrs Grigg who had a few dozen eggs, some parsley, a couple of chickens and a large enamel bowl of cream on her stall; the family always bought their cream from her. While Mrs Grigg spooned some into Ann's glass dish and tied the muslin cloth on top, Ann counted out the pennies for the cream and some parsley. She was still arranging the purchases in her basket when Miss Lucy appeared with an armful of flowers.

'Hello, Ann! That parsley looks lovely and fresh. We're having fish for dinner, aren't we?'

Miss Lucy stood close to her, smiling, and Ann caught a trace of the perfume that was kept in a cut-glass bottle on her dressing table.

'Hello, Miss! Yes, us is having halibut.' She had learnt a lot about fish since being at Castle House; in Shebbear the only fish they had were herrings brought by horse and cart from Clovelly in the autumn.

'Have you seen any sweet peas for sale? I'm meeting Miss Buckland in the church in a few minutes to do the flowers. I've bought these delphiniums but I would like some sweet peas for the windowsills.'

'Over there, Miss, in the corner, I smelt 'em as I went by. Would you like me to show 'ee?'

'No need, I see them now. Goodbye, Ann!'

She watched Miss Lucy making her way across the crowded market, her face hidden by the large bunch of flowers.

George had said Miss Lucy would be an old maid; *Her's coming up to thirty, idn't her?*

No, Ann had said indignantly, *her's not yet twenty-seven.*

Well, her idn't walking out with anyone, only talkin' with that Reverend Francis all the time, so I don't reckon her'll ever marry. Too serious, her is.

But Ann knew that Miss Lucy frequently had letters from Miss Buckland's brother; she guessed that they were love letters, but she told no one. Even the family did not mention the letters. So, she and Miss Lucy shared a secret, in a way.

She bought two pounds of broad beans and three lettuces, looking at several stalls before choosing the freshest, then had to rearrange her basket so that the strawberries did not get squashed.

'Ann? It is Ann, in't it?'

It was Lizzie, Reverend Francis' servant whom she had met in the Black Horse at Mayfair. They moved to a quieter part of the market hall to talk, though Ann warned her that she dare not be long for fear of incurring Miss Wilcox's wrath.

'Me neither, there's that much to do. And 'tis going to get even worse.' Lizzie seemed quite anxious.

'Why, what's happened?'

'I don't know that I should tell you really.' She looked around to make sure no one was listening, 'but Clara's been given a month's notice and they'm not hiring anyone else 'cept someone to do the wash once a week. Somehow I've got to manage it all! I don't know how I'll do it, I'm working every hour of the day as it is.' She was quite tearful.

'That's dreadful, Lizzie, I *am* sorry. Will 'ee look for another position? Will the Missis help out?'

'I don't want to leave, though Will says I should. Mrs Francis says her'll work with me, her's being very brave about it and I've got to like her for it, but her's never been used to work. I know why it's all come about; the shopkeepers have told me they idn't being paid!'

Ann's heart went out to Lizzie. She suggested they meet for a walk on a Sunday if George and Will could be persuaded to make up a foursome.

Ann hurried back to Castle House. Surely she was fortunate to be employed in a steady household with people she liked, even if Sarah was bad-tempered when she was preparing for dinner parties.

Chapter Fourteen

The following week, Lucy was greeted by the warm smell of baking as she hurried into the kitchen to see how the picnic preparations were progressing.

'Ah, Lucy, there you be!' Mary Wilcox was standing with her hands on her broad hips, scrutinising a collection of dishes on the table. 'Now, look, there's the boiled beef, the ham, and the tongue. I know you said as you'd carve 'em there on the beach, but just think how awkward it'd be with no table and Polly too distracted to help 'ee! So, I shall carve 'em up for 'ee and pile 'em up nicely. Then yer, see, two pigeon pies and the veal and egg pie, Sarah's done 'em bootiful. They'm easy to cut, folks can do their own with the good sharp knife I'll give 'ee. Then us've made sandwiches with salt beef and celery, and ham and cress, and over there,' she pointed, 'is your plum turnovers – they'm lovely, I couldn't have made 'em better meself – and my fruit cakes.'

'It all looks wonderful, Mary, thank you.' It really was an impressive spread. 'And these are our drinks?'

'Yes, Miss, look,' Sarah pointed at the line of bottles, 'there's ginger beer, tonic water and lemonade. But they'm awful heavy. Us'll put a few in each of the baskets to even 'em out.'

'I'm sure we'll manage, but it's fortunate that Charles is able to come. He can help Harry load them on to the wagonette here, then Harry will drive to Instow, taking us to the station on the way. He will make better progress without four people on board, and we can travel with our friends.'

There were nine going on the excursion, the second that summer, and it was Lucy and Polly's turn to provide the picnic. The beach at Westward Ho! would have been Lucy's preferred destination because she loved to see the ocean waves crashing on to the beach, but the necessity of taking an omnibus from Bideford Station made Instow a more inviting prospect, even though its position at the river estuary was no rival to the wild Atlantic shore.

'We shall need to leave in an hour, Mary, to allow enough time to reach the station. I'll see that Polly is ready on time.'

'That's all right, my lover,' Mary gave her a quick hug, 'and you see that you have a bootiful day.'

As Lucy walked through the hall, her mother called her into the morning room. In the months since Polly's engagement to Edwin Boxer, her mother's health had improved, and her headaches came less frequently. Perhaps, Lucy thought wryly, it had been the prospect of both daughters remaining unmarried that had been making her ill.

'Lucy, just a quiet word, if I may.' She closed the morning room door.

'I know it is not long now until their marriage, but I wonder whether you would keep an eye on Polly and Edwin, just quietly, you know? What with it being a warm day and the seclusion of the sandhills at Instow – I'm sure you know what I mean, Lucy.'

Lucy went to stand by the windows, looking out at the sunlit garden to hide her impatience. 'Yes, Mother, of course I do, but what am I to say? Do I order them back if I see them heading towards the sandhills? Polly is very sensible, she won't do anything that might spoil her wedding day.'

'I hope not, but perhaps if they were aware that they were being watched, if you were to call them back for some help with the picnic perhaps?' She sighed, and came to stand beside Lucy. 'I know it is not easy for you, Lucy dear, seeing Polly so happy but not knowing what *your* future will be. Have you heard from Rawlin recently? Does he say when he might return for a visit?'

She hated being quizzed about Rawlin. 'I had a letter last week but, as I have told you before, there is no agreement between us; we are friends, that is all.'

'So you say, Lucy, so you say. Well, we shall see. Perhaps it will *not* come to anything, therefore you should be more careful of the impression you make in Torrington. After all, what man wants to see his future wife striding across the Common? Anyway, if you could just keep an eye on Polly for me today.'

Was it true to say that she and Rawlin had no agreement? Lucy paused on the stairs, turning to look down the sweeping staircase to the spacious hall with its ornamental tiled floor and panelled oak doors, the flower arrangement on the side table, the hallstand with its array of coats, hats and umbrellas – the presence or absence of her father's top hat a reliable indicator of his availability – and in her imagination there came a firm knock at the front door, which opened to reveal Rawlin's familiar face smiling up at her.

In a recent letter he had written that in Australia he was missing female company.

A few of the chaps here are married, having travelled to England to find a wife. There are no other ladies here so I have no female company but, in truth, there is only one whose company I crave. It is different for you, of course, for you have all the beaux of Torrington knocking at your door. I tease you, Lucy; I hope you are not cross with me.

His words sent her into turmoil. Over the past few weeks, she had had several conversations with a friend of Edwin Boxer, being flattered by his interest in her and growing despondent of ever seeing Rawlin again. As she came to know the man better, she began to find him dull, seemingly incapable of any independence of mind or original humour. Gently, she made it clear that she was not interested in developing the relationship any further, and she wrote a playful reply to Rawlin, declaring that the queue of suitors at her door was as long as that of the princess in the story of King Thrushbeard but, like the princess, she found each to be too fat, too thin, too pale or too stupid.

One day, perhaps, she wrote, *I shall open the door to see a long-familiar and greatly missed figure.*

She posted the letter with trepidation and, the previous week, after six long months and many replies to other earlier letters, came the response.

Lucy, your words give me hope. I pray that it will not be many months before I can tell you to expect that knock upon the door.

She turned and continued up the stairs with a spring in her step.

When Polly was ready and Edwin Boxer had arrived in his blazer and boater, Harry brought the wagonette around to the front of the house for the picnic baskets to be strapped into place. Lucy ordered Alpheus to sit close to her feet – there was barely room for him – while she positioned herself next to Charles, with Polly and Edwin opposite, surreptitiously holding hands. Charles deserved a day off. He worked hard, but was so closely monitored by their father that he did not feel the pride in his achievements which he would if he was given more independence. Such a time was surely overdue; after all, he was almost thirty years old. Lucy sometimes wondered whether her father's reluctance to let Charles go was due to John's life and career not progressing in the way he would have wanted.

'Charles, I think you and Edwin should paddle today!' She looked fondly at her brother. 'The tide will be coming in and the water will be refreshing. You must make the most of the day; forget about boils and bunions, fevers and fistulas!'

They all laughed.

'And I,' said Edwin Boxer, 'shall forget about pennies and pounds, columns and calculations!'

As they passed through the Square and out of the town, the clink of bottles from the picnic baskets rang out in time with the horse's hoofs, drawing smiles and waves of recognition from people they passed.

It was a beautiful summer's day. Lucy looked up to watch a pair of buzzards circling together against the bright blue sky. When the wagonette began the descent across the Common to the station, the familiar view down to the valley and across to further hills was always sudden and breathtaking; extensive woodlands in every shade of green, fields of grazing cattle, meadows lying clean and golden after the hay harvest, and barely a house in sight. Beside the road the flowers of the meadowsweet, like cream lace above the bright green of their foliage, were attracting a cloud of butterflies, while swallows dashed and swerved above the road, almost skimming the surface before again wheeling high above the carriage. There were more of the birds this year, she was sure; she would tell Rawlin, and explain that she thought it might be due to last summer's good weather.

Mr Copp's omnibus had already arrived in the station yard and a large group of people were waiting on the platform; she could see Edith, Emily Rudd, Katherine Colling and Charles

Maxwell talking animatedly, also George Doe and Rhoda Macartney standing quietly by. And then – another familiar figure, all in black.

'Oh no, look, Charles!' She spoke quietly, not wanting Edwin Boxer to hear.

He followed her gaze. 'He has not been invited, has he?'

She had spoken to Charles of her exasperation with Reverend Francis, but not of his recent financial difficulties.

'I certainly have not invited him. Perhaps he just happens to be travelling on the same train.'

But it became clear that this was not the case when he hurried over to the wagonette, insisting on taking first Polly's then Lucy's hand with exaggerated politeness to help them down.

'Such a fine day for a picnic, is it not! What a time we shall have! *Suave mare magno*!' And he gave one of his high, foolish laughs.

What could she say without sounding rude? So she merely bowed her head politely, but Charles spoke out, being careful to engage a light, humorous tone.

'We did not realise you were able to come, Reverend Francis! I hope we shall have enough food for you!'

'Oh, do not worry about me! I do not eat a great deal!'

That laugh again. Lucy looked away down the train track. She would not let him spoil her day.

A minute or two later, a cloud of steam appeared in the distance and the engine came into view accompanied by a low roar which became louder and louder as the train approached. Edith took the opportunity to move to Lucy's side and speak quietly to her.

'I'm sorry, I know you were only expecting nine people, but Reverend Francis was visiting Father yesterday evening and the picnic was mentioned. He was very keen to come with us and I hoped you would not mind.'

The engine hissed slowly to a standstill.

Lucy hesitated. 'I wish I could be as patient with him as you are, Edith. But I would like to talk to you later, when we have an opportunity.'

She took Charles's arm as they climbed into the carriage, noticing from the corner of her eye that Reverend Francis had to step back and then go into another compartment with George Doe and Charles Maxwell, there not being room for them all to sit together. There, she need not think of him again during the journey. She settled Alpheus at her feet where he leaned happily against her legs, gazing up at her with dark, shining eyes. He loved accompanying her on a day out.

As the railway line crossed and re-crossed the meandering River Torridge, she peered out of the window to see a stalking heron stretch its neck to stare fiercely at the train, and red-beaked moorhens glide through the shallows. On some occasions she had spotted an otter, but that was usually from the late evening train. Weare Giffard came into view with its rows of white cottages gleaming in the sunshine, and smoke from the pottery drifting gently over the wooded hill. Cows grazed knee-deep in buttercups in the riverside meadows, and it all looked pretty and tranquil with the river so still and the sky a vivid blue.

Only a couple of dozen passengers had travelled on the train from Torrington but quite a crowd stood on the platform at Bideford, so there was a clamour of voices and door-slamming before everyone was settled, and then the train moved just a few yards before stopping again at the platform serving the Royal Hotel, where two more passengers boarded with their luggage. The delay gave Lucy more time to admire the view of Bideford; the river, broadening as it approached the estuary and crossed by the numerous arches of the ancient bridge; the tall-masted ships moored by the long quay from which the little white town rose steeply, dazzling in the June sunshine. In her imagination she walked the familiar route across the bridge and into the narrow shopping streets, feeling the warmth of the man who walked by her side and linked her arm with his. Perhaps, in a few months, this dream might come true.

'Lucy, are you listening to me!'

Perhaps the noise of the train drawing away from the hotel platform had prevented her from hearing what Polly was saying, but everyone was looking at her.

'I was talking about the bridesmaids' flowers, did you not hear a single word? You know that I shall carry orange blossom providing it can be got from the greenhouses, but of course we cannot be sure because by the end of September the weather can be uncertain. Oh, Edwin!' She turned to her fiancé who was smiling benevolently at her. 'Perhaps the wedding should have been earlier! If the orange blossom is not ready then I must carry roses, but then what shall Lucy and Edith carry?'

Ever since the wedding had been announced, Polly had scarcely been able to speak of anything else. Although Lucy was weary of discussing the relative merits of veils and bonnets, tulle or organza, she never tired of seeing her sister so perfectly happy. She and Edwin seemed ideally matched; he was completely entranced by Polly, but calm and sensible, teasing her gently when an excess of enthusiasm threatened to overturn common sense. The wedding and subsequent holiday in Bournemouth was, of course, Polly's main focus at present but Lucy was confident that her future happiness was also assured. Edwin's apartment above the bank in the Square would be sufficiently spacious for a few years and was just a few minutes' walk from Castle House. He had advertised for a servant, and would also take on a young girl, so Polly would not have to work any harder than she did at present.

'Why don't we carry pink roses?' Lucy suggested, 'they would go well with our dove-grey gowns, then if the orange blossom is not available you can have red or orange roses.'

The conversation then turned to the benefits of rosebuds and full-blown roses, and whether one was more suitable for a bride than the other, until the engine shrieked before puffing to a standstill alongside the Instow platform.

It would be an hour or more before Harry would arrive with the picnic baskets and rugs, so they all set off for a walk along the sands, passing the attractive, whitewashed houses that stood beyond the sea wall, and the old stone jetty where small boats were anchored on the sand. Lucy positioned herself between Charles and Katherine to avoid becoming the focus of Reverend Francis' attention, but she could hear his high, persistent voice coming along behind and, glancing back, saw that Edith and

Miss Macartney were walking with him. He was holding forth on the subject of salmon fishing about which he professed to know a great deal, and was gesticulating in the direction of two fishermen on the edge of the shore who were just then hauling in their net.

'I'm sure what he is saying is incorrect,' murmured Charles. 'They will have taken the net out by boat.'

'I was surprised to see him here,' remarked Katherine. 'Now that so many of us have deserted St Michael's, one would think he might feel surrounded by the enemy.'

'I didn't know he was coming, and would really rather he hadn't,' Lucy told her quietly. Perhaps she should not have said it, but she did not want Katherine to think she was the cause of the disharmony. 'But we must not let him spoil our day.'

They walked through the soft, white sand to watch the tide as it flowed steadily in from the sea and towards Bideford, the south-westerly breeze ruffling its surface to create little wavelets that flashed in the bright sunlight. However many times she saw it, she never tired of watching the tide race in, while feeling the fresh sea breeze on her cheeks. On the far bank of the river, where many sailing vessels were moored, the village of Appledore stood serene in the sunshine, its grand merchants' houses lining the quay, and the narrow streets of fishermen's cottages climbing the steep hill beyond. Alpheus raced off to chase the seagulls standing at the edge of the shore, bounding this way and that until they had all taken flight, then galloping back with ears flying as if to tell Lucy what a wonderful thing he had done.

They walked on past the sandhills to see the wide expanse of the confluence of the Torridge and the Taw, and the open sea beyond. The rest of the party came along behind, Reverend Francis' voice still audible above the cries of seagulls, but Lucy soon forgot about him when, with much laughter, they discussed the dubious progress of the choral group and the forthcoming concert at which she would play the piano accompaniment. Charles told them he would attend, but promised not to sit in the front row lest he should make them laugh.

By the time they returned to the village end of the beach, Harry had arrived and had driven the wagonette down the slipway on to the sand. Lucy went to talk to Diamond, their dark bay horse; he seemed confused by the lack of grass until Harry found the nosebag of hay for him, enabling him to chew contentedly while they laid the rugs out on the sand.

While everyone helped themselves to food, laughing and chattering as they passed around the plates, Reverend Francis sat in silence, as if feeling that he was being shunned. Lucy had noticed that when he addressed a remark to George Doe, George pretended not to hear and turned his back. She did not like to see anyone feeling downcast, particularly at a party that she was hosting.

'Would you like a slice of pie, Reverend Francis?' She passed him a plate. 'You must bring Mrs Francis and the children here one day, I'm sure they would like it.'

After the picnic, which everyone pronounced exceedingly good, they settled themselves for a rest, the women sitting with their backs to the sea wall while the men sprawled on the rugs. Reverend Francis sat upright, looking very uncomfortable with his legs straight out in front of him.

'Do you have recent news of your brothers, Edith?' George Doe asked. 'I really ought to write to Rawlin and Maurice but you know how it is, men are never good correspondents.'

Some are, thought Lucy. She looked down at the book in her lap, as if not much interested in the conversation.

'They are well, as far as I know,' Edith replied. 'There continues to be some trouble with natives in the Argentine, but Rawlin has a fairly peaceful time of it in Australia.'

'Let's hope things don't get as bad as they are in South Africa; it is astonishing what those Zulu soldiers have been able to do, despite some of the best battalions of the English army. Does Rawlin have any trouble with the natives in Australia?'

'A little, I think,' said Edith, 'not personally, of course, since he is not farming, but there have been some tensions between them and the Chinese farmers who have arrived in the area. Rawlin says he generally gets on well with the natives he meets when he is out riding; he says it is best to be firm but kind, and to give them honest payment for work done, much as one treats servants at home.'

It was chilling to think of Rawlin being in any danger. Lucy stroked Alpheus's head, and pretended to read her book.

'I suppose it is natural that natives should be aggrieved when land is taken from them, much as the Commoners in Torrington will fight back when Mr Rolle tries to restrict their access to the Common!' Charles's comment caused much laughter. 'But there is limitless land available in Australia and I hear farming is very successful. Do you know that meat is being packed with ice and shipped to London, and when allowed to thaw is as fresh as the day it was butchered? Extraordinary.'

Every time Lucy glanced up from her book – which was remaining unread – Reverend Francis was looking at her, his head tilted slightly and his eyes soft, as if he were watching a small child or a kitten. Annoyed, she refused to meet his gaze. How presumptuous of him to scrutinise her like that! Perhaps Charles realised what was going on, because he came to sit on her left, blocking Reverend Francis' view of her.

'It appears you are in need of some more stimulating company, Lucy,' he said sympathetically. Before long they were laughing together, and she almost forgot the curate.

When Charles and George Doe declared their intention to paddle, Emily and Katherine decided they would watch. Rhoda Macartney was talking intently to Reverend Francis about one of the families she visited in Mill Street, so Lucy took the opportunity to speak to Edith.

'Shall we have a walk together? Do you want to come, Polly?'

Polly was happy sitting in the sun with Edwin, and moved her parasol to shade them both, a manoeuvre that Lucy suspected would conceal a kiss.

The tide having risen to its fullest extent, the river now appeared motionless, as tranquil and blue in the sunshine as a mountain lake, but it would not be long before the tide turned; by the time they left it would be racing out to the sea again.

Lucy took her friend's arm, and positioned her parasol over them both. 'I hope you are able to relax today; you work too hard, you know.'

Edith took on more parish work than was good for her, and had much to do at home with two younger brothers to care for, and her stepmother losing her sight.

'I am! And thank you for providing such a wonderful picnic. But what was it you wanted to ask me?'

It would have been a relief to confide her fears about Reverend Francis' feelings for her, but she did not feel she could tell even Edith of that; he was, after all, a married man, and perhaps she was mistaken. But she did tell her what the curate had told her of his financial affairs and his inability to pay two servants.

Edith stopped suddenly and stared at her. 'I knew he was having difficulties, but I did not realise that it was so serious! Poor Mrs Francis, however will they manage? But why did he tell *you*? It is unusual to share such things.'

'I know, and I am very uncomfortable about it. Does your father realise how serious things are?'

'I know Father told him that a cut in his pay would be necessary due to the decrease in contributions, but I assumed he would manage because he also has his salary as chaplain of the Workhouse.'

'I suspect he may have been stretched from the beginning, because the rent for Torridge Villa must be high. I am very concerned for Mrs Francis, and intend to visit her more often. I know you go when you can, but she has no one else, her family being in Dorset, and she has not been able to go out visiting to make friends because she would not want to take all the children. Even doing something simple like helping us with the church flowers might raise her spirits, but how can she with four children and no nursemaid to care for them?'

Edith promised to talk to her father and see whether or not something could be done to avert the crisis. 'But the only way to bring people back to the church would be to revert to the old ways, and that would mean him standing up to the bishop and Reverend Francis too. I don't think he will do that, and I am afraid he won't take much notice of my opinion. I agree with you though – what is the point of holding services that hardly anyone attends?'

'Yes, and if the changes were made, people would soon come back.'

Alpheus was galloping through the shallows in a cloud of spray.

'There, look! Now he will be wet and covered in sand for the journey home and most of it will be transferred to me. It is as well I didn't wear my best clothes.'

They turned and wandered back to the station, savouring the last minutes on the beach. It had been an enjoyable day, despite Reverend Francis' presence.

Part Two

Chapter Fifteen

18th August 1879

Lucy walked slowly alongside the cemetery wall that separated the town from the Common. She was usually a brisk walker but it was, in truth, far too hot for taking the air and, although it had been her intention to descend the hill and follow the stream through the valley, the thought of the steep climb back up to the town was not inviting. She paused, resting her hand on the wall.

She never tired of the view from here or, indeed, from anywhere on Torrington Common; the green folds of the hills all around, the glint of running water in the deep wooded valleys of the River Torridge and its tributaries below. A blackbird was singing languorously, pausing after each phrase as if the effort required for song in this hot sun was almost too much for him. She knew a tap-tapping coming from the undergrowth to be a thrush striking a snail shell against a rock; she could picture the raising of the narrow head, the glint of the eye, the sudden oblique strike.

There was a movement from the allotments on the hill opposite, and she watched idly as the distant figure bent, straightened, and bent again as he tended his crops. Then the man remained still, seeming to stare across the valley to where she stood on the hill. She did not like to be observed, but he was far off, and it did not seem significant. Hearing the *thunk* of a bat from the boys playing cricket on the Common behind her, she turned instead to watch their studied concentration as they tracked the ball's trajectory, their tense limbs ready to run and catch.

The heat of the sun was relentless. There was perspiration running down the back of her neck, and her legs above her stockings felt damp. It was so hot she had left Alpheus at home.

She undid the top button of her dress where it constricted her throat and, putting up her parasol to shade herself, she lifted her skirt above the dusty surface of the path and turned back towards the road that led to the town.

But after walking a short distance she paused, reluctant to return home so soon. At breakfast her father had been silent, the tension palpable. John, who was staying at the house for a night or two, had come to the table late, then poured coffee and taken a small piece of dry toast. She guessed that he had again been drinking late into the night. Her father lifted his newspaper and did not emerge from behind it until John had left the table. If she returned home now, it would be too early for her father to be attending his first patients and she would again have to play the part of peacemaker, a role of which she had long grown weary.

She walked on again, slowly, undecided as to which course she should take. Her excuse for leaving the house before listening to her parents' complaints had been the necessity of calling on Reverend Francis. It was true that she needed to talk to him about the troubled family who had moved into Well Street – the husband had sustained a nasty injury at work, they had neither coal nor sufficient food – and it really could not wait until their fortnightly meeting. In the event, when she reached his house on Warren Lane, she found that he was not at home.

She stopped when she reached the road that climbed from the railway station to the town. She would *not* return home just yet. If she were to continue the walk she had planned, the air would surely be a little cooler in the valley by the stream. She turned again and retraced her steps along the track that ran next to the cemetery wall.

It was then that she noticed the curate in his long black coat hurrying across the Common from the direction of the station. Recognising her, he increased his pace and waved enthusiastically, one of those extravagant gestures that had earned him such ridicule in the town.

And, without a thought, she turned off the path to meet him.

They met in a hollow in the ground which she recognised because, as children, she and her brothers used to run down into it to hide from playmates. Having grassy walls about fifteen feet long and six feet deep, it had been an ideal hiding place; she had heard that it was an old quarry pit, many of which had been filled in when the new cemetery ground was constructed.

'Reverend Francis, I am glad I have seen you. I have to speak to you about the family who have moved into Well Street, their case is most urgent.' The mother's pleas and the desperation in her eyes returned to Lucy again, as they had frequently during the restless night she had passed; she had wanted to get up to pace around or stand outside on the balcony, being too hot even under a light coverlet, but she had been afraid of waking Polly.

Reverend Francis was a little out of breath from his walk up the hill, and seemed flustered. 'I hoped to see you too, Miss Jones, I was walking on the Common in the hope of seeing you.' He looked around at the hollow in which they stood and gave one of his high, unsettling laughs. 'This is a fortunate meeting place! We cannot be seen!'

She took a step back from him. 'There is no reason why we should not be seen, Reverend Francis.' There was something in his face which unnerved her, and she determined to leave as soon as possible. 'Please can you arrange for some coal to be delivered to this family? They do not belong to a friendly society and it will be several days before the Relieving Officer can help them, if indeed he will at all; in the meantime they are unable to cook or heat water. I can organise some food to keep them going for the time being.'

'Of course I will. I will see to it today, Miss Jones.'

She explained the circumstances of the family, where the house was, and how much coal would be needed. Then, before she had time to move away, he stepped forward and took her hand.

'Lucy.' His face softened. 'May I call you Lucy?'

Afterwards, when she went over and over it in her mind, she tried to remember just what he had said, what she had replied, when she had pulled away. Had he pursued her? Had he taken her hand a second time?

He was looking at her intently. 'I'm sure you know that I have feelings for you, feelings which I am certain are reciprocated. I have seen the way you look at me. Please tell me that I am right, Lucy? *Dear* Lucy.'

There was perspiration running down his face. He moved closer, so that their joined hands touched his chest; she had been paralysed, but that was when she recoiled, was it not? When she snatched her hand away from his clammy grip? If only she had left then, walked right out of the hollow and back to the road. She did not because, despite the shock, she wanted to make him see that he had completely misconstrued the situation so that he would never, ever refer to it again. There was only one man who could call her *dear Lucy*. When she spoke, her voice was high and unsteady.

'I do *not* have feelings for you! Reverend Francis, you are *married!*'

'I know. I know.' He spoke sadly, as if his marriage was something to be regretted. 'The path is not clear for us, I know that, yet if we can meet occasionally, if you will allow me to express my feelings for you...'

'Reverend Francis! You must not!' Her voice must have sounded foolish, she thought afterwards, she should have spoken with more power.

Perhaps she began to move out of the hollow then, because she remembered that the heads of the cricketers were visible beyond the brow of the hill, but he called after her.

'Do not leave me, Miss Jones, Lucy. I am sorry if I have upset you, but you must not leave until you are calm, you do not want anyone to see you looking upset.'

There was truth in this, she would not have wanted to meet anyone while she was feeling so disturbed, but did she really move back into the hollow again? She could not remember. But she knew that in her distress she faced away from him, her breath coming fast and uneven, as if she had been running, while he spoke falteringly of how she had helped him, how he had grown dependant on her advice, how he admired her kindness to the poor of the town. She did not want to hear any of it. She despised the sound of his voice.

'You're the only companion I could ever desire,' he said, 'I think of you day and night, Lucy. I walk on the Common hoping to see you with your dog.'

Then, suddenly, he was close behind her again; she felt his breath on the back of her neck and his hands around her waist.

It was too much. She ran, scrambled out of the hollow, but then, all was confusion.

There was a man. A man in dirty, labouring clothes. She noticed his blackened hands, and then his unpleasant grin. He had been crawling on his hands and knees towards the edge of the hollow; he had been spying on them. She started to walk quickly towards the cemetery wall and the track that would take her back towards the town, but the man ran after her, and she heard his insinuating voice close to her ear.

'No need to run away, Miss; I knows who you be, and I knows who the gennelman be, and I've see'd it all, I have.'

She whirled around and, unnerved by his proximity, took several steps backwards.

'You have seen nothing! There was nothing to see!'

He grinned at her. Several of his teeth were missing and, suddenly, she knew him; he was the man who had accosted her in Calf Street just a few weeks previously.

'See'd you from up on the hill,' he gestured to the far side of the valley, 'was doing my allotment when I see'd you and I knowed it was you. Bin sitting on the ground with the curate, bain't 'ee?'

His laugh was horrible. She backed away again.

'I have not! I have done nothing wrong!'

'I know what I see'd! If the curate don't want the town to hear of it, he'll have to act the gennelman to me.'

She looked around wildly. A passer-by further up the track had stopped to watch; to his right, Reverend Francis was walking away as fast as he could.

'Reverend Francis!' He turned around and hurried back, looking alarmed. 'This man has insulted me! He said we sat on the ground together!'

'We did nothing of the kind!'

She left them. She hurried away, so disturbed she scarcely knew where she was going. When she reached the track, the passer-by she had seen earlier was still there; it was Mr Jackson, and he took a step towards her, looking concerned.

'Are you all right, Miss Jones?'

'Yes, thank you.' She walked quickly on. It was only later, remembering that she had still been able to hear Reverend Francis' voice and the lower tones of the labourer, that she realised that Mr Jackson could have overheard the conversation.

She was walking so fast that she tripped and almost fell as she turned into New Street. A carriage was approaching; she made herself slow down, she must appear calm. She must not attract attention to herself. Perspiration was running down her face and the bodice of her dress was clinging to her body; remembering her parasol she quickly put it up, it would hide her face from passers-by as well as shielding her from the almost unbearable heat of the sun. Had she taken it down when she was in the hollow? She could not recall.

Her shoes tap-tapped on the pavement; gradually her heart began to beat more steadily. She wanted to speak to no one, to keep walking until she reached the solitude of her own bedroom. The streets were almost deserted due to the intensity of the heat, but a few people stood in shady doorways, a horse and cart moved at a slow plod. She crossed the road and walked steadily past Halsdon Terrace, along South Street and, at last, reached Castle Street, and then the gate to Castle House.

As she opened the front door she could hear the piano; it was Polly practising for the next concert when she would accompany Edwin. As Lucy walked swiftly and silently past the half-open door of the drawing room and up the stairs, Polly started to sing;

Come into the garden, Maud, for the black bat, night, has flown.

She closed the bedroom door behind her and leaned against it with her eyes closed, her pulse beating in her temples. What a blessing was the emptiness of the room; there was no one to watch her, no one to pry, and gradually her breathing calmed. With shaking hands she took off her dress and put it over the back of the chair to dry. She threw back the bedcovers and lay down with just a sheet covering her; if anyone came in she would say she had a headache – which indeed she did – and would ask to be left alone.

The events of the morning played through her mind; why had she walked across the Common to meet Reverend Francis? Why had she not left the hollow immediately when he first made those absurd statements? He must have considered her continued presence to be encouragement – had she not left the hollow once and then returned? Why had she done that? And that dreadful man who had been watching them – he must be the same man who had watched her from the allotments, he must have run all the way down the hill and up the other side of the valley until he reached the hollow. If she had returned home when she first became aware of him watching her, none of this would have happened!

But after a few minutes she sat up suddenly. How dare he? How dare Reverend Francis accost her in such a way? She was not to blame. He was supposed to be a man of God; he was married! And, for the first time, she thought of poor Mrs Francis who was already suffering; she must never, ever hear of this.

Lucy slipped out of the bed and walked in her petticoat to the open French window. The heat was even greater here, it was too hot to stand on the balcony today and, besides, she could see Harry below slowly sweeping the driveway, his usual youthful energy replaced by lethargy. She took a step back so that he would not see her. He should be wearing a broader-brimmed hat to keep off the sun; she would talk to Mary Wilcox about it.

I am calm now, she thought. *I can see the way forward.* When she next saw Reverend Francis, providing she could not be overheard by anyone, she would say, *You are <u>never</u> to speak to me again the way you did, Reverend Francis. If you do, I will at once tell Reverend Buckland.* Just that; she would speak firmly, coldly, then she would walk away. Afterwards she would make every effort never to be alone with him again.

All would be well.

And, meanwhile, she hoped that he would remember to order the coal for the family in Calf Street.

Chapter Sixteen

'The chest should be sponged with vinegar and cold water and, um,' Charles looked up at the ceiling of his father's surgery as if seeking answers from the Almighty, 'some mineral acids, dilute sulphuric, given in water.'

'Good. How much and how often?'

'Oh. Fifteen to twenty drops in cold water, three times a day.' His smile was apparent only in his eyes because he had allowed his beard to grow so thick. *I must suggest he trims it,* Dr Jones thought, *he needs to communicate effectively with older patients and the feeble-minded.*

'Or four times, I would suggest. Excellent, we will see the patient this afternoon.'

He gathered his papers together and stacked them neatly on his desk. Charles rarely made errors now; if he continued to study diligently, he should be able to pass the examination next year. 'Now, let's see whether Mary can find us a cold drink; the heat is oppressive even in here.'

As he got up, there was a knock on the inner door. Charles opened it to reveal Ann, her face flushed from the heat despite her rolled-up sleeves.

'Doctor, Mr Jackson is here to see you.'

'Mr Jackson? The one who was mayor?'

'No, sir, it be his father.'

'All right, ask him in. He's not come to the surgery door,' he said to Charles, 'so I don't know what this is about.'

Mr Jackson was perspiring freely, as well he might, wearing a wool jacket in this weather. He hesitated in the doorway when he saw Charles.

'Oh, I'm sorry, Doctor, but I think I should see 'ee in private.'

Whatever could he want? Charles inclined his head as he left the room, and Mr Jackson sat on the edge of the vacated chair, twisting the brim of his hat in his hands.

'I don't rightly know where to start, Doctor.'

'Wait, is this a medical matter? You came to the front door, so I assumed it was not.'

'No, 'tisn't medical. 'Tis about your daughter.'

He hadn't expected this. 'My daughter? Which daughter, Polly? Lucy?'

'Miss Lucy. I don't want to poke my nose in where 'tisn't wanted, but when I thought about it as a father, I felt you should know.'

He stared at the man, his mind blank.

'I was taking a walk on the Common this morning, down by the cemetery wall. I weren't going far on account of the heat. I heard voices, and when I looked around,' he swallowed uncomfortably, 'I saw your daughter and the curate, Reverend Francis, coming out from that hollow that lies away from the road. Now I'm not saying as your daughter was doing something her shouldn't, but...'

'Mr Jackson.' He had to bring this conversation to an end immediately. 'My daughter is a district visitor. She meets Reverend Francis regularly in the course of her work. I don't know what you are insinuating, but I really don't want to hear any more.'

Mr Jackson looks very uncomfortable, as well he might. 'I'm sorry, Doctor, I'm not saying anything against Miss Lucy but, the curate, I'm not so sure about he. And, you see, there was another man, and it seemed to me he'd been on his hands and knees, peering down into the hollow.'

The story was becoming even more bizarre. 'On his knees?'

'Yes, Doctor, and Reverend Francis and this other man, a rough-looking chap, they was arguing.' He stopped, looked down.

'Well? And what was this argument about?'

'I don't know, Doctor. I couldn't rightly hear.'

Dr Jones had the distinct impression he wasn't being told the whole truth. 'And my daughter?'

'Her'd gone, almost running towards the road. I asked was her all right 'cos I could see her was proper upset.'

Dr Jones stared at him. The story made no sense at all. Why would Lucy be upset?

He stood up. 'Mr Jackson, I'm sure there is a perfectly simple explanation, but I would appreciate it if you do not repeat this to anyone. Stories can get altered and misconstrued in the telling, and I'm sure you understand, as a father, that gossip would not be desirable.'

When Mr Jackson had gone, Dr Jones closed the door and sat down at his desk. The story was clearly nonsense, but he could not shake off a strange sense of foreboding. He knew that some townsfolk had spoken of Lucy and Reverend Francis in the same breath in the past, but others had been quick to quell the gossip. It was a chance she took, going about in the town in the way she did, and he admired her for continuing with her work despite the risk. After a few minutes he rang the bell and asked Ann to send Lucy to him.

He was relieved to see that Lucy appeared her usual, calm self when she came into his surgery.

'Well, Father,' she said cheerfully, 'why do you want me?'

He hardly knew how to start. It was a foolish story, he said, and the facts had clearly been misconstrued, but as he told her quickly what Mr Jackson had said, being careful not to suggest that any wrongdoing was suspected, he was alarmed to see her face change. He was reminded for a moment of a young deer he had once come across trapped in the yard of a farm he was visiting, its eyes wild as it leapt this way and that in its search for a way out.

'Father, please, don't speak of it! I met Reverend Francis to discuss a family I had visited, that is all, and then this man saw us talking, and he insulted me! But it was nothing; I just want to forget about it now.'

She did not want to tell him what the man had said, so he reassured her that it would not be spoken of any more, and calmed her by asking about the family in Calf Street, and making her laugh at an incident he had observed in the town. But when she had gone he sat for a long time, staring at his desk.

Later that evening, Dr Jones put his hands behind his head and stretched out his legs towards the empty grate. It was remarkable how a good dinner could dissipate unease. A crackling fire could help too but it was far too warm a night for that. Lucy, sitting opposite him on her little high-backed chair, was concentrating on her sewing, so did not see that he was observing her. A tendril of her dark, wavy hair had escaped its coiled plait to lie on her cheek, and she held her head a little to one side to see her needle in the best light, her lips parted in concentration. She was a little pale perhaps, but did not seem unduly anxious. He had heard her ask Mary Wilcox if there was any mending to do, for she knew that Mary struggled with it now that her eyesight was failing a little. She was a good girl, always thinking of others. Alpheus, stretched at her feet and taking up much of the hearthrug, opened an eye every now and then to make sure she was still there.

As usual, Polly was doing some sort of fancy work to adorn her new home after her wedding, now only three weeks away. He allowed some of the conversation between her and his wife to penetrate his reverie. *I think this pale blue embroidery on the pillowcases would go well with the curtains in the main bedroom, Mother, do you agree?*

Charles was sitting sideways at his mother's writing desk, his legs being too long to fit underneath. Clearly the letter he was writing amused him, for he smiled from time to time and once let out an involuntary chuckle. It was clear that he was smiling despite his mouth being hidden by his beard, so perhaps he need not trim it after all; his mood was communicated through the slight rise of the cheeks, the eyes that shone. Few men chose to be clean-shaven these days and those that did so choose were, almost without exception, high churchmen. Somehow, their naked faces made them seem not only unmanly but also less trustworthy, despite their emotions being in full view for all to see. It was strange. Certainly it was true of Reverend Francis – he felt a twinge of anger at the thought of him – for one felt that he often dissembled rather than show his true feelings. It was also true of Reverend Buckland; Dr Jones did not feel he understood the vicar well, for emotions rarely played upon his face. Charles, despite his hirsute appearance, seemed all emotion by contrast. It would be interesting to reread Charles Darwin's book on the subject.

Just as he was picking up the book that lay by his side – not Darwin, but an old favourite by Sir Walter Scott – the bell rang from the front door. This was unusual in the evening; it was not infrequent that a bell rang, but it was almost always the surgery bell. Every head in the room was raised, and they waited for the knock that soon came on the drawing room door.

''Tis Reverend Buckland, Doctor,' said Ann, drying her hands on her apron, 'and he wants to see 'ee in private, he says.'

Charlotte looked up in surprise. 'Whatever can he want at this time of the evening!'

Dr Jones took Reverend Buckland into the library. When he lit the lamp that stood on the leather-topped desk, bright light flooded out to illuminate the silver-framed photograph of his family and the colourful spines of the books on the closest shelves, and to intensify the darkness in the corners beyond its reach. Samuel Buckland declined a chair and did not seem able to meet his eyes, staring instead at the bookcase to his right, but this diffidence was not unusual for him. The subject he wanted to discuss, however, was highly unusual.

'A delicate matter, to be honest. Rather unfortunate. Concerns a meeting between Lucy and Reverend Francis.'

The doctor's heart sank.

'They met quite innocently, of course, purely by chance, talked of church matters as I understand, but unfortunately they were observed by a man whose thoughts were far from innocent. Balkwill, the name was. He demanded payment from Francis, said if he did not get it he would tell the town what he had seen.'

'But he had seen nothing! And that is blackmail – he must be brought to book immediately!'

Reverend Buckland stared intently at the wall, his mouth a thin line. 'Unfortunately, it is a little more complicated than that. Reverend Francis has, I'm afraid, been a little foolish. So determined was he that gossip should not be spread about the town, he agreed to give the man a half sovereign.'

'He did what!'

'He did not have the money about his person at that time, so he agreed to meet Balkwill later. He then gave him the money.'

Dr Jones was lost for words. What shady world was this that his daughter had become embroiled in? When eventually he spoke, it was with great emphasis. 'He has, through his actions, given the impression that he and my daughter had something to hide.'

Reverend Buckland took a long, slow breath, but still could not make eye contact. 'Reverend Francis has assured me that there were none. He simply wanted to put an end to any tittle-tattle.'

Dr Jones was not often moved to anger, but this situation was extraordinary. 'I do not need Francis' assurance! I know my daughter! It is unthinkable - Lucy involved in an adulterous relationship! Besides, she has a strong attachment to your son – you did realise that, I suppose!'

'I am aware that they write to each other.'

They stood in silence for a minute or more. His thoughts leapt this way and that; what could be done? What could be said to protect his daughter? He could see no way out, and could only wish that the day could start again, that he could sit again at the breakfast table with Lucy and say, *do not go out today, it is hot, there is work to do at home, stay here, stay in this house and this garden.* If only he had warned her against working with Francis at the very beginning; you only had to look at him to know that he was not trustworthy, and he had proved it through the turmoil he had created in the town. Reverend Buckland should have done more to keep him in check, but when faced with complaints from his parishioners, he just gave that watery smile of his; *the bishop supports Reverend Francis*, he would say, *and we should all follow his example.*

'How did you hear about this?' Dr Jones asked. 'Did Francis tell you?'

'Reverend Francis came to me after he had met with Balkwill. He realised his mistake. On my advice, he went to see the solicitor, Mr Price, and he wrote to the bishop to tell him what had happened. What we must now hope is that Balkwill honours his side of the bargain and keeps quiet.'

'Balkwill!' Only now did he comprehend the man's name. 'I hope that is not William Balkwill who lives in Well Street?'

Reverend Buckland inclined his head.

'He is notorious, has been in trouble with the law on numerous occasions! Do we really believe that he will keep quiet about this story he has concocted?' He had visited the house once or twice, and also the parents' house when the boy was growing up, one of the roughest, most disorderly households in Torrington. He could imagine that Balkwill would like to boast of the money the curate had given him, and would not the whole town then believe that Francis had something to hide, and Lucy too?

'Whatever was Francis thinking?' He found he was gripping the back of a chair, and made a conscious effort to calm himself. 'He should resign! This matter would soon blow over if he was to leave the town.'

'I think we must wait to hear the bishop's opinion.' Reverend Buckland spoke very calmly. It was not *his* daughter who was embroiled in this! 'I believe Reverend Francis when he says they met quite innocently, but perhaps we should also talk to Lucy for her account of what happened.'

'No!' Of this, at least, he felt certain. 'I will talk to her myself but I will not have her interrogated about this.'

As he accompanied Reverend Buckland through the hall, neither man spoke, and when they nodded curtly to each other at the door, their eyes were sombre.

Dr Jones returned to the library and sat at the desk, gazing unseeingly at the shadowy room with its book-lined walls. If this distasteful story were to get out, not only Lucy's prospects but the prospects of the whole family could be damaged; his practice, John's practice, perhaps even Polly's marriage. Should he now confide in Charlotte? But it was late; she would be distraught. If he spoke to Lucy tonight he would upset her again; she would not sleep. And he must be careful, so careful, that when he did speak to her he did not in any way communicate to her this nagging doubt that would not leave him, but kept demanding why Francis would hand over a half sovereign if there was nothing to hide?

Ann scuttled into the kitchen corridor when she heard the library door open. She pressed herself against the roughly whitewashed wall and listened while two sets of footsteps moved across the hall. The front door was opened and then closed without a word being spoken. How strange it was that the two men did not say goodbye! Dr Jones returned to the library - she knew it was him because his slippers made a soft padding noise on the tiled floor – so she edged a little closer to the hall, and when, after a few minutes, he crossed the hall again and she heard the drawing room door close, she took a chance and dashed silently out to listen at the door.

'A church matter? At this time of night?' she heard Mrs Jones say.

'He just wanted my opinion on something before the vestry meeting tomorrow. I think I helped him get his thoughts straight on the matter.'

Polly spoke then, and a chair creaked; Ann turned and fled back to the kitchen.

'Well, there's something up, I'm sure of it.' She carefully closed the kitchen door behind her in case a member of the family came down the corridor. 'That's Mr Jackson *and* the vicar have called and they've both said something about Miss Lucy!'

Sarah looked up in surprise from her scrubbing of the kitchen table. 'The vicar! What did he have to say then?'

'I couldn't hear it all, but it was something about Miss Lucy and Reverend Francis, another name too, but I couldn't quite make it out. Dr Jones weren't pleased, I could tell that, but he didn't tell the truth when he went back in the drawing room, he said it was a church matter.'

She was close to tears. It had been such a very hot, fatiguing day, and she just couldn't bear the thought of upset in the household, particularly if it involved Miss Lucy. 'It must be dreadful news if he's keeping it to hisself.'

She couldn't help remembering what George had said about Miss Lucy and Reverend Francis. It sounded as if the gossip might have started up again.

Sarah sat down wearily at the table, pushing a lock of hair out of her eyes. 'You said as Miss Lucy looked out of sorts earlier, so her must know something about it. It may just blow over, you know.' She sighed. 'Look, it's late, I've still got the china to put away and the floor to clean, and you haven't done the bedrooms yet, have 'ee?'

'No.' Ann was so very tired. She went upstairs, pausing first in the hall to make sure that the drawing room door was still closed, and the voices low. Moving swiftly from room to room, she turned down the beds, closed the curtains and checked that the chamber pots were in place, but when she reached Polly's and Lucy's room she paused, and she laid her hand gently on Miss Lucy's pillow, deep in thought.

Chapter Seventeen

When Lucy awoke, there was no sun shining through the curtains. She would hardly have known that it was morning but for the distant sounds from the kitchen and Ann's steps on the stairs, telling her that a cup of tea would soon be arriving. She was too hot in bed; Polly was still deeply asleep, the coverlet rising and falling with each breath, so she carefully pushed the bed clothes back a little and eased herself up to lie against the pillows.

When the memory of the previous day returned to her, it was as if she had been slapped; the meeting in the hollow, the words she did not want to hear, and that other man, his ghastly grin. The images would not go away, even when she closed her eyes. But it was over now, she reminded herself, it would never happen again, and Rawlin need never know that she had been involved in such a shameful incident. Her life could continue as it was before; there was the inconvenience of having to avoid Reverend Francis, that was all.

There was a quiet knock at the door. Ann came in, balancing two cups of tea on a tray, and whispering her greeting when she saw that Polly was still asleep.

'Are you feeling all right this morning, Miss?'

'Of course I am, thank you, Ann. How is the weather today, will it be as hot, do you think?'

Ann went to the window and drew the curtains back a few inches. ''Tis very overcast, Miss, can you see those clouds building up? But just as hot, seems to me.'

'Well, I hope it doesn't rain, I'm out visiting today.'

Yesterday afternoon she had felt she never wanted to leave the house again, but thankfully she had come to her senses now; there were many people who depended on her, she could not stay at home.

Polly stirred, then stretched luxuriously and sat up.

'Is that the time? I must hurry, Katherine is calling for me after breakfast and we are going to Barnstaple. Did I tell you?'

She yawned. 'I just cannot buy ribbon in the right shade in either Torrington or Bideford!'

'You did tell me. I hope you find it.' Lucy could not remember what the ribbon was for, but no doubt it had something to do with the wedding.

'I've been thinking,' said Polly, 'about my arrival at the church. Would it be best if you and Edith alight from the carriage first so that you are ready to help me with my dress, or would it look better if I descend first and you follow? You see, there is certain to be quite a crowd there to see me arrive, so we must get it right.'

'I think you must get out first. You are the one the crowd will be waiting to see.'

Also, she thought, everyone would then be gazing at Polly, and she could descend from the carriage unnoticed.

When she came downstairs, her father was already finishing his breakfast. He patted his mouth with his napkin and pushed back his chair.

'Could we have a quick word, dear?'

'Of course, Father, shall I pour you another cup of tea?'

To her surprise, he said he wanted to talk to her in his surgery. As they walked through the hall together, Ann called after her.

'Don't you want your toast, Miss Lucy?'

'She won't be long, Ann,' her father replied. His manner seemed strange, he was not whistling to himself as he usually did when walking about the house.

He closed the door of his surgery and invited her to sit down.

'Lucy, I'm afraid I have to talk to you again about the events of yesterday.'

He looked grave, and a wave of fear washed over her.

'Father, I really don't want…'

'I know, and I'm sorry. But it was due to those events that Reverend Buckland visited last night.'

She was shocked. How could the vicar know?

'After you left the Common, the man you told me about, Balkwill, threatened Reverend Francis. He said that unless Francis gave him money, he would tell the town what he had seen.'

He told her that Reverend Francis had given the man a half sovereign, not then, not in the heat of the moment, but afterwards, an hour or more afterwards, at an arranged meeting place. Then, realising that he had been foolish, he visited the vicar, he wrote to the bishop, he spoke to a solicitor.

She could scarcely take it in.

'Lucy? Do you understand how serious this is?'

She did not reply. It could not be anything to do with her.

'If news of this gets out,' he said gently, 'do you realise what people will think?'

'Of me?' Her reply came as a whisper. 'What they will think of *me*?'

Her father stood up, walked to the door and back. 'Lucy, I know you would do nothing wrong. We will hope that this will blow over. But I am acquainted with Balkwill, and he is not trustworthy. If he tells people what he claims he saw, naturally they will think Francis has something to hide and, by implication, that you have something to hide too.'

He was looking down at her; she met his gaze but could say nothing. She felt that all the blood had drained from her face.

He sat down, and spoke softly. 'Lucy, I must know, otherwise I cannot help. When you were in the hollow, did Reverend Francis do anything or say anything to you that you would not want other people to know about?'

Her mouth was dry. 'I cannot say.'

He stared at her, and she had to look away at last.

'Then he did.' His voice was a whisper. 'And did you encourage him in any way?'

'NO!' She jumped up. 'I detest him! I hated what he said! How can you suggest that I encouraged him!' She leapt up, but as her hand grasped the door handle her father was suddenly there, turning her around and leading her back towards the chair.

She was struggling to breathe, and trembling all over.

'Lucy, tell me what happened, please.'

She shook her head. 'I cannot.'

'No one else need know.'

She could not look at him.

'Remember,' he said, 'that I have taken an oath of confidentiality. I am well-practised at keeping my counsel. But you must realise,' she saw his fist clench in his lap, 'that if Reverend Francis has done anything criminal...'

She shook her head. 'It is not that. I do not believe it was criminal. It was foolish, stupid, and the reason I do not want anyone to know...'

She paused. She could think of a thousand reasons why she did not want anyone to know, but one was stronger than all the rest.

'I cannot bear for his wife to know what he said to me! She is suffering enough without that! She has lost a child, she has lost her standing in the community and her hopes for the future through the foolishness of her husband. She is struggling to run a big house with the help of only one servant, work to which she has never been accustomed – just imagine if she were also to discover that her husband loved another woman, someone who professed to be her friend!'

She told him, then, exactly what had happened, and what Reverend Francis had said. How dreadful it was to put it into words!

Her father shook his head in bewilderment. 'What I would give for that man never to have come to Torrington! Perhaps you are right in wanting to keep the truth to yourself; I am less concerned for Mrs Francis, but the chance of your reputation becoming tarnished could be greater if the truth were known. And what if Francis denied it?'

Suppose Rawlin were to hear of it, would he believe her to be entirely innocent? She could not bear for him to know what had happened.

'Father, do we have to tell Mother? It would upset her dreadfully and she has so much to think of for Polly's wedding. And you won't say anything to Reverend Francis, will you? I just want to be able to forget all about it.'

She had never seen her father so downcast. He sat in silence for a minute or more before replying.

'No, we won't tell your mother, not yet, and we will hope that it will never be necessary, that no one else hears of what has happened. As for Reverend Francis, I must wait until I feel calmer but I will speak to him, eventually. What I will say will be short, and to the point. Just to ensure, my dear, that he never, ever speaks to you in such a way again.'

Despite her trepidation, it was reassuring to think of her father taking control. 'And you won't tell anyone else? You won't speak of it to Charles or John?'

'No, I won't. But, Lucy, we will have to see what the coming days have in store for us, whether the story gets out.'

They both looked up as a sudden flash lit up the room, followed by a low rumble of thunder which made her father smile ruefully. 'There is drama in nature, also. I must let my first patients into the waiting room before the rain comes, as I am sure it will.'

As he gave her hand an affectionate squeeze, she began to feel a little more confident that everything would turn out well; she would never meet Reverend Francis alone again, her mother would not hear of what had happened, Polly would have her wedding and - she hardly dared to think of it - perhaps, one day, Rawlin would return.

She managed to speak of everyday matters as she ate her breakfast with her mother and Polly. But as they talked, there were flashes of lightning from the sky beyond the river, then the rumbles of thunder grew louder, and gradually drew nearer to the town on the hill.

'Pass me the next one.' Lucy reached down from the small step ladder to take the ironed and folded sheet that Mary Wilcox held up to her, and stacked it neatly on the top shelf of the linen cupboard. It was pleasing to see the piles of freshly-washed bedding and pillowcases, to breathe in their clean, crisp smell, especially, she thought, when you had not been responsible for washing or ironing them.

'Nearly done, just these now,' said Mary, 'then do be careful how you come down, I'm glad 'tis not me up there. Don't forget to scatter the lavender bags around.'

They walked downstairs together, Mary pausing to run her finger along the hall table in the hope of finding some dust.

'Mary!' said Lucy. 'I saw Ann dust the table this very morning! Poor girl, I would not like to work under you.'

Mary took Lucy's arm affectionately as they went into the drawing room where the plans for the wedding were laid out on the table.

'Would you like me to go through the wedding menu with you?' Lucy asked, 'though I am sure if Polly and Mother are happy with it, there is no need.'

There would be fifty guests at Castle House for the wedding breakfast, quite the biggest party Lucy could remember. Her mother was confident that it would be a success, having been accustomed to much bigger gatherings when she was young, but it was causing Mary Wilcox a good deal of anxiety.

'If it will only stay dry!' she said yet again.

'I'm sure it will, but if it should rain we will manage, we can easily accommodate people in the hall and dining room.'

'But then the guests will be in two rooms, and 'twill be harder for me to keep an eye on the servants.'

Servants were being sent from the Vicarage and from Lucy's great-uncle's house in Mill Street which would ease the burden on Sarah and Ann, but Mary was particularly wary of Colonel Palmer's Clara who considered herself very experienced in managing large parties.

'Now, look!' Mary pointed to the first list. 'We will have mayonnaise of chicken and lobster galantine. I do hope we can get the lobsters but if the weather is rough and we can't, then we will have duck galantine. Then there will be cold ham and game, and all these pastries, you see? Then ices, and of course the cake.'

'And that will be made by Brown's?'

'That's it, and if 'tis anything like Jane's 'twill be bootiful.'

The tables were to be decorated with a central band of white satin bordered with maidenhair and white flowers. Lucy felt now that she would enjoy the day. She looked forward to giving Polly her carefully-chosen present of gold and pearl earrings, and as the attention of all the guests would be focussed on Polly, she hoped she could observe the celebrations quietly in Edith's company.

Just then, the front door opened and Polly appeared with Edwin.

'What's the matter?'

Polly was close to tears.

'She's had a shock, she needs to sit down,' said Edwin, 'but you're getting over it now, aren't you, dearest?' Putting his arm protectively around her, he gazed at her anxiously. 'Perhaps she should have a little brandy, Mrs Wilcox.'

Mary rushed to get the brandy while Lucy led Polly to the sofa by the window.

'Whatever happened? You were only going to the post office!'

Polly had gone out looking happy and confident but now her shoulders were drooping, and her face pinched and pale.

'I went to the post office,' she told Lucy shakily, 'then I went into the bank to say *hello* to Edwin, but when I came out two men, horrible men, insulted me.'

Edwin took her hand. 'Polly came to find me again and I came straight out, but they had gone. I didn't want to leave her on her own while I searched for them.'

'But who were they? What did they say?' Lucy tried to ignore the cold feeling in the pit of her stomach.

Between sobs, Polly told her that the men, who were no more than boys really, looked familiar but she did not know who they were.

'They insulted you too, Lucy,' Edwin said quietly. 'One of them pointed at Polly and asked whether she was the one who likes…who likes… the curate, and the other said, *No, this one prefers bankers.* If I can find them…'

'He said *bit of snug,*' Polly sobbed. 'He said, *Is her the one that likes a bit of snug with the curate*, then they laughed! Lucy, if you weren't doing your stupid district visiting, this wouldn't have happened! How can I show my face in the town now!'

Lucy stared down at her lap, only half-aware of Mary murmuring soothing words to Polly while giving her little sips of brandy.

'Lucy!' Mary's presence was insistent. 'Come on, dear, you'd better have some brandy too.'

'I don't want it.'

'You must take no notice of what folks say, they'm not worth the time of day. There's always folks as will say unkind things, I've heard some meself these last few days and I just walk away!'

'What have you heard?'

'Now, no need to bite me head off! You've nothing to hide, I hope!' Mary gave her a searching look, her eyes wide and anxious.

Lucy left them as soon as she could, calling to Alpheus and going out on to the Common.

The intense heat that had led to the storms had passed. The day was still; the sky grey. When she reached Castle Hill, she turned left, following the path that zig-zagged down the steep slope until, still high above the river, she came to the monument, the tall steep-sided stone structure that was erected by the ladies of Torrington after the Battle of Waterloo. She sat on the low seat that was little more than a perch cut into the side of the tower, and stared blankly at the view before her; the river winding its way through the valley, the patchwork of fields on the far hills, the distant Darkham Wood. There was not the slightest breeze, the only movement the rapid rise and fall of her chest.

She would not cry; not here.

Was it chance that those men had spoken of Reverend Francis? It must be, surely. They could not know what had happened.

But what of Mary Wilcox – had she heard something?

She took a deep breath. *I must not speculate, I must not worry myself unnecessarily.* There were visits to make, sewing to be done, every inch of the house to be made spotless for the wedding. She had no time for anxiety.

Gradually her breathing slowed, other movements caught her eye: Alpheus's tail waving back and forth amongst the bracken; the flitting of small birds in the bushes, a blue tit, and a robin which flew to the path at her feet, hopping forward experimentally, its head cocked and its eye bright; a man driving a herd of goats coming into view almost a quarter of a mile away as they followed the path on the opposite side of the valley, and the sound of distant hoofs alerting her to a farm cart descending the hill from Little Torrington. She leaned back against the stone side of the monument to watch a buzzard soaring slowly in the warm air rising from the slopes of the Common.

Whatever happens, she thought, *I cannot be confined within the house. I must be able to walk on the Common.*

Over the next few days she kept busy, but the sense of unease persisted. When visiting Mrs Gent, it seemed to her that the woman's manner was less respectful. When she was shopping in the Square, two women appeared to nudge each other and whisper when they saw her. She thought she caught a remark from a man outside the Black Horse. Probably she imagined it; she had had a shock, it was only natural she should take a little while to get over it.

But then, after a meeting with Edith, Miss Macartney and Reverend Buckland – he had agreed to take over the meetings from Reverend Francis for the time being, much to the bewilderment of the other two – the vicar took her aside.

'Would your father be at home this evening, do you suppose?'

The evening was well advanced before the meeting was over and her father returned to the drawing room. She knew at once that the news would not be good.

'I need to talk to you all. It is a serious matter, I'm afraid.'

Her mother, Polly and Charles looked up in surprise, but Lucy continued to focus on her mending.

'Lucy knows a part of the story I am to tell you, but I am afraid there has been a further development.'

He went on to describe the meeting in the hollow, the appearance of Balkwill, the giving of the half sovereign by Reverend Francis. He emphasised the innocence of the meeting, and she glanced up at him in gratitude for honouring her wishes.

'Lucy! Why did you not tell me of this?'

She had known her mother would be horrified.

'I didn't want to worry you, Mother. I hoped it would blow over.'

'Unfortunately, it hasn't,' her father said quietly. 'It would appear that Balkwill has not kept his word, but has told others of what he claims to have seen. Of course, there are those who are pleased to spread gossip about Francis; but all that matters to us is that Lucy, through no fault of her own, has become caught up in this.'

'That's why those men insulted me!' cried Polly. 'It is even worse that I thought, they really believe those stories about you, Lucy!'

'Lucy, if you had not started this district visiting this would not have happened! I knew it would lead to no good!'

She could neither reply nor meet their eyes, and was grateful when Charles spoke for her.

'Lucy's work has achieved much that is good, Mother. I'm sure it is not her fault that she has become embroiled in this.'

'I agree,' her father said. 'But there is more to tell. It seems that Francis hoped that the whole thing would blow over, but now it is clear that Balkwill has spread his lies, Francis intends to bring a charge of libel against him in order to clear his name, and Lucy's. He has taken legal advice and has the support of the bishop. Until his name has been cleared, he will take no more services at St Michael and All Angels.'

Lucy stared at her father, trying to take in what he had said, but it was again Charles who voiced the questions that were beginning to form in her mind.

'What will that mean? Need it involve Lucy?'

'I have been discussing that with Reverend Buckland. Unfortunately, Francis has already shown himself in a bad light by giving Balkwill money, whether or not it was demanded. We understand that an initial hearing to decide whether there is a case to be met will likely concentrate on exactly what happened when Reverend Francis and Lucy met. If it is decided that they are innocent, the charge of libel can go ahead.'

There were exclamations of shock from Polly and her mother. Lucy could not take it in; it was all too horrible.

Charles spoke quietly. 'Will Lucy have to give evidence?'
'I believe so.'

It was as if she had been struck. 'Father! I cannot! I cannot speak publicly of such a matter!'

'Lucy, I am afraid that you must, because a refusal might imply guilt. All you will have to do,' he looked at her steadily, 'is to tell what happened, that you met by accident on the Common, that you discussed the district visits you had made, that Balkwill appeared. Nothing else.'

She heard her mother's loud complaints that the whole family was disgraced by her actions, that the story would be the talk of the town, that her prospects were for ever ruined, but all she could see was the sea of faces as she stood exposed in the courtroom.

She stood up and moved towards the door. 'I'm going to bed.'

As she left the room, Polly shouted tearfully after her, 'Lucy, do you realise you've ruined my wedding?'

She kept walking. She could not think; she could not feel. When Charles ran up the stairs after her, she turned to him reluctantly.

'Lucy, I'm so sorry. It is going to be hard for you, but I'll stand by you whatever happens, do you understand? And don't take too much notice of Mother and Polly, it is natural that they should be upset, but their anger will pass.'

She managed to hold back her tears as she thanked him. Tentatively, he laid his hand on her shoulder, then she continued to her room, and closed the door.

Chapter Eighteen

Ann carefully placed the dustpan and brush and a bowl of tea leaves in the corner of Lucy and Polly's bedroom, then returned downstairs for the bowl of hot water and the cloths. As she passed back through the hall, she could hear Lucy and her friend, Miss Buckland, talking quietly in the library. It was tempting to pause outside the door, but Miss Wilcox was around somewhere and Ann had no wish to provoke her.

It had been an extraordinary morning. She and Sarah had known, of course, that something was up. They had heard the raised voices, and when the family came down to breakfast you could have cut the atmosphere with a knife, but it was only when luncheon was over that Miss Wilcox asked her to call Harry into the kitchen.

'I've something to say to the three of 'ee,' she said.

And she told them the whole story; Miss Lucy's meeting with Reverend Francis, and the man who had threatened them. Miss Wilcox said they had to know the truth because they were bound to hear all sorts of stories, and needed to be able to put people right.

'And us'll stand by the family, and do our best to make things easier for 'em, especially with the wedding coming up.'

They had all nodded earnestly.

She still could not quite take it all in. Why had Reverend Francis given the man money? Miss Wilcox said it only went to show that he was even more foolish than he looked, but they weren't to repeat that.

She folded and put away the dresses and petticoats that had been left on the chair, then stripped the bed of all its linen and brushed the mattress with the soft brush, before remaking it with clean sheets from the linen cupboard and covering it all with a dust sheet. Then she cleared the dressing table of all the little bits of china, hairbrushes and perfume bottles, shook out the curtains, and proceeded to sprinkle tea leaves on the carpet prior to sweeping it.

'Oh, Ann, I didn't realise you were doing the bedroom today.'

Miss Lucy was standing in the doorway. She looked tired; perhaps she had hoped to lie on the bed.

'Oh, I'm sorry, Miss, but it *is* Friday and I usually does it on a Friday. Would you like me to stop? I can soon make it comfortable for 'ee.'

'No, it's all right, Ann. It's just that I hardly know what to do with myself, I can't go out alone, you see.' She walked to the French window and looked out on to the garden.

Miss Wilcox had said they should speak up when the opportunity arose, but Ann stammered over the words.

'Miss, I just want to say how sorry I am about what's happened. Miss Wilcox told me, you see.'

She stood awkwardly by the bed. It would seem rude to continue with her work. Miss Lucy turned to smile at her – the very smallest smile – then stared out at the garden again.

'Thank you, Ann. It is all so stupid. I wish it had never happened, but I don't know what I could have done to avoid it. We just have to make sure that the thought of what is to come does not spoil Polly's wedding. She is very cross with me, you know.'

'I'm sorry, Miss.' What else could she say?

'I think I shall sit in the garden, perhaps take some of Polly's sewing to do because at least then I can be outside.'

Ann knelt with the dustpan and brush, but after a few minutes she got up and looked out of the window, being careful not to stand too close. Harry was carrying out a chair, then Miss Lucy followed, pointing to a shady spot under the tree and sitting down wearily, as if all her usual energy had drained away.

She looked so alone sitting there with her sewing basket unopened on her lap. Beyond the garden, the slopes of the Common fell away into the valley and the distant wooded hills stretched up to the sky. There was not another person to be seen.

Of course, some would feel sorry that Miss Lucy was caught up in the scandal, but there would be loud laughter from others, men mostly. Ann knew that things would be said; she had heard stories from George even before this happened. The thought of Miss Lucy hearing them made her shiver.

And what of Reverend Francis! He was a curate. He should teach others how to behave.

She turned away from the window to wash the bowls and water jugs, then wiped down the washstands, and cleaned the skirting board with a damp cloth. She straightened up and paused, staring into space. Miss Wilcox had said that if they heard any stories, they must put them right, so perhaps she could persuade George to do the same. He knew far more people than she did. If only the gossip could be stopped before the wedding! It would be too awful if people turned up outside the church to gawp at Miss Lucy rather than to admire Miss Polly.

When she had been serving breakfast there was a tense silence, but once, while she was coming through the hall, she heard Polly cry,

'How will I tell Edwin? Suppose he were to call off the wedding now that the family is disgraced?'

She had hesitated for a moment outside the door, but could not stay there with the eggs growing cold, so she took a deep breath and walked in, keeping her eyes lowered. When she left the room, she had heard Dr Jones begin to talk in a low voice.

Surely Mr Boxer would not call off the wedding; he clearly adored Miss Polly.

She carefully dusted the dressing table ornaments and cleaned the windows. Trying to push thoughts of Miss Lucy aside, she scrutinised the room to make sure she had not missed anything.

Down in the kitchen, Sarah had her hands in a basin of water, scrubbing carrots. She rolled her eyes at Ann.

'Anyone about?' she asked.

'No, bain't no one in the hall. I believe I heard Miss Wilcox with Mrs Jones in the drawing room.' Mrs Jones had been in bed with a headache all morning, but had got dressed before luncheon.

'You'll never credit it, Mrs Jones has changed the wedding menu again! Says us has got to have chicken crockets or some such thing I've never heard of, and almond puddings, and that's on top of everything else us has got to do!'

'Whatever has her done that for? Us don't need more!' It was already hard to see how they could manage all the cooking.

'Miss Wilcox says 'tis only natural that Mrs Jones'd want to make a 'specially good impression on the guests 'cos of all that's going on. But her don't stop to consider how us is going to do it! I'll be up all night, I shouldn't wonder.' She threw a carrot back into the basin, splashing water out on to the table.

'Another couple of weeks and it'll be all over and us can get back to normal.'

But then she remembered that after the wedding Miss Lucy would have to stand up in front of a room full of people; she would have to answer questions about the curate. It would be a long time before things were normal.

After dinner, Ann took the bucket of scraps out to the yard where it would be collected the next day for Mr Moore's pigs. Just as she was checking that the lid was sufficiently secure to keep rats out, a low whistle came from the other side of the high wooden gate. It was George; he sometimes called by on his way home from work. Now was her chance to talk to him about Miss Lucy. It would be wonderful if she could help to put things right. Glancing back through the kitchen window to make sure that Miss Wilcox was not watching, she slipped through the gate.

George was waiting in the lane that led from Castle Street to the Common. She looked around apprehensively when he put his arm around her waist and pulled her close, but there was no one in sight so she let him kiss her despite the faint smell of the tannery that still hung about him.

After just one kiss he pushed her away. 'You amn't told me what's been gwain on!' He sounded annoyed.

'What do 'ee mean?'

''Bout the curate. I should've been the first to hear! Whole town's talkin' about him - and your young lady.'

His tone was sneering, and her heart sank. 'It idn't true! I know there's stories, but her met him by chance, they was talking 'bout church business, that's all.'

'That's not what folks is saying.'

'Well, what be 'em saying?'

He grinned at her. 'Don't know as it's fit for the ears of a nice maid like you.'

She felt her irritation rise. 'Tell me, you'm bound to now.'

'They was out on the Common, close to the Old Bowling Green. There's a hollow just down over the hill, I've seen it meself, and that's where they met, then after a while some chap came along and saw 'em, and there her was with her skirts over her head and him pumpin' away....' George could hardly speak for laughing.

'Stop it! It bain't true!' She was appalled. ''Tis lies, all for it, Miss Lucy would never... with him of all people!' She had pushed George away and was fumbling to open the gate, but he grabbed her arm.

'Hey, come on, 'tis only a bit of foolery, some folks think it's true, but I never did. Mebbe he gave her a kiss or a bit of a cuddle, I dunno, I always said they spent too much time in each other's company, didn't I, and him a married man.'

'No! Not even that! Her just wouldn't, I know it!'

'No need to get in a huff! Anyway, some good may come of it, he'll have to leave the town now, folks'll make sure of it, that's what they say.' He pulled her close to him again, and she yielded reluctantly, her mind elsewhere, but after a few moments he put his mouth to her ear and with a throaty laugh, whispered, 'How 'bout you and me go to this hollow on Sunday?'

She wriggled away from his embrace. 'No, George! I've told 'ee, it bain't funny!'

She had to leave, she would soon be missed, and in any case she no longer wanted him close to her.

'You've got to tell everyone the stories idn't true!' She fixed him in her gaze, determined to make him listen. 'You will, won't you!'

'I might.' He grinned, teasing her. 'Give us another kiss and I might think about it.'

Reluctantly, she let him, while looking over his shoulder to make sure no one was about.

'Promise!' she said again, when they had said their final goodbye. But as she watched him walking away whistling to himself, she had a premonition that he would not keep his word.

Lucy wrapped the shawl tightly over her nightgown to keep out the chill of the early morning air, and moved the chair a little closer to the open French window. Now, she could make out the silhouette of the thrush that was singing so joyously from the top of the lilac tree. There was a scent of damp grass, along with a hint that summer was ending, although the leaves had not yet started to turn.

It was some time since she had heard Sarah and Ann tiptoeing down the stairs. She turned back into the warm and lightly perfumed atmosphere of the bedroom where the clock on the mantelpiece told her that it was now seven o'clock. Polly was lying on her back and breathing deeply with her mouth open.

Perhaps the worst was over. That first night, when her father told the family what had happened, was dreadful. She had pretended to be asleep when Polly came to bed but her sister immediately started to rail against her, accusing her of selfishness, of caring only for herself and the 'paupers' she visited. 'And that curate!' she added, 'I believe you think more of Reverend Francis than you do of your own family.'

Lucy would like to have responded calmly and rationally but her anger got the better of her at last.

Later, before they went to sleep, she was able to speak more calmly.

'Polly,' she said, lying with her back to her sister, for she could not yet look her in the eyes, 'I have done nothing wrong, but I am truly sorry that I have upset you and taken away some of the pleasure of your wedding. I will do all I can to make it up to you.'

The next day their father told Edwin what had happened. Polly had been a little happier when he reassured her that he would not dream of calling off the wedding.

The thrush flew to a higher branch and was now close enough for Lucy to see its bright yellow throat when it sang. Most of the thrushes on the Common had stopped singing and would not start again until spring, but this one seemed to know how much its song consoled her.

Today was a new day. She must not worry about Rawlin hearing of the scandal, he was too far away for that, and she would not allow Reverend Francis to make her miserable. Tomorrow she was to go out visiting again, because Edith had been very kind to her when she heard the story, although she had been puzzled about what had really happened.

'Why did Reverend Francis give the man money if he had seen nothing?' She gave Lucy a very straight look and there was doubt in her eyes.

She could not lie to her friend, but neither did she feel she could tell her the whole truth. Mrs Francis did not know what had really happened, so it could not be right for others to know.

'Edith, please believe me when I tell you that I did nothing wrong.'

Edith took her hand. 'I do believe you.' She spoke sincerely but looked thoughtful, perhaps suspecting that Reverend Francis had not behaved well.

'I knew something must have occurred when Father took our fortnightly meeting in Reverend Francis' place. The next few weeks are going to be difficult for you, Lucy. Do you perhaps want to give up your district visiting?'

'There are so many who depend on me, yet I don't see how I can continue at present. Mother has told me not to go out on my own and, perhaps it's silly, but I have no desire to do so. Every time someone passes me on the street, I will be afraid they will look at me with either amusement or scorn. And if I walk on the Common, people will think I am hoping to meet Reverend Francis!'

She had tried to speak lightly, but her predicament filled her with foreboding. She had dreamt the previous night of seeing the curate in the distance and being unable to move as he approached, grinning and waving. As he came closer, he changed into that man, Balkwill.

'Suppose I were to accompany you on your visits?' Edith asked sympathetically.

'Come with me? On all my visits? But you would not have time!'

'I think I could find the time, and sometimes I could safely leave you in a house whilst I visit elsewhere. You are not easily replaceable, Lucy! And perhaps we can sometimes walk on the Common together. Poor Alpheus will be missing his walks! We need not go anywhere near Torridge Villa.'

It had been a great relief. She had been worried about Mrs Gilbert, and knew that old Mr Rattenbury would miss her visits very much. If either of *them* heard the stories circulating about her, they would dismiss them as nonsense. Some of the younger women might be more curious but, with Edith by her side, she would feel brave enough to face them.

She knew, too, that she should visit Mrs Francis. The thought filled her with dread; what could she say? How much did Mrs Francis know?

Now, as Polly stirred and stretched in the bed, she had another obstacle to overcome. She waited while her sister sat up, smoothing the plait that lay over her shoulder and yawning.

'Did you sleep well?'

Polly looked up, surprised to see her sitting by the window.

'I think so. Didn't you?'

'I awoke quite early. Polly, I have to ask you, do you still want me to be your bridesmaid? Because if you would rather I didn't, I will understand.' There, it was said.

'Oh, Lucy.' There was sadness and regret in Polly's sigh, and Lucy turned to the window again to hide her emotion. 'I just wish none of this had happened, for your sake and mine too. But how can I marry without my sister by my side? We must just make the best of it.'

'Thank you, Polly,' her voice came as a whisper, 'in that case, I will be there.' Feeling the need to be busy, she rose to get dressed.

Downstairs, she was surprised to find her mother already at the breakfast table with her hair done and her jewellery on. Her father lowered his newspaper for a moment to wink at her in acknowledgement of the unusual occurrence.

'Good morning, Lucy.' Her mother's tone was unusually brisk. 'Ann, some fresh tea please. Lucy, I have some calls to make this morning and I would like you to accompany me. I have decided that if we are to survive this ludicrous situation unscathed, we must make it clear to everyone that we have nothing to hide. We will go out into the town together to visit the shops and call on Uncle John.'

'Oh, Mother. Perhaps not today, I don't think I feel ready…'

It was one thing to walk through the town purposefully as she would with Edith, quite another to be out with her mother when the aim of the outing was a social one. Charles intervened on her behalf. 'Perhaps it would be better to wait a few days, Mother. It is all rather fresh in people's minds at present.'

'Nonsense. We need to be seen out and about. I understand from your father that people are already inventing stories.' She paused, buttering her toast with great deliberation while Ann brought in the tea. 'And, as I was saying, the sooner we are seen out, the sooner people will decide that we have nothing to hide. The Palmers and the Stawells have never had anything to be ashamed of.' Lucy saw her father, who was still hiding behind his newspaper, raise his eyebrows a little, whether at the truth of this statement or at the implied criticism of his own family, she was not sure. 'You must change your dress; put on the dark blue silk and the little hat with the feather that complements it.'

'Mother, I really do not want to talk to anyone about it. And suppose we should see Reverend or Mrs Francis, have you thought of that?'

'Don't be foolish, we will not *talk* to anyone about that absurd event, except of course your great-uncle. And I'm sure if Reverend or Mrs Francis are reckless enough to go out into the town, it will be possible to avoid them.'

There was nothing to be gained from further argument. When she had finished her breakfast, she went upstairs to dress all over again.

Castle Street was quiet. Two of Mr Copp's boys were kicking a pig's bladder to and fro, but ceased and waited by a house wall when they saw Lucy and her mother approaching.

'Disgusting habit; I don't know why their parents don't buy them a ball,' her mother said, even though they were within earshot.

'It's quite simple, Mother, they don't have the money.'

'Then they should at least take it to the Common.'

'I don't see why they should not play on the street. It may be that they cannot go far because they will be called in to keep an eye on younger brothers and sisters.'

When they came to the junction of Castle Street and the Square, her mother spoke more hesitantly. 'This is not easy for me either, Lucy. Can we try to speak as one, do you think?'

It was unusual for her to issue a plea, and Lucy was touched. Faced with her mother's usually abrasive attitude, it was easy to forget how hard this must be for her; the family's good name meant everything to her.

Lucy took her arm. 'Yes, Mother, come on, we will do this together.' And they strolled along the busy street as if they did not have a care in the world.

'We will go into the market first.'

'Are you sure, Mother?' Lucy asked quietly, 'You do not usually like to.' Her mother often said that the market was dirty and best avoided.

'I don't like to now, Lucy, but we want as many people as possible to see us looking calm and contented. Are you ready?'

They passed arm-in-arm through the iron gates and walked slowly between the rows of stalls where farmers' wives in white aprons displayed their eggs, trussed chickens, vegetables and posies of autumn flowers. Lucy concentrated on keeping her face relaxed. Many of the shoppers had come on foot or by carrier's cart from surrounding villages, so surely would not have heard any stories about the Torrington curate, and indeed did not seem to be taking any notice of her and her mother.

'Shall we buy a jar of honey to take Uncle John, Lucy? I do not like to go empty-handed.'

While her mother was paying for the honey, Lucy noticed two women watching her. One whispered something, and the other laughed, all the time keeping their eyes on her. Her mother saw it too, and squeezed her arm in an almost affectionate way, saying quietly, 'Look right back, and smile.'

I will, she thought, *I will not be intimidated by them, I have done nothing wrong*, and she looked directly at first one and then the other while smiling graciously, as if flattered by their attention. They stopped laughing then, and looked away as if confused. She had done it. It had not been too difficult. Her mother patted her hand.

'Let us look in the window of Mrs Charles's shop.'

They crossed the road by the drinking fountain to stand outside the shop admiring some rolls of serge and a display of ribbons in which they had no interest.

'Now here comes Mrs Colling; this will be a trial,' her mother murmured.

Lucy had felt uneasy at the thought of meeting friends, knowing that they were sure to be curious to hear her version of events, but here came Katherine and Marion's mother, bearing down on them with a determined look in her eye. As the widow of a solicitor she commanded respect in the community but Lucy knew, from hints dropped by her daughters, that the family struggled financially.

'Mrs Jones, Lucy, how lovely to see you!'

Both Lucy and her mother inclined their heads politely, but it was to Lucy that Mrs Colling made a direct approach.

'I am so sorry to hear of your difficulties, Lucy. My son, as you know, works with Mr Boxer and was given some intimation of the sorry tale. How are you?' She peered at Lucy with her head on one side, her expression suggesting she was trying to appear sympathetic rather than just curious. Her daughters would have been far more considerate.

'I am quite well, thank you, Mrs Colling. It is much ado about nothing, as Mr Shakespeare would say. I was merely discussing my district visiting with Reverend Francis, as I often do.'

'The only person,' her mother said emphatically, 'who is in the wrong is that dreadful man who attempted to extract money from Reverend Francis. And he will receive suitable punishment, I'm sure, then we can all forget about this.' She smiled sweetly at Mrs Colling.

'But am I mistaken in thinking that Reverend Francis *gave* the man money? How very foolish of him! But then we have become rather accustomed to such behaviour from him, haven't we? I'm sure we all wish he would move away from Torrington. Tell me, Lucy,' she dropped her voice a little, 'is it true that you met Reverend Francis in a rather secluded place?' She turned to Mrs Jones and laughed lightly. 'It is quite a trial, isn't it, having daughters; they are so independent these days!'

Lucy opened her mouth to reply, but her mother was quicker.

'Lucy has done nothing wrong, Mrs Colling, and we are not in the least bit concerned, though I admit the curate has made himself look rather foolish. Now tell me, is it true that Katherine is applying for a post as a governess? Has she had any success yet?'

This was clever, if rather unkind. Mrs Colling was sure to be embarrassed that her financial situation necessitated her youngest daughter seeking employment, although Katherine herself was quite sanguine about it. After a short conversation about Katherine's prospects, Lucy's mother, smiling happily as if she had not a care in the world, said goodbye, and they strolled on past Mr How's refreshment house and the Plough Inn.

'There; that's over for now. I hope she will tell others that we are quite unconcerned. Let us go right around the Square before we continue along South Street. I can call at Mrs Rowe's to ensure my hat will be ready in time for the wedding.'

When the little bell rang above the door of the milliner's shop in Cornmarket Street, Mrs Rowe's expression suggested that it was not merely the readiness or otherwise of Mrs Jones's hat that surprised her. Lucy looked away in embarrassment, pretending to be interested in the display of clocks and pocket watches that ticked discordantly on the shelves, for Mr Rowe, a watchmaker, shared the shop with his wife.

Mrs Rowe assured her mother that the hat would be ready in a few days.

'And Miss Jones, is she still to be bridesmaid?' Her voice brimmed with sympathy, and Lucy could be silent no longer.

'Of course I am, Mrs Rowe, I would not miss it for anything. Why did you suppose I might not?'

'Oh, I just thought, with the recent trouble, – so unfortunate…' The woman looked uncomfortable, it was impossible not to feel sorry for her.

'It's nothing, Mrs Rowe,' Lucy's mother said briskly, 'Just a silly misunderstanding. We do not intend to bother ourselves with it.'

Next door, Eliza Down stood at the door of her shoe shop. She was a strange little woman who, despite her humble station in life, wrote poems of high romance and drama, and had attained some local fame by having them published the previous year. She smiled at Lucy, creating wrinkles all over her pixie-like face. 'Chin up, Miss Jones,' she said, 'Remember the strength of the Valkyrs!'

For a moment, Lucy's troubles melted away. Stifling a laugh, she replied warmly. 'Thank you, Miss Down, I will try to do that!' Eliza Down, with her tiny stature and rather masculine clothes was such an unlikely romantic.

'Whatever is she talking about?'

'Oh, it's a reference to one of her poems, Mother, we had a conversation about it once. The Valkyrs were female spirits in the northern legends Miss Down is so fond of.'

'I fail to see what that has to do with you. But you see what we have to contend with, when even Miss Down, who keeps so much to herself, has heard something of the gossip.'

They passed the end of Castle Street. If only she could go home to sit alone in the library, or her bedroom, but her mother walked on so she had to follow.

In South Street, they paused outside Mr Willmer's shop to admire the display of green, red and russet apples, a pyramid of oranges, a basket of carrots and some carefully arranged cauliflowers.

'Mr Willmer is going to deliver some of his best quality fruit to display at the wedding breakfast,' her mother said, 'but your father is also going to ask Mr Rolle if he might have a pineapple from the hothouse. It would provide a wonderful finishing touch.'

The delivery boy, coming out of the shop with a sack of potatoes in his arms, stared at them, then looked back over his shoulder several times as he walked up the street. Lucy pretended to be interested in the fruit, while watching from the corner of her eye. He stopped outside Mr Short's bakery whereupon another young man came out and with a grin and a toss of his head, Lucy was identified. She was the object of their attention. She could not look away; she saw their crude gestures, the thrusting of their hips, she heard their guttural laughter.

She turned her back on them. 'Mother, we must return home.'

Her mother was immediately alert. 'Why, what is happening?' She spotted the two lads, laughing now, the play-acting over. 'Come; I have something to say to them!'

'Mother, no, please.' She clutched her mother's arm.

But the two realised they were being observed and quickly went on their way.

Her mother had not seen the gestures, and it took Lucy a moment or two to understand their significance. As she walked on, she responded automatically to her mother's remarks, but she could not smile, nor feign interest in shop windows.

Did people really think that of her? Did they believe that she and Reverend Francis…

Her mind reeled with the impossibility of it, the shame.

Despite her reluctance to visit her great-uncle, all she wanted now was to escape the gaze of all these people, and his house would give her shelter.

Rack Park House, Colonel Palmer's home, did not hold good memories for Lucy. A very large, three storey house set back from the road, its rather forbidding appearance used to inspire her brothers to tell stories of monsters that lived in its attics, causing her to listen with trepidation for sounds from above while she sat obediently on her great-uncle's huge leather chair, the grown-ups' conversation passing to and fro above her head.

One of the young servants opened the door. She and her mother walked through the dimly-lit hall which was full of dark furniture, potted ferns and a stuffed bird; the walls were festooned with gloomy hangings collected during the Colonel's service overseas. Then they were introduced into the drawing room where the old man sat reading.

'Charlotte, Lucy!' He reached for his stick and struggled to get to his feet until Lucy's mother assured him that they would not take offence at his remaining seated.

Lucy perched on the edge of her chair, the faces of ancient family members gazing disapprovingly at her from the portraits on the walls as if they, too, had heard the stories circulating in the town.

Her great-uncle's house smelt musty, as if the windows had not been opened for many months. Coffee was served, and her mother answered questions about the health of the family, deflecting her uncle's gruff comment about John – *still drinking too much, I expect* – with assurances that he was busy building up his practice. Then, she looked meaningfully at Lucy and launched into the reason for their visit.

'There is a tale being spread maliciously about the town, and I wanted you to hear the truth from me before any lies reach you from elsewhere.'

'What the devil's that, then?' Great-Uncle John was eighty-five years old but his eyes, amongst the folds of skin, were as sharp as ever.

So, her mother told the story. It was an innocent meeting she said, naturally nothing untoward occurred. It was the man, Balkwill, who had made claims with the aim of extorting money, then spread lies about the town.

'But Francis did what? *Gave* money?' His mind was still sufficiently astute to leap on the most worrying element of the story. Lucy shifted uncomfortably on her seat.

'The man is a liability,' her uncle's voice was a low rumble, 'totally untrustworthy, I have said so all along, and a papist to boot. This is the last straw. He must go, I shall write to the bishop, see what can be done on a local level also.' He looked at Lucy. 'You'll give evidence at this hearing, hm? An ordeal for you, I daresay.'

She could do no more than nod.

'Once it's done, it's done. But I'll write letters, get up a petition perhaps. I could name fifty in the town who'd be glad to see him gone. Need to return to the tolerant spirit of the true church; had enough of these arrogant Romish pretensions. Reminder of the Inquisition, in my opinion.'

'But would the hearing still have to take place?' asked her mother. 'If it could be stopped…'

'Don't know about that; if he retracted his accusation, it wouldn't look good for him, would mean he was guilty, you see.' He mumbled to himself, deep in thought, while Lucy and her mother sipped their coffee.

On the way home, her mother continued to smile, and to greet the people with whom she was acquainted. For Lucy, it was scarcely bearable. Everyone knew, she could see it in their eyes; some were compassionate, some were amused. But others looked shocked when they saw her, remembering what they had been told. They, especially, were the ones from whom she turned away in shame.

'Mother, I will not do this again. I will not stroll around the Square making a spectacle of myself.'

They were turning into the gateway of Castle House, and her mother withdrew her arm.

'Very well. But you will have to face the crowds at the wedding, Lucy, and at the hearing.'

Chapter Nineteen

The day of the wedding dawned dry and bright. When Lucy walked out on to the balcony in her nightgown, the sky was so blue, even at this early hour, that it could have been a June day rather than the end of September. Only the size of the fruit on the apple trees in the garden and the wheeling flock of gulls following a plough across a distant field told her that autumn was on its way.

'Polly! It's a beautiful day!' She hurried back into the bedroom. 'I knew it would be! No more worries about rain spoiling your dress.'

Polly, peering into the mirror, turned around with a smile. 'I know! I've been up for ages. After all our worries, I think we can now enjoy the day, don't you? Though I will be relieved when Miss Bright has done my hair to my satisfaction.'

She looked radiant, even now with her hair in curl papers and her dress waiting in a heap of lace and silk on the chair.

'You sit and rest; I'll ask Ann to bring you up some breakfast and I'll help you dress later.' Lucy threw a shawl over her nightgown and hurried down the stairs. She wanted to help Sarah with some last minute preparations in the kitchen before she helped Polly and then got dressed herself. Later, Edith would arrive, and they could all travel in the carriage together.

She paused in the hall. Everything was ready. Each window, each wooden surface and every floor tile in the house gleamed, for she, Ann and Mrs Wilcox had worked together to a careful plan, and now the aroma of soap and beeswax mingled with the delicate scent of the floral decorations, cream-coloured lilies and pink roses, completed by her mother the previous evening. In the carriage house the wagonette shone and in the stable Harry would be giving Diamond a final groom, having washed the horse's mane and tail the previous day. Charles had been helping Harry, for there had been the additional tasks of removing every last weed from the garden, sweeping the driveway and giving the entrance gates an extra coat of white paint.

She was determined that she would enjoy the day. Edith has ascertained that Reverend Francis would not be in or anywhere near the church, indeed she said that her father had stipulated that he was to carry out only limited parish duties until the hearing was over. It was with Mrs Francis that Lucy's sympathies lay, having heard from Ann, who heard it from the Francis' servant Lizzie, that Mrs Francis considered the gossip to be nonsense, and scorned the people of Torrington for believing it.

Probably she had not heard the worst of the rumours that were circulating in the town.

Lucy shook herself out of her reverie and hurried into the kitchen. Today she would not entertain any thoughts of what had happened, or what was still to come. This was Polly's day.

By the time Diamond stood waiting on the drive with white ribbons in his mane, Polly was ready. Lucy and Edith guided her down the staircase, anxiously trying not to trip on her train or dislodge her veil. Their father waited below, and Lucy saw that he had tears in his eyes as he moved forward, murmuring his approval, to take Polly's arm. Before they reached the front door they had to turn around again because the servants were hurrying out from the kitchen to see the bride; Ann, Sarah and Mary Wilcox having been joined by five others from the Vicarage and from her great-uncle's house in Mill Street. They clapped and gasped in admiration when Polly turned around, her delighted smile clear for all to see, despite the veil of frothy lace.

'Oh, that scent!' said Ann, and Polly held up the posy of orange blossom which had, after all, opened its flowers in time.

'Now, stand either side, Lucy and Edith,' insisted Mary Wilcox, 'for us to see 'ee, 'cos you'm very nearly as lovely.'

And Lucy, wearing her dress of dove-grey silk and clasping her posy of pink rosebuds, found that she did not, after all, object too much to being on show, at least in front of the female servants whom she knew and liked so much.

When they were settled in the wagonette, Polly sitting next to her father and Lucy with Edith, and when Polly's dress was carefully arranged with no trailing lace to catch in the wheels,

Harry clicked his tongue and their short journey to the church began.

As they turned into Castle Street she saw that all the children from the school were lined up on the pavement, and well-wishers stood outside the door of every house, their numbers swelled by friends and relatives who had come from other parts of the town to see the bridal party set off. Mrs Copp was there with her newest baby in her arms; Mary Curtice, continuing to sew the glove she was making while she watched and smiled, and old Mrs Thorne who had been helped out to sit in a chair on the pavement. A cheer went up and, as they passed the rows of smiling faces, Lucy glanced at Polly whose cheeks were pink with pleasure as she tried her best to look demure, as someone about to be wed surely should. How she had longed for this day! As a small girl, she would dress up in her mother's castoffs and demand that Lucy play the part of her bridesmaid, or else of the horse that pulled her carriage. The bridegroom had rarely appeared in these childhood games, but Lucy was confident that Polly had now found someone who would make her happy. Perhaps the apartment above the bank was not as grand as she might have wished, but Edwin's prospects were good.

When Harry, in his best jacket and cap, shook the reins and Diamond broke into a gentle trot - for they must not be more than a few minutes late - the measured clip-clop of hoofs was drowned out by more cheers from the groups of people lining Cornmarket Street. Polly was waving now, a gentle wave she knew would become her. Lucy kept her gaze low, but through her lashes she scanned the faces in the crowd. Reverend Francis was not there, nor was William Balkwill. All were smiling, all were admiring, and their gaze when it left Polly for a moment to light on Edith, her father and herself, was just as generous. She saw one woman whisper and point, but there were no cruel jokes, there was no unkind laughter; she need not have worried. Her faith in the people of Torrington was almost restored; after all, were they not just like everyone else in their craving for entertainment, whether it was a wedding or a scandal? There was sometimes ignorance of the pain that could be caused, but no malice.

Diamond, fully aware of the importance of the occasion, held his head high as he turned into the narrow, cobbled entrance to the churchyard where more well-wishers had gathered to see Polly enter the church. Reverend Buckland waited by the door, his white surplice stirring in the breeze and a rare smile on his face. Polly descended carefully from the wagonette with the help of her father, then Lucy and Edith stepped down to help her straighten her veil and arrange her train.

'Here; let me.' Lucy reached under the veil to push back a tendril of hair that was trying to escape, and she touched her sister's cheek, feeling closer to her than she ever had before. 'You look absolutely beautiful.' Polly smiled at her wanly; her mingled excitement and nerves were palpable.

Then, as they stood in the church porch, the rousing opening notes of Mendelssohn's Wedding March sounded from within. Polly took her father's arm and they started their slow, stately walk up the aisle. Lucy matched her pace to Edith's and kept her eyes on Polly's veil trailing in front of her, partly to avoid stepping on it but also so the throng of people she glimpsed on either side would not know that the passionate music had caused her eyes to brim with tears.

She glanced up to see the love in Edwin's eyes as he turned to Polly, then she slipped into the pew next to her mother, with Edith by her side. Now that the organ had fallen silent, the church was hushed but for the rustle of a silk dress here, the clearing of a throat there, then Reverend Buckland's deep, reassuring voice rang out, echoing around the walls.

Dearly beloved, we are gathered together here in the sight of God...

She listened as never before to the words, the solemnity of them.

Marriage was ordained for a remedy against sin, and to avoid fornication.

It was ordained for the mutual society, help, and comfort, that the one ought to have of the other, both in prosperity and adversity.

Then came the dreadful warnings, and the searching questions;

Wilt thou love her, comfort her, honour, and keep her, in sickness and in health; and, forsaking all others, keep thee only unto her, so long as ye both shall live?

Edwin's voice rang out, strong and true. *I will.* For a moment she forgot about Polly and Edwin; it was Reverend Francis who came into her mind. He had made these promises to his wife, not only as a husband but as a man of God. How dare he act as he did? How dare he implicate her in his wrongdoing? She despised him for it.

The moment passed. She listened intently to Polly's certain, if rather soft, response, then as she drew strength from Edwin's confidence, her next response became clearer.

I, Mary Elizabeth, take thee, Edwin Sturdee, to my wedded husband, to have and to hold from this day forward, for better for worse, for richer for poorer, in sickness and in health, to love, cherish, and to obey, till death us do part.

When their mother took out her handkerchief, Lucy touched her arm in sympathy.

At last the organ sounded again, the bells rang out triumphantly, and Polly and Edwin turned, smiling broadly now, to walk back down the aisle to murmurs of pleasure from the congregation. Lucy walked out on Charles's arm, and her brother Henry, who had arrived by train late the previous night, followed behind along with John and his wife Rose, who wore a bright red dress that had made Lucy's mother shudder.

Outside in the sunshine everyone crowded around to congratulate Polly and Edwin, laughing as they raised their voices to make themselves heard over the clamour of the church bells. Now that the ceremony was over, and she was no longer sitting safely in the carriage or the pew, Lucy looked around with some trepidation at the huge crowd of people. As some were glancing in her direction, she moved a little closer to Charles.

Henry came over to greet her.

'Lucy, I have not even had the chance to say hello yet!'

'No, I was asleep when you arrived, Henry.' They embraced and he kissed her lightly on the cheek. 'Did you travel up from the station on Mr Copp's omnibus?' she asked.

'No, I walked up the hill. I had been sitting for far too long and needed some bracing exercise. Mr Copp carried my portmanteau for me.' He leaned towards her to whisper. 'Father told me a little of what has happened; it was the first I knew of it because he had not liked to put it in a letter. I can see it is difficult for you, and I'm sure you must regret your actions.'

'Regret my actions?' She stared at him. 'But I have done nothing.'

'Oh, I just mean walking out alone, and putting yourself in the way of trouble. You always were a tomboy, Lucy.'

Charles came to her rescue. 'Look, Lucy, I think you should stand with the bride and groom now, can you see Edith is beckoning to you? Come, I will walk with you.'

'I would rather stay next to you,' she said, as they moved away, 'but I suppose I must go. Does Henry really feel I am to blame?'

'Take no heed of him, we'll talk more of it later if you wish.'

She squeezed his arm gratefully as they made their way towards Polly, but first Emily Rudd stopped her, putting her arm affectionately around Lucy's shoulders.

'You look beautiful, Lucy! And I just wanted to say,' she dropped her voice, 'I'm so sorry to hear of your recent trouble. No one believes that *you* have done anything wrong, you know, but clearly Reverend Francis has acted very foolishly. My father has told me that there are moves afoot to make him leave the town, and I'm sure we will all be glad to see the back of him.' She gave Lucy's shoulder a squeeze. 'Now go and join your sister, Mrs Boxer!'

As she moved through the crowd with Charles, replying to greetings and agreeing that Polly did indeed look beautiful, she felt reassured after the shock of Henry's words. Emily had chosen to speak to her, and had brought good news. If Reverend Francis could be persuaded to leave the town, perhaps the hearing would not have to take place. What a relief that would be!

She kissed Polly and her new brother-in-law, congratulating them both. Edwin seemed almost overcome.

'This is the happiest day of my life!' he declared, kissing Lucy on the cheek once more.

Lucy's father consulted his watch. 'It is time we returned for the breakfast. We have to adhere to a strict schedule if Polly and Edwin are not to miss their afternoon train.'

As the laughing bride and groom moved towards the carriage, a dozen or more people suddenly ran forward to throw handfuls of rose petals and call out congratulations, causing Diamond to throw his head up in surprise as more of the fluttering cloud landed on him than on Polly and Edwin.

Once Lucy was settled into the wagonette with Edith, their journey was repeated in reverse, except this time Edwin took the place of her father. The other carriages that had been waiting outside the churchyard followed close behind and, as they passed through the Square, they were joined by a large group of people who had walked through the narrow, cobbled path from the church, making quite a procession.

At Castle House, the tables stretched along the lawn for the full width of the house, the crisp white tablecloths swaying gently in the breeze. Lucy quickly checked that everything was as it should be. She knew that once the tables had been laid with the silverware and crystal, and the bowls of fruit and flowers had been put in place, one of the servants from the Vicarage had stood on guard lest birds came to leave their droppings or steal the fruit before the guests arrived.

Before long, the guests were seated and the servants were bringing out the first dishes. She stole a glance at her mother, who was looking magnificent in her dark, plum dress and little matching hat. She was smiling and nodding while she pretended to listen to her cousin sitting opposite, but her eyes darted this way and that, observing Ann placing another bowl of salad on the table, Mrs Loveband admiring the display of fruit, and Polly looking radiant as she talked to the guests seated opposite her. The weather was perfect; warm, with the gentlest of breezes and the sun not too hot but, later on, guests were to be offered the option of moving into the house to drink their tea if they were feeling the effects of too much sun. After all, her mother had said, so much work had gone into ensuring that the house was immaculate, it would be a pity if no one were to see it.

Lucy tried a chicken croquette. It was very good; Sarah had excelled herself. She managed to catch Mary Wilcox's eye as she was pouring some more wine for Colonel Palmer, and their moment of silent communication told her that Mary, too, was relieved that the meal was going well, despite the anxiety that no doubt reigned in the kitchen. Nodding politely as she half-listened to the rather dull story her cousin was telling her, Lucy let her mind wander. She would be able to tell Rawlin about the wedding in her next letter, describing the scene here on the lawn so that he could picture it exactly, emphasising the pride she felt in Polly, and telling him the amusing little details of the preparations. Her last letter to him had been brief. For the first time ever, she had been unable to write of the things that were on her mind. What could she possibly say? *I was seen on the Common with the curate...* The very thought of him knowing even a part of the story made her feel sick to her stomach. What would she tell him after the hearing? But perhaps it would not happen. Perhaps Reverend Francis would leave Torrington first. Meanwhile, she could write about the wedding, and it would be a happy letter.

After the servants had taken away the dinner plates and the ices had been served, some of the guests started to push back their chairs, retiring to the house for a cup of tea or wandering around the garden to admire the dahlias, or stare at the view and point out landmarks on the distant hills.

'No, look,' Lucy heard her brother Henry correcting old Uncle Charles Palmer, 'that is Caddywell Lane and there, you see, Burwood Farm.'

She felt herself to be in danger of interrogation now that the guests were mingling freely, indeed Mrs Loveband, seated at the end of the far table, was peering at her through her lorgnette, and Mrs Sarah Balsdon was already moving purposefully in her direction, so she was relieved when her mother reminded her that it was time for Polly to go upstairs and change.

'Oh, Lucy!' Polly sat down on the bed and held her face in her hands as she gazed up at her sister. 'What a day! What a simply marvellous day!'

'It's been perfect, hasn't it? And you look radiant, you really do.' She meant it, and felt almost overcome with relief that the day had been everything that Polly wished. 'Now we must hurry or you will miss your train; Harry is already harnessing Diamond.'

Polly's cases were already packed for her holiday in Bournemouth, her dresses carefully layered with tissue paper, her underclothes pressed and folded with lavender, her hats safely stored in separate boxes. In a corner of the bedroom two trunks containing all her remaining belongings were stacked ready to be taken to her new home on the Square, so that everything would be ready for her return. Lucy had promised to arrange everything the way she liked it.

Harry and Charles came to carry the cases downstairs while she was still in her petticoat, so Lucy had to hold up a sheet to shield her from the male gaze, while they all laughed helplessly both at the absurdity of the situation and from relief that the day for which they had all prepared for so long was almost over.

At last Polly's violet travelling dress was on, and her hat adjusted at an angle that satisfied her.

'There; now you are ready.'

They stood and looked at each other. Lucy felt real affection for her sister at this moment, and knew that her feelings were reciprocated.

Polly's eyes shone. 'I have even more pleasure ahead, you know.'

Lucy knew that she was thinking of the night to come. She was not surprised; it was clear to anyone who took the trouble to look that the physical attraction between Polly and Edwin was strong.

'I hope you find someone one day, Lucy, who will make you as happy as Edwin has made me.' They embraced then, and held each other tight. 'I do believe that you will.'

As they left the bedroom, Lucy turned back for a moment to look at the open cupboard door revealing empty shelves, the dressing table that looked so bare, and the high double bed with its colourful counterpane and two piles of pillows in which tonight, for the first time in her life, she would have to sleep alone.

MARRIAGES.

BOND—VILE.—Sept. 24, at the Parish Church, Barnstaple, Mr. Arthur H. Bond, of Exeter, to Miss Bessie Vile, of Barnstaple.

BOXER—JONES.—Sept. 29, at St. Michael's Church, Great Torrington, Devon, Edwin S. Boxer, third son of Commander J. F. Boxer, R.N. "Staff," to Mary Elizabeth (Pollie), elder daughter of Chas. R. Jones, Esq., M.D., of Torrington. No cards.

COLLINS—HARDING.—Sept. 25, at the Church of SS. Philip and James, Ilfracombe, Mr. William Collins, of Ilfracombe, to Miss Mary Harding, daughter of the late John Harding, of Ashford.

North Devon Journal, 1879

Chapter Twenty

The pleasure the whole family had taken in the wedding lasted for days. It was not often that Dr Jones was able to share so thoroughly in domestic affairs, but even he was happy to agree that the wedding was everything they had hoped it would be, and he felt proud to be head of such a family.

But after every detail had been pored over, his thoughts inevitably moved to other matters. For a week he went about his work in a sombre mood that would not lift, but only deepened as the day of the hearing approached. Quietly, he observed Lucy when they came together at the dining table, and he saw that she, too, was filled with foreboding, but he could conjure no words to reassure her. When he pictured her standing in front of a large crowd, having to answer questions about a subject of which she could not bring herself to speak even to her own family, his blood ran cold. If only he could take her place! He sighed, and Diamond flicked back his ears in sympathy.

He was on his way to Frizenham Farm to see James Balsdon. His was a sad case, and he had sympathy for the man. He was in the prime of life, master of a four-hundred-acre farm, Justice of the Peace, Mayor of Torrington last year too, but he had been brought to a standstill by the agonising pain of gout which was recurring with increasing regularity. There was no cure; it was probable he would have to give up farming because there was no son to take on the farm.

With the town behind him and the Common ahead, he rode past the Workhouse, glancing towards it in case Reverend Francis was passing through its austere arched entrance. Wherever he went in the town, he kept his eyes open for the curate, for Francis did not intend to leave, but most of his duties had been temporarily withdrawn from him so he was rarely abroad. It was now only the unfortunates in the Workhouse, the choir and the parish council who had the pleasure of his company. The doctor could only hope that once Balkwill was convicted, the whole thing would blow over.

As he turned Diamond's head towards Taddiport, he caught the full strength of the moist south-westerly breeze, so was glad when they reached the shelter of the valley and the old stone bridge over the Torridge. He paused to observe the deep, autumn flow that swirled between the arches, carrying fallen leaves and small branches down towards Bideford. Sometimes he saw an otter or a heron from here, but not today, so he continued on his way. His road wound up through the woods for almost a mile until he turned off on the track leading to Frizenham, where a black-and-white sheepdog ran out wagging its tail and giving short, sharp barks to greet him. As he dismounted, James Balsdon appeared from the yard behind the substantial, well-built farmhouse, raising his hand in greeting as he limped slowly towards him.

In the large farmhouse kitchen Mr Balsdon sat on the wooden settle by the fire so that the doctor could ease off his boot. The big toe was swollen and red.

'Do you have much pain now?'

'Yes, but 'twas worse in the night. And 'tis in my knee now too. I was taking hay to the horses when it came on and 'twas all I could do to get in yer to sit down.'

'It was the heavy load, I expect, that set it off. You took the medicine I sent?'

'Yes. It does help. But I've taken heed of your advice, Doctor. I've put in for a man and his missis to come and run things yer.' He was silent for a while as he stared out across the kitchen, his expression bleak. 'No good carrying on if I be crippled. Granfer had to do the same, but he had Father to take it on.'

It was his life's work. The doctor put a sympathetic hand on the man's shoulder. 'I've made up some more solution for you, take it whenever the pain comes on. Will you stay here at the farmhouse?'

'For the time being, but I reckon us'll take a house in town in due course. Can't sit here watching another man doing my work, giving my workers their orders. I'd be in the way.' He looked up and made an attempt at cheerfulness. 'Town'll be a better place once us gets rid of the curate, eh, Doctor? But I was sorry to hear 'bout your family getting tangled up in his affairs.'

The doctor busied himself with finding the medicine. 'I'm not too hopeful that we will get rid of him, but once Balkwill is convicted perhaps the whole sorry tale can be forgotten.'

'No, Doctor, us is seeing to it that he goes! Not me personally, you understand. I shall be sitting in judgement on the case alongside Mr Mallett, deciding whether there's a case to answer, so I can't involve myself in such things beforehand, but there's plenty that can, and they'm doing so.'

'Doing what? I don't understand.' Mr Balsdon's confident tone was disconcerting.

'It all hinges on whether Balkwill demanded money, or was offered it, see? The curate wouldn't offer money unless he was guilty, would he? So, there's to be a public subscription to pay for a defence lawyer for Balkwill, cos if he gets off, then the curate is the guilty one for offering the money. He'll have to leave then!'

He felt a sense of foreboding. If Francis was considered guilty, then Lucy would be too. 'Surely there will not be enough money raised? Lawyers do not come cheap.'

'Enough?' He laughed. 'There'll be enough for half a dozen lawyers from what I hear! There's only a handful of folks that support Francis and the rest want him gone. The whole town wants him gone! They've had enough of him, they want a peaceful life again and to be able to worship in their own church! Look at me! I've not set foot in St Michael and All Angels for more'n a year now, and the wife and I allus used to alternate with Little Torrington Church, turn and turnabout. No, as long as Balkwill gets off, then the curate'll have to leave.'

Although, as he rode back through the woods, the doctor saw that the leaves of the hornbeam were already turning yellow, and the hawthorn berries glowed like drops of blood against the silver-grey sky, he could think only of James Balsdon's news. The hearing was a gathering of evidence to decide whether Balkwill should be sent for trial. A defence lawyer would fight hard for him, he would ask searching questions of Francis but also of Lucy. He would challenge their responses, try to catch them out. It would be a dreadful experience for Lucy. And if the case were then to be dismissed, the implication would be that Francis had offered money because he had something to hide. On the other hand if Balkwill were charged, Lucy would be called to give evidence again, perhaps in Exeter Court. Whatever happened, the prospect was appalling. Would his daughter forever be remembered as the one who had met the curate on the Common?

Lucy walked with her parents into the Square. Mrs Charles and Mrs Fowler were watching from their shop doorways, then she saw the large crowd around the colonnades of the Town Hall. She reached for her father's arm.

'We'll pass straight through the crowd,' he said quietly. 'We'll say nothing.'

Mr Doe, the town clerk, was shouting *Make way, there!* She held on to her father as they pushed through the throng; people were staring, she heard their comments and kept her head down. More people were queueing on the stairs. As Mr Doe went ahead to clear the way she glimpsed Mr Copp, the washerwoman Mrs Smale, Mr and Mr Loveband, then she and her parents passed into the crowded courtroom and heads turned as they were taken to the seats at the front. Ahead of her there was a dais with a heavy oak table and some chairs, and then the tall windows that looked out on to the Square.

If she were a bird, she could fly out of that window, soar up into the open sky above, far away from this place.

'The court is already almost full,' her father murmured. 'Many people will be turned away.'

Lucy's mother sat to her left, her spine rigid, her hands in their cream silk gloves gripped in her lap, and beyond her, on the other side of the aisle... Lucy quickly turned away. It was only a glimpse, but she had recognised Reverend Francis' profile and, beyond him, the pink hat Mrs Francis was so fond of.

Her father lowered his head towards her. 'Don't look that way,' he whispered, 'Balkwill is there as well.' He laid his hand on hers for a moment.

She stared up at the dais. She could hardly breathe. Where was the courage she had been determined to show? Where was her indignation, her anger?

A letter had come from Rawlin that morning. She had almost cried to see it, for she could not savour it in the way she wanted. She had read it quickly; the light, easy tone, the amusing stories, the affectionate phrases. He knew nothing of what was happening. She thought for a moment of putting the letter in her pocket to give her strength through what was to come, but thought better of it; if the letter was with her, it would be as if he were with her also, and she could not bear for him to know anything of her shame.

Behind her, there was a shifting of chairs and the clearing of throats as people settled into their seats, then the sound of measured footsteps. Reverend Buckland came and sat near Reverend Francis then, one by one, five men in black stepped on to the dais and sat down. Their eyes searched her out. She made herself meet their gaze until they sought others in the room. Mr Mallett, the mayor, was there, Mr Balsdon, and Mr Doe. She did not know the other two.

The room was very quiet now. Dust floated in the shimmer of heat from the cast-iron stove that stood against the wall.

Mr Doe stood up. He said something about Reverend Francis, *the complainant*, and William Balkwill, *the defendant*. She was relieved that he did not say her name. Then one of the other men stood up.

'I would ask please that the witnesses leave the courtroom.'

Mr Doe was coming towards her. 'Miss Jones, please,' he turned to the seats on the other side of the aisle, 'and Reverend Francis.'

She could not move. Her father leaned towards her. 'Lucy, you must go. Charlotte, you go with her.'

She stood. She moved towards the aisle. Reverend Francis was there, he saw her. With an extravagant gesture, he indicated that she and her mother should leave first, and then she was walking through the room, staring straight ahead, knowing that every eye was on her.

Outside the courtroom she and her mother were ushered into a small antechamber containing a table and chairs, and tall wooden cupboards against the walls. They sat, and they stared at one another.

'Well, at least that man is not with us,' her mother said. 'That's one thing to be thankful for.'

Mr Thorne from Barnstaple, a personable young man with dark hair and beard, started by setting out the details of the case for the prosecution. Reverend Francis might be foolish, the doctor considered, but not so foolish that he employed a Torrington lawyer, knowing that there was so much feeling against him in the town.

'The charge against William Balkwill, a young man of the labouring classes,' said Mr Thorne, 'is that on the eighteenth of August he indirectly threatened to publish certain false libel, matter or thing, of, concerning and touching one Herbert Oldfield Francis of Great Torrington, Clerk in Holy Orders, with intent then and there to extort money from him.'

Mr Thorne walked along the dais for a few steps, then turned to face the crowd again, his hands behind his back.

'The case is one of a rather unusual character; at the same time it is by no means of the sensational description many persons believe it to be. Rumours have been circulated very freely, some of which are most gross exaggerations.'

There was a murmuring, and a few suppressed laughs. Mr Doe stood up and glared at the crowd.

'Anyone interrupting will be ejected from this court.' He sat down again.

Mr Thorne continued. 'The charge against Balkwill was that he said to Reverend Francis that he had seen him acting improperly towards a young lady, Miss Lucy Jones, one of the district visitors of the church and daughter of Dr Jones, and that he said, in effect, *If you don't give me ten shillings to hold my tongue, I'll go into the town and tell all that has taken place.*'

There, it was said. Dr Jones sat absolutely still, but closed his eyes for a moment in gratitude that Lucy was not present. How shocking it sounded when stated in plain words in front of perhaps a hundred people. It brought shame on the whole family.

Mr Thorne went on to admit that Francis had acted unwisely by promising to pay the money, and subsequently doing so; however, this had no bearing on the case. Having reminded the magistrates that they did not have to try the case but only decide whether there was such a *prima facie* case as should go for trial, Mr Thorne stated that he was perfectly certain that a decision would be reached that was impartial and unbiased. He then called for Reverend Francis, who returned to the room.

Dr Jones sat up in his seat and fixed his gaze on the curate. If anything was said against Lucy, or anything that was untrue... Francis saw him sitting there in the front row and quickly looked away, clearly discomfited.

As he gave his account of the events of August the eighteenth, his voice was as loud and his manner as rumbustious as ever, but his eyes darted nervously this way and that, towards the doctor, towards Mrs Francis and then the lawyers, and, from time to time, his gaze flew skywards as if hoping for help from the Almighty. He explained how he and Lucy had met by chance on the Common; how they did not remain in conversation more than ten or twelve minutes. Then he described how Balkwill had crept up on them as they were leaving the hollow, claiming to have seen them sitting on the ground together and threatening to go into the town to tell what he had seen unless he was given money to keep quiet; and how subsequently he had given Balkwill a half sovereign. He could have been an actor in a show.

Mr Thorne then questioned him.

'Will you tell us exactly what the defendant said when you met on the Common?'

'He said he had seen me and Miss Jones on the ground with my arm around her waist, behaving improperly.'

'Now, Reverend Francis,' Mr Thorne's voice was as smooth as treacle, 'did you and Miss Jones sit on the ground at all?'

'Never!'

'Is it true that you placed your arm about her waist?'

'It is quite untrue.' Had there been a shadow of hesitation?

'Did you behave improperly towards her?'

'Never.'

'Thank you, Reverend Francis.'

Mr Bencraft, the defence lawyer for Balkwill, stood up. He had a round face with fleshy lips, his hair was red, and his eyes were disconcertingly blue.

'Reverend Francis, just now you were asked to repeat what Balkwill said you were doing. The first time you said he claimed to have seen you sitting on the ground together, yet when asked to repeat this, you said he claimed to have seen you with your arm around Miss Jones, behaving improperly. What was your reason for forgetting this detail?'

Francis looked startled. 'No reason at all. It did not come into my mind at that moment.'

'Do you think that there is anything else that occurred that will come into your mind?'

'No, of course not, I do not think so.' He was clearly alarmed, and it occurred to the doctor that when he brought the summons he never imagined that he would be the subject of such questioning.

The lawyer took a few steps across the dais as if deep in thought, then turned back to Francis.

'May I ask from whence you were coming when you came up the hill?'

'I had left my house to go to the station to enquire about excursion trains, but I turned back.'

'You turned back? Had you any idea the lady would be there?'

'I had not the slightest idea of meeting Miss Jones and, so far as I know, her being there was quite fortuitous.' He tried to sound indignant, but it was not convincing.

'Is it not a fact that when in the trench, people on the brow of the hill would not be able to see the persons?'

'Probably that would be so.'

'Is it not strange, then, that you happened to meet in this trench?'

The doctor groaned inwardly. Mr Bencraft was sharp, and Francis was no match for him.

'Was it while in the trench that you saw this man?'

'Yes, it was.'

'Was that what made you leave it?'

'I saw Mr Jackson and the man coming. We walked out of the trench.'

'Were you walking pretty fast?'

Looking nervous, Francis flung out his arms in an attempt at humour. 'We divided and went different ways.'

'So you wouldn't appear to be together, perhaps. Is that correct?

'No! I didn't think about it.'

'When Miss Jones told you that Balkwill had insulted her, did she say anything about an arm and a waist?'

'No.'

'Reverend Francis, have you known this young lady very long?' Mr Bencraft's tone was unctuous, as if making pleasant conversation at a tea party.

'Yes, all the time I have been in Torrington.'

'Have you ever walked on the Common before with her?'

'No, never.' He shook his head seriously. It was as if he were play-acting, which of course he was and, on hearing his reply, a rumble of laughter went around the court. Mr Doe looked up sharply and glared at the audience. Why had Francis said that? It was a lie; there had been quite innocent walks, at least in Lucy's eyes, and she had usually been accompanied by Edith Buckland, but it was a lie nevertheless, and everyone knew it.

'Have you ever taken any little trips with her?'

He hesitated. 'Yes, I have.'

'By railway?'

'Yes, once or twice.'

'Have you ever been to Exeter with her?'

'Yes, once.'

'Were there any members of her family there besides herself?'

A pause. 'No, there were not.'

Mr Bencraft nodded slowly as if deep in thought, then took a stroll along the dais again.

'I believe, Reverend Francis, that you did not take out the summons until you discovered that stories were being circulated in the town about you and Miss Jones.'

There was a long pause. 'Yes, that's correct. I have heard some very gross remarks, and all sorts of stories.'

'You said that when you gave the money you were off your guard. You remained off a long time, Reverend Francis, considering that more than an hour elapsed between your first interview with Balkwill and your paying him the money.'

'Yes. I went home quite bewildered,' his voice rose to a high pitch, 'and sat down in my study to think.'

'And when, Reverend Francis, did you get your guard *on* again?'

Francis replied with irritation. 'When I went to the vicar for the purpose of telling him what had happened.'

'Reverend Francis, as the defendant is not permitted to speak, I will ask you this. Did you say to him, "I will give you half a sovereign if you will say nothing about it"?'

The strain was clear to see in his face now. 'No, I did not.'

'Thank you, Reverend Francis.'

Mr Thorne then asked him a few more questions in a vain attempt to repair the damage. It was clear to see which way the verdict would go. Why could they not make their decision now and spare Lucy the ordeal of being questioned?

She returned to the room with her mother who slipped into her seat as Lucy stepped up on to the dais. A murmur of interest travelled around the courtroom. Her father saw her look around; she must have seen Francis and Balkwill sitting there in the front row because she flinched a little, then she looked at him and he held her gaze, giving her an encouraging smile. How out of place she looked in this room, where men were discussing immoral activities, and the sordid machinations that resulted. As she stood there in her dark green dress and little jacket, her hair arranged in careful folds and pleats, there was a simple, straightforward honesty about her. He saw, despite the hands that were clasped to stop them shaking, that she was determined. Her chin was raised, her mouth was set; she did not intend to let them intimidate her, and he felt an overwhelming pride in his daughter.

Mr Thorne stepped forward. 'Miss Jones,' he looked at her encouragingly, 'do you recall the events of August the eighteenth?'

'I do.' Her voice was hesitant, those sitting at the back of the room would not hear it.

'Would you care to tell us what happened?'

Quietly, she cleared her throat and fixed her gaze on a point across the dais, a little to the left of Mr Thorne.

'On the afternoon of that day I was walking on the road outside the cemetery wall. As I was going along I saw Reverend Francis approaching.' Her voice broke a little as she said his name. She hesitated for a moment but when she continued, her voice was strong and clear. 'I walked across the turf towards him, and ultimately we met in a hollow in the ground, but it was within sight of the road leading to Furzebeam Hill. There were some cricketers on the Common, and from where I stood I could see the allotment gardens on the other hill. We remained in conversation about five or six minutes.'

As she continued her testament, so her voice grew in confidence. You could have heard a pin drop in the room. Dr Jones hardly dared to breathe.

She went on to describe how Balkwill appeared, telling her he had 'seen all' and that she and the curate had been sitting on the ground, and how she had called to Reverend Francis to tell him she had been insulted.

Mr Thorne asked, 'Is it true that you were sitting on the ground?'

'No, it is not true.' Her voice was emphatic.

'We have heard something about your going to Exeter with Reverend Francis. Did you travel alone with him?'

'No, there was a gentleman in the carriage nearly all the way. We merely happened to be travelling on the same train.'

'Thank you, Miss Jones.'

Mr Thorne returned to his seat and Mr Bencraft stepped forward. *Surely*, Dr Jones thought, *he would be gentle with a lady, please God he would.*

'Miss Jones.' Lucy glanced towards him nervously. 'You have told us that the defendant said that he had seen all, and that he had seen you sitting on the ground. Nothing else?'

'No, nothing else.' She looked apprehensive, sensing a trap no doubt.

Lucy, he thought, *take care.*

'He did not say he had seen anyone taking liberties?'

'No.'

'There was no reference to anybody having his arm around somebody's waist?'

'No, nothing like that.' She looked shocked, her voice was strong.

'You are quite sure of that?'

'Yes, quite sure.'

'Miss Jones, you said you were in conversation with Reverend Francis for five or six minutes. If anyone said it was for ten or twelve minutes, would that be incorrect?'

She hesitated. 'We were holding a conversation, and it might have been longer than I stated.'

It had been clever of Mr Bencraft to ask for her to leave the room while Francis gave his evidence for she did not know what he had said, and in any case did not know whether it was best to contradict or agree with his statements.

'How long were you in the trench altogether?'

'I might have been there for ten or twelve minutes.'

'Is it not a curious thing that you met in this trench?' Bencraft's tone was exaggerated, as if their meeting was the most curious thing he had ever heard, and his very blue eyes widened.

'Yes,' she answered abruptly, 'but we met there by chance.'

'It is rather a deep place?'

'Not very deep.' He could see that she was beginning to grow angry at all the questioning.

'Anyone who is on the brow of the hill cannot see persons who are down in the hollow, can they?'

'Decidedly they can, unless the persons in the hollow are sitting down.'

'Have you tried it?'

Laughter ran around the courtroom. Dr Jones clenched his fist in his lap.

'Did you go out that morning in the expectation of meeting Reverend Francis, Miss Jones?'

'Certainly not.'

'Yet I have heard that you were walking up and down by the cemetery wall, as if waiting for someone.'

There was a long hesitation. 'It was a hot day. I was merely taking the air.'

'Thank you, Miss Jones.' Mr Bencraft inclined his head with exaggerated politeness, and returned to his seat.

She looked confused, unsure whether the ordeal had finished, and Dr Jones jumped up to help her from the dais and back to her seat between him and her mother. He touched her hand and whispered *well done*. His wife sat motionless, and he saw that she, too, was in shock.

After scribbling a few notes, Mr Bencraft stood again. He strolled to the side of the dais where he could address both the audience and the magistrates.

'Gentlemen, the prosecution has utterly failed to make their case. They have made a mountain out of a molehill! My client, William Balkwill, is not permitted to speak, but if he were to give evidence I don't know that he would say he had seen anything very remarkable. While working on his allotment he noticed a lady walking up and down by the cemetery wall as if waiting for someone, then he saw a gentleman walking across the Common towards her and, being curious, he ran down the hill and up the other side to see what was occurring. The reverend gentleman's statement as to my client saying that he had seen him sitting on the ground with his arm around Miss Jones's waist, acting improperly, was entirely uncorroborated and it seems to me the defendant must have been dreaming when he made that statement!' A ripple of laughter was heard in the room. 'God forbid that I should say anything, gentlemen, but the circumstances are peculiar. If the reverend gentleman thought that extortion had taken place, why did he not at once go to the police and meet the man in company with the superintendent? My client tells me that there was no attempt whatsoever to extort money and, the money having been freely given, he kept faith with Reverend Francis and said nothing of what he had seen, but another person told Dr Jones. If my client were to be proved guilty, he would be liable to three years of penal servitude. The case is really an attempt to whitewash Reverend Francis at the expense of my unfortunate client and,' he looked meaningfully about the room, 'I am confident that it will fail. Thank you, gentlemen.'

Lucy watched as Mr Mallett and Mr Balsdon left the room in the company of Mr Doe.

'They will make their decision now,' her father whispered, 'I don't suppose they will be long.'

She did not reply. She did not know which way the decision would go, and she did not much care now. Whatever happened, people would believe that she had intentionally met Reverend Francis; they would believe that he had put his arm around her waist, or worse, and that she had let him. Her name would always be linked with his.

She was aware that the people sitting behind her were growing restless, but then the door at the back of the room opened and it was quiet except for the sound of measured footsteps. The three men stepped on to the dais and Mr Mallett spoke.

'Before the decision of the bench is given, we hope there will be no expression of feeling whatever, either for or against.' He stared challengingly at the crowd. 'We have carefully considered the case on its merits only and, from the contradictory evidence of the witnesses, we both consider there is no *prima facie* case made out on which to send the case for trial.'

There was a slight attempt at applause which was immediately checked by Mr Doe, then the men in black walked back down the aisle.

'Come; we will leave quickly.'

Her father stood, she hardly knew what was happening, but then she was walking between the rows of seats, keeping her gaze on the ground. The hum of voices was increasing, from the corner of her eye she saw people rising from their seats, then she was following her parents down the staircase, almost running, her father taking her mother's arm to steady her. As she emerged into the fresh air she looked up, and there was a sea of faces, a roar went up, a prolonged *ahhh*. She could not move, she was fixed in the gaze of the crowd, then her father pulled her away and she was hurrying from the Square with her head down, her eyes on the dark green skirt gathered in her hand to keep it from the dirt of the street, as she hastened towards the safety of Castle House.

Chapter Twenty-One

Lucy lifted the crumpled dark green dress from the chair and shook out the folds. She had grown careless since Polly had left; being untidy seemed to matter less when the room was so empty but it was unfair to expect Ann to pick up after her.

Several minutes passed before she realised that she was still standing in front of the wardrobe, the dress in her hands. She had been like this all morning, distracted, unable to concentrate. She was tired, of course, that was it, she had slept only fitfully. She had tried to put it behind her, but the scene of the courtroom kept returning to her; the smell of polished wood, the murmuring and fidgeting of the crowd, and the confident gaze of Mr Bencraft's pale blue eyes as he threw question after question in her direction. It had been like a terrifying game of tennis, and she had always hated tennis.

As the scene replayed in her mind, in her imagination the questions grew ever more searching and personal. *Did Reverend Francis suggest that he was in love with you, Miss Jones? Perhaps you had encouraged him in some way? Why did you not leave the hollow immediately?* And always the eyes of the crowd were on her, watching, listening, sometimes laughing at her answers. By now, the whole of Torrington knew of her shame.

When Polly came to Castle House soon after the hearing ended, Lucy and her parents were still sitting in shocked silence in the drawing room.

'What happened? Is William Balkwill to be charged?' Polly was bright and fresh in her new pink dress; she had not been sullied by the courtroom.

Her father spoke quietly. 'No, he will not be sent for trial. The magistrates considered that Francis had sufficient reason to offer him money.'

'Sufficient reason? Why?' Her innocence had been painful to see, and her father had hesitated before replying.

'They believe that he and Lucy met intentionally.'

Polly had been shocked, of course, and anxious about the effect of the scandal on the family. When she embraced Lucy kindly, promising to visit again the next day, Lucy struggled to contain her tears because it was surely more than she deserved. Polly would never do anything of which society might disapprove.

She hung up the dress and picked up her shoes, retrieving one of them from under the chair. She had not taken them down for Harry to clean last night. Well, she would not be needing them today. Her father had advised her not to go out. *It is inevitable, I'm afraid, that people will talk at first, but there will soon be something new to distract them. You'll see, it will soon be forgotten, especially once Francis has left the town.*

But *when* would Reverend Francis go? He had to find a new position, a new home for his wife and children. Having been involved in a scandal, he would have to take whatever position he could obtain, and it would certainly not be the promotion he so desired. She did not care about him, but she pictured Mrs Francis with the new baby in her arms, her startled blue eyes looking accusingly at Lucy, and little Jessie with her disconcertingly serious gaze.

Her mother had not been as understanding as Polly. In the evening, when she had recovered from the initial shock, she accused Lucy of ruining the family's reputation.

It would never have happened if you had not become a district visitor and gone into such disreputable houses! You brought it on yourself!

The respectability of the family was everything to her; was she not descended from the Palmers, the most well-thought-of family in Torrington? Lucy had long since grown tired of hearing stories of the wealth and the achievements of her forebears. She suspected that her mother would like to have married someone with better connections, and blamed Lucy's father for the shame that John, through his unsuitable marriage and his liking for alcohol, had brought on the family. Lucy found this hard enough to bear, but it was devastating to know that she had added to the disgrace. She should have apologised to her mother for upsetting her; instead, she had argued.

Edith is a district visitor! Her family's reputation is not ruined!

When Mary Wilcox eventually intervened, Lucy ran upstairs to bed where her anger and the stresses of the day came to the fore at last, and she sobbed into her pillow until there were no tears left.

Knowing that she was the subject of such gossip appalled her. She would always be *Miss Jones, the one who got tangled up with that curate, remember?* She would have to live with it, forever.

She walked to the French window, and gazed unseeingly at the garden and the drizzling rain. She would have to live with it, but she would not let it define her. She had done nothing wrong! *And it's over now;* she told herself, *it was dreadful, but it is over.* She would continue with her district visiting, Edith would come with her until people were used to seeing her out on the streets again. In time, she would walk on the Common again, there would be no reason not to, once Reverend Francis had gone. She would make a life for herself. She did not know what sort of life it would be; perhaps not one that she would have chosen. For a moment, Rawlin came into her mind but she thrust the thought away, she could not bear to think of him yet. He would not know what had happened, and she thanked God that local English newspapers did not reach Palmerston.

Newspapers. It was Thursday, so that morning Mary Wilcox had placed the North Devon Journal on the breakfast table as usual, but her father had not opened it. She had thought it odd, and remembered that he had warned her the affair would be covered in the newspaper. Surely it would not be published so soon?

She carried her shoes out on to the landing. Ann was cleaning Charles's room – she could hear the broom knocking against the skirting board – and her mother was still in bed. At the bottom of the stairs, the hall was empty but for Alpheus gazing up at her. Knowing he was not allowed upstairs, he put his front paws on the bottom step and his whole body wagged along with his tail as he whined to persuade her to join him. She walked down to him and stroked his soft head.

'We'll go in the garden later, Alph, I'll see if I can find a stick to throw for you.' He whined again, his expressive eyes looking lovingly at her.

When she walked through to the kitchen both Sarah and Mary looked up and smiled sympathetically.

'Hello, my lover, how are you feeling?' Mary asked. 'Can I get you anything? A cup of coffee, perhaps?'

'I'm all right, thank you, Mary. I'm going to read in the library.'

She put her shoes by the back door and walked back through the hall. Her father had gone out in a hurry after the surgery bell rang, but she was not sure where Charles was. She knocked on the surgery door. No answer; he had probably gone to the Workhouse Infirmary. Hesitantly, she turned the handle.

The room was empty. There was the usual faint smell of disinfectant, and the sense that someone had left in a hurry. Her father's worn leather chair was pushed back, and Charles's was set at an angle to the side of the large desk. On the back wall were the shelves of glass jars and bottles, and the scales used for measuring their contents; on the adjacent wall were shelves of medical textbooks. A fly buzzed loudly, repeatedly knocking itself against the window before coming to rest against the frame. Lucy glanced back towards the hall, then slipped through the door.

Her father's desk was strewn with papers; letters from patients, receipts from local businesses, notes scribbled on scraps of paper. His account book lay open next to his brass penholder and inkwell. She stepped forward. There was something under his leatherbound blotter; she lifted it, and there was the newspaper. When folded, it was just a little smaller than the blotter, and she knew that it had been placed there quite deliberately to keep it hidden.

Holding it in her hand she walked back to the door to stand there for a moment, listening. There was silence but for the buzzing of the fly. If she stood here, she would hear if a door opened, or if footsteps crossed the hall to come down the passageway; in a moment she could replace the newspaper under the blotter, she could be at the door claiming to be looking for her father. Carefully, she unfolded the paper.

The first page carried large ornate letters declaring the paper's title, and numerous advertisements for auction sales, farm sales and houses to let. She was familiar with the paper's layout; on the second page were letters to the editor, on the third was national news, then advertisements for servants, coach companies and private schools. She turned the pages rapidly, then, there it was. *Torrington. Serious Accusations against the Curate.* Quickly, she scanned the words, saw that there were two whole columns of dense print, but certain words and phrases leapt out at her: *rumours respecting his relations with a lady of this town,*

Miss Lucy Jones, daughter of Dr Jones.

And here were her words, the questions and her answers exactly as she had given them, in print for anyone to see, and Reverend Francis' answers which she had not heard the previous day.

Is it true you placed your arm around her waist? Quite untrue.

Did you behave improperly towards her? Never.

It was appalling that these words had been heard by a roomful of people; now they could be read by anyone in Devon. Her breath was coming in fast, uneven gasps. She tried to calm herself, took a deep, slow breath and looked out towards the hall to make sure that no one was coming. Then she started to read, slowly, from the beginning.

The next day, after Lucy had helped Mary Wilcox to candy orange and lemon peel for fruit cakes, and had endured a stiffly polite luncheon with her mother, eased only a little by Charles's helpful chatter, she retired to the library.

She had started Mr Hardy's *The Return of the Native* the previous week and had, at first, found it rather too sensational. She returned to it in the hope that it would throw her own predicament into perspective – after all, Egdon Heath was not unlike Torrington Common – but it was hard to find parallels between Eustacia Vye's problems and her own, so she put it down to search the shelves for a more comforting read.

Before she had chosen a new book, the front doorbell rang, and Ann showed Edith through to the library.

'Lucy.' Edith took Lucy's hand. 'How are you?'

Edith's expression told Lucy that she could imagine exactly how she was feeling, and she could not reply except by squeezing her friend's hand.

'Would you like me to bring some tea, Miss?'

'Yes please, Ann.'

She tried to regain her composure as they settled themselves at the library table.

'You look tired, Lucy. I wish I was bringing you good news, but…' Edith looked down at the table, as if lost for words, then took a deep breath. 'I'm afraid Reverend Francis is not leaving the parish. He wrote to the bishop immediately and has now received a reply which says there is no reason to doubt the truth of Reverend Francis' statements, and so Father can allow him to officiate as usual.'

'He's going to stay?' She could hardly take it in. 'But at the hearing he was not believed! How can he stay?'

'Lucy, it's the bishop who decides whether he can retain his post, not the magistrates. And remember, this means the bishop believes you, too, to be innocent of any transgressions.'

'I don't care what the bishop thinks, I've never even met him!' She lowered her voice, seeing that Edith looked rather shocked. 'The magistrates and the people of Torrington believe he has done wrong, so how can he stay? The church will lose its entire congregation!'

She did not much care what happened in the church; she just wanted to know that she would never see the curate again.

'I know, it is going to be very difficult.' Edith looked troubled. 'Father believes the decision was wrong, he says that the magistrates had made up their minds before they even heard the evidence; after all, Mr Mallett and Mr Balsdon have been two of the most vociferous critics of Reverend Francis. Father hopes that people will forgive and forget eventually but, in the meantime, it will be very hard for you.'

'I cannot see him, Edith! I cannot go out if he may be in the town!' She broke off as Ann came in with the tea and Edith changed the subject, remarking on the rain that had fallen in the night.

'I cannot go to the meetings and sit looking at him after the things that were said at the hearing! Edith, if you'd been there…'

'I was there.' She spoke gently.

'Were you?' It had not occurred to her that Edith would attend the hearing. 'I did not see you, but I hardly dared to look at the crowd.'

'I sat near the back with Mother. You were very brave, Lucy, and spoke out so well. You know, I don't think anyone holds a grudge against you; the talk in the town is, I understand, all about Reverend Francis. He seems to have very little support.'

'What of Mrs Francis? Should I go to see her?' The thought filled her with dread.

Edith hesitated. 'I think perhaps not. I have seen her, and naturally she is confused and upset. I think it's best for you to stay away for the time being.'

'I was supposed to be her friend.' Lucy closed her eyes for a moment. If only she could go back in time, do things differently. 'Mary Wilcox told me that there is talk of little else in the town. She says that people are particularly angry at him saying that he and I had never before met on the Common, when clearly we had. You and I were often together when we met him!'

'Yes, some people say he should be charged with perjury for that statement.' Edith's eyes were wide with anxiety. 'I told Father that I was sure you would not want to attend meetings with Reverend Francis, so he has agreed to continue taking them for the time being. And perhaps next week we will go visiting together, we could visit Mrs Gilbert. Would you like that?' She took Lucy's hand. 'Our passage through this world is beset with difficulties; we may not be able to understand God's plan, but we know that it is there, it is our duty to accept the ills that befall us. I'm sure life will get easier in time, Lucy.'

She could not imagine that it would. 'Will I ever be able to walk alone on the Common again? I feel as if I will be watched every time I go out. And, Edith, what about Rawlin?' The words were hard to say, and her voice broke a little. 'He will want no more to do with me.'

'Lucy, I cannot believe that.'

She felt her eyes fill with tears at Edith's kindness.

'Remember that news takes three months to reach him,' Edith said. 'If you wrote to him telling him of all that has happened, by the time he read the letter it might all be forgotten, and he would have been upset unnecessarily. Why not wait a while?'

Dr Jones picked up the first of the letters Mary Wilcox had brought to the table for him. He was enjoying a more relaxed breakfast than usual because Charles was taking surgery, on the strict understanding that he would call his father in for any difficult cases. Lucy, having finished eating, had taken Alpheus into the garden.

'You have a lot of letters this morning. Are there none for me?'

He had been pleased to see his wife dressed for breakfast; she seemed to have recovered her spirits somewhat after the initial shock of the hearing. He quickly checked the names on the envelopes. 'No, all for me this morning.' The size of the pile was unusual, and he picked up the first with some trepidation.

It was from his old friend Dr Blagden, with whom he usually exchanged letters only at Christmas. *Dear Charles,* the letter read, *Naturally the enclosed article will not be news for you, but I wanted to express my sincere sympathies and hope the extraordinary story, which seems to me to be more molehill than mountain, will soon be forgotten.* The headline on the cutting, which was taken from *The Stroud Journal* and formed a half column, read *Charge of Libel against a Clergyman.* As he scanned the text, phrases leapt out at him; *improper behaviour with a young lady of position; Miss Lucy Jones, daughter of a local medical man.*

Hurriedly, he folded the paper inside the letter and returned both to the envelope.

'What is that, dear?' Charlotte asked, looking up from the magazine she was reading.

'Oh, nothing of interest.'

He opened the second letter, which carried a Yorkshire postmark. It was from Dr Swanson; he had not heard from him for several years. *Dear Dr Jones, the enclosed cutting will not be a surprise to you except perhaps to learn that the news has travelled as far as York, but then there has always been great public interest in scandals involving clergymen. I hope the impact on your family will not be too great. I thought I would take the opportunity to write and express again my thanks to you for the help you gave me...* He dropped the letter and unfolded the cutting.

Singular Charge of Libel. His daughter's name was again printed for all to see. He looked at the remaining letters; surely they could not all be on the same subject?

The next was from his cousin in Exeter. *Dear Charles, I am writing to express my sincere sympathies...* No cutting this time, but a mention of *The Express and Echo*.

There were further letters from Norfolk, Wales and London.

'Charles, what *are* all those letters?'

He could not keep their contents from his wife any longer, however much he would like to have protected her; she too would receive condolences from friends and relatives in time, and would know then how far the news had spread. He had, eventually, shown her the article in *The North Devon Journal*, so the tone of these pieces would not come as a complete shock to her.

'I'm afraid the newspapers cannot resist a tale of a disgraced clergyman.' He took out the cuttings and handed them to her, being careful not to point out that their daughter was also disgraced.

She sighed in despair as she read the cuttings. 'York? London? Is there a town in England which has not heard the news? Charles, Lucy's prospects are now completely ruined!' The colour had drained from her face, and he reached out to take her hand.

'Charlotte, this is the worst time. Things will get easier, time will heal.'

CHARGE OF EXTORTING MONEY FROM A CLERGYMAN.
SINGULAR CASE.

At Torrington, North Devon, yesterday, a labourer named Balkwill was charged with having threatened to publish certain false libels concerning the Rev. Herbert Oldfield Francis, curate of Torrington. Mr. Francis's evidence was to the effect that on August 18th, whilst walking on Torrington Common, he met Miss Lucy Jones, daughter of a local medical man. They met by accident in a kind of gully, remaining in conversation a quarter of an hour. Shortly after they parted defendant accosted Miss Jones, telling her he had seen them sitting on the ground in the gully behaving improperly. Miss Jones shouted for Mr. Francis, and to him the defendant repeated the accusation, and demanded money, saying he would let all Torrington know if he did not behave like a gentleman and pay. Mr. Francis offered him half-a-crown, but defendant insisted on having half-a-sovereign. The rev. gentleman, not having the money, met him later in the day, when the money was paid. Complainant denied any impropriety between Miss Jones and himself in the gully, and explained that when he paid the money he was taken off his guard by the defendant's demand. Ultimately Mr. Francis reported the circumstances to the vicar. The Bishop of the diocese was written to, with the result that the present proceedings were taken. The defence was that the money was paid to Balkwill to induce him to hold his tongue, and he had fulfilled his part of the contract. The bench considered the evidence unsatisfactory, and dismissed the case.

Bristol Mercury, 1879. (Public domain)

The story was reported by fifty-two newspapers throughout Britain and Ireland.

'But will they get easier? While that man is still in the town, no one in Torrington will forget!'

'I know. I told you, didn't I, that I intend to visit the Vicarage once surgery has finished and hope to persuade Reverend Buckland to put pressure on him to leave.' The task was weighing heavily on his mind. 'But my dear, please do not blame Lucy for this! I consider her quite blameless, and she needs our support if she is to get through this without breaking down completely.'

'But if she could only have behaved properly! Walking alone on the Common! She always did go her own way, and now look what has happened!'

'Charlotte,' he spoke quite firmly, 'I will not have Lucy upset, Francis is to blame, no one else, and I want you to promise me that you will not say anything to the contrary. Let us all get through this together.' When he held her hand and made her look at him, she eventually acquiesced. 'That's it; now why don't you take a walk in the garden, the fresh air will do you good. We will not say anything to Lucy about these letters just yet.'

It was only a five minute walk to the Vicarage, but one which necessitated Dr Jones battling the northerly breeze which had sprung up. There were few people on the street, so perhaps he was imagining that he was being greeted less often than usual, but he walked fast with his head down so that he would not have to see people turn away from him.

Emerging from Potacre Street, he crossed the main road, passed through the open gates of the Vicarage, and rang the bell firmly before he changed his mind. While he waited, he turned to gaze out on the garden. Rooks were squabbling noisily over roosting perches in the elms that grew alongside the boundary wall. The lawn was neatly cut but the shrubs needed trimming and there was little colour. Now that Mrs Buckland was nearly blind, the garden was somewhat neglected, and the vicar showed no interest in it.

Samuel Buckland had come to live at the Vicarage only a few years before the doctor had moved into Castle House. As vicar and doctor, their paths had often crossed right from the beginning and, their children being of similar ages and social standing, it was natural that the families should become close, but somehow that closeness had never extended to the two men.

The housemaid took him to the study, and the vicar rose from his chair. He had been sitting at his desk reading a leatherbound book, and the doctor glimpsed the title on the spine as he put it down, *The Lives of the Saints.*

'Come in, Charles, take a seat.'

He sat, and took a deep breath. He had no time for polite chatter. 'I understand Francis intends to stay in the town.'

'Yes, indeed.' Reverend Buckland gave a watery smile. 'Perhaps you heard that the bishop advised him to resume his duties?'

'And do you really believe that he should?' He was aware that he sounded unusually confrontational, but he did not care.

'It is the bishop who decides these things; it is my duty to follow his advice. I'm sure you know that, Charles.' He appeared to be looking at the arm of the chair which only served to increase the doctor's irritation.

'Have you considered how you would feel if it were Edith rather than my daughter who was caught up in this affair? If it were Edith who had to stand up in front of a large audience to be asked personal questions, then have the answers to those questions printed in every newspaper in the land? Would you not feel it inappropriate that she had to fear meeting Francis every time she left the house?' His voice had grown louder, and a pained expression had developed on Reverend Buckland's face.

'I'm sure it must be difficult for Lucy, and I am sorry for it, but it is out of my hands!' He lifted his palms to demonstrate his helplessness.

'All you have to do is strongly advise Francis to resign! You would not be disregarding the bishop's instruction, for it would be up to Francis to decide, but he could hardly continue to work with you in such circumstances!'

Reverend Buckland looked at the floor. 'I'm sorry, but I cannot do that.'

The doctor took a deep breath and made an effort to lower his voice. 'Have you considered the result should he stay? Already the congregation is greatly depleted and there is discord in the town. It will be much, much worse if he stays. The whole town is against him – the bishop does not see that!'

'I'm sure the whole unfortunate affair will blow over in due course and there will again be harmony.' He attempted to smile.

The doctor was afraid his anger would get out of hand, and knew he had to leave. He spoke quietly, but with great emphasis. 'In the past few years my family and I have continued to support St Michael's despite our distaste for the doctrine being disseminated. But as long as Francis remains in post, we will not be crossing the threshold again. Others will follow suit. I advise you to reconsider your decision.'

He turned on his heel and strode through the hall, almost bumping into William, the second youngest son.

'William, I'm sorry.' He put his hand on the young man's shoulder, and let himself out without waiting for the housemaid.

Chapter Twenty-Two

'So, you see, the doctor said *I* could go to church even though the family bain't going, that way I can come home and tell'n if I was the only one there, or no.'

Miss Wilcox tugged self-importantly at her best jacket to straighten it, and looked at the reflection of her hat in the glass door of the kitchen dresser.

'What'll 'ee do if *he*'s there?' Ann asked. 'Would 'ee walk out?' She could not imagine being brave enough to do such a thing.

'Of course I will!' She turned to face Ann and Sarah, who had paused in their work to hear the news. Her face clouded a little. 'Though I must say I hope I wouldn't be the only one to do it. Then I'm coming home, I'm not gwain to my cousin's this week, there's too many yer needs my help.'

Although Ann usually enjoyed Sundays without Miss Wilcox's eagle-eyed presence, and having Miss Lucy's help instead, on this occasion she was glad she would be returning. Every time she saw Miss Lucy, she was overcome with pity for her, and it did not feel right to be asking her if she had seen the big serving dish, or whether more carrots were needed.

They were all waiting to hear whether Reverend Francis would leave the town. It had seemed that he would not, but then something else had happened.

'Listen to this!' Miss Wilcox had said, holding up the newspaper. 'The Chairman of the Workhouse Guardians says as Reverend Francis can't be the Workhouse chaplain no more. *He has brought discredit upon himself and his office,*' she said, reading from the newspaper, '*by his familiarity with Miss Lucy Jones, daughter of Dr Jones.*' Ann and Sarah gasped at Miss Lucy's name being in the newspaper again so soon, and promised to keep the paper hidden.

'The Chairman,' Miss Wilcox told them, 'is Mr Moore-Stevens, and you can't cross him! He always gets his way, the doctor told me so hisself.'

Ann had heard about Mr Moore-Stevens when she lived with her family near Shebbear, and had even seen him once when he rode past in his carriage.

'Quick! Curtsey!' her mother hissed, and they had both kept their gaze on the dusty road while they held their skirts and bent their knees, because it was said that Mr Moore-Stevens would punish anyone who did not curtsey or doff their cap to him when he passed. He was very important, so perhaps he would be able to make the curate leave the town. Miss Wilcox had heard that Reverend Francis would try to take the Sunday service at the Workhouse Chapel as usual that afternoon, and they were all keen to find out what would happen.

When Miss Wilcox had left for church, Ann went to the dining room to lay the table. She paused in the doorway; it was a task she and Miss Lucy usually did together on Sundays, and she enjoyed the shared work and companionship. The atmosphere in the house was very different now; they all felt they had to move around on tiptoe, being very careful not to say or do the wrong thing.

Today, Miss Polly – or Mrs Boxer as she must now remember to call her – and Mr Boxer were coming to luncheon, so she must lay for six. She shook out the tablecloth and spread it on the table, making sure that all the sides were of even length, but then, with the place mats in her hand, she wandered over to the window to look out at the garden. Miss Lucy was standing on the lawn with a flat wicker basket on her arm, cutting the dead flowers from the dahlias that grew tall in the border; Ann could just hear the snip-snip of her scissors. She was working slowly, and every now and then she stopped and stared straight ahead, although there was nothing to see. Perhaps some company would do her good. Boldly, Ann opened the window and called out to her.

'Please Miss, be there some flowers for the table? Some of they would look proper!'

Miss Lucy looked up and smiled. 'Oh yes, Ann, I'll pick some now.'

She came in a few minutes later with a bunch of bright dahlias; orange ones with deep red centres, and yellow ones with apricot tips to their petals.

'I'll put these in a vase, then I'll come and help you.'

'Oh Miss, you needn't, I can manage.'

'I know you can, Ann, but I've finished in the garden now.'

When she came back, she placed the vase in the centre of the table, then started laying the silverware while Ann found the glasses in the sideboard.

'It doesn't feel like a Sunday, Ann, does it? Father says next week we may go to Little Torrington Church, or perhaps St Giles in the Wood.'

Ann wondered whether she should mention Reverend Francis. She didn't want to upset Miss Lucy. 'I'm sure you'll be glad when things get back to normal, Miss.'

'I just want Reverend Francis to go, Ann! Nothing can be normal until then. Did you know he has been dismissed as chaplain of the Workhouse? I'm hoping he will *have* to leave the town now.'

So, she had heard; Ann was glad, it did not feel right to have secrets. 'I'm sure we'll all be glad when he does. You'll see, Miss, before long it'll all be over and done with, and you'll feel like it never happened!'

Lucy smiled sadly. 'I hope you're right, Ann.'

They continued working in companionable silence until the table was done.

'There we are, Ann, there's only the mustards and sauces to come from the kitchen now and I expect you'll do those later, won't you? I had better change out of this old dress now, look, I have pollen all down the front!'

'Don't worry, Miss, I'll sponge and press it for you later.'

She was watching admiringly as Miss Lucy walked up the stairs when the front door opened, and in came Miss Wilcox looking rather flustered.

'Oh, you'm back already! What happened?'

'He came! He were there!' As she bustled in, Miss Lucy came back down the stairs and Mrs Jones appeared at the door of the drawing room to hear what she had to say.

'There were only a handful of us in the church, twenty or thereabouts I'd say – all them empty pews and every footfall echoing! – and I were sitting near the back so I were the first to see him as he walked up the aisle along with Reverend Buckland. I were that shocked to see him!'

'How did he look?' Sarah had come from the kitchen to hear the news.

'Peaky, I'd say. Like something's keeping him awake in the night, and so it should.' She gave a grunt of disapproval.

Ann glanced over at Miss Lucy; she was standing at the foot of the stairs as still as a statue.

'So, what happened, Mary?' asked Mrs Jones.

'Soon as ever he reached the front of the church, Mr and Mrs Doe got up.'

'Mr Doe! He hasn't been to St Michael's for months!'

'Well, he came this time and soon as he got up, so did Mr and Mrs Stoneman, and then Mr and Mrs Lake and Mrs Colling and half a dozen others and they all walked right out of the church and I followed on behind. I'm glad I did too!'

'Was Mrs Francis there?' Miss Lucy asked quietly. The colour had drained from her face, Ann wanted to reach out to her, but did not like to with Miss Wilcox and Mrs Jones there.

'Yes, she were, with the little maid too, poor mite.'

'Was there much conversation outside the church?' asked Mrs Jones.

'Well, folks gathered together you know, and I heard Mr Lake say that the situation can't go on like this, but I didn't like to join 'em so I came on home.'

'You did well, Mary, it took some courage to walk out.' She turned to Ann and Sarah. 'Now, this is nothing to do with you two and you have work to do! I'm sure the luncheon isn't ready yet.'

Ann hurried back to the kitchen to help prepare the meal.

'Could 'ee ever credit such a thing?' asked Sarah. 'You never hear of the Methodists getting in a stew like that! Where will it all end?'

> THE CURATE RESUMING HIS DUTIES.—For some weeks previous to Sunday last, in consequence of the reports in circulation respecting the conduct of the Rev. H. O. Frances when he met a lady parishioner on the Common on the 18th August last, the reverend gentleman has taken no part in the Sunday services at the Church or Union Chapel. After the hearing of the charge made by Mr. Frances against Wm. Balkwill before the Borough Justices on Wednesday in last week, it appears that the vicar (who probably is acting under the authority of the Bishop) considered that there was no reason why the curate should not resume his usual duties at St. Michael's Church. Accordingly on Sunday morning last Mr. Frances was present, and at the appointed time emerged from the vestry in his robes and took up his customary position at the desk on the north side of the reredos. Scarcely had he done this when several respectable people left the church in ill-concealed disgust. The vicar preached the sermon on the occasion from the words "Judge not, that ye be not judged," &c., and gave some very good advice to his audience about "first casting out the beam out of their own eyes, before seeking to cast out the mote of their brother's eye," &c. Some little curiosity was excited with respect to the usual afternoon's service at the Union Chapel, especially as a report had been circulated that the chairman of the Board (and donor of the chapel) had given directions to the Union Master to lock the door against the curate if he should attend. Several persons went to the Union Chapel, but found the door closed. They, however, waited some time in the rain, and when the time for the service had considerably passed without the curate putting in an appearance, they returned home.

North Devon Journal, 1879

When she had finished clearing up after luncheon, Ann changed her dress and went to call for George at his lodgings in Calf Street, where she found him waiting for her at the door.

'There you be! I thought you must've gone to chapel instead!'

'Course not!' He was looking handsome in his Sunday coat and with his curly hair neatly combed. She took his arm happily and they set off for a walk while she told him what had happened at the church that morning.

'Have 'ee heard he's banned from going to the Workhouse Chapel?' he asked. 'Let's call by there, see what happens.'

The chapel, being set behind the Workhouse, was invisible from the road, but by walking up New Street and taking the path across the Common, they could make their way to the back entrance. This was also the quickest way for Reverend Francis to walk from his house, so they were sure to see him if he tried to get into the chapel.

It was a grey, windless afternoon with the threat of rain in the air. As they turned off the road, the steep valley leading down to the village of Taddiport came into view, and a chink of sunlight found its way through the clouds, illuminating the ochres, russets and browns of the pockets of woodland on the far side of the valley, and the cows and sheep dotting the patchwork of green fields. When they stopped to admire the view, George pulled her close to his side and she leaned her head on his shoulder for a moment, breathing in his Sunday scent of soap and clean linen, overlaid with something more masculine. She always treasured dry Sundays; when the weather was wet, they had no choice but to go to chapel where the chairs were hard and the sermons long, and even surreptitious hand-holding was frowned upon.

As they approached the wall marking the boundary of the Workhouse garden where vegetables were grown by the inmates, she saw that there was already a large group of people standing by the back entrance.

'What be gwain on?'

George laughed. 'I reckon us isn't the only ones looking for some fun!'

There were men and women of all ages in the crowd, although no one from the better classes. Ann recognised one or two, and guessed that most lived nearby on New Street. The back of the chapel was visible from their vantage point, and Torridge Villa, where Reverend Francis lived, lay just a few hundred yards further along the path. He was sure to come this way.

'A man came half an hour since and locked the chapel door,' a woman told them. ''Us wants to see the curate's face when he finds he can't get in!'

Those around her laughed, but Ann could not help feeling apprehensive. 'Be us doing wrong by waiting here?' she whispered to George.

'Course not, 'tis the Common, us can do as us please! Us can wait here all day if us wants, 'tis our Common, they can't make us leave!'

They waited for ten minutes or more, gazing up at the bleak walls of the Workhouse beyond the vegetable garden, and along the path in the hope of seeing an approaching figure in black, but none came, and they began to grow weary.

'I reckon he's heard 'tis locked,' a woman said, and a few people began to drift away.

'Just as well,' said another, 'why should those poor folk have to listen to him just 'cos they're in the Workhouse? *They've* got no Baptist or Wesleyan chapel to go to and it idn't fair.'

Eventually, two people coming along the path created a buzz of interest amongst the group, but it soon became apparent that neither of them was the curate, and as the couple drew nearer, Ann recognised Lizzie and Will. Lizzie seemed startled to see the group of people on the path, and looked relieved when Ann moved forward to speak to her.

'What's going on yer?' she asked.

It was an awkward thing to describe because when she tried to put it into words, it seemed to Ann that it would have been cruel to laugh at Reverend Francis, had he tried to get into the chapel. 'Can us walk with 'ee and I'll explain?'

Lizzie shook her head sadly when she heard the story. 'A man came to tell 'im the chapel was locked, that's why he didn't go. I know he's made mistakes, and I s'pose he really should leave the town now, but oh, Ann, if you could have heard 'im this last week or so! He don't worry about me hearing, nor the Missis neither, and I feel so very sorry for 'em, but so wearied of it all too!'

George and Will had walked on ahead, having lost interest in the curate, so Ann and Lizzie were free to talk openly together. Probably Will had heard the story already, but Ann did not feel George should know what was going on in the curate's household, although she could not quite have said why that was.

'So what does he have to say?'

'One minute he's downcast, desperately so, says he's frit they'll all be in the Workhouse before the month is out, then next minute he's glad and laughing, certain he'll be given a new job as vicar of a big parish somewhere; that was after the bishop said he'd stand by him. And now he knows he's not the Workhouse chaplain no more, he's wailing an' complaining again, says they can't live without the money an'll have to go away or starve. But then, just before I came out, he was saying it was wrong to shut him out of the Workhouse Chapel and he would write to London to complain. And those poor chiels hear it all along with me, standing there listening with their eyes wide!'

'They say he'll never win against Mr Moore-Stevens, no one can.'

'I know,' said Lizzie, 'I heard that too, but once Reverend Francis gets a notion in his head, there's no stopping 'im.'

It was appalling, but fascinating too, to imagine the scene at Torridge Villa. 'What 'bout Mrs Francis?'

'Oh, Ann, I feel that sorry for her! Her does her best to cheer 'im up, speaks calm and sensible to 'im when he's all worked up, but then I hear her crying when her's alone in the bedroom. I went into her once when I couldn't bear to hear it no more, and her clung on to me, crying *What's to become of us? What's to become of my children?*'

Lizzie's voice was unsteady, and she had to stop talking for a while. Ann put her arm around her friend's waist.

'You can't do more than that. I'm sure her's comforted to have you there.'

'Maybe. But I keep wondering when I'll have to look for a new job.'

''Tis hard at Castle House too, but not so bad as that. Does Mrs Francis believe the stories about him and Miss Lucy?'

'Her says not, her says folks have made it all up, but I've seen her look at him sometimes as if her's wondering if there's any truth in it. An', of course, her doesn't want to see Miss Lucy.'

'Those stories bain't true, though! For sure they bain't!'

'I suppose not.'

Lizzie looked thoughtful, and Ann wished she could make her see that however foolish the curate might be, Miss Lucy would not have done anything wrong.

So involved had they been in the conversation, they found they had crossed the road without even noticing and were now walking down the hill towards the stream.

'Look,' said Lizzie, 'us have just passed the hollow where they'm supposed to have met!'

Ann looked back. It was plain to see how the ground dipped suddenly to form a deep trench, and she could imagine how anyone going into it would be hidden from sight.

'Well, us won't go back to look at it.' George was busy talking to Will and she did not want him to make fun of the meeting in the hollow.

It was not something to laugh about; there was far too much heartache for that.

Yet again, Dr Jones turned restlessly in his bed. He could not make himself comfortable. It did not help that the room was cold; there was a frost tonight, the first of the autumn, Diamond's hoofs had slipped a little on the sparkling road when he returned from his final call. Perhaps he should have told Ann that he required a fire but it had been late, and he had not had the heart to ask her to bring up the coals.

Ever since Lucy's fateful meeting on the Common, and in the weeks since the hearing at the Town Hall, his sleep had been restless. There had been no respite, because almost every day there was some new development.

Of course, few of his patients and acquaintances spoke openly to him of the affair, knowing that his own daughter was implicated in it, but he had come to realise that it was the curate they were interested in, the curate they wanted to be rid of, and the young lady was of no importance.

But she was important to him. She was his daughter, her prospects were now irreparably damaged, and his reputation was also affected.

There was the matter of the Workhouse Chapel. Because Moore-Stevens had locked Francis out, and demanded that he resign, the curate had made a formal complaint against him. How could the man be so foolish? He was merely adding fuel to the fire because Moore-Stevens would be enraged by someone making a complaint against him – the doctor knew that only too well – and goodness knows what retribution would result.

Every time there was a new development, there was another article in the local press, and his daughter was again brought to the public's attention. This week it had been the story of the outgoing mayor, Mr Mallett. It was the custom on the last Sunday before the mayoral election for the mayor and the corporation to put on all their finery and process from the Square to the parish church in the company of the officers and members of the Volunteer Corps. When the bugle sounded, a crowd had gathered to see them process to St Michael and All Angels. It was noticed that there were surreptitious smiles and knowing glances amongst the company as they set off, striking up with *Onward Christian soldiers, marching as to war*, then they strode right past the entrance to the church, continuing along New Street and out of the town. There was much bemusement as the crowd followed them part way down the hill towards the railway station, until eventually the followers turned back, not being in the mood for a lengthy walk. It was later understood that the company had continued all the way to Frithelstock for the service at St Mary and St Gregory, finding a march of more than two miles preferable to attending the church associated with Reverend Francis.

As for that fellow Balkwill, he had now made his true colours known. At the hearing he was portrayed as a poor working man who had been dragged into the affairs of those who should be setting him an example, but within a week he had savagely beaten his wife and her sister, and when Constable Howe was called, he attacked him as well, punching him in the mouth and breaking the strap on his helmet. He had been sentenced to six weeks in Exeter Gaol. Meanwhile, his brother had been sentenced to two weeks' hard labour for indecently assaulting a girl on a dark lane near Cranford. Their father, Samuel, visited him in Torrington lock-up and was afterwards fined ten shillings for using obscene and abusive language outside the Town Hall.

It was sordid, all of it. His family was in the midst of something appalling, something so disgraceful he wondered whether the town would ever forget it, and all because of that wretch Francis.

It was a blessing that John remained in Sheepwash, the village being at a sufficient distance from Torrington to spare him daily exposure to the family's troubles. He had, nevertheless, turned up at the house once or twice too inebriated to return home after a night in the town's public houses, and had blamed his distress at his sister's humiliation. Probably it was true – John was very fond of Lucy – but having an inebriated son staggering around the town's inns did nothing to enhance the family's reputation.

John had mentioned that there was much laughter in the public houses about plans for revelry on the Fifth of November; no one had been willing to divulge the details, but the doctor felt a sense of foreboding. Feelings against the curate, both from those who were quietly determined to oust him, and those who were inclined to violence, were rising to dangerous levels. The previous year a small group of roughs, delighting in the opportunity to make fun of one of their superiors, had made an effigy of Francis and burnt it on the Common. It was Guy Fawkes' night in two days' time, and the doctor feared the sport would be repeated.

They surely could do no worse than that, could they?

Chapter Twenty-Three

Lucy pushed the darning needle through the wool one last time, and cut the end with the sewing scissors. She dropped the sock on to the stool, and sighed. There were two more of Charles's socks to darn, but she felt too restless to start another.

The lamp by her side cast a pool of light around her, and a second lamp illuminated the figure of her mother, fast asleep on the other side of the fire with her embroidery in her lap. The two bright lights intensified the gloom in the corners of the drawing room, and cast shadows on the deep reds and golds of the heavy curtains, tightly drawn to shut out the November night. The room was silent but for the ticking of the glass-domed clock on the mantlepiece, and an occasional genteel snore from her mother.

The surgery bell had rung shrilly half an hour earlier, followed by a demand for her father's help at a difficult birth. He had asked Charles to accompany him, declaring it to be a valuable learning opportunity. Lucy tried to imagine the young woman's feelings; would her relief at seeing help arrive overcome her embarrassment at having two men witness the most intimate and dramatic of moments?

How quiet this room was by comparison, and how dull. She would read for a while, the darning could wait. She rose to fetch the book which she had left in her bedroom.

There was enough light from the chandelier in the hall to light the way up the stairs so she did not trouble to take a candle, but felt her way into the dark bedroom and over to the bed where the book lay on the counterpane. The curtains were not yet drawn, and something caught her eye. Was it a light? She moved over to the French window. The moon, almost full but partly obscured by thin cloud, allowed her to make out the silhouette of the lilac tree by the wall, and the apple trees at the end of the lawn. But there was something else; a dancing light in the lane beyond the garden, and then another beyond the bowling green, moving up and down and from side to side like fireflies, but surely much bigger than insects if she could see them from such a distance.

She pressed her face against the cold glass and, as she watched, more lights appeared as if by magic, waving and bobbing as if they had a life all their own. She saw that they were flames, yet this was not a conflagration for they appeared to be suspended above the ground, burning nothing but air. Drawing her shawl about her against the cold, she opened the French window and went out on to the balcony.

There was a roar, a deep, prolonged *Woaah!* Was it the roar of flames? Was something alight? But there was no house out there to burn, no trees beyond the garden, nothing but the smooth sward of the bowling green and then the Common, falling away to the river far below.

The noise continued, a low rumbling now rather than a roar, and more dancing lights appeared beyond the garden, where usually there was only silence and the occasional slow glide of an owl.

What could it be? She felt she was in the throes of a strange dream where all was confusion, where nothing made sense. Then, perhaps the clouds drifted away from the moon, or maybe the swaying lights increased to illuminate the scene, but as she gripped the balcony rail and peered out into the gloom she made out human shapes, moving, gathering, their numbers increasing, and she realised that the rumbling was the sound of many voices. What were people doing out there on the bowling green? Now that she had discerned them, her sight became clearer; there were a lot of people, a hundred, perhaps more, some holding flaming torches above their heads and all facing in her direction as if she were on a stage and they formed the audience. How strange it was, and how fortunate that she stood here in the darkness, invisible.

Then, as she watched, a figure rose up above the others in awkward, jerky movements, almost falling sideways before straightening again. How tall it was! Could it be human? Then torches were raised as men clambered on to the shoulders of others and in the light of those torches she saw its black clothes, its face, its ghastly grin.

It was Reverend Francis.

For a moment she believed it really was the curate, that the crowd had found him wandering on the Common, but then she saw the way the awful figure bobbed up and down, lurching sideways as if inebriated, and she knew that it was a mere puppet, an effigy made in malice.

Why had it been brought here? Why come to the bowling green?

The crowd was roaring now and there was the blowing of horns and the crashing of drums, sounds that must surely be heard all around the town, and as the noise increased another figure rose up beside the first, wobbled, steadied, then as the torches were lifted again she saw its face. Her face.

It could not be. But there it was, the prim mouth, the dark eyes, the brown hair looped back from the face. And the dress. Her green dress, the shade exact, the high neck, the flounces.

Why? Why were they doing this?

She watched, transfixed. She could not move. And then she realised; the crowd was not the audience; *she* was the audience. They were here to show her this.

The two figures - Reverend Francis, herself - moved towards each other. The noise from the crowd grew louder, roars of laughter, chanting, she could not make out the words. The figures met, their faces pressed together, she knew they were kissing.

Her legs weakened, she tightened her grip on the balcony rail. *Father!* But it would be no use to call, he was not here. There was only her mother, the servants.

The figures moved again. She could not look away. By some subterfuge, some sleight of hand, the hem of the green dress, her green dress, rose. Instinctively she grabbed her skirt, held it down, as the skirt of her alter ego was lifted up beyond her waist, the figure of Reverend Francis moved forward and, as the roar of the crowd grew still louder, began to thrust against her.

'Lucy!'

When an arm came around her she screamed, and her legs buckled.

'Quickly! Come away!'

She was in the bedroom, Charles was guiding her to a chair.

'What were you doing out there? Lucy! Did you see…?'

She could not answer.

'Why were you out there, Lucy?' He leapt up to draw the curtains, returned to her.

'I didn't know what was happening. It's dark, they couldn't see me.'

'Lucy.' He took her hands. 'You were standing in the moonlight.'

She could not speak.

'Look, it's all right now.' He held her hand tightly. 'Stay here, don't get up, I've asked Harry to lock all the doors, I'll make sure he's safe then I'll be back.'

She sat in the dark room. She could hear the roar of the crowd. Was it getting closer? Was that awful figure of Reverend Francis coming this way? Suddenly Charles was back, beside her again.

'Why have you locked the doors?' She was almost afraid to hear the answer.

'Just in case. It's probably not necessary.' He went to the window, moved the curtain an inch or so. 'I think they're moving away. They'll be going to Torridge Villa.' He spoke quietly, as if to himself.

'Torridge Villa?' she cried. 'Why?'

'To put on the same show. Lucy, you know what this is, don't you? A skimmington, rough music as it is sometimes called. They will go to each of the houses…' he hesitated, unsure how to continue.

'I know what it is. I didn't at first, but I do now.' She was appalled. 'But they're wrong! I've done nothing!'

'I know, Lucy, I know.'

'And Mrs Francis! Will she see that? She mustn't! Where is Father?'

'He had to continue to the confinement, he couldn't turn back. As we rode out on the Huntshaw road, we saw many people walking into town, some of the men masked, some carrying horns to blow or pots and pans to strike. We guessed what they were about and I returned at a gallop, but I'm so sorry I was not in time to save you that sight…' His voice broke.

'But Mrs Francis mustn't see it, we must stop it!'

'Lucy, we cannot. There is nothing we can do. It is a very large crowd and growing all the time, I saw people coming from all directions. If we could have got a message to Torridge Villa, told them to lock the doors and stay away from the windows, - but it is too late now.' He peeped through the curtains again. 'The crowd is moving on already. They will go along Castle Hill, it will not take them long.'

She pictured that dreadful effigy in the dress that was so like hers, being carried along the path in the dark, the torches illuminating the way, the grazing sheep scrambling away in terror from the sight. It was as if she were really there, with the figure of the curate swaying at her side along the path to Torridge Villa, to repeat the performance...

'Lucy, look at me. Come on, that's right. We will go downstairs now. We will sit by the fire in the drawing room. Mary Wilcox is sitting there with Mother. Up you get now.'

'Does Mother know?' She could not bear it.

He hesitated. 'She knows why the crowd was there, but she did not see what you saw, Lucy.'

'I'm going out! I'm going to try to stop it!' Ann looked wildly around the kitchen. 'Where's my jacket?'

'Ann, you can't! What'll Miss Wilcox say?' Sarah grabbed her arm. 'Besides, 'tis too dangerous! You saw what they'm like!'

The three of them had gone out into the yard when they heard the shouting. They crept around the house together and had seen the crowd gathering beyond the garden wall, heard the shouts and the laughter. They ran back inside then, knowing beyond doubt what was happening.

'I'm going to find George! His uncle's been made mayor again, he'll be able to stop it! He'll call in the constables! George needs to know!' She found her jacket hanging on the back of the scullery door, and as she pushed her arms into the sleeves they heard the roar of the crowd grow still louder, and the clamour of pots and pans being struck.

LIZ SHAKESPEARE

'Ann, do be careful, there's awful rough types out there! But
what about Miss Wilcox? What'll I tell her?'

'Her won't notice I'm gone, her's too busy with the Missis.
But tell her I'm sick and have gone to bed if you have to. Now
let me out the back door, will 'ee?'

Castle Street was quite deserted, but she hurried from the
safety of one streetlight to the next, reassured by the soft pools
of gold cast by the gas lamps. Surely George would be at home.

Two men were walking quickly along Calf Street, then a
group of lads laughing and talking excitedly.

'Come on, us mustn't miss it!' one said.

The crowd was shouting in the distance, but it was impossible
to discern whether they were still at Castle House or whether
they had started to move towards Torridge Villa. If only she
could warn Lizzie! For a moment she hesitated, wondering
whether she should go there first.

Her heart was beating fast as she knocked at George's door.
He *must* be in. She waited, longing for the reassurance of his
arms around her, but there was no light in the front window, nor
the sound of footsteps in the hallway. She knocked one more
time, then turned away.

Where could he be? Then she thought of the lads hurrying
along the street, and with a rush of anger she guessed that
George, too, had gone to watch that dreadful entertainment. He
would not be able to keep away, and she despised him for it.

She walked slowly back along the street. If she could find
him, perhaps she could show him how wrong it all was; perhaps
it would not be too late to find his uncle. She made up her mind,
and began to walk quickly along New Street to reach the western
edge of the Common.

She had assumed that the people would gather within view of
Torridge Villa, but beyond the boundary wall of the cemetery
there was a very large crowd gathered close to the hollow where
Reverend Francis and Miss Lucy were supposed to have met.
Another group was chanting and singing loudly as they marched
up the hill from the direction of the railway station. The leader
was a man wearing women's clothing, the skirt dragging along
behind him, others were wearing scarves over their faces and

carrying old pots and pans to bang together. As they drew nearer, she made out the words of the chant that they were roaring out, and which was soon taken up by the waiting crowd.

Us saw him! Us saw him!
In the hollow with a lady, and his hands inside her gown,
Us saw him! Us saw him!
He said that us was sinners, but look who's sinning now!

She backed away until she felt the cemetery wall behind her. There was violence in their voices; there was no telling what they would do. She should go home, there was nothing George or the mayor could do, half a dozen constables could not stop this. Keeping close to the wall on her left she started trying to push through the crowd to get back to the road, but more and more people were arriving all the time, men wearing masks, men carrying cow horns or makeshift drums, women too, their faces glowing with excitement, and all were pushing forwards to get closer to the hollow.

The noise of the chanting and the smell of unwashed bodies was overwhelming as face after face loomed out of the darkness towards her, all of them unknown. Where was George? Why could he not think of her, and come to find her? She pushed her way back to the edge of the throng and stood up on a little hummock of grass with her back to the cemetery wall. At least here she was out of the way of the main thrust of the crowd so might be able to see George if he passed close by, and as soon as the crowd thinned she would go home to the warmth of her bed. If only she had never left!

After a few minutes, a shout went up.

They'm coming!

Lights were swaying and dancing up the road that crossed the Common, then, as they got closer, she saw that they were flaming torches carried by another throng of people; this was the crowd that she had seen from Castle House, they had been to Torridge Villa.

There was a roar of laughter, cheering. Everyone was watching the approaching mob. And then she saw her.

It was Miss Lucy, held up on the shoulders of the crowd, they had got her.

'No! No, please!' She screamed as she tried to push into the crowd.

'I must help her! They can't do this!' She was sobbing, but a woman held her back, spoke kindly to her.

'Harken to me! Look at me, maid!'

Ann looked, she had a kind face, perhaps she would help...

''Tis only a puppet! 'Tisn't really her! Look again!'

'A puppet?'

The woman was holding her shoulders, looking into her face.

'You a friend of hers? You'm as white as she is, look! Her face is made from a bedsheet!'

Ann looked at the approaching figure. It *was* Miss Lucy, her arched brows, her dark hair, and that dress, an exact match or nearly so, but the face was indeed white. It did not have life.

'Come back where you was, maid, 'tis safer there.'

The woman pulled her back through the crowd until she was back on the hummock, her head a little above the others. It was then, by the light of the torches, that she saw Reverend Francis.

Of course, she should have realised, they would not have made an effigy of Miss Lucy alone. There was his white collar, his black coat, his face with lips pursed and eyes wide as if he were shocked at what he saw, there at the end of a long pole, above the heads of the crowd. The two figures were now being carried side-by-side and the chant started up again.

He said that us was sinners, but look who's sinning now!

The woman next to her laughed.

'They'm taking 'em to the hollow and I can guess what they'll be up to there! Wish I was close enough to see!'

Ann could not reply. She felt she were turned to stone. She looked towards the road, but the way was still quite impassable. More people were running up the hill now to join in the excitement, they came from Frithelstock perhaps, or Monkleigh.

There were roars of laughter from the direction of the hollow. She leaned back against the wall and closed her eyes for a moment, relieved she could not see the horror of what was occurring there, feeling sick to her stomach that Miss Lucy should be involved in this.

But before long, the effigies were carried back again, their clothes grubby and stained now from the violation that had been enacted. Miss Lucy's head was leaning at a strange angle as if her neck had been broken. They were set on a platform a short distance away, and a man leapt up beside them. She saw that the platform had been built above a large pile of wood.

'You saw what 'ee did!' he yelled at the crowd.

Us saw him! Us saw him! they roared in reply.

He said that us was sinners, but look who's sinning now!

'And what do us do to sinners?'

This produced a cacophony of shouted answers and the clanging of pots and pans.

'Burn 'em!' yelled a man in front of Ann, and others took up the cry. Looking towards the road, in the hope of finding a way out, she saw another group of people, about fifty strong. They stood in twos and threes at a decorous distance from each other, and there was no shouting or waving of arms. It was too dark to see them clearly, but Ann knew that they came from the better classes of the town.

'Look!' she said to the woman next to her. 'Even they cannot keep away!'

The woman laughed. 'Everyone likes a bit of fun, maid.'

'But it's so cruel! Miss Lucy's done nothing wrong!'

The woman looked at her curiously. 'Do 'ee work for her? I do feel a bit sorry for her I must admit, but not for the curate! Not after the things he said about us! Why should us put up with it!'

Something was happening on the platform; Ann did not want to look, but could not help herself. While flaming torches were held up so that everyone could see, two men climbed up on to the platform and between them lifted a large bucket which they tipped over the heads of the effigies, coating them in a thick, black substance.

The crowd went wild, the commotion intensified by the crackling and booming of fireworks being ignited somewhere near the hollow. Ann closed her eyes, and when she opened them again a white sheet was being shaken over the figures to release a cloud of feathers, many of which stuck to the tarred effigies while others floated away into the darkness, much to the hilarity of the onlookers who leapt up to catch them.

She was glad, afterwards, that the tarring and feathering had been carried out, for the figures were then barely recognisable as Miss Lucy and the curate. If they had retained their likenesses, she did not think she could have borne what was to follow but, even so, the event stayed with her for many months, disturbing her sleep and distracting her from her work.

Orders were shouted for the crowd to stand back, then men carrying flaming torches moved forward, one to each corner of the platform, and they bent to ignite the huge woodpile beneath it. As the flames leapt up, engulfing the feet of the effigies, there was a terrible cacophony of horns being blown, pans being clashed, jeering and cheering. When the green dress started to burn, Ann covered her mouth with her hands, trying to remind herself that it was not Miss Lucy who was burning, it was a merely a puppet, a cruel likeness covered now in tar and feathers. Nevertheless, as the flames leapt ever higher, orange, red and yellow tongues of fire reaching up to the face, the hair, she cried out and would have fallen if the woman beside her had not grasped her arm.

'Come on, maid, 'tis only a bit of cloth and some feathers remember!'

She leant against the woman, glad of the human warmth. It was a cold night, but the heat of the fire was intense even where they stood, and she knew that her shivering was not due to the temperature. The fire crackled and roared, the flames surging so high they must surely be seen for miles around, and a column of black smoke reached high above the Common. As she watched, it billowed out into a dark cloud which spread across the sky until it obscured the almost full moon.

'What's that?' Could it be snowing? Dozens of fluttering white flakes floated over her head and she reached up to catch one, but quickly shook it away from her hand when she saw what it was. In the heat, some of the feathers were breaking away from the effigies and being carried on the breeze towards the town.

The fire was enormous now, and the shapes of the effigies could only just be seen in the midst of the conflagration. She could not look away until at last the dark shapes crumbled and fell.

The woman looked anxiously into her face. 'You'd best head for home, maid, soon as ever you can get out of this crowd. A warm bed is what you need. I'll walk along with you if you want. 'Tis a dark night.'

She did not feel strong enough to walk through the town alone. There would be crowds of people on the streets, many of whom would, no doubt, make their way to the public houses when the dreadful entertainment drew to a close.

'That's kind of 'ee. Could you walk to the beginning of Castle Street with me? I'd be safe from there on.'

It was then that she looked for one last time at the burning platform and the smouldering pile of fabric which was all that was left of the effigies.

One of the four men who had started the conflagration threw his torch on to the pyre and turned away, pulling the scarf from his face.

It was George.

He had been there all along. He had helped to make this happen.

As she pushed through the crowd towards him, never in her life had she been so angry.

She threw herself at him, pulling at his hair. He whirled around and grabbed her wrists.

'What the devil?'

'How *dare* you! How dare you do such a dreadful thing!' She fought to escape from his grasp, wanting to scratch and bite like a wild animal. 'I've been trying to find you!' she screamed. 'And all the time you were the one doing it! Let go of me!' She fought against his grip. 'Why didn't you tell me what you was doing!'

'I weren't going to tell you! Why should I? You'd only try to stop it.'

He released her wrists but held his hands high to ward off any further attack.

'Of course I would! It were terrible, how could you do such a cruel thing! Suppose Miss Lucy had seen it...'

He laughed, his blue eyes shining with pleasure. 'Oh, her saw it! Her saw it all right, stood right there on the balcony!'

She struggled, at first, to take in his meaning. 'Her was on the balcony? And you was there, outside Castle House?'

'Yes! Pity there idn't a balcony at Torridge Villa as well, us couldn't have done it better if us had planned it!'

He meant it. He felt no remorse whatsoever. She stared at him, and her heart turned to ice.

'I *hate* you, George Chapple! I hate you for what you've done and I never, ever want to see you again.'

Shaking with anger and disappointment, she turned and pushed back through the dwindling crowd, never pausing when he called plaintively after her.

'Ann! Don't be silly, maid, please! I'm sorry, honest I am!'

But he did not try to follow her as she strode back through the town, and the people who had gathered on dark street corners and outside the public houses moved out of her way, perhaps sensing that any attempt to interfere with her would lead to trouble.

It was the worst night of her life.

GUY FAWKES.—The celebration of this annual event here on Wednesday night last was carried out upon a scale and in a manner to attract an immense concourse of people, and it is computed that between 2,000 and 3,000 persons assembled on the spot, to witness the unusual display of fire-works, &c. The principal feature in the programme was a procession from the Barley Grove to the Hollow on the Common, which consisted of a number of men, wearing masks, and carrying two effigies (male and female), with a number of torches. To avoid passing through the streets they went down over Castle Hill and then mounted the Common. A pile of wood was prepared on the common just above the memorable Hollow, and on the procession reaching this spot, one of the party (masked) got on the top of a barrel, and read a paper to the effect that the two effigies had been found under very suspicious circumstances : their case had been brought before public opinion which had found them guilty, and sentenced to be tarred, feathered, and burnt as a caution to other young persons not to do likewise. A short visit was then made to the Hollow, and on returning with the effigies they were fixed on the pile, and the whole was soon consumed. A number of tar barrels were burnt and fireworks let off on the green.

North Devon Journal, 1879

Chapter Twenty-Four

In the days following the burning, Lucy hardly knew when it was day and when it was night. She went to bed earlier than the rest of the family but, once free of their well-meaning but ineffectual attempts to distract her, she relived the events of November the Fifth again and again. She saw Reverend Francis' white face with its ghastly fixed grin coming closer, and her limbs tensed as the memories played out before her. How could she have been so stupid as to go out on to the balcony? Why did she not realise that she could be seen? She had made it so much worse. When eventually she fell asleep, she was woken frequently by her body convulsing in terror at the sound of the wind in the chimney which, in her dream, resembled the roaring of flames. Then, as often as not, she would fall into a deep sleep shortly before dawn, and wake at ten or eleven o'clock in the morning, a cup of cold tea at her bedside.

She had asked her father to tell her exactly what had happened after the crowd left Castle House. He had been reluctant to divulge anything, of course, but she explained that she had to know the truth, or her imagination would conjure even worse scenarios. If she ever went out into society again, she would want to know exactly what people were thinking when they stared at her.

He told her that there was a large crowd, and that the effigies had been burned. He did not say that there were almost three thousand people, or that the effigies were taken to the hollow - she knew what would have been enacted there - or that they had been tarred and feathered before being burned. She found that information, along with her name, in the newspaper.

Three thousand people; that was almost the entire population of Torrington. Three thousand people came to see her being abused and burned. How they must hate her.

She should have realised that she should not spend time alone with Reverend Francis. She should have realised that he was developing feelings for her. It was her fault that this had happened.

During the daytime, she tried to occupy herself. She did some mending, tidied her father's surgery when he was out, polished the silver. But she found she had used dark blue thread on Charles's black jacket, and after sitting for two hours with the cutlery she left smears on the spoons because she had spent much of the time staring into space. She could not bear to be near her mother, but found some comfort in the kitchen, because the servants were gentle and considerate towards her.

On the second day, Polly came to see her. Lucy was sitting in the library watching the drops of rain running down the windowpane while beyond, in the garden, the wind tore the last withered leaves from the apple trees.

'How are you?' Polly sat alongside her on the window seat and held her hand.

What could she say? Polly looked fresh and young in her mauve dress, her fair hair looped attractively away from her face, her complexion perfect. *How can she bear to touch me?* Lucy thought. *Would she touch a stray dog on the street, a dirty, flea-bitten dog, something offensive? For that is what I must seem to her.*

'You look tired, dear. Are you sleeping?'

'No, not really.'

'Lucy, what happened was appalling, I can hardly believe it. I'm sorry that I didn't come yesterday but I did not like to leave the house, and Edwin thought it best that I should stay in. But today, two people greeted me quite sympathetically as I walked here, and Edwin feels there is much regret for the evening's events. One man told him that the bad feeling was all against Reverend Francis and many people thought it wrong that you had been included.'

'If they thought it wrong, why did they continue?' She did not want to discuss this with Polly, or with anyone.

'Edwin believes there were some very rough types present, many people had come in from the villages, and it is likely that, even if they had heard of Reverend Francis, they did not know who the female effigy represented.'

'Everyone in Torrington knew.' *Everyone*, she thought, *every single person knew that it was me.*

'But in time they will forget.' She took Lucy's hand again. 'In a few months it will be as if it never happened.'

If only that were so! 'Polly, they will never forget! You did not see it all, you did not see what I saw from the balcony, it was far worse that you could imagine! My name has been besmirched, for ever. Even if the events that caused it are ever forgotten, I will be seen as someone unfit for society, someone dishonourable, scandalous... I am only glad that you were able to marry before this happened, because I never will.' Her voice had become too unsteady, she could not go on.

Polly looked shocked, but did her best to comfort Lucy, reminding her that only a few days had passed, that time would heal.

'Mother wants me to go and stay with Cousin Jane in Wales,' Lucy told her. 'She is ashamed to have me in the house.'

Jane Herbert and her husband lived in a huge, draughty vicarage in a small Welsh village. Lucy had nothing in common with them, and they would undoubtedly disapprove of her.

'Oh, that would be dreadful! I will talk to Mother. Now, why don't we go upstairs together, I can do your hair for you, and we'll find you a clean dress.'

She meant well, of course, but Lucy did not have the energy for it. 'Anyway, it does not matter, there is no one here to see me,' she said.

'Then why don't you come to my house tomorrow? Spend the day with me, it would do you good to have a change of scene.'

It would be a relief to spend a day away from her mother's recriminations, but the thought of walking along the street to reach Polly's home terrified her.

'I cannot, not yet. But come and see me again soon, Polly.'

She felt a quiet horror at knowing that she could not leave the house.

Dr Jones watched the rain streaming down the carriage window. The high hedgebanks of the narrow lane obscured more distant views, except when a gateway allowed a glimpse of empty fields.

'Would a vapour bath not have helped Mrs Moore?'

Charles was trying to make notes with a pencil as the carriage creaked and swayed along the rutted lane. It was surprising that he could concentrate when there were so many mental distractions; perhaps he would not find it so easy if he were ever to become a father. A particularly sudden jolt of the carriage, which almost dislodged Charles's top hat, reminded the doctor that he had not replied.

'Not in someone so elderly, I think. I suspect there is also dropsy of the heart, you saw how short of breath she was. The diuretic we have given will suffice for now, but tapping may be necessary sometime in the future.'

The farm where Mrs Moore lived had been the last in a series of calls around the villages of Merton and Peters Marland, a journey which involved passing Winscott, the home of Mr Moore-Stevens. It was the machinations of that gentleman rather than Mrs Moore's dropsy that was occupying his mind.

Since the events of the Fifth of November, events that had shaken him to the core, many issues had preoccupied him. Francis had still not left the town, but was determined that he would again officiate in the Workhouse Chapel and, without that extra salary, he could not afford to stay. The doctor just wished him gone. But foremost, of course, was his concern for Lucy. He had observed how pale and withdrawn she was as she moved her food around her plate at mealtimes, but ate little, and he knew there was a danger that her dejection would develop into melancholia, for there was little to lift her spirits. Perhaps it would be better for everyone if she were to go and stay with her cousins; her presence in the house was dispiriting.

His concern for his daughter led, naturally enough, to anger at those who had caused her distress. Of course, there were many who would enjoy a spectacle without considering how it might damage others; it was thoughtless, but not malicious. His anger was directed at those who organised the event, knowing the anguish it would cause his daughter.

'The handbills that were distributed; the cost would have been significant, beyond the means of an ordinary working man.'

'Pardon?' Charles looked up from his notebook.

'The handbills. The engine driver, Pope, could not have met the cost of them without support.'

Francis has written a public letter to the London and South-Western Railway Company, complaining that Mr Henry Pope, an engine driver at Torrington Station, had organised the event and as such was not a fit person to continue in that employment.

Charles put away his notebook, and gave his father his full attention. Dr Jones knew he had been deeply shaken by the insult to his sister on that fateful evening.

'Do you think someone else was behind it?'

'The event had been carefully planned: the making of the effigies - their clothing would have been a significant expense; and the handbills advertising the event which no one would share with me, of course, until it was too late. Then there was the timing, who should meet at the Bowling Green, who should wait by the cemetery wall.'

'No, it was not something that happened spontaneously.'

Dr Jones looked out of the carriage window at the tower of Little Torrington Church in the distance. He was somewhat reluctant to voice his thoughts, but knew he could rely on his son's discretion.

'I believe Pope was the chief organiser and probably, as Francis has claimed, he collected money from passengers on the station platform to pay for it, but why would a working man risk his job in that way unless he was assured by someone in a position of power that he would not find himself in trouble?' He took a deep breath before he continued. 'Who is it who has organised a counter-petition in support of Pope? Who has made it his mission to rid the town of the curate?'

Charles stared at him. 'Moore-Stevens? Do you really think...?'

Mr Moore-Stevens had sent a petition to the London and South-Western Railway Company stating that Pope was a steady, reliable man, and the events of November the Fifth *were*

promoted and shared by the inhabitants of the town generally.
Moore-Stevens had obtained the signatures of more than a
hundred of the gentry and principal inhabitants of the town in
support of the petition.

'I believe that as soon as Francis lodged a complaint with the
Local Government Board at being locked out of the Workhouse
Chapel, his fate was sealed. One should not challenge Mr
Moore-Stevens! I may be wrong, but I would not be surprised if
he were behind the burning of the effigies. And now he will
ensure that the hearing of the Local Government Board will
result in the dismissal of the curate.' He sighed. 'Lucy will have
to give evidence again, but at least we shall then be rid of
Francis, at last.'

THE CURATE AND THE EFFIGIES.—It was thought
and hoped by many in this town that the burning of
effigies, &c., on the night of the 5th November would
constitute the last act in the drama of the painful scandal which has gathered around the curate, the Rev. H.
O. Frances. It appears, however, that such is not to be
the case, as the curate, assisted by a few of his friends,
has within the last few days sent a memorial to the Secretary of the London and South Western Railway
Company calling attention to the action taken by one of
their *employés* (Mr. Henry Pope) in connection with the
burning of the effigies. A copy of the memorial has
been forwarded to Mr. Pope, so that he may have an
opportunity of replying to the allegations laid to his
charge.

North Devon Journal, 1879

That evening, there were only a few patients in the waiting room.
It was a relief, for he was tired, but he resolved to see them alone
and sent Charles to keep Lucy company. The last patient was a
lad of fourteen or fifteen years old with a bandaged hand, who
shuffled into the surgery and sat looking at the floor.

'Well, what have we here?'

'Hurt my hand.' He lifted it an inch or two to indicate the problem.

'And are you going to let me see it?' He spoke encouragingly; young lads invariably found a visit to the doctor difficult. He moved his chair closer and untied the bandage. The hand was in a shocking state, swollen, purple and infected.

'How did you do this? You should have come to see me before!' He looked closer. 'It's a burn, is it not?'

The boy nodded, his gaze still fixed on the floor.

'Who has been dressing it for you?'

'My mam.'

'Well, your mam should have sent you to me several days ago.' He started to clean the wound. 'What were you doing, playing with fire?' Suddenly, he stopped. His patient raised his head and their eyes met. The boy's gaze was full of fear, and it was then that he knew.

He continued his work on the hand. 'The bonfire, was it? November the Fifth? Did you get too close?' He was careful to keep his touch gentle.

The boy nodded, clearly feeling ashamed. 'Thought I'd take a piece of clothing as a keepsake.' His voice was no more than a whisper.

The doctor controlled the impulse to yell with exasperation at the lad. 'Well, I hope you've learnt your lesson.' He kept his voice light. 'You had an enjoyable evening, no doubt, but the fire has hurt you, and it has hurt others also, very badly. Did you think of that?'

The boy, staring at his lap again, nodded. He looked rather as if he might cry.

When the wound was clean, the doctor applied Goulard's lotion and wrapped a clean bandage around the hand, keeping the fingers free as far as possible so that the boy might have some use of them.

'Where do you work?'

'Mr Chapple's tannery, Sir.'

'And have you been able to do your usual work?'

'The maister's put me in the packing room.'

'Very well. You need to keep this dry.'

When the boy stood and started to move towards the door, the doctor saw that his frayed trousers barely reached his ankles.

'Come back to see me in two days' time. I won't charge for redressing the hand.'

The boy muttered his thanks.

When the door had closed, Dr Jones shook his head ruefully. His anger had almost consumed him in recent days, but it was time to let it go. There were occasions, he thought, when doctoring could be a healing process for the doctor, as well as the patient.

Ann sat back on her heels. There was still half the length of the surgery passage and then the hall floor to wash before she could move on to a less onerous task. From the surgery, she heard a man cry out, then Dr Jones's reassuring voice. He was setting a broken arm, Miss Wilcox had said. Ann often heard cries and moans from beyond the surgery door, and sometimes there were drops of blood to mop from the entrance passage.

At least I have a job, she reminded herself, as she wrung out the floorcloth in the bowl of hot soapy water again. Her friend Lizzie had been told by Mrs Francis that the family would have left Torridge Villa by the time Christmas came, so she would need to look for a new post.

Perhaps when the New Year came, things would be easier. Perhaps she would be able to forget about George.

She did not feel as angry as before, just very sad.

She remembered how they used to meet on a Sunday afternoon, either at his house where he would try to pull her inside for a kiss before they set off for their walk, or in the Square where he would be leaning against the drinking fountain, looking handsome in his best Sunday coat. She remembered the sensation of his hand holding hers as he strode by her side, large and warm and protective, making her feel she would never have to worry about anything ever again.

But then there were the times when he did not consider her feelings.

'Well, aren't all young men thoughtless?' Sarah had said. 'Mine is steady, 'tis true, but then he's been through a lot, losing his wife and being left with a little chiel.'

Sarah had been kind to Ann when she returned to the house that night.

'Are you sure you'm doing the right thing?' she asked, when Ann was able to talk about it. 'I think George is quite handsome,' she blushed a little, 'and he's got very good prospects, you could be comfortable if you married him. You'm throwing all that away, remember!'

'But, Sarah, when I think about what he did! 'Tis worse than other people that night because he *knew* Miss Lucy'd done nothing wrong, but he went ahead regardless! He knew 'cos I'd told him, so either he was very cruel, or he set no store on what I'd told him time and time again. Either way I can't forgive him!'

She felt the tears starting again so rubbed harder with the floorcloth, cleaning four tiles at a time as she worked her way up the left side of the room.

She had hoped never to see George again, but he had started calling at the house. Right from the first evening after the burning, she heard him whistle outside the yard gate. She hurried back into the kitchen, but when she opened the kitchen door just a crack twenty minutes later, she heard him again, that low, questing whistle that reminded her of the call of a curlew, and used to make her heart pound with excitement rather than anxiety. He came the next evening, and the next, until finally Miss Wilcox heard him and demanded to know what was going on. Ann had to tell her that she was no longer walking out with George. She could not say that she had been out on November the Fifth so she told a white lie, saying that he had called to tell her he had been involved in the burning. Miss Wilcox was so indignant at this that she told Ann she was proud of her for doing the right thing.

'But you must go out now and make him see that you mean it, else he'll be out there whistling 'til Kingdom come.'

So, she went out. He tried to take her in his arms, but she pushed him away.

'I've only come to tell you not to come here.' She tried to sound stern, but her voice was shaking. 'I meant what I said, I don't want to see you again.'

'But, Ann! You can't say that!' He was distraught. 'Us is meant to be together! It were nothing, the other night, just a bit of fun, nothing compared to you and me!'

If he hadn't said that, she might have wavered. 'It were *not* nothing! If you could see the state poor Miss Lucy's in!' She tried to keep her voice low despite her fury. 'I can't ever forgive you that!'

He tried to persuade her to change her mind, their arguments and counter-arguments going back and forth until finally he strode off, shouting over his shoulder, 'All right then, see if I care!'

When she went back into the kitchen, she could not stop crying with the shock of it all. Miss Wilcox had pretended to be exasperated, but let her go upstairs to calm herself.

Now, there were all the Sunday afternoons to fill.

Reaching the final corner of the hall, she returned to the kitchen where Sarah was scouring pans in the scullery.

'Do you reckon you'll marry Henry Davey one day?' Ann asked.

Sarah glanced up. With her hair wrapped in a cloth and a scowl of concentration on her face, it occurred to Ann that she did not seem the sort of woman a man would immediately fall for.

'Probably. Samuel needs a mother, my parents can't look after him forever.'

'But do you love him?'

Sarah seemed taken aback. 'I like him well enough. Us have known each other for years.'

It did not seem much to Ann. 'Perhaps I won't marry. Perhaps I'll be a housekeeper like Miss Wilcox one day.'

'Would you want to be like her?'

Ann emptied the bowl of dirty water into the sink. 'I don't know,' she said, 'I don't know what I want.'

Chapter Twenty-Five

Lucy sat down at the little desk in the library. She was determined that she would, this time, do what had to be done but first, she carefully unfolded Rawlin's letter again. She would read it one more time, then she would place it with his other letters and lock them in the jewellery box that she had been given for her twenty-first birthday and never used. She would place the box at the back of her wardrobe and *never* read the letters again.

She raised her head and stared bleakly ahead. *Never*. That was a harsh word; maybe, when she was old and alone, she would allow herself to read them once more and remember what might have been.

Dearest Lucy, her eye ran over the loops and firm, downward strokes of the handwriting that had become so familiar, and so loved. *I was so pleased to receive your most recent letter. I could picture you enjoying your walk on the Common and I wished that I was by your side. A marsh fritillary! I don't believe I have seen one there before. There is a similar butterfly here but, like most things, it is larger than our native British one. By the time you read this letter, the butterflies will have long since departed, and you will be wrapped in your warmest coat for your walks on the wintry Common.*

It was eight weeks since she last walked on the Common. She went into the garden most days to throw a ball for Alpheus and look longingly over the garden wall at the distant hills with their narrow winding lanes and inviting field paths. She could hardly bear to picture her favourite spots on the Common, and experienced a quiet horror when she thought of the weeks and months of confinement inside Castle House. Her only outing was to be the ordeal of yet another hearing when she would again have to stand before an audience and relate the dreadful story in all its detail.

Both Edith and Polly had suggested she go out for a short walk with them. She knew they had her best interests at heart, but she could not go walking about the town or on the Common as if the public disgrace she suffered had never taken place.

Everyone who saw her would be reminded of the scandal; images of depravity would play out before their eyes, and they would turn away from her in disgust. It would not matter that she was innocent of any wrongdoing – her presence alone would distress people.

She had been reading Mr Hawthorne's *The Scarlet Letter*. Poor, dear Hester Prynne. Having had a child out of wedlock, she had to stand on the scaffold for three hours, exposed to public humiliation, and then wear a scarlet letter A, for adulteress, for the rest of her life. Hester made the letter herself in the most beautiful embroidery, as if determined that some good should come from it.

Lucy could not think that anything good would ever come from her humiliation. She could not be brazen about her shame as Hester Prynne had learned to be.

Rawlin, too, would find her loathsome when he heard of her disgrace.

He might have heard already. It was entirely possible that one of his many friends had written to him by now, not knowing that he had feelings for her. *There has been quite a scandal in Torrington concerning the curate and Lucy Jones, the papers are full of it. Who would have thought it of her? Quite the dark horse, Miss Lucy Jones.*

He would then write to express his utter disappointment in her, and to forbid any further contact. The thought of receiving such a letter made her sick to her stomach; she must write to him immediately; she had put it off long enough.

She took a sheet of paper from the box inside the desk, placed it on the blotter, and removed the cap from her pen.

Dear Rawlin,

It is with a heavy heart that I write this letter to you. I have valued your friendship ever since we were children together.

She paused, picturing the two of them playing on the Common, the way Rawlin chose her company above that of the other children, the consideration he showed her.

During your absence I have eagerly awaited the arrival of your letters, and I have cherished the hope that we might one day meet again. It causes me distress, therefore, to tell you that there can be no further letters and, should you ever return to England, there can be no meeting.

I have, quite unintentionally, become involved in a series of events which have resulted in my name being for evermore associated with feelings of revulsion. Naturally, you will not want be the friend of someone who is the subject of such intense public disapprobation, nor would I want you to be. I hope, however, that you will hold in your heart the memory of the person I was, and remember her with kindness and some affection.

Quickly, she signed the letter, placed it in the envelope, and wrote Rawlin's name and address on the front, knowing that she would never do so again. She carried it through to the hall where, through the window, she could see Ann sweeping leaves on the terrace. Alpheus followed her hopefully to the door.

'Ann.' She stopped and took a deep breath to stop her voice from shaking. 'When you have finished, would you take this letter to the post office for me? Here is sixpence for the stamp, it will be no more than that, being only a single sheet.'

'Yes, Miss, of course.'

She walked back into the house and up the stairs, remembering to turn right instead of left at the top. She had been in the same bedroom since she was a child, but now she could not look at the window without seeing the effigies. She closed the door of her new room at the back of the house, and curled up on the bed. She could not even cry.

Dr Jones helped his wife and daughter down from the carriage. The hearing was to be held in the Board Room at the Workhouse, and he had asked Harry to drive right into the courtyard so that there would be no one to observe Lucy's arrival.

He had been anxious about her having to attend another hearing, but once she understood that no members of the public would be present, she seemed indifferent. This did not reassure him, for he considered it yet another indication of her low spirits.

Reverend and Mrs Buckland arrived on foot with Edith. He had not spoken to the vicar since the burning of the effigies, and had no intention of doing so now. They stood together uneasily while the ladies greeted each other.

'Come; I think we should enter.'

The boardroom, a whitewashed room devoid of decoration, had a dozen chairs arranged in a semicircle facing a table. As they entered, Mr Doe stepped forward to ask the ladies to accompany him to an anteroom where they would wait until it was time for Lucy to give evidence. The doctor took a seat next to the vicar and nodded to the mayor, Mr Chapple; the former mayor, Mr Mallett; and James Balsdon, all of them here in the hope of seeing Francis humiliated. At the other end of the semicircle sat Reverend and Mrs Francis and their solicitor, Mr Thorne. After a minute or two's silence, Mr Moore-Stevens walked in, his bearing imperious, and his expression impassive.

Before Mr Doe took her aside, Lucy glimpsed the men sitting in the boardroom. It would be as before; male eyes perusing her, judging her. Whatever she said, they would believe her to be guilty. She sat in the anteroom with her mother, Edith and Mrs Buckland, the four of them in a row on the hard chairs.

None of them spoke. The walls were bare, a wooden cupboard stood in the corner. Somewhere beyond the Workhouse yard, a distant child was crying.

Mrs Buckland turned to Edith. 'Are we the only ones here?' she whispered. Her sight had quite gone now.

'Yes, Mother. We will wait here to keep Lucy company.'

She would almost have preferred to be alone. She could not be comforted.

The door opened. Expecting Mr Doe, she glanced up, but it was him, it was William Balkwill, the man she dreaded most of all. He saw her and grinned, that awful sneer that had haunted her dreams, displaying those blackened teeth. She could not look away; she was caught like a rabbit in the gaze of a hawk.

His eyes travelled slowly down to her feet, and up again to her face.

'Well, fancy you being yer!' He laughed. 'Be lookin' for another curate, be 'ee?'

There was a sudden commotion; Mr Doe appeared, he grabbed Balkwill's arm.

'The *second* door, did you not hear me? This room is for lady witnesses!'

She barely noticed when Edith took her hand, or when Mr Doe returned to apologise. She hardly cared about the forthcoming ordeal; she could not feel any worse than she did now.

THE CLERICAL SCANDAL AT TORRINGTON'

H. Courtenay, Esq., Local Government Inspector, held an enquiry in the Board room at the Torrington Workhouse on Monday, into the circumstances under which the Rev. H. O. Francis, curate of Torrington, as Chaplain of the Workhouse, had been refused admission to the chapel to perform his official duties. The refusal arose out of the case which came before the Magistrates a short time ago, in which Mr. Francis (who is a married man) charged a man named Balkwill, a labourer, with obtaining half-a-sovereign from him under false pretences. The actual reason for the Board's refusing to allow Mr. Francis to continue his services was contained in a letter written by the Local Government Board to Mr. Francis, in answer to a request that an enquiry might be made into the matter. It was to the effect that the charges against him which had led to the action of the Guardians was that he had brought discredit upon himself and his office by his familiarity with Miss Lucy Jones, that he and Miss Jones had been frequently seen together in the country alone, and that his conduct on some of such occasions had been unduly familiar, and of a very questionable character; and it had been further alleged that, on one occasion, he was observed with Miss Jones in a gravel pit on the Common, and that he afterwards gave to a man who had observed them together, a half-sovereign in order to induce him to observe silence as to what he had seen.

Mr. J. A. Thorne, solicitor, of Barnstaple, appeared for Mr. Francis; and J. C. Moore-Stevens, Esq., Chairman of the Board of Guardians, represented the Board. The witnesses were ordered out of the room and the Inspector asked that no speeches should be made on either side, as all he had to do was to collect evidence and to report to the Board above.

Exeter Flying Post 1879
(Public domain.)
Part of a much longer article.

The doctor sat very upright on his chair. The meeting started with Mr Courtney, the inspector for the Local Government Board, reminding Reverend Francis of the reason for the enquiry taking place. *The Guardians of the Torrington Union have requested your resignation because they consider you have brought discredit against yourself and your office by your familiarity with Miss Lucy Jones; that you and Miss Jones have frequently been seen together in the countryside alone, and that your conduct on some of such occasions has been unduly familiar and of a very questionable character.*

It had not become any easier to hear. Dr Jones realised he was clenching his teeth, and made a conscious effort to relax his jaw.

Mr Doe called in the first witness, Balkwill, who had been made to look respectable in a new suit of clothing. As Mr Moore-Stevens asked Balkwill to give his version of events, the doctor watched Francis from the corner of his eye. His habitual air of overarching confidence had gone; he seemed a broken man. He had developed a tic which caused the left side of his face to perform an exaggerated wink every minute or so, and his gaze was unable to settle in one place.

As a doctor, he could not help but feel some sympathy for the man's suffering but, as a father, he could feel nothing but anger. *Lucy and I are the only ones who know the truth of what happened that day in the hollow*, he thought. Would it have been better if she had agreed to bring charges against him? Perhaps the ordeal would have been no less distressing for Lucy, and certainly it would have been far worse for Mrs Francis. Watching the curate's wife now, he could understand his daughter's decision a little better; she looked like a frightened child who was trying her utmost, in very difficult circumstances, to be brave. If only Francis had never come to Torrington!

Balkwill's cross-examination being over, the engine driver, Henry Pope, was called in. He looked earnestly at Mr Moore-Stevens, as if promising to remember every detail of evidence required of him; the doctor felt sure there was an understanding between them. It would have been quite simple; Pope would provide evidence of Francis' wrongdoing and in return Moore-

Stevens would ensure that he came to no harm for organising the burning of the effigies.

In response to Moore-Stevens' questions, Pope began his litany of damning evidence. He had seen the curate and Miss Jones travel together by train to Exeter, also on many occasions to Instow, Bideford and Barnstaple. He had seen them walking on the Common together as they went to or from the station.

Then Mr Thorne cross-questioned him.

'Did you take part in the events that took place on November the Fifth?'

Pope hesitated. 'Yes, Sir.'

Mr Moore-Stevens stood up quickly. 'I must object to any more questions on that point.'

But Mr Thorne addressed Pope again. 'Who paid the expenses for that evening's events?'

Moore-Stevens glared at him. 'I must *object* to that.'

The inspector raised his eyes languidly from his notepad. 'I think we can simplify matters by not discussing anything that has happened since the enquiry was requested. If the witness was given money to buy a Guy Fawkes, it has nothing to do with these proceedings.'

Mr Thorne replied politely but firmly. 'It was not a Guy Fawkes; effigies of Reverend Francis and Miss Jones were burnt, which demonstrates that the witness is biased against them.'

The inspector looked impatient, and would surely have consulted his pocket watch if it had not appeared overly rude. 'I don't think it worthwhile to go into that.'

Mr Thorne conceded rather sarcastically that it was not worth asking questions if the answers were not to be included in the inspector's notes, and Pope was dismissed. Still, the doctor felt his suspicions were confirmed; Moore-Stevens would stop at nothing to get his way.

Henry Curry, a railway guard, was called and declared that he, too, had seen the pair travelling by train on many occasions, also walking on the Common together.

Walter Cull, a railway goods clerk, was next. The doctor had ministered to his children on several occasions, and was rewarded now with a nervous look.

I have seen them, he said. *I have seen them walking on the road when I was going to or from the station.* He could not meet the doctor's eyes when he was eventually told he could leave the room.

Mr Vicary, a bellringer, had seen Miss Jones and Reverend Francis go into the church vestry together. James Beer, when tending to his sheep and cattle on the Common in the evening, had seen them together on several occasions, but he concurred that Miss Buckland was usually with them. Richard Pettle, a farmer's son, had seen them talking for upwards of half an hour at Goose Green, and Mrs Ward of Calf Street had seen them conversing on several occasions; she supposed it was due to Miss Jones being a district visitor in the street. The doctor had the distinct impression that she had no idea why she had been called to give evidence.

The case for the Guardians was now complete, and that for Francis commenced, with Lucy being called as the first witness. Yet again, Dr Jones was struck forcefully by the irony of her having to support her persecutor in order to exonerate herself. She stood before the inspector like a prisoner resigned to her fate, knowing that not only had she been utterly disgraced herself, she had also unwittingly brought shame and disgrace on the entire family. The change in her appearance since the first hearing was distinct; the lively determination was gone, her eyes were dull, her face was pale and drawn. It broke his heart to see how her dark blue dress hung loosely on her thin frame. He managed to catch her eye and give her a reassuring smile; there was the smallest flicker of recognition in response.

The evidence she had given at the previous hearing was read out to save her having to repeat it; that was a relief, he had wondered how she would get through it.

'Now I must ask you the question, although it is a disagreeable one.' Mr Thorne's tone was quietly sympathetic. 'Did any impropriety ever take place between you and Reverend Francis?'

'No, never.' Her tone was flat. A few months ago she would have been horrified at being asked such a question, but now displayed only shame and despondency.

The inspector was observing her closely; it was clear that he felt pity for her.

He addressed Mr Thorne. 'She has not been charged with impropriety by any of the witnesses; however, it is quite proper for you to ask the question.'

Mr Thorne then questioned her about the journeys by train, giving her the opportunity to say that the trips to Instow were picnic parties with a large group of people, and on other occasions Miss Buckland or other ladies were present.

'I believe, Miss Jones,' the inspector intervened, 'that you are a district visitor?'

'Yes, I am.' She hesitated for a second, no doubt wondering whether she would ever again carry out the work.

'And, as such, you constantly meet the clergymen of the parish?'

'Yes, I do, very often.'

'Thank you, Miss Jones. Mr Moore-Stevens, do you wish to ask Miss Jones any questions?'

Moore-Stevens looked up, and his face was impassive. 'No, that will not be necessary.'

The doctor sighed with relief. Thank God; Moore-Stevens was able to show some compassion after all.

When Lucy had returned to the anteroom with her mother, Francis stood to give evidence. He lifted his chin as if the coming examination held no fear for him, but the increasing frequency of his facial twitch gave him away. The inspector started by saying that although he had not insisted on the lady being fully examined, he must do so in the case of Reverend Francis. And so, the whole sorry tale was told again, or at least the version that Francis chose to tell; how they met by chance in the hollow, the events following Balkwill's appearance. When he reached the end, he produced a letter from the bishop expressing satisfaction with his work, letters of encouragement from other clergy, and a letter of support from his previous parish signed by the principal inhabitants. The papers were passed around.

'I see no supportive letters from this parish,' remarked Moore-Stevens.

'There is one letter here from Bideford; none from Torrington,' said the inspector, passing it to him.

Francis looked on nervously, like a boy awaiting judgement from his headmaster.

When the cross-examination began, Moore-Stevens showed him no mercy. After an hour and a quarter of intense questioning, the doctor's back was beginning to ache from sitting so long on a hard chair, but still it went on. Moore-Stevens questioned every aspect of Francis' conduct on that fateful morning and on previous occasions, exposing the weaknesses in his replies and destroying his credibility. Moore-Stevens remained calm and in control throughout, but by the time he brought the questioning to an end with the observation that a great many people had left the church as a result of the curate's conduct, Francis' hands were shaking and perspiration running from his face.

The inspector stood up. 'I will make my report to the Local Government Board. The Guardians and Reverend Francis will be acquainted with the decision in due course.'

It was clear that they would find against Francis. He would have to leave the town. As everyone filed slowly from the room, Dr Jones went in search of his family. At last it was over; they would return home. They would attempt to rebuild their lives.

Chapter Twenty-Six

Slowly, Lucy pushed back the bedclothes and swung her legs out of the bed. She sat for a few moments, the dread of what she was about to do dragging like a stone in the pit of her stomach. But it would soon be over. No more nightmares, no more visions of flames and sly, leering faces.

She had wanted a quiet, respectable life. She had achieved it, until this year, had she not? She was the younger Miss Jones, not so pretty as her sister, not one to court attention, but reliable, helpful. A comfort to those in trouble. Independent too, not afraid to be a little different. Sometimes rather odd perhaps; all that walking in the countryside, chasing butterflies, unperturbed by muddy boots and hems.

But then, everything changed.

She could not endure this new life. A life without Rawlin, a life without useful work, confined to the house day after day, year after year, because the story of her disgrace would always be remembered, people would always stare and laugh behind cupped hands, wouldn't they? Probably it was a weakness in her, that she could not withstand the shame. She would be remembered for her weakness, as well as for the scandal. She would bring further disgrace to her family for what she was about to do, and she was sorry for that.

She lit a candle. The clock told her that it was a quarter to six, and she knew she must leave before daybreak. She put on her underclothes, then chose the navy dress on account of its deep pockets, but hesitated as she took her wool jacket from the shelf. Ann had once admired it, and Polly might think of passing it on to her, when it was all over. She put on the grey jacket instead.

Carefully, she opened the bedroom door. Downstairs in the hall the lamp was lit, giving just enough light for her to find her way down. As she reached the bottom step a clatter from the kitchen told her that Ann was lighting the stove; Lucy moved swiftly to the front door and turned the key. A sudden noise made her turn, and there was Alpheus, his claws clicking on the tiled floor as he trotted from the kitchen, his whole body wagging along with his tail, and his eyes shining. He pushed his wet nose against her hand and whined pleadingly.

'Ssh, Alpheus, no; not this time, my boy.'

She hesitated, longing to kneel and put her arms around his warm body, but then pushed him gently back and slipped through the door. She was out. The night-time air was cool on her cheek, but any relief she might feel at being outdoors was crushed by the fear of being seen. As she walked quickly towards the gate she glanced up at her father's bedroom window. The curtains were still drawn so it was not one of his early mornings, and she experienced sudden, overwhelming sadness at the suffering she was going to impose on him. But she must not think of that; it would pass, better that than her presence remind him daily of the shame she had brought on the family.

She walked quickly along the path leading to the Common, holding out her arms lest she stumble against a wall in the dark. When the path started to descend, she slowed, placing each foot carefully in turn until she detected level ground, and then she stopped.

She was standing at the top of Castle Hill. She knew that, just a few steps away, the ground fell precipitously for almost three hundred feet to the river. Never before had she stood here in the dark. Yesterday's rain had passed, and the wind she had heard in the night had dropped; in this stillness and the silence before dawn there was a sense of anticipation, as if something momentous was about to occur. It was a sense, almost, of hope, but she knew that to be a trick of nature. Today marked an end, not a beginning.

It was here that she had sat with Rawlin, gazing out at the view but aware only of him at her side; here that she had come to read his very first letter. She used to feel his presence even though he was on the other side of the world, but ever since her disgrace she had known that she was alone. He would despise her when he heard of her involvement in the scandal.

She sensed a subtle change in her surroundings, and saw that above the eastern horizon a narrow band of sky was lightening; where there had been nothing but darkness, she could now discern the land dropping away and the shadowy outlines of distant hills. The harsh, guttural cawing of crows started to echo from the slopes below her. She must hurry, before long the graziers would be coming to check on their sheep.

She walked as fast as she could in the dim light, taking the path that zigzagged first right, then left, down the steep hillside, choosing the way that would lead her most directly to the river. She was barely able to make out the rough path but felt she could have followed it even in complete darkness, so well did she know it. Here was the place where she had once found a wren's nest with Rawlin; here was Sliding Rock, the steep, flat surface down which she and her brothers, as children, had loved to slide, despite Mary Wilcox's threats that their clothing would be spoiled.

She pushed these thoughts aside; she was no longer the person who found such pleasure in life.

The darkness was more intense at the bottom of the hill, but she could discern the outline of Rolle Road which had been constructed over the old canal bed. And there, beyond the road, lay the river.

She crossed the road and looked down at the water beneath her, sensing its depth, the speed of its flow. During several days of heavy rain, water had been running in little rivulets from the high lands, along the sides of deep lanes into little streams and under small stone bridges, until it swelled the waters of the river. Here, the Torridge was deep; it flowed fast and sure. She watched it, her eyes widening against the gloom.

By the side of the road were many stones left from its construction. Boys from the town liked to lob them into the water. She crouched, feeling for them, gathering the largest, and putting them into the pockets of her skirt.

When her pockets were full, she stood. They dragged at her, as they should. She hesitated, then collected more stones, smaller this time, tucking them into her bodice, pushing them into her sleeves, turning the cuffs to prevent them falling out. Her mind was empty, concentrating only on the task she had to complete, but her hands shook and some of the stones fell to the ground.

When she was ready, she climbed up on to the riverbank.

She looked down at the deep, dark water.

She thought, at first, that it was the sound of stones on the riverbed that she heard. She lifted her head. It *was* the sound of stones, but the scrabbling came not from the water below but up on the hillside behind her, and it was getting closer. Someone was coming.

She turned quickly back to the river. She could do it now, she could scramble down the bank into the water, or she could jump, but if she was seen... The thought of rescue was appalling, worse even than the deed, what should she do?

The sound was louder, something rushed at her, jumped at her, almost knocked her over.

'Alpheus!'

He leapt at her joyfully, thrusting his wet nose at her face, licking her hands, whining with pleasure at having found her. She crouched down and put her arms around him, her heart thudding against his side. Ann would have let him into the garden; he would have been desperate to accompany Lucy on her walk; he would have found the place in the corner behind the old apple trees where the wall was tumbling down. He had escaped from there once before, she had forgotten to ask for it to be repaired. And then he would have followed her scent across the Common.

She held on to his collar. Now that he had found her, he lost interest in her; the scent of rabbit in the undergrowth and mallard on the riverbank was far more enticing, and he fidgeted against her restraining grip.

What should she do? She sat down on the bank and made Alpheus sit next to her. The act she had been about to perform seemed suddenly absurd; Alpheus would follow her into the water, he liked swimming and would think it a great game. Should she go home, return to the river tomorrow?

Even at this, she thought, *I am a failure.*

She sat, her mind empty, hopelessness dragging her down as surely as the stones in her pockets.

After a few minutes, there was the sound of footsteps, many footsteps. Startled, she looked up. Coming along the road were four goats, three white ones and one brown-and-white, their hoofs tapping as they trotted along the rough surface, and their heads nodding wisely in time with their steps. Behind them walked an old man wearing a battered hat and an overcoat tied with string; she had seen him before, he took his goats out to graze each morning. What would he think of her, sitting here by the river so early in the day? She could not bear anyone to see her. She felt she should stand, but suppose he should notice the stones weighing down her dress?

'Good morning, Miss.'

'Good morning.' Her throat was dry; she could barely speak.

''Tis master early to be out with your dog, Miss, but 'tis good to see 'ee. Us've missed 'ee out on the Common, us was only saying so a day or so ago, me n' William what runs the sheep.' He paused, looking at her. 'You all right, Miss?'

'Yes, thank you. I was just having a rest, and watching the river.'

'That's all right, then. 'Tis running proper now after the rain, bain't it? Good morning, Miss. Take care now, won't 'ee?'

And he went on his way, chivvying the goats that had stopped to graze on the verge.

She sat very still, hardly daring to breathe.

Suppose she had done what she intended, and he had found her in the river? What a dreadful thing it would have been for him to see!

And it was then that she realised what a monstrous act it was that she had planned. How could she have thought to do such a thing?

She put her arms around the dog and hugged him to her. 'Alpheus! Oh, Alpheus!' He was soft and warm, he was so alive, and the water would have been cold, it would have swept her away.

Aroused by her unusually demonstrative affection, Alpheus forgot the rabbits for a while and leaned into her embrace, licking her face and trying to climb on to her lap. As she stroked the silky hair on his ears and his chest, she started to sob uncontrollably, and her body was convulsed by her shuddering breaths. All the dreadful events of the last few months ran through her mind: the unwanted attention of Reverend Francis at that meeting in the hollow; the knowledge of the vile, untrue stories that had spread around the town; the humiliation of being questioned before a large audience, then the horror of seeing her effigy, and hearing afterwards that it had been burned. It had all become too much for her, it had worn her down; it would have worn anyone down, would it not?

But I did nothing wrong! She sat up straight, letting go of Alpheus, who took the opportunity to bound off into the undergrowth. At the beginning she had been angry at the false accusations, but over time she had somehow forgotten that she was innocent, so humiliated had she felt by everything that had happened. The old man who had just spoken to her knew she had done nothing wrong; he would not have been so kind otherwise. Perhaps there were other people who believed in her innocence.

She stood up and reached into her pockets. One by one, she took out the stones and dropped them on to the ground where they landed with deep thuds. She was able to stand up straight again now. Her skirt was damp from sitting on the wet ground, her pockets muddy from the stones, but she shuddered to think of her clothes streaming with water, the ripples on the surface closing over her face, her throat filling with river water. How could she ever have contemplated such a horrible deed?

Although the light was still dim down here in the valley, the sky had brightened; high on the hill above her, a shaft of weak, winter sunlight illuminated the monument. The Common had changed in the three months since she last walked here, the bracken had turned brown, the trees across the valley had lost their leaves. It was going to be a steep climb back up to the top; she was out of practice, she had done nothing but wander aimlessly around the house and the garden for so long.

She called to Alpheus, and she set off.

Part Three

Chapter Twenty-Seven

Two weeks later, when Edith came to see her as promised, Lucy had already put on her warm winter coat.

'How are you, dearest?' Edith regarded her anxiously.

'I think perhaps I am a little better.' She had been ill with a cold but, of course, Edith knew that it had been more than that. 'Edith, would you accompany me for a short walk on the Common?'

The sun was trying to break through the dark cloud as they took the path towards the monument, sending an optimistic shaft of dazzling sunlight down over Darkham Wood, but Lucy faltered. She could see a man leading a donkey along a lower path just a few yards beneath them.

'Come, there is no need to worry.' Edith spoke quietly, and put her hand on Lucy's elbow to guide her forward. When the man glanced up and wished them a good morning, she answered for them both in a loud, clear voice.

'There, you see,' she said, 'he barely gave you a second glance.'

Lucy was not so sure; it seemed to her that the man had looked at her curiously. 'I could not reply to him, Edith, my throat closed up.'

'It does not matter; remember, this is the first time you have ventured out, it will become easier. People will get accustomed to seeing you out and about again.'

'I don't think I will ever be able to walk alone again.'

'Then I will walk with you.'

They sat on the low seat at the base of the monument, gazing out at the expansive view over wooded hills and a patchwork of fields, the river winding its way through the valley far below. Lucy breathed deeply, feeling the tension she held within beginning to dissipate; she had thought she would never sit here again.

'You know, do you not,' Edith spoke tentatively, 'that Reverend and Mrs Francis have now left the town?'

Lucy had known that it was their intention to leave, but no one in her family would mention the curate's name in front of her.

'Where have they gone?'

'To Mrs Francis' parents in Bridport initially, but Reverend Francis will take up a new position in the new year.'

'Oh!' She had not known he had found another position. 'Where is his new post?'

Thinking of them brought a wave of confusing emotions; anger at him for what he had done, pity for Mrs Francis and the poor children, and guilt at her own involvement in their downfall, despite it being unintentional. Why had it all had to happen?

'They are going to Sussex; Father says Reverend Francis is to be chaplain to the navvies who are building the Lewes and East Grinstead Railway. It is a lowly position and not well paid, but at least he has somewhere to go; having been publicly disgraced, he had few options.'

Lucy knew that the Inspector had decided there was no evidence that any familiarity had taken place between her and Reverend Francis, but that the enquiry was justified because Francis' action in giving Balkwill the half sovereign aroused strong suspicion of misconduct. By then, Francis had already agreed to resign.

'Have they found somewhere to live?' She thought of Torridge Villa, now standing empty.

'Reverend Francis has been offered a small, terraced house with three bedrooms, and he has had to take it. I am very sorry for his family but I cannot help feeling, Lucy, that he has brought all this upon himself.'

For Edith, who always saw the best in everyone, this was strong criticism.

'Poor Mrs Francis. I wish I could have seen her before she left, but I did not feel strong enough, and I doubt she would have agreed to meet me.'

'Probably not, but I think, Lucy, that was more through embarrassment than dislike for you. I'm sure she knew you were not in any way to blame.'

'I hope so.'

'The navvies will be Irish; probably they will not object to Reverend Francis being high church. Father and Mr Rolle have now appointed a new curate with more moderate views. I hope I am not upsetting you, Lucy, by talking of this, but I thought it might help you to know that he has gone.'

'I think it does help a little; thank you, Edith.' She took her friend's hand. She would never have to see Reverend Francis again; certainly, it was a relief.

'Perhaps, in time, you will feel able to carry out some district visiting again. We miss you terribly! I will be able to tell you whether the new curate seems sympathetic, and don't forget that I could accompany you at first.'

'I don't know, Edith. I can't imagine that I will ever be able to go visiting again, but I'm grateful for your offer.'

Twice, Polly had come to collect her and together they had walked to her home in the Square. Lucy had found walking through the town difficult, and had kept her gaze on the pavement, but once in the house it had been wonderful to have a change of surroundings, and to be shown the new furnishings of which Polly was so proud. The thought of walking about the streets in the poorer parts of town however, subject to the ridicule of all and sundry, was another matter altogether.

Christmas came and went. Lucy's father grew less anxious about the future of his practice, despite having lost a few patients through the scandal. Her mother was pleased, of course, that Lucy was at home more often and able to help run the house. John, whose drinking had increased in the autumn, was being more sensible, but came to stay at Castle House from time to time when he had fallen out with his wife.

For Lucy, the days were long. She set herself tasks; she cleared out the linen cupboard, giving the oldest sheets away to charity, mending others, and ordering new. Glad of an excuse to be outdoors, she pruned the roses, dead-headed the winter pansies and completed other jobs in the garden that Harry did not have time for; she dusted all the books in the library. The jobs kept her busy, but she found little satisfaction in them.

What is my future now? she wondered. *What will I become?* She supposed she would stay at home to look after her parents, take more responsibility for the running of the household as her mother and Mary Wilcox grew older. When her parents died, she would be homeless; perhaps one of her brothers would take her in. She thought of the two unmarried great aunts who had lived at Castle House when she was a child; everyone was kind to them, but the truth was, they were somewhat of a nuisance in the busy household.

Some educated single women were being trained as nurses at St Thomas's Hospital in London, but the thought of living alone in a big city did not appeal to her at all; besides, she was not brave enough to withstand the sight of blood.

One afternoon, bored with dusting books, she was sitting next to her father's globe, spinning it around slowly in its polished wooden mount. England was tiny, the area that was Devon not even marked. Torrington, had it been shown, would be smaller than a pinhead. When she considered the extent of the Common, the miles and miles of paths, the day-to-day concerns of the people living in the town, it was extraordinary to think that Torrington did not even appear on the globe, and that events in the town were of so little importance. She traced her finger down across France, Italy, Greece, and then her hand strayed gently down towards Australia. It would have been wonderful to see such places, but her chances of a life beyond Torrington were over.

She tried not to think of Rawlin. Her dream of marrying him had gone; probably it had never been anything but a dream. A letter from him had arrived just a week ago, an affectionate, humorous letter in which he told her he had joined the Palmerston Dramatic Club, and taken part in an entertainment. It would be the last letter she received. She had read it once, quickly, before putting it in her box with the rest of his correspondence. This week he would receive the letter in which she told him that they could no longer be friends; she had counted the days, and it was now three months since she posted it. It was the first thing she pictured each morning, Rawlin opening the letter, reading it. Would he be disappointed? She was sure that he would, for a little while, but then he would forget.

She would never forget.

When she thought of him reading the letter, perhaps throwing it aside in disgust, she wished that Alpheus had not come to find her, that morning by the river. Then she would pinch herself, hard, and set about another household task.

Sometimes, when Polly visited, they walked together to Castle Hill to sit on one of the seats and admire the view. Lucy was not the only one to notice that spring was approaching, for while they talked, a thrush celebrated by singing from the oak tree by the old castle wall. Polly spoke of her hopes for the new baby that was expected, of the goings-on in the town, and gave her news of their friends. Another day, Emily Rudd and Katherine Colling joined them for a while. When townspeople passed by, Lucy would see that they were trying not to stare at her and she knew what they were thinking, the pictures their minds were conjuring. It was with difficulty that she wished them a good afternoon.

One day in February, when she was sitting at the little desk in the drawing room trying to balance the household accounts, Mary Wilcox bustled in.

'There's a little maid at the door asking for 'ee! 'Tis one of the Gilberts I do believe, they'm as alike as peas in a pod. Will 'ee see her?'

The Gilbert family were part of Lucy's previous life; she had not seen Ellen Gilbert since the scandal, but surely a child would not be judgemental.

'I can't imagine why she's here, but I suppose you had better show her in.' She closed the account book and pushed back a lock of hair that had escaped from its pin.

Ellen Gilbert appeared in the doorway in a shabby dress. She looked rather overwhelmed by her grand surroundings but, when she saw Lucy, she marched up to her with her customary aplomb.

'Mary says you must come now.' Once her message had been delivered, she allowed her eyes to wander about the room, taking in the colourful carpet and the chandelier that hung from the ceiling.

Lucy could not help smiling. 'Does she? And why is that, Ellen?'

'Her's had a baby, another little chiel. And her wants you there, her says.'

'Oh, I didn't know she was expecting again! Is all well?'

'The chiel looks viddy to me.' Ellen crossed her arms and sighed self-importantly. 'But Mary thinks it'll die same as the others, so her wants you to come.'

If the child were ill, it was Lucy's father that was needed, but if Ellen were right – and she probably was – it might be that Mary just needed reassurance. Lucy knew that she should go, but dare she walk through the town?

'You got to come,' said Ellen firmly. She edged over to the window and touched the curtain with her forefinger. 'Be that velvet?'

'Yes, it is. Ellen, if I come now, will you walk with me?'

As they walked along Castle Street together, Ellen looked up at her knowingly.

'Don't go out much now, do 'ee, Miss?'

What complex emotions the question evoked! It was hard to know how to reply.

'Well, no, I suppose... the weather hasn't been too good, has it? Perhaps when the spring comes...'

'Don't worry, Miss, you'm with me now.' Ellen reached up to take her hand, and together they walked through the Square, attracting some surprised stares. Lucy looked steadily ahead, trying to be brave, and hoping that Ellen would not be spurned for associating with her.

In the small, terraced house in Calf Street, Mary Gilbert sat crying by the fire with the baby in her arms. Ellen's mother, who was washing dishes in a bowl on the table, looked relieved when Ellen and Lucy entered.

'Oh, Miss Jones, thank 'ee for coming. Mary won't listen to no one else.'

Lucy quickly cast her eyes about the room. It was clean and neat; Mary was dressed and had some colour in her cheeks.

'You're looking well, Mary! And the little one, what is her name?'

'Her's called Annie.' Mary looked anxiously at the baby. 'I've asked for her to be baptised, but the vicar's not come.' She looked imploringly at Lucy. 'Look, Miss, how her's breathing, 'tis too fast, just like George was, and Mary. Her's going to die, I'm sure of it. I'll lose her like the others…' She started weeping again as she clasped the baby to her breast.

Lucy soothed her, gently unwrapping the blanket to look at the baby. The truth was, she did not know a great deal about babies, but she had seen Mary's last child before it died, and she had seen healthy newborn babies. This one definitely fell into the latter category; she was an endearing little thing with dark eyes and rosebud lips. She showed Mary what a fine colour the baby was, how plump her cheeks and how bright her eyes.

'Look how she's gripping my finger, Mary! She's so strong! Does she feed well?'

'Her's always hungry, Miss, her oughtn't to be so hungry.'

'But that's a good sign! Your other babies were sickly, Mary, they didn't feed well, but little Annie will thrive, you'll see!'

'Then the vicar needn't come yet?'

'No, she can be baptised later, when you feel stronger.'

Mary dried her eyes and managed a weak smile.

'There!' said Ellen's mother. 'I knew her'd listen to you!'

While Lucy drank a cup of tea, they talked about babies' propensity to survive, putting forward a convincing argument between them, and Mary looked greatly encouraged.

Lucy felt it was the most useful thing she had done in months.

'If you would like me to call in again,' she said, 'just send Ellen along for me.'

'Miss Jones,' Mary beckoned her over so that she could whisper to her. 'I just wanted to tell 'ee, your recent trouble – no one in *our* family was involved in it, Miss.'

As she walked home hand-in-hand with Ellen, she thought that perhaps, one day, if she could overcome her fear of meeting William Balkwill, she might feel brave enough to start district visiting again.

A few days later she came downstairs to find Mary Wilcox standing by the front door.

'Look.' Mary held up a paper, her eyes wide.

'What is it?'

'A telegram. It's for you.'

'For me?' Very occasionally her father received a telegram, but no one else in the house had ever had one. She took the envelope from Mary.

Miss Lucy Jones, Castle House, Great Torrington, Devon, England.

'Shall I open it?'

'Well, of course, chiel, whatever else would you do with it? But I hope 'tisn't bad news.'

Lucy went into the drawing room to find the paper knife, and then, with a feeling of dread deep in the pit of her stomach, carefully slit open the envelope while Mary looked on.

She stared at the words on the slip of paper, unable at first to take in their meaning.

Arrive England end May then to Torrington. Your friend Rawlin.

'Well, what is it?'

'It's Rawlin. He's coming home.' Her throat had constricted, she could barely speak.

'Well! There now, didn't I tell you? I knew he'd come back!'

Lucy looked at her, appalled. 'You don't understand, Mary, I can't see him! He doesn't know what happened, what people think of me now! I tried to tell him in a letter but I couldn't write the words I needed!'

He would hear all about it, though, when he came to Torrington; there would be some who would tell him, he would learn every vile detail, he would find her odious, the very idea of her company would be repugnant…

'I won't see him! I don't have to, he'll want to spend time with his family, perhaps he has work to attend to. That will be why he's returning, it is probably just a short visit!'

Mary was looking at her dubiously.

'I know what you're thinking, but you're wrong!' She ran back up the stairs and closed her bedroom door.

If only he were not coming! She cannot have been clear enough in her letter about the seriousness of the situation, how her position in society was for ever changed. She paced up and down the room. Perhaps he was not thinking of her anyway; perhaps he had to come to England for work and the telegram was sent out of courtesy. She threw herself down on the bed, then a moment later stood again, every muscle in her body tense. She had just begun to recover some equanimity, to accept her new situation, and now this had happened. She could not bear it.

She knew she must speak to Edith. She dared not walk to the Vicarage, she was not yet able to do that alone, but perhaps she could send Ann with a note asking Edith to visit.

In the event, she did not need to, for Edith arrived after luncheon, looking rather flustered.

'Lucy, we have had a telegram from Rawlin.'

It was a relief that hers was not the only telegram, it might even be one of many.

'I have too. So, he is to visit.' She spoke dully, and could not meet Edith's gaze.

'Lucy, surely you are pleased? I believe he is coming especially to see you.'

'Then he must not! I cannot see him, Edith, you must realise that. When he hears what has happened, he will want nothing to do with me and I cannot bear to be rejected by him! Can't you tell him not to come?'

Ann, bringing in the tea, gave Lucy a sympathetic look which only added to her anxiety. When Ann had returned to the kitchen, Edith walked over to the window and stood with her back to Lucy.

'Lucy, I have to tell you something, and I hope you will not be too cross with me. When you told me you had just posted a letter to Rawlin telling him you could no longer be friends, I

289

knew he would be dismayed, so I decided to write to him myself. My letter was posted the day after yours. I told him that a scandal, linking your name with that of Reverend Francis, had shocked the whole town but that you were entirely innocent of the charges and greatly upset by them. He had not mentioned an imminent visit in previous letters, so I'm sure that these telegrams, sent just a week after he would have received our letters, indicate that he is returning because of you.'

She turned back towards Lucy, her face a picture of sympathy.

'Then, Edith, you must stop him! Can your father send him a telegram?'

Edith's eyes widened. 'But he is already on the ship to Singapore! And, besides, it costs at least three pounds to send a telegram to Australia; I'm sure Father would not agree.'

'Edith,' she took her friend's hand, 'I don't think you realise the seriousness of what happened; you did not see the effigies, you did not see what was enacted, people will not describe to *you* the horrible details of what they believe I did. No respectable person can be associated with me either now or in the future because this will never be forgotten. Rawlin will realise that, when he hears the full story.'

Edith tried to argue with her but she would not be swayed. If Edith was right and Rawlin was travelling across the world especially to see her, it was the most dreadful waste of his time and money. She could only hope that seeing his family and friends would be some recompense before he travelled back to Australia.

The next three months passed slowly. Lucy started attending church services again with her parents; unwilling to meet the eyes of other members of the congregation, she kept her gaze on the stone floor, but was aware that the new curate was serious in his manner and quietly spoken. With Edith, she visited some people she knew in Calf Street, choosing those who were most likely to be forgiving towards her. Sometimes she went for a short walk with Charles in the evening, but they never went far from the house. She did not think she would ever be able to walk on the part of the Common where the effigies had been burnt, but it was wonderful to be out; she saw the first primroses opening deep in the hedgerows, then the wild daffodils pushing shyly through the dead bracken, and, one sunny evening in April, she and Charles saw the first swallows skimming the slopes of Castle Hill and swooping low over the river in search of insects. It was always here, on the sheltered southern side of the town, that she saw the swallows arrive after their long journey from Africa, and it brought joy to her heart.

Rawlin was constantly in her thoughts. She dreaded having to see him. Surely it could be arranged that they need not meet? But her mother told her she was being ridiculous, and even Edith told her gently that she must, out of courtesy, meet him at least once.

Polly brought up the subject of Rawlin after they had walked together through the Square to her house. Two people greeted Lucy politely, but she saw one woman pointing at her from across the street, and two boys whispering and laughing as they watched her.

'There, what did I tell you, Polly? Nearly six months have passed but I am still the woman who, who… *did those things* with the curate. I always will be, they'll never forget!'

She usually saved her tears for when she was alone, but she could not help herself this time.

Polly led her to an armchair and sat on the floor next to her, stroking her hair.

'It is so very hard for you, and I wish I could do more to help. But Lucy, Rawlin is coming, and although I know you would never admit it, you did, I think, hope that you and he might marry one day. And now he is coming right across the world to see you! If he were to ask you to marry him you could…'

'Polly, stop, please.' She could not bear to hear it. 'Don't you see? I am not fit to marry anyone, and when Rawlin hears what happened he will think the same.' She pictured again his apologetic expression when he explained his reason for rejecting her, the spring in his step when he walked away from her for ever. It was better not to see him at all.

Chapter Twenty-Eight

The month of May arrived with its usual burgeoning of new life, but Lucy could not take pleasure in watching the vivid green fronds of bracken unfurl, or admire the frothy pink-and-white flowers of the hawthorn against the perfect blue sky. She tried to distract herself by reorganising her father's surgery shelves, wiping the dust from the glass bottles and writing new labels for them, but she could only think of the days passing, and the end of the month approaching. Perhaps by the time June arrived, the meeting she dreaded would be in the past, enabling her to adjust to this new, lonely life.

At last the day came when Edith told her that Rawlin's ship had docked; he was on his way to Devon.

She hoped that Edith would be present when she and Rawlin met but, despite her protestations, it was arranged that he would come alone to Castle House for tea, and her mother decided that a table for two would be laid in the garden.

Lucy stood at her bedroom window looking out at the table with its white cloth, its cut-glass vase of rosebuds, the waiting chairs set at oblique angles. The lawn was freshly mown, the branches of the lilac tree weighed down with blossom, the clear blue sky a perfect backdrop to what should have been such a consequential meeting. With what anxious excitement she would have stood here, had the circumstances been different! She would have longed for the sight of his face, and carefully rehearsed her words of greeting but, as it was, she felt nothing but dread.

Her stomach clenched with anxiety; taking slow, deep breaths to calm herself, she turned to look at the mantelpiece clock; another hour, and it would all be over. She would get through it, would she not? She must not break down in his presence.

There were voices; she stepped back from the window. Her mother led the way on to the lawn, a man beside her, broad-shouldered, loose-limbed, wavy brown hair reaching his collar. He turned in response to a comment from her mother; that face, so often pictured. Her heart was pounding; she sat in the chair, her back to the window.

'Lucy!'

She could not do it. She could not face him.

'Lucy!' Her mother's voice was insistent.

Shakily, she rose and walked down the stairs.

The lawn was yielding beneath her feet, like velvet, she thought. He was facing away from her, looking out over the garden with its beds of hollyhocks and columbines. Then, he turned.

She could not hold his gaze, she looked down at the grass.

'Lucy.'

His hands were firm and warm around hers. She must be courteous; he must not think her ill-tempered.

'Hello Rawlin, it is good to see you.'

His face was browned by the sun, there was warmth in his eyes. She looked away. 'Did you have a pleasant journey?'

He cleared his throat, he seemed lost for words.

'Let us sit down, Lucy.' There was bewilderment in his eyes as he searched her face, and she felt a pang of sympathy for him as she looked down at her hands folded neatly in her lap. Their meeting should not have been like this, they should have been open, if tentative, in their approaches to one another.

'I would not call the journey *pleasant*.' He hesitated. 'We had some very bad storms, I was quite ill at times. It seemed interminable and... not the journey I once imagined. I would not have minded the storms, or the length of the journey, but ever since I received your letter, Lucy...'

She looked at him. His brow was creased, as it always was when something troubled him, and she knew that he was now going to reject her.

She spoke quickly, trying to keep her voice level. She knew she would not be able to do so for long. 'It does not matter. You do not need to explain, I know we cannot meet again. You must enjoy your time with your family and not worry about me.'

'That is not what I mean!'

Before he could continue, Ann came walking carefully across the lawn with the tea tray. They sat in silence while she placed the best silver teapot, the milk jug, sugar bowl, cups, saucers and plates on the table.

'I'll go back for the cakes, Miss Lucy.'

'Thank you, Ann.'

He waited until Ann reached the door to the kitchen, then started to speak again.

'I have come to see *you*, Lucy, there is no other reason for my journey. The duplication the Port Darwin cable is complete now, so that part of my work is done, and I would have come to see you anyway in a few months' or a year's time, but I have come now because of your letter.'

'You should not have come! You could have written to me if you felt the need to reply, that would have sufficed!'

Her voice rose unsteadily; she took a deep breath and clasped her trembling hands in her lap. If she could, she would have leapt up to run back to the house, but she must control herself, she must be polite. She could not bear for him to think even worse of her than he already did.

From the corner of her eye, she saw her mother at the drawing room window. She was standing next to the curtain where she imagined she could not be seen.

'We are both unsettled, and now your servant is coming with the cake. Let us talk of other things for a while.' He spoke quietly to her, then raised his voice as Ann approached. 'Ah, fruit cake! I have not had such a cake since I left England! And Alpheus too, come here, boy, do you remember me?'

Alpheus, accompanying Ann from the kitchen, came to Rawlin with his head held low and his tail wagging with pleasure. Of course he remembered – had he not accompanied them on many walks? Rawlin told her about the wild dogs in Australia which, he said, were sometimes domesticated by the natives, then went on to tell her about the specimens of butterfly, moth and insects he had brought back with him and which he intended to donate to a museum.

'The one of which I am most proud is the Canopus swallowtail. Do you remember there was an illustration of a swallowtail in my book of butterflies, and how we wished we could see one? This one is different but just as handsome, its velvety black wings having a broad white band and a row of red and blue dots on the hindwings. I believe one of my specimens may be an unusual subspecies, but I will have to wait to see what the museum has to say.'

When she was able to compose herself, she poured the tea, and cut two slices of cake. As she sipped her tea, she glanced surreptitiously at Rawlin. His eyes shone with boyish enthusiasm as he described the swallowtail butterfly, as if he had forgotten the awkwardness that had arisen between them. His beard was neatly trimmed, his hair a little longer than he used to wear it, and she fancied that he was rather thinner than when she last saw him more than four years ago. His turn of phrase was just the same as in his letters; it was as if she had conjured his presence by reading one of them aloud – and how often had she wished to do just that! She must treasure these moments, for they would not come again.

'There now, I will bore you, and my tea will grow cold! But I would like to show you my collection, I think you would be impressed, although of course it is better still to see them in their own habitat. Now that *is* a sight!'

She had, once, cherished a secret hope that she might be able to see the sights he had described in his letters. He sipped his tea, and took a bite of fruit cake. She *must* think of something to say.

'To which museum will you donate your specimens?'

'I wrote to the Natural History Department at the British Museum in London during my voyage, and posted the letter when I arrived in England. I will see whether they will be interested, but I believe they will. I have learnt how to mount the specimens correctly, a very different process from the one you and I used when we pressed them between the pages of a book as children!'

She looked away. The reminder of the many connections they shared was hard to bear.

'Those were happy days, were they not, Lucy?'

She nodded, unable to reply.

'And we will have happy days together again, I hope?'

How could he say that? Did he not understand the seriousness of what had occurred?

She shook her head, and struggled to speak. 'No, Rawlin, never. I can't have made myself sufficiently clear. We can never be friends after what happened.'

She started to get up, but he put a restraining hand on her arm.

'Lucy, I have talked with Edith, I know what happened.'

He looked at her steadily. She could not leave, his hand was still on her arm. It was what she had most dreaded, that he should see her as others saw her. She looked away, struggling to control herself. She must not sob, not here, beside him.

'It was appalling,' he said, 'and I am so very sorry that this has happened to you. But, Lucy,' his hand squeezed her arm gently, 'you have done nothing wrong, it was not your fault. You are still the same sensible, principled young woman whose company I have treasured all my life.'

His voice faltered, and she knew she must take the opportunity to say what had to be said, however hard it was to do. He must not leave without hearing the truth.

'If that is what you think, Rawlin, then you have not heard the whole story. How could you have heard it? Edith cannot tell you, she did not see it, she does not know all the terrible details.'

'Lucy, I heard enough, I can imagine the rest.' His gaze, although sympathetic, seemed to reach into the deepest, most shameful part of her.

She leapt up. 'Then you know that I'm no longer the same person, in the eyes of the world I am forever tainted by what happened.' Her voice was shaking, she could stay no longer. As she turned towards the house, she saw her mother step back out of sight. 'I'm so very sorry, Rawlin, but I am no longer fit company for you.'

She stayed in her room for the remainder of the afternoon. She had not looked out of the window after she ran upstairs, so did not know how long it was before Rawlin left, or whether he spoke to her mother. When she finally went to the window, the table had been cleared away. It was as if he had never been there.

After an hour or two, Ann brought her up a cup of tea.

'Will 'ee be coming down for dinner, Miss?'

Ann spoke gently. She would know that the meeting had been difficult but, of course, neither of them would mention it.

'I suppose I must.'

'I expect 'twould be best, Miss.'

Lucy's mother had not been up to see her, and made no reference to Rawlin during the meal, an unusual reticence for which Lucy was grateful. She must have spoken to Charles and to Lucy's father for they did not ask after him either, and the conversation, in which she took little part, centred around the construction of the new Marland railway which would carry clay to Torrington.

While discussion about the new viaducts passed back and forth across the table, she considered that perhaps Rawlin never would be mentioned. He would become part of her past, and she would have to face her bleak future alone.

Chapter Twenty-Nine

The next morning, when she had finished breakfast and been persuaded by Mary Wilcox to help with planning the week's menus, Edith came to call. *Rawlin has sent her*, Lucy thought, *he has decided that our friendship must end immediately*.

'Lucy? Don't look so alarmed!' Edith took off her gloves as she came into the drawing room. 'I have come to ask whether you would come to tea this afternoon.'

It was not what she expected to hear, and she turned away to the window to hide her shock. 'Thank you, Edith, but I don't think I will.' She would stay here; she would help Mary Wilcox, or do a little gardening. 'Rawlin would not want me to come.'

'He *does* want you to come, Lucy, he said so quite clearly.' Edith hesitated. 'I'm not going to ask what happened between you yesterday, it is none of my business, but I could tell that Rawlin was very unhappy when he returned.' She moved a little closer. 'I thought if we could have tea together, just the three of us, we could talk of old times perhaps. He said he would like that very much.'

'I'm sorry, Edith, but I cannot.' She turned around, and her hands were shaking. 'Everything has changed, I can no longer sit in the Vicarage making conversation! I'm so sorry, Edith!' And she walked quickly out of the room and up the stairs.

Three days passed, then four. She could not settle to anything. What must they think of her? Edith had shown her so much kindness, and had had it thrown back in her face. And Rawlin had travelled across the world to see her! It distressed her to be so close, yet unable to meet him.

Then on the fifth day, Edith came to call again.

She spoke hesitantly of the fine weather, the warmth of the sun, while observing Lucy anxiously.

'I wondered whether you would like to accompany us on a picnic tomorrow, just Rawlin, William and myself. We intend going to Westward Ho! to walk on the beach and perhaps have tea in the hotel. Rawlin has ascertained that the tide will be out.'

For a moment she let herself imagine walking on the sand with Rawlin. But, of course, it was impossible.

'I cannot, Edith, not if Rawlin will be there.'

'But he has particularly asked me to arrange a picnic, providing you will come. Father has said we may take the landau, so you need have no worries about travelling on the train.'

She had not taken the train since the events of the previous year, but to sit close to Rawlin in the landau, with no escape should a difficult situation arise...

She shook her head, but Edith was persistent.

'Rawlin and William have much to talk about, I'm sure they will be deep in conversation. It will be as if you and I were on our own.'

'Of course you must go, chiel!' Mary Wilcox bustled in, doubtlessly having listened at the door. ''Twould do you good, have a bit of sea air to put the colour back in your cheeks! Would 'ee like her to bring something for the picnic, Miss Edith?'

Eventually, Lucy gave in. It *would* be wonderful to walk on the beach; it was almost a year since she had done so, and she would like to be able to observe Rawlin with William if she could do so safely in Edith's company.

The landau arrived as promised at half-past ten the next morning. She dressed in her grey dress and refused to change into anything brighter despite her mother's protestations; after all, she was not aiming to impress anyone.

She felt some trepidation when the coachman helped her into the carriage, but Rawlin greeted her in a friendly manner. Edith had arranged for her to sit alongside him so that she need not look directly at him, but she was acutely aware of his presence nevertheless: the humour and goodwill in his voice as he talked with William; his hand resting on his thigh just a few inches away from her; his masculine scent. It was difficult to concentrate on what Edith was saying.

After a while, when Rawlin was telling William about the easier journey by steamship through the Suez Canal, and the development of Palmerston, he included her in the conversation.

'Do you remember that I told you, Lucy, about the new library? Well, a few months ago, public meeting rooms were also built – the town is becoming quite civilised!'

Murmuring a reply, she turned towards the window to hide her confusing emotions. *He seems glad that I am here.* Despite herself, she was thrilled. Looking beyond her reflection in the window, she could see the river flowing slowly beside clumps of oak, ash and alder, for the road to Bideford followed its meanderings. It was to this river that she had gone, early on that fateful morning just a few months ago, a mile upstream. *But I am here*, she thought, *and Rawlin is here next to me. I am thankful to be alive, even if things can never be as I had hoped.*

And for a time, the four of them sat in companionable silence, broken only by the creaking of the carriage and the horse's trotting hoofs.

When they reached Bideford, Rawlin looked eagerly out of the window. 'I used to take these beautiful old buildings for granted but they seem quite extraordinary now, for there is nothing of this kind to be seen in Australia.'

'Why not?' asked Lucy, so surprised by his comment that she forgot to be wary of him.

He smiled at her. 'Because Australia is such a new country. In Palmerston, before the arrival of the Europeans, there were only the most basic of native huts. No building in the town is more than ten or so years old, and most have been built rapidly to a simple single-storey design, the only exception being the Government House which is as grand a villa as any that have been built on Warren Lane in Torrington!'

She looked out at the buildings lining the Quay, the grander ones at least a hundred years old, the inns, the back-street cottages and the church very much older. How strange to be in a place where everything was new! But perhaps there were benefits in leaving the past behind.

The High Street was lined with horses and carts, and shoppers crowded the pavements; on the Quay, people gathered beside the moored ships, and gulls wheeled over the fishing boats. She had almost forgotten what a pleasure it was to be out in the world.

William was now talking about his plans for the future; he would soon leave school and thought of going into the Church, but would also like to travel abroad. While pretending to look out of the window, Lucy listened as Rawlin described the opportunities, offering to help find him a position should he ever wish to travel to Australia. *He is kind and thoughtful*, she thought; *being away has not changed him.*

The horse slowed to a walk as they began to climb the hill to Northam, the winding road affording glimpses of the grand houses that lay beyond tree-lined driveways, then took the road that led to the top of the ridge above the coastal plain. Extra brakes were fitted to the carriage at the Upper Lodge, a house with a pinnacled roof and mullioned windows that marked the entrance to Westward Ho!, then, when the lodge keeper had opened the gate, they started the steep descent, laughing and holding on to their seats. She and Rawlin, who were facing forward, were in the most uncomfortable position.

'Take my arm if you wish,' he said.

It would surely appear churlish to reject his offer. Tentatively, she placed her hand on his upper arm, saved from embarrassment by the magnificent view opening suddenly in front of them, an immense expanse of tranquil, turquoise sea cradled by a sweep of land that stretched from the resort to the twin estuaries of the Taw and Torridge, and beyond to Baggy Point, while further to the east the distant hills of Exmoor gleamed in the sunshine. As all four leaned towards the window, she helped to point out the landmarks, but her awareness was focussed on the warmth of Rawlin's arm beneath her hand.

Reaching the bottom of the hill, they drove past the grand entrance to the Westward Ho! Hotel and on into the resort, passing the new church, the ladies' baths and the guesthouses until they came to the shore where the coachman pulled up the horse.

'Will this suit you, Mr Rawlin? If you want to get out here, I'll take the horse on to the Burrows. There's precious little grazing but I've brought the nosebag for him.'

Lucy stepped down on to the pavement. The tide was out, exposing the full breadth of firm, gleaming sand alongside the two-mile-long pebble ridge. The distant roar of the waves, and the wonderful aroma of salt and seaweed cleared her head and lifted her spirits. Well-dressed couples of middle age were walking along the sea front, two or three families were taking the air; all were visitors to the area, there was no one here who knew her. There were no grinning Torrington boys, there was no William Balkwill. She could almost imagine that dreadful time had never been.

'William and I will carry the picnic basket down to the beach,' Rawlin said, addressing her and Edith, 'then perhaps you would like to walk on the sands or out on the cliffs. Or would you rather take a stroll around the village to see the new villas that have been built?'

How many times had she imagined walking arm-in-arm with Rawlin, talking freely as they climbed the steep paths of the Common or strolled across the sands? But while she hesitated, she saw his gaze cloud with anxiety. It was as she thought; he was ashamed to be seen with her, he hoped she would not want to walk with him. It was quite understandable, there might be someone here who knew her.

She turned away, unable to reply. The beach directly below her consisted not of sand but of rock, and amongst the rocks were many pools. Seeing the rockpools, she realised that she could let Rawlin spend time with his brother and sister unencumbered by her company.

'Last year I read *Glaucus* by Charles Kingsley,' she said, staring out across the beach. 'It is a book that describes the creatures that can be found on the seashore and particularly in the rockpools. I would love to see whether I can find some of them but, if the rest of you want to walk first, I will be happy to spend some time here alone.'

She was surprised to see Rawlin smiling warmly.

'I remember you telling me about it in one of your letters! What a good idea, I would like to join you. What about you, Edith, and William?'

'I'll come!' said William.

Edith was more doubtful. 'I'll be happy to watch you all clambering over the rocks, but I think I will sit safely on a large pebble to do so, if you have no objection.'

They scrambled down on to the beach together, and Lucy tried to gather her thoughts as she led the way to the rockpools. Rawlin had asked her to come on the excursion, and now he had chosen to accompany her rather than walk with his family. Despite herself, she felt a kernel of optimism beginning to form in her breast.

'Did I tell you,' she asked, turning back to him, 'that Charles Kingsley mentioned your cousin William Buckland in the book? He spoke of him as a very great naturalist, one whose sole aim was the advancement of knowledge.'

Rawlin came to walk by her side. 'I wish I could have met him, I was just a small child when he died. I know his son, Frank, of course, and have told you stories about him, I think.'

She laughed. 'You have indeed, especially his strange eating habits!' Frank Buckland, like his father, was a well-known naturalist but had a penchant for eating the animals he studied, and had been known to try stewed mole, mice in batter and squirrel pie.

'I like to think I have inherited the family affinity for natural history but have no intention of following Frank's culinary interests. Now, be careful, the rocks are slippery here.' He took her hand as they clambered across.

The first rockpool lay like a deep, mysterious, underwater forest in a crevice between rocky plateaux. She crouched for a closer look.

'Take care,' said Rawlin, 'your hem is in that puddle, it will get wet through.'

'Oh, I don't mind, I'm bound to get a bit wet on the beach.'

'That's my girl.' He smiled as he crouched down beside her. 'You always were practical when it came to things like that. Now, what have we here? This is bladderwrack, of course.'

The olive-brown, branching fronds of the seaweed were covering the rocks around the pool and growing down into its depths.

'I remember coming here as a child with Father, we used to like to pop the little sacs.' She pressed one between her fingers. 'He told us that the air sacs enable the weed to float to the surface when underwater.'

'Let's look underneath.' Rawlin lifted a handful of the weed and a dark green crab scuttled out sideways, dropping into the pool with a plop and making them both laugh.

The rockpool was like a magic land, a forest of gently swaying growth in every shade of green and brown from the brightest emerald to the darkest ruby, and amongst the luxurious growth were translucent shrimps darting this way and that, sea snails moving almost imperceptibly down the rocky walls, and a shell with protruding claws that scuttled across the bottom of the pool like a miniature disembodied hand.

'Look, that's a hermit crab, I'm sure of it!' In her excitement, she almost lost her footing. 'Did you see it? It's gone under that weed.'

'Yes, did you see its eyes? Extraordinary! And here is a sea anemone, move your finger towards it and see how it reacts.'

Lucy reached into the water, which was surprisingly warm. When she gently touched the wavering rusty-red fronds of the anemone, they closed around her finger, trying to draw it into the soft, jelly-like mouth.

'We don't have those where I live; at least, I have never seen any.' Rawlin's voice was very close to her ear; his hand was on her arm to prevent her toppling into the pool. 'I would like to find out more about the creatures of the seashore. Could I borrow the book you mentioned?'

'Of course.' She had not dared to ask how long he intended to stay, but it seemed it would be long enough to read a book. Now that she had withdrawn her fingers from the pool she was no longer in danger of falling in, but he did not remove his hand, and she did not move away. They stared into the pool together.

When at last she glanced up, she saw that William had wandered on and was holding his arms up for balance as he negotiated a particularly fissured section of rock.

'Look.' As Rawlin pointed, she felt the warmth of his hand leave her arm. 'Do you see that limpet beneath the surface? I can just discern that it is moving, and that must be the mark to which it will return.' He indicated a faint circle on the side of the rock. 'They always return to the same spot, I think, and only move when underwater.'

'Yes, I remember how we used to try to shift them from the rocks, it's quite impossible!'

Together, they stood and continued across the rocky surface, turning to wave to Edith who was shading her eyes to watch their progress.

The next pool was even more wondrous than the first, a miracle of underwater cliffs, caves and chasms with small, mottled-brown fish that darted from the hair-like fronds of bright green seaweed. Lucy was so entranced by what she saw that she forgot to be self-conscious. When she told Rawlin how Miss Macartney, during their last visit to Westward Ho! two years previously, had slipped on the rocks and fallen right into a pool, she found she was laughing so much she could hardly get the words out.

'I hope she wasn't hurt!'

'Only her pride! And her dress soon dried in the sun.'

The tension between them had gone; it was like old times.

She stood up to stretch her legs and pin back a tendril of hair tugged from its confinement by the fresh breeze, then gazed at the vista of sparkling water that met the cloudless sky at the horizon miles and miles away, and the white-crested waves rolling in, each as strong and bold as the last, to crash and froth on to the sand. She breathed in, taking the clean, salty air deep into her lungs.

William had ventured as far as the seashore and, with trousers rolled up and his shoes dangling from his hand, was paddling in waves that sent semicircles of swirling water over the shining, wet sand. As she watched, he turned away from the waves and ran over the sand towards them.

'Rawlin! I'm very hungry!' he shouted across the rocks.

So, they returned to Edith who had begun to lay out the picnic as best she could on the pebbles. While they ate, Rawlin asked for news of Torrington, who had married and who had not, which businesses had thrived and which had closed, old disputes resolved and new ones started. She was aware that they all avoided talking of the church, and of curates.

While she joined in with the conversation, her gaze kept returning to Rawlin as he sat with legs outstretched on the pebbles. He had a habit of looking down when expressing an opinion, but then looking very directly at the person to whom he had addressed his remarks, his dark eyes alive with interest. When he looked at her, she felt he was looking straight into her soul.

When Rawlin was speaking, Lucy saw that Edith watched him, glancing now and then at Lucy, and there was a quiet pleasure in her gaze. *She knows that he and I are feeling hopeful,* thought Lucy. *She, too, hopes that the understanding between us will grow. But whatever the future might bring, I will have this day to remember.*

After lunch, they all agreed they should stroll up to the promenade to find a seat, for the pebbles were not conducive to relaxation, and for the next half an hour they sat with the sun on their faces listening to the roar of the waves, and remarking on the antics of the gulls that wheeled and squabbled on the shore. They watched the emergence of a large sailing ship from the distant Torridge estuary, and the smartly-dressed couples who strolled past, taking in the sea air.

'Now,' said Rawlin, 'who is ready for a walk? I think we need to work up an appetite for tea, don't you?' He looked affectionately at Lucy, as if she were the only one whose opinion mattered.

They elected to walk on the beach. The tide was coming in, but it would be another hour or two before it reached the pebble ridge and, meanwhile, a two-mile stretch of sand lay ahead.

'We can walk through the village if we come here another day,' said Rawlin. 'The tide might be high then.'

Could there be another day such as this?

At first she walked with Edith, but after a while Rawlin turned to address a remark to her and she soon found she was walking by his side, with Edith and William in front.

'Would you like to take my arm, Lucy?'

'Of course.'

He held his arm close so that her hand rested against the warmth of his chest, and so they walked, the firm sand under their feet and the sea breeze in their hair.

'I have waited so long to walk with you like this, Lucy.'

She could hear the emotion in his voice, and she knew that he meant what he said. He really was pleased to be with her.

She could not reply. Her heart was too full.

The next day, Lucy stood at the open window in the drawing room. It was a fine June morning, and the sky above the bright green foliage of the apple trees at the end of the garden was of the deepest blue. She lifted her hand to shield her eyes from the sun which was just beginning to lift the dew from the grass, and she watched a thrush as it ran across the lawn. It stopped, its head cocked to listen for the small subterranean sounds that no human could discern, then hopped forward to pull a worm from the soil, pecked at it once, twice, then swallowed, its speckled throat working.

She smiled, and turned away. Rawlin would like to have seen that; he would have remarked on the acute senses enjoyed by birds, he would have been amused by its intense concentration. He noticed such things.

They were to meet in the afternoon. He was to call for her and together they would walk to the Vicarage where they would have tea, and he would show her some books he had brought from Australia. They had been walking back along the beach when he invited her, and she had hesitated.

'Are you apprehensive about walking to the Vicarage? Edith told me that you do not often go out now. Perhaps I could send the carriage for you.'

It sounded so foolish. How could she be nervous about walking through the town where she had grown up? But she must be honest with him.

'I am, a little.'

'I will be with you, Lucy, we will walk together, just as we do now.' He sounded determined, so perhaps it was true; he was not ashamed to be seen with her.

When he expressed a wish to see Polly and to meet her new husband, Lucy had promised to arrange it. She wandered out into the hall, stopping indecisively near the front door. Usually, she waited for Polly to call; she had never walked to the house in the Square on her own, but she would like to be able to tell Rawlin that arrangements had been made. When Mary Wilcox came into the hall carrying a dustpan and brush, Lucy made up her mind.

'Mary, I'm going to see Polly.'

'On your own? You'm sure? That's it, chiel, you do that.' Dropping the dustpan on the hallstand, she gave Lucy a hug. ''Tis about time, i'n't it!'

Both Mary and her mother had been intrigued by her meeting with Rawlin, but had been careful not to ask too many questions when she returned from Westward Ho! the previous day. Her mother merely declared that she hoped the day had been successful, but Mary had squeezed her hand and whispered, ''Twill all be well now, chiel, you'll see!'

'I will take Alpheus with me, just for the company, you know.' She would feel braver with the dog by her side.

It was barely a five-minute walk, but Alpheus's pleasure at being taken out was quite out of proportion to the distance, as he bounded beside her while looking up into her face and trying to hold his lead in his mouth. As they walked, she watched his antics rather than look to see who was on the street, and she only had to wish a good morning to two people who passed close by. She arrived at Polly's home so quickly, and without incident, that she could scarcely believe that for nearly nine months she had been afraid to venture out.

After questioning her about the day at Westward Ho! – *Were you civil to him this time*? *Did he* choose *to walk with you*? –

Polly immediately decided that she would hold a dinner party for Rawlin and Lucy.

'It will not seem too presumptuous, will it, asking just the two of you? Should I ask Edith as well, in case people think…' She broke off.

'Polly,' said Lucy, 'I don't give a fig for what people think.'

Chapter Thirty

During the next two weeks, Lucy went again to Westward Ho! with Rawlin; she spent several afternoons taking tea with him in the Vicarage gardens when the weather was fine, or indoors when it was wet; they had dinner with Polly and Edwin a most enjoyable evening; and travelled on the train together to Exeter, the first time she had used the railway since the events of the previous year.

Then, one day, when he called at Castle House, he suggested a walk on the Common.

'I've taken several walks since my return, but it is not the same without you.' He was sprawled in the drawing room with his leg hooked over the arm of the sofa. 'The scabious are in flower and the air is alive with butterflies – I saw a marsh fritillary near the river the other day.'

It did not take her long to decide.

Pausing at the garden gate to put on Alpheus's lead, Rawlin gave her one of his very direct looks. 'Now, tell me where you would like to go. Just to Castle Hill? Is there anywhere you want to avoid?'

She thought of all the places where she had loved to walk, places that had been overlaid by darker memories, but of what significance were those brief events compared to the happier times which had been such an important part of her life? They were in the past now; one day they would be forgotten, and she wanted to relive those earlier times.

'No, there's nowhere I want to avoid. Let's walk right around the Common!'

Rawlin offered his arm as they walked along Castle Street and she took it, knowing that people would notice and whisper to each other, but why should she care? She had nothing to be ashamed of now.

In the Square, Eliza Down was standing at the door of her shoe shop wearing a man's jacket that was far too big for her; she looked very directly at Lucy, then their eyes met and she gave a small smile and a nod of approval.

'Isn't that Miss Down?' Rawlin whispered. 'The one who writes poems? As a child, I was rather nervous of her, and perhaps still am.'

'She is a little eccentric, she knows her own mind, you see.' She looked at him archly. 'Men aren't accustomed to that in women.'

He squeezed her hand. 'No, but I shall have to get used to it, won't I?'

Trying not to smile, she walked on through the Square with her head held high, both she and Rawlin wishing curious onlookers a good afternoon, and Alpheus trotting happily at her side.

They had not discussed the future, nor had she thought much about it. When she was not with Rawlin, she was reliving the things that he said, the way he looked at her, the touch of his hand on hers, and anticipating their next meeting. If she ever had doubts about his feelings for her, they disappeared the moment they met, and she saw that the emotion she felt was mirrored in his eyes.

'Has he said how long he will be in England?' her mother had asked.

'No,' she replied, looking down at her mending.

'And he has not,' her mother hesitated, '*spoken* to you?'

'No.' And she hid her smile when she heard the sigh of exasperation.

Leaving the town behind, they walked along Gas Lane between hedgebanks bright with red campion, buttercups and cow parsley; a pair of bullfinches uttering low, whistling calls as they flitted shyly ahead, giving glimpses of bright rose-pink and white plumage.

'You are no longer nervous to be walking through the town, are you?' Rawlin asked.

She considered carefully before she answered. 'I can walk through the Square quite confidently on my own now. I would not like to walk alone on particular streets or parts of the Common for fear of seeing William Balkwill – he is the man who spread the rumours about me.' She shivered a little at the memory; walking past the hollow, as they were sure to do that day, would not be easy. 'But when I am with you, I am not afraid.'

He pressed her hand. 'I am glad of it. We haven't talked of this before, I didn't want to distress you, but perhaps we may do so now?'

She nodded, but could not meet his eyes. She would not cry; she was past that now, surely.

'I have talked with Edith and I have questioned my father; he is reluctant to speak about it but from what I understand he is partly to blame. It is clear that Francis was deeply unpopular in the town and his presence was damaging the reputation of the church. My father should have acted sooner by insisting that he change his ways; if Reverend Francis could not do this – and from what I hear, his character unsuited him to the role – then he should have been asked to resign. I'm sure the bishop would have agreed if my father had put the case forward with sufficient determination. But then, that never was his strong point.' These last words were spoken quietly, as if to himself.

'But what happened – it was not your father's fault.'

'But it was! In a way, it was. I hope I am more effective in my treatment of the men under me. He did not act, so the people took the matter into their own hands. They disliked Reverend Francis so much they were willing to believe concocted stories about him, and grew even more determined to be rid of him. Such resolve leads to change, and that can be a good thing, but the cruelty of it was that you were involved through no fault of your own! The hearings were bad enough, but that dreadful night of the effigy-burning was positively heathen! One knows there are such incidents of rough music in the villages occasionally, but this was on an unprecedented scale!' She squeezed his arm; his voice had risen in anger, and a woman in an old-fashioned bonnet was walking up the lane towards them. When they wished her a good afternoon she replied politely, but eyed Lucy curiously.

'I'm sorry,' Rawlin said, 'I hope she did not overhear, but I am appalled when I think of how unjustly you were treated. If only I had been here!'

Her mind reeled - how different things might have been! Surely none of it would have happened if Rawlin had been in Torrington.

'I think,' she said, 'that they considered me to be of no significance because I am a woman, and the same went for Mrs Francis. I hope that, one day, women will be thought to be as worthy of consideration as are men.'

'I think that may come to pass, in time. After all, there are some who now call for equal rights for women.'

It was in the past now; he was here beside her, his arm strong and warm beneath her hand; the valley before them was loud with birdsong; the rowan trees held their creamy-white blossom up towards the azure sky as if to celebrate her return to this place after so many months.

'Let us talk no more about it, for now anyway.'

They walked alongside the Common Lake, watching Alpheus as he ranged happily back and forth between the gorse bushes on the slopes above them, nose to the ground and tail waving. She pointed out the speckled trout gliding almost invisibly above the stony streambed until a flick of their tails gave them away. A little further on, they disturbed a couple of bullocks that had come down the hill to drink. Eyeing them warily, the dark red cattle backed away, blowing through their noses as if astonished to see a lady and gentleman on the Common.

Lucy laughed. 'We are not so extraordinary, are we?'

'You are, Lucy; you are extraordinary.'

They had stopped to watch the bullocks, and he turned to face her. Her heart was pounding; they had never kissed, and she ached with longing for him. For days she had dreamt of his lips touching hers, his body pressing against hers; she had lain awake, faint with desire.

His eyes were soft, his lips parted. He took her hands and squeezed them gently. 'Not now; not here. I think we would be within view if someone came from the allotments.' He gave her a wry smile; they turned and walked on.

He was right, of course, she would not want anyone to see them. They walked in silence for a while. Rawlin had again offered his arm, and through the warm cloth of his jacket she could feel the muscle above his elbow tense, then relax, as he moved. When she turned her head just a little to look at him, she could see his neatly-trimmed beard, his brown hair curling over his ear, his dark lashes. He seemed thoughtful.

He spoke quietly. 'I would not have offended you, would I, if I had…?'

'No, of course not.' Her reply was little more than a whisper. Had he heard her? He gave her hand a gentle squeeze with his arm, and she moved her fingers a little closer to his chest.

'I'm glad,' he said.

Alpheus, returning from an adventure of his own, raced back along the path towards them.

'Alph, you are wet! Get down!'

They dodged him, laughing, and the spell was broken.

Rawlin pointed out a bank of foxgloves where the mass of purple flowers was attracting hundreds of bees.

'Now, that's something we don't have in Australia. I miss the foxgloves, they've always been one of my favourites. But I don't think I've ever seen such tall flower spikes as these, they must be three feet high!'

The bees were landing on the speckled lower lips of the flowers and buzzing contentedly as they moved deep inside to reach the nectar. 'I remember telling you not to touch them!' she said. 'Father used to remind us of that. He uses them of course, as a tincture and in an infusion.'

'No doubt the natives have a similar plant. But we have a doctor's surgery now in Palmerston.'

Two men in working clothes passed them on a higher path. She looked straight ahead, but Rawlin replied to their greeting.

'There, that was not a problem, was it?'

'No.' It wasn't, but she knew the men had recognised her; she would not like to have been alone for fear of what they might have said. Perhaps in time they would become accustomed to seeing her about again.

As if reading her thoughts, Rawlin said, 'Eventually, everyone will forget about it, you know.'

'Yes, perhaps.'

But would Rawlin be here with her until that time? He had not spoken of his return to Australia, and she had barely considered it, immersed as she was in the delightful experiences that each day brought. She could not think of it now; for Rawlin to be on the far side of the world seemed an impossibility.

When they reached the Roman road, he paused.

'Would you like to go as far as Furzebeam Wood?'

'No, I think not.' Now that she was so close, she had to continue to the place she had avoided for so many months. They followed the road up towards the cemetery wall. There was no one in sight either on the road or up on the Old Bowling Green. When they drew level with the hollow, Lucy stopped.

'This is where it happened, isn't it?' said Rawlin quietly.

'Yes'

It seemed an ordinary place, unremarkable, tranquil now in the afternoon sunshine. She moved a few steps closer. Now, she could see the path that ran across the Common from the direction of the railway station. It did not run straight to the hollow, and surely she had been further up the road? Had Reverend Francis deliberately taken a different course, so that they would meet there?

'I thought it must be here, from the description in the newspaper,' said Rawlin.

'You read the newspaper articles?'

'My father had kept them.'

Three children ran down the hill from the Old Bowling Green; of course, school was over for the day, they were taking a shortcut across the Common. When they came near to the hollow, they changed direction to run down its steep side. One, a boy in a large cloth cap and a tight jacket long since outgrown, shouted to the others to wait, then, running around to reach the high slope of the hollow again, jumped, giving a yell of mock fright as he landed at the bottom and rolled on to his back. Laughing, he jumped up, and all three ran whooping down the road towards their home in the valley.

Rawlin laughed. 'I remember doing that as a boy, though perhaps I was not so raucous.'

'Yes, I remember.'

The place seemed cleansed by the children's game. So many had played there over the years; the meeting with the curate had lasted only a few minutes.

'Let us walk over the grass.'

Rawlin was quiet, and she sensed that he understood that these moments held great significance for her. She walked slowly, looking at the sheep-grazed ground; there were droppings, but the grass was still lush. There was nothing to see. Rawlin had dropped back, but was not far behind her when she paused, seeing something at last. There was a low gorse bush, and at ground level its branches were blackened, burnt. New fresh shoots had grown up, almost hiding the damaged trunk. She pushed at the ground with her shoe. Underneath the grass, the ground was black; she moved several paces to the left, and then to the right, until she found the extent of the burnt area.

Rawlin was by her side. 'This was the place, then.'

'Yes.' She looked up at the distant, wooded hills, the steep slopes, the glint of the river in the valley. All unchanged. 'I thought it would be bigger than this, I imagined the whole hillside burning, and blackened still, all these months later.'

'But look how the grass has grown back. Soon there will be nothing to see, even for those who search.'

'Yes, it is in the past now. It is over.' Relief flooded through her, overwhelmed her, her eyes filled with tears.

'Oh, Lucy.' He was a few paces away, watching her, his eyes soft with sympathy, and she knew that if he could have held her, here on the Common, she would have sobbed, and neither of them would have minded.

But she must not, not here.

'Look, a kestrel.' When the sudden movement caught her eye, she was glad of the distraction. The bird had swung into view and hung now above the gorse-covered hillside, its wingtips shivering to maintain its stillness, its chestnut plumage bright in the sun. They watched as the bird's steely gaze searched for some small, unfortunate creature far below, before slipping away and swinging up again to hover above a different piece of rough ground.

'Beautiful.' Rawlin had moved a little closer. 'They are called mosquito hawks in Australia, but are much the same.'

After one last look, they walked on, crossing the road to take the path down across Mill Street Common, with Alpheus on the lead for the sake of the hens that scratched and pecked on the steep slopes. The beauty of the kestrel had chased away thoughts of scorched ground, smoke, and ash; the air was pure and fresh, the sun warm on her face. As they walked, she told Rawlin about her work as a district visitor, the people she had helped, how much she had enjoyed being useful.

'I can see that it must be rewarding. A small group of ladies in Palmerston who, like you, wish to be useful, have been carrying out similar work in the community.'

'Rawlin, you are far more understanding than my mother ever was!'

They crossed Mill Street with its long terraces of thatched cottages and started the steep climb across the Common towards Castle Hill.

The path was narrow and Rawlin took the lead, striding confidently up the hill, turning now and then to point out an orange-tip butterfly, then a common blue.

'Lovely!' she said. 'But look, you missed this brimstone.'

They stopped to watch the yellow butterfly feeding on the deep purple knapweed, its wings slowly opening and closing as if in ecstasy.

Lucy was out of breath from the climb, and glad of the rest.

'Am I walking too fast for you?' Rawlin asked, regarding her with concern. He, too, was breathing fast, he had loosened his collar, and she could see the pulse beating in his neck.

'Not as long as we can rest occasionally, it is pleasing to be doing something more energetic than wandering around the garden!'

They set off again, continuing up the hill until they came to a seat that had its back to a high stone wall, providing a breathtaking view down across the precipitous slopes of the river valley and over to the distant fields and pockets of woodland. There was more privacy here than at the highest point of Castle Hill; here, no passers-by could approach unseen. They did not need to confer but sat down together, and Alpheus flopped down on the grass next to them, panting happily in the sun.

So often she had dreamed of sitting here with Rawlin; now that the moment had come, she did not know what to say, and Rawlin, too, was quiet. His shoulder was only an inch or two from hers, she could feel his warmth, and see the gentle rise and fall of his chest.

Below them, where the land fell steeply away, swallows dived this way and that as they hunted for insects, their glossy dark-blue backs and long tail streamers bright in the afternoon sunshine. Rawlin turned his head to watch one bird as it performed a particularly agile aerial feat, before swooping down towards the river to hunt the insects over the water.

She wished he would turn to her, take her hand; they could move apart if someone came into view. Perhaps they could kiss now; the thought made her dizzy with longing.

He leaned back, sighing a little. 'Lucy, you know, do you not, that I have to return to Australia.'

She could not reply. Why did he have to speak of this now?

'I have to return to my work, a lot of people depend on me and there is still much to do.' He cleared his throat, looked down at his hands. 'I would have been lonely, you know, these last few years, so far from home, but your letters kept me going. I can't tell you how much they meant to me.'

He paused, and she could sense that he was struggling to keep his voice steady.

'But I can't go back to that, Lucy, I can't go back to waiting six months for your replies to my letters, not after what we have shared these last few weeks.'

She could not feel; she could not think. He was going to leave, and she could not bear it.

He turned towards her. She stared straight out over the precipitous hillside, she could not meet his gaze.

'Lucy, look at me, please.'

He took her hand, and then he gently turned her face towards him. She was afraid she would cry, but even in the sadness of the moment she knew she would never forget the sensation of his hand on her cheek.

'Will you come to Australia with me, Lucy? Could you bear to undertake that difficult journey, and to live in such a remote outpost as Palmerston?'

'Come to Australia with you?'

Could he mean it? In his eyes, she saw the same doubt, the same longing that she was feeling.

'I know it is a lot to ask, to leave your family, your friends, your hometown, but please don't say *no* immediately, Lucy. Perhaps you could think about it for a while?'

She stared at him. His face was just a few inches away.

'Do you mean…?'

'I mean, Lucy, will you be my wife? But I cannot ask that unless you feel able to come to Australia with me, because I must return there.'

She started to cry, she could not help it; the doubts, the fears, the strain of all she had gone through came bursting forth.

'My dear girl; my dear, dear girl.'

His arms were strong and warm around her, and the sobs would not cease but they were sobs of relief now, and happiness such as she never expected to feel.

'Of course I will, Rawlin, of course I will.'

He pushed her gently away so that he could look into her face, his eyes full of love and wonderment.

'You'll come to Australia with me?'

'Why would I not?' Her voice was shaky with emotion. 'I'd go to the ends of the earth with you, Rawlin.'

She realised immediately the absurdity of what she had said, as did he, then they were both laughing, and he took out his handkerchief and dried her face tenderly as one would a young child.

'You see what a lot I ask of you! It *is* the very end of the earth, but you'll come? You really will?'

She nodded, then they drew together again, and their lips met in a deep, long kiss such as she had not been able to imagine even in her most fevered dreams.

When at last they parted, she looked along the path, remembering.

He smiled. 'Don't worry, there's no one coming. It's just as well, for I gave it no thought.'

They talked then of delightful things; of dates, and journeys, and a wedding, which he agreed could be a simple affair, if that was what she wanted.

She sat up suddenly. 'You must ask Father's permission!'

'I have! I spoke to him on Tuesday before you came downstairs.'

'Did he agree?' The thought of him refusing made her head reel.

'Yes, he did not say much when I explained about Australia, but I think, now, that he knew it was what you wanted.' He stroked her hair. 'I was not sure! I was so afraid that you would not want to leave Torrington.'

'I *will* miss this.' The green and gold patchwork of distant fields and woodland gleamed in the afternoon sun; she would never forget it. 'But there will be other wonderful places, will there not?'

'There will, my darling girl, and they will be especially wonderful because we shall see them together.'

As Rawlin drew her close, she glanced once more at the dizzying view across the Torridge valley, and she visualised her future outlook in a magnificent rush of light and joy.

BUCKLAND—JONES. — At St. Michael and All Angels', Great Torrington, Devonshire, Mr. Rawlin G. S. Buckland, to Lucy B., daughter of Dr. C. A. Jones, of Great Torrington, Sept. 18.

St James's Gazette. (Image copyright The British Library Board)

Dearest Polly,

As I write this, I picture you in your drawing room with little Florence in your lap, while down in the Square beyond your window the residents of Torrington go about their daily business. How extraordinary that I am so far away!

As you will have guessed, we are at last in Palmerston. The first part of the journey by steamship through the Suez Canal was so much easier, Rawlin tells me, than the 'Great Circle' voyage by clipper. From Singapore to Port Darwin was rather more arduous, the ship being crowded and the weather inclement, but we arrived only slightly dishevelled, no more so than after a windy walk on the Common, Rawlin said!

Oh Polly, such things I have seen and experienced since I left Torrington! When I used to stare at Father's globe I never dreamed I would visit such places, but with Rawlin at my side I feel safe even in the most alarming storm.

I have so much news, I hardly know what to tell you first. Palmerston is smaller than I imagined, smaller even than Torrington. And very different, all the buildings being single-storey and detached from one another. There are less than a thousand Europeans here but many more Chinese, most passing through on their way to the goldfields. I have already made a friend whose husband is a friend of Rawlin's.

Our house is larger than most. It has a long central room with bedrooms, bathrooms and pantries opening off it; the kitchen is in a separate building alongside. We have a garden which brings me much joy and occasional surprises – yesterday there was an iguana on the lawn! Another day, a wallaby bounded off into the forest. Rawlin and I are compiling a list of all the species we see in the garden, and another for those we see elsewhere. The colours of the birds and the butterflies are much brighter than those at home.

Rawlin has given me a pet cockatoo! It is grey and white, quite affectionate, but its language is rather less than polite. He is also buying me a horse so that we may ride together in the forest. As you can imagine, I am a little nervous, having not ridden for so long, but being brave will have its compensations, because around

Palmerston there are lush forests where one can find orchids and lilies, inland cliffs, dramatic waterfalls and smooth white beaches bordered by rich, green vegetation. The sunsets are extraordinarily beautiful. At night, the only sound is the washing of waves over shingle, and the wind rustling in the palm trees.

We have two Chinese houseboys who are sweet-natured and hard-working. There is still much for me to do, especially in the kitchen, but I do not mind. Rawlin is always home for dinner; his place of work is close by, so we are never apart for long.

Such happiness, Polly, as I never imagined.

Of course, if I could have Mary Wilcox here, and Ann and Sarah, life would be better still! They must be very busy now that I am not there to help. I do hope Ann finds time to take Alpheus out on the Common sometimes.

I must finish now because we are reaching the part of the day when it is too hot to think or to write. Rawlin will come home for an hour or two, and we will rest together.

I hope, Polly, that you have forgiven your wayward sister who brought such trouble to the family.

I am writing separately to Mother and Father, and to Edith, but will send yours first. Please give Florence a kiss from me, my best wishes to Edwin, and my love to you.

Lucy

Historical Note

Ann White was a servant at Castle House in 1881, but then
disappears from the historical record.
Sarah White married Henry Davey of Shebbear in 1884.
Dr Jones died in 1888, having retired through ill health. Shortly
after his death, Mary Wilcox, having worked for the Jones
family for more than forty years, married Torrington widower,
James Barrow. She was seventy years old.
Rawlin and Lucy Buckland lived in Palmerston (later renamed
Darwin) for several years before moving to Cable Bay, New
Zealand, where Rawlin was superintendent of the Eastern
Extension Telegraph Company. They had three children,
Trevelyan, Effie and Harold, who were educated in England.
Later, Rawlin and Lucy lived in Macao, Borneo and Malaysia.
By 1911 Rawlin had retired; they lived in Orchard Hill,
Northam, then returned to Torrington to live at 26, South St.
During the First World War, Lucy volunteered with the Red
Cross at Torrington Hospital, and Rawlin was the Red Cross
Commandant, for which he was awarded the M.B.E.
Lucy died in Torrington in 1923, aged seventy.
Rawlin died in 1940 aged eighty-six.
Their son Trevelyan, after working overseas, was twice
Mayor of Torrington.

Great Torrington Cavaliers

The Old Bowling Green on Torrington Common is still the
setting for public bonfires today. Since 1970, the Great
Torrington Cavaliers have staged popular community events
every few years to raise money for local charities. Volunteers
work together for many months to create an elaborate replica of
a well-known structure which is then burnt, people coming from
miles around to enjoy the spectacle. Structures have included the
Houses of Parliament, Torrington Church, and a life-size replica
of the Mayflower. The bonfire in 2021 attracted nine thousand
people and raised eighty thousand pounds for charity.

THE SONG OF THE SKYLARK
LIZ SHAKESPEARE

"Mary Mitchell, nine years old. Draw your straws, gentlemen, and we'll see who's to win this prize."

It is 1842, and this method of assigning parish apprentices has died out, except in North Devon. This story is based on the actual experiences of one such apprentice sent to work on a remote farm.

Mary is fearful of her master's volatile temper and, despite the comforting presence of her older brother Thomas, she finds the harsh regime of physical labour hard to bear.

When a series of failed harvests makes life on the farm intolerable, the brother and sister take daring action in an effort to change the course of their lives.

This novel draws on original documents to shine a light on the farming and chapel communities of nineteenth century Devon.

THE POSTMAN POET
LIZ SHAKESPEARE

As a boy, Edward Capern is desperate to read and write, but has to work an eighty-hour week in Barnstaple's lace factory.

Edward's fortunes change when he finds employment as a postman, allowing him to spend his days walking the Devon lanes he loves. He begins to write poems and songs that express his delight in the countryside and the people he meets, but neither he nor his wife Jane can foresee the profound impact his poetry will have on their lives.

Liz Shakespeare's novel, telling the story of Bideford's Postman Poet from obscurity to national renown, captures the opportunities and inequalities of the Victorian age.

Also available: *The Poems of Edward Capern*

All available from www.lizshakespeare.co.uk

ALL AROUND THE YEAR
Liz Shakespeare

These twelve poignant stories, deeply rooted in the Devon landscape, are each linked to a month of the year from January through to December. You will be transported from a sleepy village square to the wilds of Exmoor and from a summer beach to the narrow streets of a small Devon town, and introduced to a variety of memorable characters. In January, a young Croyde surfer tries to come to terms with her uncertain future. As signs of spring appear in the hedgerows, a farmer's wife starts a new venture. In August, a bereaved woman is deeply affected by an unexpected sight on Lynmouth beach. A Bideford man searches for a special Christmas present.

These stories of love and loss, of separation and reconciliation, will stay with you throughout the year.

THE TURNING OF THE TIDE
Liz Shakespeare

Young and vulnerable Selina Burman from Clovelly and her two young children are confined in the harsh environment of Bideford Workhouse. Her prospects improve when she meets Dr Ackland, a popular G.P. committed to social change. He employs her as a servant in his own household, despite the doubts of his wife and the Bideford community. Selina's work gives satisfaction, but her search for love and security does not conform to the expectations of a middle class Victorian family and threatens to damage both her own future and Dr Ackland's career.

Set in Bideford and Clovelly, this novel draws on newspaper articles, letters and census returns, and powerfully brings to life the factual origins of the story.

All available from www.lizshakespeare.co.uk

FEVER

A Story from a Devon Churchyard
Liz Shakespeare

How many of us have wandered through a country churchyard and been moved by the memorials to young children? In this book the author sets out to discover the truth behind a number of graves dating from just one year in a nineteenth century Devon village. Her compelling investigation reveals the harsh reality of life in a small village before the days of effective medical care. By skilfully weaving social history, research and imaginative reconstruction she builds a sympathetic portrait of a community in the midst of adversity.

THE MEMORY BE GREEN

An Oral History of a Devon Village
Liz Shakespeare

When she first moved to Littleham near Bideford, Liz Shakespeare decided to capture a vanishing way of life by recording the memories of elderly men and women who were born early in the twentieth century. Farmers, housewives and labourers tell stories of oil lamps, outdoor privies, communal harvests, cattle drovers and the arrival of the first tractor. They describe in their own words the days when families kept a pig to supplement a simple diet and water had to be carried from the village pump.

In this remarkable book, the voices of a generation who are no longer with us reveal changes in village life which have been reflected throughout Devon and beyond.

All available from www.lizshakespeare.co.uk